I0745305

VICTIM ELEVEN

BY TOM CHORNEAU

Copyright © 2021 by Tom Chorneau

All rights reserved. No part of this publication may be reproduced, distributed or transmitted in any form or by any means, including photocopying, recording or other electronic or mechanical methods, without the prior written permission of the publisher, except in the case of brief quotations embodied in reviews and certain other non-commercial uses permitted by copyright law.

This book is a work of fiction. Names, characters, places and incidents are either the product of the author's imagination or are used fictitiously, and any resemblance to actual persons, living or dead, events, or locales is entirely coincidental.

Printed in the United States of America
Print ISBN: 978-1-953910-61-5
eBook ISBN: 978-1-953910-62-2

Library of Congress Control Number: 2021907969

Published by DartFrog Blue, the traditional publishing imprint of DartFrog Books.

Publisher Information:
DartFrog Books
4697 Main Street
Manchester, VT 05255

www.DartFrogBooks.com

Join the discussion of this book on Bookclubz. Bookclubz is an online management tool for book clubs, available now for Android and iOS and via Bookclubz.com.

To the Brotherhood of the Rewrite: Peter and Paul, Chris, John and Jim.

ONE

The old cop heard about the arrest a day ahead of the press. His former son-in-law, a prosecutor in the U.S. Attorney's Office in San Francisco, texted him: *Big news, Pop. They got the Ransacker! He's in booking right now at the Sacramento County Jail. You were right all along; the guy's a former badge. Sleep well, Skipper.*

It stunned him. Not the news but the message itself. A text. He never got them. His grandson had given up sending them. His daughter never tried. The unfamiliar buzzing from the phone started him. *Why not just call? All that typing on such a small keyboard. Why not just call?*

That's what he was thinking when he heard the news.

He stared out the glass doors at the lush conifer forest on the other side of the river. The sun was going down. *People who text don't really want to talk to you. It would be odd, anyway, talking to Donny after all these years.*

He wanted a cigarette. He could smell dinner from the kitchen. He looked at the phone. *Donny said the bird had been a cop. We always thought so. Should I call someone? Share the news? They got the Ransacker, the East Area Rapist, the Golden State Killer.*

He tried to remember. May, 1974.

***

The bureau was just a block from the Capitol back then, the investigation unit occupied a corner of the seventh floor in the old federal building at 17th and L streets. By then, Skip was a second year GS special agent, but the guys in the bullpen still called him rook because he was the youngest. He didn't mind, he was all hustle in those days.

The Visalia Ransacker had made the overnights several times during the past year. A break-in artist who never left a trace. He hit all over town at least a few times a week. During the Thanksgiving holiday alone, the locals suspected him of 13 burglaries. To date, investigators at the Visalia PD counted more than 80 of them with the same M.O. He'd rummage through the house, throwing things around. Seemed to have a thing about women's underwear.

Until February, the Ransacker had limited his work to homes and businesses inside the city. Nothing for the bureau to get involved with. That changed when he hit the forest service building in Porterville. A few weeks later he broke in there again.

Skip took notice, even if the bosses upstairs didn't. Tulare County was supposed to be part of his assignment. Initially, no one thought it was the Ransacker. The Porterville chief said it was kids because nothing much was taken: a worn-out scout hat, a coin box, rifle ammo, and a Smokey the Bear doll.

Then came the third hit, yesterday. This time, the overnight report strongly suggested it was the Ransacker all along. This time, he'd found the superintendent's locker and her clothes. She arrived in the morning to find her panties and bras laid out on her desk like paperwork.

Skip was pretty sure he'd be called upstairs. He knew the superintendent of the Sequoia National Forest was a big deal, she was one of only three females to have risen that high in the service nationwide. It wasn't quite ten when he was summoned to the big boss's office.

"You know about Visalia?" the boss asked him.

"You mean the Ransacker? Yes, sir."

"Do you know they've been finding footprints outside bedroom windows all over town?"

"Heard that."

"Well, we have a problem."

Skip nodded, keeping his mouth shut. He wasn't sure if the boss was asking for input.

"I want you to go down there. Organize things with the Porterville PD. I want a show. She needs to feel like we're doing something. She needs to feel secure in her damn building."

"I understand."

"Do you, Haskins? Do you know what you're dealing with?"

Skip nodded again.

"I'm asking rook."

"The guy is light, in and out. Leaves behind just enough to make a show. He's a gamer. Likes it that the locals are getting desperate. Likes the ink, the attention."

The boss folded his arms. "I've called ahead," he said, signaling toward the door with a jerk of his head. "Talk to her first and then meet with the Porterville chief. There's people in D.C. watching this."

Four hours later, Skip found the forest service headquarters a couple of miles out of town on a lightly used road. Row crops and cattle pastures surrounded the place. The sound of big rigs moaning on the highway. His reaction? Remote. No neighbors. No one would hear a thing.

He met her in the radio room, working mic.

"10-9, Kings12, 10-9 please." Her voice was horse and irritated. There was a young man in uniform sitting in front of the radio console. She stood over him, holding the mic and looking off into the distance. "Clark is such a nervous Nellie," she said in a softer tone to the young ranger with the mic closed. "Get a damn grip, the kid hasn't been missing even an hour yet." The younger man smiled and looked at Skip with a wink.

"Sequoia One, Sequoia One," the speaker cracked with the fuzzy sound of a man's voice. "Be advised, eight-year-old male missing near Mineral Peak. Requesting backup."

The super straightened. She was tall and lanky, all arms and legs. Her face might have been pretty once, but it was weathered by decades of cold winters in the mountains and hot summers in the desert.

"Negative, Kings12," she said firmly. "Stay tight until sixteen hundred and then check back in. Sequoia One out."

She set the mic back on the table in front of the young ranger and waved for Skip to follow her. "Are you my GS agent?" she asked, walking quickly out of the radio room and into a hallway and then to her private office.

"Yes ma'am."

She closed the door behind him and took a moment, Skip thought, to size him up. *She thinks I'm too young.*

There was fresh coffee brewing on the counter. She got two cups and put one in front of Skip.

"All I got to say is you'd better find this sonofabitch first, because if I do, I'll put a fucking bullet between his eyes." her voice was a low growl, her coffee-back eyes sparking.

"I believe that," Skip said with a grin.

He asked about the new security features. She said they'd installed better locks on the windows in back after the first break-in. Better outdoor lighting too after the March incident. "Made no difference, did it?"

"No," Skip answered and then waited a moment. "What about your house? Do you live here in Porterville?"

"Visalia."

"Alone?"

"My sister and her kids were with me for a while. Now it's just my cat." She tried to smile.

"I'll need the address."

It was a two-story bungalow near the center of town. Most of the neighbors had well-kept yards. Kids riding bikes. Skip took that as a good sign.

Her place was newly painted a bright blue, but the lawn was yellow and dotted with weeds. The front door was solid. The windows facing the street, too. He walked around to the back. The gate was unlocked. More weeds and dead grass. He inspected the flower bed and the windows. No prints. A sliding glass door led from the den to the garden. The lock looked old and easy to jimmy. He juggled it and tried to push it open. Nothing. A 2X2 stud on the bottom rail floor jammed the door shut.

There were two other windows on the backside. Both standard wood sash with thumb-turn locks that seemed pretty stubborn against a stiff jolt. Not too much to worry about there. He moved on to the downstairs bath. The window was overhead height. It had a slider pane, unlocked and ready for the Ransacker. He made a mental note.

Behind the back fence was an alley. Garages up one side and a long, empty lot on the other. He walked both before returning to her yard.

The neighbors had a huge oak. He knocked on the neighbor's door and asked if he could look around. He found cigarette butts on the ground near the base of the tree. Three of them. He noticed a sturdy limb six feet up and shimmied to it. The perch gave him a clear view into the superintendent's house through a second-story window. He could see the pillows on her bed through the lace curtains.

Skip called his boss, told him about the bungalow and the cigarette butts and the oak tree. The boss called the Porterville chief and the day commander in Visalia. A joint surveillance operation started that night. One team from Visalia sat on the house; Skip and a car from Porterville took up watch at the forest building.

The teams worked two nights before replacements took over. Four nights went by. Five. Nothing happened. The Porterville chief pulled the plug after that; the stakeout was taking up too much manpower.

"What do you think?" the boss in Sacramento asked.

"There's a little blaze going, just south of the park," Skip said. "If it is the Ransacker, he'd know her schedule. He'd know sometimes she'll be working alone during a fire."

"You said a little blaze and south of the park."

"We could get her to call the radio station, make a bigger deal out of it than it is."

"Do it."

Skip was on his own now. After the first night, he made sure he slept eight hours during the day. He called home. His wife said not to worry; her mother had arrived yesterday to help with the baby. He got in his run, too. Ate a good meal around sundown. Prepared his equipment and set up for another vigil.

He sat in a ranger unit parked on one side of the motor yard. Each time, the burglar had broken in through a window in the men's bathroom. It had a new lock, but from what he'd heard about the Ransacker, it wouldn't stop him. Skip had an unobstructed view of the window, even though two big evergreens were shading it. They'd left the lights on inside the communications center, lights that could be seen from the street.

Around four, Skip got out to stretch and to piss in the bushes behind the truck. Still keeping a sharp eye. There had been rain earlier in the week, and a tule fog rose from the moist soil.

He got back in the truck.

There. A shadow. A movement.

He took one slow breath and exhaled even slower. He checked his revolver and got the heavy steel flashlight off the passenger seat. He paused, considering the handset radio on the dashboard. Agency protocol wasn't definitive. If he tried to raise the Porterville PD, he might spook his prey.

Skip opened the truck door without a sound. The air was thick with moisture, but he could still make out a figure in the bushes. Dark clothing, a mask, gloved hands working the window screen.

Boots on the ground. One step. Two. He crept around the truck. His breathing controlled. He approached from behind. Close enough now. Skip sparked the light, his weapon poised.

"Police!" he shouted, excitement elevating his voice. "Show me your hands."

"Oh God, no!" the suspect cried before leaping back into the brush and disappearing behind one of the trees.

"Stop!" Skip called, hurrying to close the gap between them. "Stop or I'll shoot!"

"No! Please don't hurt me!"

Skip heard the suspect running.

The glare of the bright light reflected in the mist and near blinded him. He resisted taking a shot. The sounds of soft shoes on the pavement came from the corner of the building and were heading for the street. Skip, still chasing, fired a warning shot into the ground.

"Don't shoot me!" the suspect screamed in a high, almost female voice. He was headed for a car parked a half-block up on the other side of the road. Skip fired into the ground again, hoping a Porterville unit was close enough to hear.

The suspect got to the car and hid behind it.

Skip was exposed. Alone and unprotected. He had moved too quickly. He ducked low, still running, trying to make it across the street to another parked car on the other side.

He didn't succeed.

Skip caught one off the shoulder and it knocked him down. The glancing shot disoriented him, keeping him on the ground long enough for the suspect to get in the car and drive off.

***

The old cop could still feel it. In his shoulder and in his gut.

TWO

The morning James J. Cole learned of the rape and murder, he woke ahead of the alarm, just down the hall from where the attack might have taken place forty-three years before.

The sheets were wrapped tightly around his torso. His one blanket was gone somehow. He struggled to free his arms; his right hand tingled and there was a sharp pain in his neck when he peered over to look at the time. Six fifteen.

He didn't need to remember that it was Thursday. His schedule was full for the first time in months, and the anticipation for each event had tortured him all night long.

He rolled out of bed wearing boxer shorts and a tee-shirt, even though April mornings in the Valley were still chilly. The bathroom first and then to the fridge for a swig of juice from the jug. Coffee on and outside to get the paper. The *New York Times*, his last luxury.

The paper was where it should be, middle-right in the driveway. It was also in the dead center of a growing pond of water flowing from under the backyard gate. The paper was wrapped in plastic, but moisture was setting in on the edges of the front page. He got his feet wet snatching it off the ground. He considered the water's source, kicking at the puddle with a heel before following it into the backyard.

There, near the tree. Something awry, but also something whimsical, even delightful—a four-foot fountain rained unrestricted from the irrigation system. The offending sprinkler head lay a few feet away, lifeless as a corpse.

He slapped the paper against his thigh. He'd spent the better part of Wednesday afternoon fixing that specific point in the system after the gardeners had broken it. Cole had dug it out, taken it to the hardware store, and picked up a replacement with glue and instructions for the repair. *Now look at it*, he thought with disgust.

He didn't have time for this. Before he could leave, he needed to vacuum the living room, brush the pool's walls, and rake around the raised beds. *A mess*, he thought. *This is how things turn out whenever I try to fix something.*

The shutoff valve was near the front door, but that would cut service to the whole house. He still needed to shower. *And what if I need to pee?* The sound of the water squelched against the ground, heavy droplets landing again and again in the same spots.

The timer in the garage will eventually shut this damn thing off, he thought. He drew the paper to his chest, turned, and walked away.

He poured a cup of coffee and started to read the paper. Only a few minutes. At seven, it was time for his daily stretch. Cole laid out his yoga mat in the living room and pondered a piece of music to start the day. Three big drawers inside the TV cabinet were lined with a couple hundred CDs.

Fauré Pavane? Elgar? Enigma? Maybe. *Symphony on a French Mountain Air.* Just right.

On his back first. Hamstrings. Leg lifts. Downward Dog. Child's Pose. A couple more moves he'd invented to loosen a back injured long ago in a car accident. He ended with a few moments of mindfulness, sitting in a modified lotus.

His breathing slowed. He concentrated—and a sound from the bedroom pulled him out of it. Buzzing. The alarm. *Damn.* It was set for seven fifteen.

He tried to ignore it, but it was no soap.

The clock had a touch plate. The alarm was supposed to terminate with just the tap of a finger. He slapped it, patted it, then slapped it harder. Still going. He reached behind the bedside table, defiantly jerked the clock's power cord from the wall, and watched with satisfaction as life drained from the appliance.

He made the bed. Wiped down the guest bathroom. He'd just started to vacuum when his cell rang. It was his sister, Kim.

"Jamie, you were supposed to text me back," Kim said, exasperated. "Can I bring the Kimbels by or not?"

"Of course. I'm getting things ready right now."

"Good. Did you cook last night? Did you cook fish again?"

"No." He noticed a cobweb hanging in a corner. "Nothing smelly, anyway."

"What about the guest bath? Please make sure the toilets are clean this time. And empty the recycling bins in the garage. There cannot be anything less attractive than looking over a week's worth of a bachelor's dining discards."

"I'm on it. Anything else, sis?"

"Yes. You should shave."

"What does that have to do with selling the house?"

"Has to do with you, big brother, shaking out of this rut you're in. What about today? What else you got going?"

"I got a date for coffee this morning," he announced with a bit of pride.

"Really? Someone nice? Or one of those awful Trump girls you keep meeting online?"

"Online."

"My goodness, Jamie, an attractive man like you having to fish around like that."

"It's how it's done these days, Kimmy."

"Well, I hope it goes well. You are a great guy, JJ. Don't ever forget it. You'll make someone a great husband."

"I already did."

"You know what I mean. Annie cannot be better off without you. And you, you'll find someone. Just hang in there."

"I intend to."

"Give this one today a chance," Kim said. "Be charming. God knows you're blessed with enough of that. And don't mention being out of work. Make something up."

He snorted. "Got it, sis."

***

The café where Cole was meeting Shari wasn't far from his house in the suburban bliss of eastern Sacramento County. The traffic on the freeway was as slow as a falling tide.

He clutched the wheel. His stomach churned. He should have eaten something. He pulled off at his exit, joined a big avenue jammed with more cars, more anxious drivers. He thought of the sprinklers. *Damn, I didn't check it. Maybe the timer didn't go off.* He envisioned Kim and the Kimbels showing up to find the backyard a flooded mess.

He put it out of his mind. Nothing he could do about it now.

What about this girl he was meeting? He thought of her photos on the dating site. Maybe she'd be the one. Shari, forty-four, who liked wine-tasting, long walks on the beach, and dancing to live music. Not exactly groundbreaking details. They'd talked on the phone the other night. She said teaching was a second career after spending fifteen years working as an administrator at Folsom Prison. *At the prison?* Cole had asked. *Yes,* she had answered, laughing.

She didn't look in her photos like someone who'd work at a prison. He wondered when they were taken. Some women posted decades-old images as if their dates somehow wouldn't notice.

Cole punched into a break in the oncoming traffic, took a left into the parking lot, and followed a black SUV to the security entrance. He didn't realize his mistake until he got up to the guard shack and saw a familiar sign: *Sacramento Journal Employee Parking.*

The kid in the shack recognized him and opened the gate. Cole smiled weakly and rolled through. *What the hell else can I do?* To get out, to turn around, meant driving the length of the first row of employee vehicles. The publisher's spot, the executive editor, the managing editor, and so on. Halfway down, he had to pass the spot that had been his during his five-year tenure as head of the paper's investigative team.

The space was empty. No name on the plaque. *Still no replacement?*

He got turned around and headed out wearing a small grin. They hadn't found anyone. Was it just money or was it that they still couldn't find anyone as good?

No one as good. Let's go with that.

He checked the time; he was late.

He found the shopping center and the coffee bar. Inside, he looked around and didn't see anyone who might be Shari. The clock above the menu chart said it was 9:10.

He'd brought the paper with him. People were often late. He got a small coffee and took a table with a clear view of the parking lot.

He opened the paper to the corrections, always his favorite. Something about the public airing of errors committed by others soothed him.

An article on Monday had confused the proportion of black Cubans with college degrees with the overall number. Tuesday, some reporter had fouled up an explanation of the Obama administration's 'wet foot, dry foot' immigration policy so bad it took the editors three paragraphs to untangle all the mistakes.

In Saturday's Style section, the *Times* had incorrectly reported Scarlett Johansson's departure from some charity. She had resigned as a spokeswoman; *she was not dropped.* Cole could see himself making that error. He could almost hear the condescending tone of the actress's publicist demanding the skin back.

He drifted through the rest of the paper. It was a quarter past. He checked his phone, thinking Shari might have texted him, alerting him to a delay. Nope.

Cole moved to the Business section. When he finished that, it was almost nine thirty. He sent her a note. "Are you coming?"

"Of course," she responded after a moment. "I just parked."

That frosted him. No apology. No explanation. Discounting the ten minutes he was tardy, she was late by a full twenty. He had half a mind to walk out on her. *To hell with this.*

She spotted him and waved. The photos were recent. She was even cuter in person.

He stood politely when she got to the table. She gave him a weak hand before putting her bag on a chair. "You've already got a cup," she said. "I'll get mine and be right back. By the way, I like the beard."

Cole absently touched his face. He'd forgotten his photos on the dating app were more than a year old.

The line started on the opposite side of the café from where Cole was sitting. It also placed her directly in front of him. He stole a glance, and when he did, he found her looking back at him. She giggled awkwardly. Cole took it as a good sign.

He relaxed some. Women usually liked him. For the date, he was in a flannel shirt, jeans, and a pair of trendy slip-on hiking boots. Eddie Bauer comfortable.

She was dressed for work, with big earrings and red nails. There was an energy about her as if she'd already been up for hours. He liked her.

When she returned to the table, she tucked a leg under and gave him a smile before starting in on all the usual first date questions. How long have you been divorced? Five years. Do you have any kids? No. Do you want kids? Maybe with the right partner.

Next, she would ask about his job, his career. This was usually where Cole killed it.

"So, you're a writer," she said, looking up at him expectantly. "What do you write about?"

"I was twenty-two years in print news," he answered with confidence and eye contact. "The last five as the associate editor of the investigative team at the *Sacramento Journal*."

"Wow, that must have been exciting," she said, bobbing her head.

"Sometimes." Cole leaned back and put his hands on the table. "What about you? A schoolteacher?"

"I'm at a small Christian charter school."

Cole's mouth fell slightly open. His fingers scratched at a spot on his chin and he smiled weakly.

"What age group?" he asked.

"Kindergarten through sixth grade."

"That must be rewarding," he said, still stroking his beard. "There's probably no more important job in the world than educating the next generation."

"Oh, yes. Very much so." She shifted slightly in her seat, but her eyes remained happy and engaged. "What do you do now?"

"I'm sorry?"

"You said you *were* with the newspaper. What do you do now?"

Cole shifted his shoulders and cocked his head. "I'm transitioning into books," he said. "I'm doing some freelancing."

Concern flashed across her face. "That sounds a lot like you're unemployed," she said bluntly.

The tone braced him, and he measured her for a moment before breaking into a wide grin. "It does, doesn't it?" He fiddled with a wooden stir stick, face frozen. "I think of it as being just a phone call away."

"Away from what?"

"A job in the Capitol working as the communications guy for a lawmaker or some state agency." He stared at his coffee. "Something like that."

"Sounds promising. Why not?"

"Exactly."

She frowned. "I feel like we're swimming here."

Cole raised his eyebrows, trying to read her. "I also have a thing going with a law firm in town. Background interviews, pretrial leg-work, document research, that sort of thing."

"Hmm."

Cole could see the bright blue eyes turning a shade darker. Her lips pouted, and a frown formed across her brow.

"Jamie," she said, looking past him. "You seem nice. You're good-looking and obviously intelligent. But I've got to be honest with you. At this stage of my life, I can't be with someone who isn't financially self-sufficient. Been there, done that."

"Wait, what?" His whole body jerked back in his chair. "Did you just say that?"

"I did."

"Let me tell you something, I-I've—" He stopped. "You don't know me well enough—I'm—I'm no jerk."

"I didn't say you were."

"Yes, you did. What makes you think I'm not financially self-sufficient?"

"Everything," she said. "The beard. The hair. The clothes. Everything you've told me about yourself."

"The beard? The clothes?" Cole jeered. "I did shower, though. You don't give me any marks on hygiene?"

"It's how I feel. I'm sorry, Jamie." She looked him over as if giving him one last chance on appeal.

He straightened his back and shoulders and crossed his arms. "Who was it, Shari? Who was the guy that gave you such a high opinion of men? Was your last boyfriend a con?"

Her mouth pinched and her eyes got wide. She blushed.

"Ha!" Cole cackled. "He was, wasn't he? You dated an ex-con! Shit. And you're worried about me. Unbelievable."

She fumbled with the plastic top to her coffee, grabbing her bag with the other hand. "Go to hell." She was out the door in a flash, never looking back.

Cole sat for a moment, still grinning, and then he looked around, wondering if anyone in the café had heard any of it. At a table nearby, a college-age kid with a laptop and headphones around his neck caught his eye.

"Better off without that one, bro."

Cole smiled and bit his lip. "Yeah, but she was cute, man, real cute."

THREE

Cole got in his car, still grinning. *She had me on the ropes, he thought. I was down for the count. Yeah.* He laughed. *What a scene.*

He pictured her waiting in some corner of the prison admin building. He's dark and handsome and wearing orange. They make out in a stall in the men's room. She's waiting for him when the gates open and she takes him back to Folsom. He's gone the next morning. Her pocketbook empty, her car gone.

A sudden sense of regret washed over him. She was probably crying her way home. Jeez, he hadn't meant to hurt her. *Still, she called me a loser. And she had an affair with a guy like that.*

The traffic had eased, but it was still slow. His exit approached. Rancho Cordova, population 70,000: a name, not a place. A blah, insular community of strip malls; fast-food outlets; and meandering, tree-lined neighborhoods.

Cole turned onto ever smaller streets until he arrived at the cul-de-sac where he lived. Halfway down, he saw two people standing in his driveway. *Damn it.* He wasn't thinking. Kim was showing the house. The dashboard clock said ten on the nose. *I'm not supposed to be here.*

He looked at the clock again. He'd been wrong about the date, too. He'd arrived twenty minutes early. He remembered asking Shari to meet him at nine thirty so Kim would have time to show the house.

It was too late to stop. Cole would just roll by, turn around at the end of the street, and go get another cup of coffee some place else. As he passed, he saw Kim, but not the young couple. She was talking to Susan, his neighbor. Kim waved a signal to stop.

"It's good you're here. We need to decide something," Kim said. Susan, a retired widow at forty and never out of heels, showed no sign of leaving.

"What about the showing?" Cole asked, getting out of the car.

"They're running late," Kim said. She pointed at Susan. "Tell him what the mailman said."

"You know about the Golden State Killer?" Susan asked. "The mailman said one of his victims was raped and murdered in your house."

"The what?" Cole asked. "Who?"

"The Golden State Killer," Kim repeated. "It's been all over the news. He committed like, fifty rapes and a dozen murders back in the seventies. The police arrested him over in Citrus Heights yesterday. He's been living here all this time, quiet as a mouse. Good Lord, Jamie. With all your newspapers, you're telling me you didn't hear about it?"

"No." Cole put a hand to his forehead and slowly drew it through his hair. He looked at Kim.

"If it's true, you'll have to disclose it to the buyers," she said. "Technically, it might not be required under the law, but it's the right thing to do."

"A rape and murder?" Cole repeated. "You sure? Here at my place?"

"That's what the mailman said," Susan explained. "He was here just a minute ago."

"The mailman?" Cole looked around.

"He said there were only a few houses on the block back then. Yours was one of them." Susan touched his hand. "It'll be all right. Who knows? Maybe someone wants a house linked to the crimes. The Golden State Killer was, or is very big."

Cole rolled his eyes. "Like hell. This is not good."

A car came from the open end of the street. "That's the Kimbels," Kim said. "What do you want me to do, Jamie?"

He started back to his car, and Kim followed him a few steps. "I think we need to be sure about this before you say anything," he said. "I mean, the mailman? I'll look into it."

***

Cole drove to another coffee bar and bought a water bottle, a breakfast sandwich, and this time, a copy of the *Journal*. There it was, a banner headline: "Forty Years On The Lam Comes To An End For Golden State Killer." The accused was a guy named Joseph J. DeAngelo Jr., seventy-two, a former police officer and a retired mechanic. They ran his mug shot on the front page. He looked beefy and dim; his mouth was slightly open like he wanted to say something but couldn't form the words. A crusty ding marked the top of his bald head like he'd been bumped during the takedown.

The DA had announced the arrest at an afternoon news conference. Cole had wondered why the *New York Times* didn't cover the story; it was big news. The announcement probably came too late for the western edition.

The sandwich, egg and ham, was slathered with mayo. Cole hated excessive mayo. A dollop fell on the paper. He got a plastic knife from the counter and lifted some of it away.

The report said the decade-long crime spree started in Visalia in the mid-seventies, moved to Sacramento, and later to the Bay Area. In the 1980s, he'd started killing people down in Southern California.

The guy was responsible for more than three hundred crimes. *Good Lord*, Cole thought, *my house was just one.* He scanned the story, looking for a reference to Curtis Court in Rancho Cordova. There wasn't one.

He waited until almost lunchtime before returning home, and then he walked around a little. He kept seeing an image of a girl, surprised from behind.

Here, he thought later, sitting in one of the two leather chairs facing the flatscreen in the living room. *Here's where it happened.* His chest tightened. His head started to ache.

He went to the bedroom, changed into a pair of workout trunks, and pulled on his running shoes. He had an hour before he needed to get ready for the thing with Abe. He laced up and headed out the door.

The spring air was warm but still fresh and the neighborhood streets empty. The weight of an already disorienting day dropped off his back as he got to the park. His mind was clear as he reached the mall and turned around at Mather Field, an old airbase. Five miles.

***

Abe's shop was a converted firehouse, open and airy, with lots of exposed oak beams and brass fixtures. It was off Broadway, south of downtown. Not a trendy location, except that it was.

Cole had met Abe when he was working for the wire in San Francisco and Abe was general counsel for a string of nonprofits people working for then-Governor Schwarzenegger were using to hide where he was spending his campaign money. Cole and another reporter won a big award after unraveling the scheme.

When Cole came to Sacramento as a political reporter for the *Journal*, Abe was careful to feed him tips and keep him at arm's length. By the time Cole was promoted to the investigative team, he and Abe had become friends, and the attorney was no longer worried that his reporter buddy might jump one of his clients. They got close after Cole's divorce and closer still since Cole left the paper.

Cole turning his investigative skills into a service aimed at the legal industry had been Abe's idea.

"This is not going to be a walk in the park, kid," Abe said, his Basset-Hound-face looking even sadder than normal.

"What?" Cole said, getting up from a soft leather sofa in the waiting room. "What now, Abe?"

"I'd forgotten your history with Dwayne Reston. He's been with us since January. He threw a little fit when I told him you were coming in today."

"What's that mean?"

"You'll just have to finesse him. You got eight friendly faces in there. Billy and I have talked it out. We want to do this."

"Then why not just do it?"

"Come on, JJ, we work on consensus here. Reston is a partner. Just don't let him roll you."

"Great." Cole followed his friend into the conference room, checking his tie and running a finger over his upper lip.

The lawyers took turns introducing themselves. Cole passed out the folders he'd prepared containing a two-page business plan, his resume, news clippings about a pair of former *Wall Street Journal* reporters who had pioneered the same service in DC, and a proposed fee structure. He stood at one end of the table and worked his way through the material before asking for questions.

"Here." Dwayne Reston was waving his hand. He was short, soft all over, hair plugs, an American flag pinned to his lapel. Three years back, Cole had busted one of Reston's clients in a bribery case involving a building inspector and a call girl.

"Your reference to Fusion GPS is curious," Reston said, looking around the table. "That's the company founded by the *Wall Street Journal* reporters."

"Curious? How so?" Cole asked, trying not to sound defensive. "I'm proposing a similar service."

"Well, I hope you're aware why these guys are so well known," the attorney said with a smug toss of his head. "Do you?"

Cole did.

"You're talking about the Steele dossier," Cole replied, staring Reston down. *Yes, you little shit. Yes, I read. I'm aware of the Steele dossier, jackass.*

"Right." The attorney turned to his partners, some of whom looked perplexed. "The Steele dossier was a bit of illusionary espionage that surfaced just as President Trump was being sworn into office. You guys remember that nonsense about hookers and Putin plotting over the Moscow Trump Tower?"

"We remember, Dwayne," Abe interrupted. "What's your point?"

"That report, the dossier, has been thoroughly discredited,"

Dwayne replied. "It's basically a boatload of lies and innuendos, and here we have a guy pitching us a service based on that same faulty model. Seems like a bad idea all the way around."

"I'm not proposing any MI6 escapades," Cole answered. "Just another set of eyes looking at things from a completely different perspective."

"What's that supposed to mean?"

"You guys are attorneys, constrained by evidence and what you can prove," Cole said. "I can follow motive. Tug strings you can't. And when I do, often new bits of evidence emerge."

"This is such a load of crap."

Abe cleared his throat. "Let's dial it back some, please."

Dwayne looked around. "Look, I'm not saying a good staff investigator couldn't help us. But this guy isn't that good. He's the wrong man."

Cole's jaw jutted forward. "Good enough to get your guy, Doo-wayne."

"Picking up the phone isn't investigating. You got tipped."

"I did. The call girl." Cole looked around the room, smiling slightly. "It's always the help, Dwayne. She didn't get paid. Trump made the same mistake with the girls in the shower."

That drew chuckles.

"Please," Abe said, taking control. "Jamie, I think it's time you step outside so we can talk about this. I'll walk you out."

In the hallway, Abe put a hand on Cole's shoulder. "Damn it, Jamie, I wanted you to hold your end up. I didn't want you to pick a fight."

"That guy's a dick."

"Yeah, well, he could can this venture. Now I've got work to do."

"I'm sorry. I couldn't help it," Cole said "It actually felt good jamming that prick. I feel like myself for the first time in months."

"Whatever works. Listen, there's a couple straightforward assignments I want to throw you, but it'll take a couple days to set up."

"That's fine," Cole said. "I can keep busy."

FOUR

Cole had acquired a log-in and password to the *Journal's* online news archives from a friend. He was surprised when both still worked.

The paper had published 2,076 stories on the Golden State Killer. He chose one at random near the top of the list.

> Dateline: Citrus Heights, May 17, 1977.
>
> Man and wife went to bed late. They awoke about three. An intruder stood at the foot of the bed, a flashlight burning in their eyes. He said he had a gun. He threatened to kill them if they didn't do what he said. He had a string of shoelaces and tossed them on the bed. He ordered the wife to tie up her husband. "Tie them tighter or I'll kill you!" he shouted at her.
>
> He tied the woman, too, and then searched the house. He went outside at one point and then returned to the bedroom with a cup and saucer. He placed them on the man's back.
>
> "If I hear this move, I'll slit her throat," he told the husband.
>
> He took her to the living room.

Cole didn't want to read further. His chest had tightened again. A girl he'd known in high school had been attacked at a party. He remembered the guys hanging around after, drinking beer, laughing about it. They were older, and Cole hadn't known what had happened until later. A sinking pain struck him whenever he thought of it.

He got up, made himself a cup of coffee, and went outside to sit by the pool. It was warm. The water was clear. Later in the week, it might just be warm enough to jump in. He could see the living room from where he sat. He thought about the girl in his house. His right hand closed into a fist.

He wanted to know what happened. He wanted to know about the victim, her family, and how she had been killed. Somewhere in there was where it had taken place. Dark. Vicious. Evil.

An image popped into his head. Wall art in his grandfather's guest room in San Pedro. Something Cole had stared at since he was old enough to walk.

A man's silhouette. His back turned, contemplating a dark alley shrouded in fog. Under it was a quote from the Bible: "Do justice and righteousness." Jeremiah 22:3–5.

Is that what this is? He wondered. He relaxed his hand, grabbed the coffee cup off the table, and returned to the dig in his office.

***

The *Journal*'s first mention of a serial rapist operating in eastern Sacramento County came in November 1976. By then, he'd attacked eight women—two of them in Rancho Cordova. The cops had been trying to keep a lid on it.

At a routine community meeting on crime prevention in an upscale neighborhood of Carmichael, two sheriff's deputies were accosted by a crowd of several hundred. They demanded to know about the rapist running amok among them.

After that, the stories were frequent and delivered with ever-increasing alarm. The press was calling him the East Area Rapist. By the time he hit the house in Citrus Heights in May 1977, there had been nineteen attacks. The victims described him as five foot nine or ten with a stocky build. He wore a mask and often brandished a knife or a blue steel .45 automatic.

By the summer of 1978, he'd expanded his territory. Attack number thirty-two took place in Modesto. Number thirty-three in Davis. Number thirty-seven in Concord. The cops in the Bay Area believed their perp was a different man and gave him another nickname, the Original Night Stalker.

The first murders happened in 1979, or at least that's what the cops thought at the time. The killings were all down in Southern California. Authorities were sure it was the work of yet another criminal, the Golden State Killer.

Cole spent most of the day reading the old stories. The *Journal* published some reports from other papers. The *San Francisco Chronicle*. The *Los Angeles Times*.

After the crime spree seemed to stop in the mid-1980s, teams of investigative reporters would pick up the story, trying to piece the evidence together, trying to explain why he was never caught or where he might be hiding. TV specials too. The guy seemed to have vanished.

Cole found two books written by investigators who had worked the case. He was surprised to learn that, just a few months before the arrest, a woman who wrote for *LA Magazine* had published a new account of the case. It was rising on the bestseller list.

And no mention anywhere of Curtis Court.

He looked up the woman's book online and considered buying it. Maybe he could get a copy at the library. She got a lot of good reviews, and Cole recognized the name of M. Downes, one of the reviewers.

Murray Downes was a guy Cole had worked with at the *Journal*. Downes had won a Polk Award while he was with the *Sacramento Star* after covering the E-A-R case. Cole had forgotten.

Cole opened a new browser and plugged 'Murray Downes' and 'Sacramento Star' into the search box. A long list of articles came back. Cole narrowed it down by including 'E-A-R' in the search string.

First up was a story from 1978. In it, Downes broke the news that the police believed a notorious cat burglar from the Central Valley town of Visalia was also the one committing all the rapes in Sacramento. The Visalia Ransacker and the East Area Rapist were the same man. It was big news at the time. Cole opened the link and read the story. *Damn. Downes was a hell of a reporter.*

A map that went with the article caught Cole's eye. It was more detailed than any he'd seen before. And it located one of the crimes on the east side of Rancho Cordova and north of Mather Field, the former Air Force base. That put it close to Cole's neighborhood. Too close to ignore.

A friend of a friend gave him Murray's phone number. He was living with his son in San Mateo.

"JJ!" the voice was weakened but still the same.

"Hey, Murray! How you doing, man?"

"Ahh, you know. The doc says I gotta do this and I gotta do that and I gotta stop doing this and I gotta start doing that. I'm seventy-six. What are you going to do?"

"Rage, man, right? Rage at the dying of the light."

"Christ, Cole! Always one to overwrite it. What's up?"

"I'm working a thing tied to the Golden State Killer, and I found something you did while still with the *Star*."

"Jeez, you gonna try to get me to remember that far back?"

"You'll remember this one. You scooped the world."

"I did that a lot." He laughed. "Which one?"

"You got Visalia PD and Sacramento City cops to say the Ransacker and the E-A-R were the same guy. Seemed to make the sheriff piss in his pants."

Murray grunted. "He did. And then did his best to get me reassigned."

"I want to know about this map that went with the story," Cole said.

"You serious? You think I could remember a map? Why?"

Cole's line went briefly dead, and he ran outside for better reception. "This map seems more accurate—or at least more specific—than any of the others the *Journal* published back then."

"I don't know, Jamie. What are you looking for?"

"The source. Any chance you remember where you got it? Was it something you guys created yourselves?"

"I have no idea."

"What about the story? Who tipped you?"

"FBI."

"Really?"

"Yeah, this agent assigned the case was sick of the bullshit the county sheriff was putting out," Murray said. "People in the sheriff's office were trying to downplay the number of attacks and, really, the whole public threat the rapist posed."

"You got a name?"

"Sure, but he's been dead about ten years."

"Anything more?"

Murray was quiet for a moment. "Well, this case stoked a fairly intense rivalry between police agencies. Especially between the county sheriff and Sac City PD. The brass didn't like each other and tried to keep the line officers from coordinating because they both wanted credit when they got the guy. The FBI was the referee."

"How so?"

"The Bureau kept everyone working together as much as they could. They were also the final arbiter over the list of crimes."

"A list?"

"More like two. The FBI had one and, for a while, the sheriff had his own."

"And the FBI list was longer?"

"It was," Murray said. "That reminds me, we always used the FBI's list of attacks and that pissed off the sheriff too. The *Journal*, which was still run by a bunch of homers then, would use the sheriff's list."

"All of this is sorted out now, I assume."

"I suppose. It's only been about forty-five years." Murray started to cough and broke away. "God, getting old ain't for sissies." Then it sounded like he took a sip of water. "What is it you're looking for, Cole?"

"You'll love this. Apparently, my house was the site of a rape and murder the E-A-R may have committed."

"Lovely."

"And I've got it on the market."

Murray grunted again. "Good luck with that."

***

Abe's assistant sent Cole a note explaining his first two field assignments for the firm. One was a woman suing a downtown department store over a malfunctioning entrance door.

"We represent the store owners," the note said. "All we need is a basic assessment. We've seen the complaint. Abe wants to know if we should settle. An appointment has been scheduled for noon today."

The second sounded like a punch line to a bad joke: a dairy farmer just north of Sacramento had filed a complaint with the county zoning board about the odor coming from a fertilizer yard more than half a mile away. Cole couldn't believe it. A dairy farmer complaining about a smell.

"This is serious," the assistant wrote. "If the yard owners are forced to discontinue operations, it could cost them more than a million dollars a year. Try to figure out a compromise."

***

The woman with the broken hand looked too healthy and too strong to have been overwhelmed by a random burst of wind. Cole checked with the store manager, who said the door was working properly on the day of the accident. The attorney representing the woman gave Cole ten minutes with her and then cut it short, complaining about the "interrogation" his client was subjected to.

He walked out convinced the suit was bogus. Did that mean Abe should settle? Cole had no idea.

FIVE

Top's was a dive bar near the courthouse between the bail bondsmen, immigration attorneys, and payday lenders. It was also the watering hole of choice for the underbelly of the city's legal community. Jesse Topper, the owner, was one of the first people Cole had met when he came to Sacramento. He'd been assigned to profile the bar owner who'd foiled a sixth robbery attempt at his establishment in less than ten years.

Top's had a backroom with a big sky light. It was once a private billiard den, frequented by some of the best players on the West Coast. By the time Topper bought the place, the skylight leaked and ruined the table. He used the room for liquor storage. There was a desk and phone. When Cole was working the courthouse, he sometimes used the backroom as a second office.

"JJ, how you been?" Topper asked as Cole approached the bar. "You want a beer or a menu?"

"Nothing, thanks. I only got a minute. Have you seen Spadron around lately? He still eat here?"

"Pablo? Yeah, some. Not here now."

Cole looked at his watch, twelve fifteen. He had an hour's drive to make his next assignment. "Maybe I can wait a bit, see if he shows up. How about a Coke?"

"Sure, JJ."

There were a couple other customers having lunch or drinking at the bar. The TV was on. A patron sitting next to Cole pointed up at the screen where the noon hour news was on. Cole had seen the guy around but didn't know his name.

"My old man lived just a block away from this dude," he said.

Cole looked up at the monitor. The big story was still breaking. *Serial killer arrested in Citrus Heights,* the news crawl explained at the bottom of the screen. The volume was turned down, but the breathless zeal of the young woman reporter radiated from the TV screen as she stood on a lawn on an otherwise quiet street somewhere in Citrus Heights.

Cole took the stool next to the guy and started to say something about the nasty business in his living room and then decided against it.

"Did your dad know him?" Cole asked.

"Nah. That's the thing about these kinda criminals. They know how to blend in. And this guy was an expert."

"No kidding."

Cole asked Topper to turn up the volume, and the reporter's voice filled the bar.

"Taken into custody was Joseph James DeAngelo, a 72-year-old retired truck mechanic and former police officer," the reporter continued. "Authorities said he was visibly shaken and could only mutter that someone needed to attend to a roast cooking in his oven."

"Did she say a roast?" Cole asked.

"Yeah," the guy said with a snicker. "That's what this creep was thinking about when the law closed in. A goddamn pork loin."

A familiar face approached the cash stand on the other side of the room. Cole excused himself and weaved his way through the busy cantina until he caught up to Pablo, getting lunch to go.

"Let me get this, counselor," Cole said, coming up from behind and handing a twenty to the cashier.

Pablo turned with surprise. "Cole? Thanks." He shook his head. "Wait. What the hell do you want?"

"Just to chat. Let's go to a table. Please. Won't take but a minute."

Reluctantly, Pablo followed.

"You back on the beat?" Palo asked. "I thought I heard something about you working with Abe Metzger."

"I am."

"Since when does Abe care about anything in criminal court?"

"I've sort of got a side deal going," Cole said. "Has to do with the Golden State Killer."

"I'm not on that."

"But you know a lot about a lot of things," Cole said with a pleading smile. "Where can I get a copy of the arrest warrant?"

"I think it's been posted on the web."

"I mean one that hasn't been redacted," Cole said. "The public version is a mess. You can't really tell what DeAngelo has been charged with."

"Can't help you there," Pablo said. "The final complaint is probably weeks away. Maybe months. They're still investigating. Some charges might be dropped, others might be added."

"I'm just looking to confirm if a murder and rape took place in my living room back then," Cole said. "I got a goofball source that says the E-A-R did it."

"Seriously?"

"I'm thinking about filing a records request with the sheriff."

"You won't get anywhere. Anything remotely tied to the DeAngelo case is completely exempt from disclosure."

"Can't you just ask?"

"No, Cole, I cannot."

"You got anything that might help me?"

Pablo thought for a moment. "There's an old investigator. I don't know if he's still with us, but he was on the task force. He might be able to help."

"Who?"

"Skip Harkin."

"How do I get in touch with him?"

"You know Scotty, right?"

"I do."

"I'm sure Scotty can put you in touch, or one of his guys could."

***

The fertilizer yard was out in the country, between Woodland and Yuba City. Spring poppies splashed orange and yellow along the roadside. Big, ship-sized clouds sailed past on the breeze, casting shadows on the pastures.

Cole met the manager in his office, and then the two of them took off in a pickup for a tour.

"There's been a soil yard on this property since the sixties," the guy said. "And we've had dairy farms around us all that time. Never had a problem before."

"Why do you think there's a problem now?"

"Well, we've started a special brew that I'll admit carries a bit of a tangy scent."

"What is it?" Cole asked.

"Organic horse and cow manure, grape pumice, rice hulls, and some rock phosphate," he said. "What makes it special is the turkey and chicken excrement. We get it trucked in from the big poultry farms south of Fresno."

The windows in the pickup were down. Cole put his face outside and couldn't smell anything too offensive. "Doesn't seem that bad."

"Wait until we get closer. We're upwind right here." He drove slowly between a skip loader and a big delivery truck. Further down the yard, the manager brought the pickup to a stop, and he and Cole got out. "Over there." He pointed.

Cole boldly stepped closer to a big pile of compost and a man operating a tractor. The machine scooped a load of the fertilizer from the bottom of the pile and dumped it back on top. Each time a load was lifted, a puff of steam billowed from inside the pile. Cole was just a couple feet away when a whiff blew his way.

It hit him like a nightstick to the forehead, followed by a barrel of freezing cold water dumped from behind. Cole jumped back with his sleeve covering his face, instantly choking. The manager and the guy running the tractor broke up watching Cole dancing in agony.

"Jee-sus!" Cole bent over, his hands on his knees, his eyes tearing. "Good Lord!"

The manager rescued him, leading him a safer distance from the pile. "You OK?" he asked. "Someone get this guy some water."

Once Cole had recovered, they drove back to the office. The yard manager claimed the stuff was crazy good for growing almost anything and that his employers would fight to keep producing it. He said they would, however, consider a compromise. He told Cole about a couple of ways they might be able to adjust the mixture or mitigate the fumes by using a tent. Cole took some notes.

That damn Abe, he thought after finishing the interview. *He must have known what I was literally going to be stepping into.* Cole stripped down to everything except his boxer shorts and stuffed the soiled garments in the trunk before getting into his car and driving home for a shower and a change of clothes.

***

Brownie's Saloon didn't shout cop bar. It didn't have to. It was strategically located just up the block from the regional offices of the state police and about halfway between Sacramento City PD headquarters and the sheriff's main office near the old rail yard. It was owned by a former Sacramento City Police Sergeant, Scotty Walsh. Scotty only allowed a few PD logos on the wall from local departments and just one Irish flag in back, opposite the Stars and Stripes.

Cole had crossed paths with Scotty when he was still a detective, years back. They'd collaborated on a story once, as much as a cop and reporter could. Cole had come to trust Scotty's intel—and that of the loose network of retired officers he kept busy with private security work.

"Mr. James Cole, to what do I owe the bloody honor?" Scotty said, applying a bar rag to a wine glass.

"I'm working again."

"I heard," the big Irish cop said, putting the glass away. "You're some kind of Charlie's Angel now."

"Yeah, I'm the easy blonde."

"More like the bitchy Asian. What's up? Beer?"

"Yep," he said, laying a five on the counter. It was a game they played. Cole had to pony up the price of a beer before anything else. If he really wanted a wet one, he had to ask again and pay out a second time.

"And?" Scotty slid two dollars and two quarters in change across the bar.

"Do you know any ex-Bureau guys that might have been around during the seventies?"

"No."

"Know anyone who might?"

"Usually helps if I know what the hell you're looking for," Scotty said.

Cole told him about his house and the crime, the map, and what Murray had said about the list of victims the FBI had tied to the E-A-R.

"The E-A-R? Before my time," he said. "I can ask around."

"What about a guy named Skip Harkin?" Cole asked.

"Sure, I know Skip. But he weren't no Bureau man. A fed, yes, but not FBI."

"He worked the case?"

"He did. Best buddies with the man that ran the task force, a dude named Donovan."

"Can you hook me up?"

"Donovan's dead two years now. Don't know about Harkin." Scotty threw a bar towel over his shoulder. "He ain't young. Last I heard, he was in and out of the hospital."

"Can you?"

"Cost you another beer."

Cole pushed the change Scotty's way.

***

He checked the time. Almost four fifteen. He'd need to hurry back to Rancho. Cole wanted to talk to the mailman. Maybe he knew something more.

He got to the post office closest to his house and waited in a long line. When it was his turn, he flashed his press credentials at the teller. Cole asked if he could speak to the carrier for his neighborhood. "It has to do with a news story about the Golden State Killer."

The woman didn't look too closely at the press pass, which had expired at the first of the year. The credentials and the mention of the big deal crime story sent her looking for the boss. The postmaster came out and brought Cole to a bench inside the employee's lounge, telling him to wait.

Fifteen minutes later, a tall, thin man in his forties with glasses and goatee came through the doors. Cole recognized him. He tried to remember what exactly Susan had said. This guy was way too young to have been delivering mail in the 1970s. Isn't that what she'd told him?

"You're 3631 Curtis, right?" the guy said with a smile. "How can I help you?"

Cole hesitated and ran his hand through his beard. "Yes, that's me. About three weeks ago, on a Thursday, could someone else have delivered my mail?"

"Three weeks ago?" The guy shook his head slightly. "The boss said this has something to do with the Golden State Killer. What's up?"

"That's just it, I don't know. The day after the killer was arrested, my neighbor said one of your colleagues was at my place. He told her one of the Golden State Killer's victims was raped and murdered in my house."

"Damn, well, I wouldn't know anything about that."

Cole got out his phone to get the exact dates. "The suspect, this guy DeAngelo, was arrested on Tuesday night, the twenty-fourth of April. The cops didn't announce his capture until the next day, Wednesday. It was Thursday, the twenty-sixth that this other carrier was at my place. Do you remember anything unusual with your schedule on the twenty-sixth?"

He shook his head again. "Nothing. Same as every workday."

"You sure?"

"I haven't taken a sick day or vacation since Christmas."

"OK." Cole rubbed his beard again. "What time do you normally get to my house?"

"Mid-afternoon, two or two thirty."

"Man." Cole put his hand to the back of his neck. "What about a special delivery?"

"I don't know. Did you get one?"

"No, what about one of my neighbors? Don't you keep records on things like that?"

"Nothing that we can share unless you were the recipient."

"OK, thanks."

Cole rolled home and went straight across the street to knock on Susan's door.

"That thing about my house," he said. "I've just been to the post office. Our carrier is about forty. Didn't you say the mailman you talked to said he delivered mail here during the seventies?"

She frowned. "No, he only said that there were a few houses on the block back then."

"What did he look like?"

"Sixties, short, shorter than me," Susan said. "Light eyes, sort of gray."

"I just talked to our carrier," Cole said. "I recognized him. Tall. Barely forty. He probably wasn't even born when the rape spree was going on."

"Jamie, I could have told you that."

"OK, but who was the old man that knew about the murder?"

Susan touched her lips. She stepped outside and pointed to the row of succulents growing out of clay pots on one side of her yard.

"I was watering the plants, and I saw this mailman coming out from your backyard and I thought, that's strange, so I called to him."

"The backyard?"

"Yes, and I asked if he needed help, you know, like what are you doing in my neighbor's backyard, right?"

"What did he say?"

"He said he was making sure you weren't home, that they had a delivery, but you had to be here and because you weren't, he couldn't leave it."

"Hmm," Cole said. "Registered mail, maybe? That still doesn't explain going into the backyard."

"No, they never do that."

"No, they do not." Cole scratched his beard. "What about after that? How did the topic of the Golden State Killer come up?"

"Your sister drove up and she was all about it."

"And the mailman just blurted it out? That my house was a crime scene?"

"No, I think Kim said something about how she'd heard on the radio that the killer attacked all over Rancho Cordova."

"Then what?"

"He told us about the murder."

Cole was looking across the street at his driveway. "Was he in uniform?"

Susan nodded.

"Was he walking? Did he have a mailbag?"

Susan thought for a minute. "No, he had a truck," she said. "No, wait. He had a white car."

"Not a mail vehicle?"

"I don't know. Do they have sedans?"

"I don't know," Cole said. "This is getting weird."

SIX

Someone impersonating a mail carrier wanted Cole to know about the murder. That's the only way any of it made sense. Cole also decided that whoever this guy was, he wanted Cole to take up the chase. *He must know who I am*, Cole thought, *or who I was.*

Then again, he could be just some nut.

The morning music was Shostakovich, Piano Concerto no. 2..

After the paper and coffee, Cole went into his home office. Easy enough to check. If he's a nut, my house wouldn't have even been built in the 1970s. He found his property tax bill, but there wasn't a construction date listed. He'd need to pull his records downtown at the assessor's office.

Property records were things that Cole had a lot of experience with. He waved to an Asian woman he recognized on his way to the public terminal. He punched in his address, 3631 Curtis Court, and quickly clicked through a series of screens until he found the original property documents.

The developer of the neighborhood was an outfit called M&M Partners. It looked like construction on his house was completed in March 1975. Yet, M&M still owned it three years later. He thought that interesting. Developers usually sell out quickly and move on to the next project. What made them hang on this place so long?

He went to the counter and asked the girl to look up his address, and then he showed her the same set of early documents. "The subdivision was developed by M&M," she said. "Your house was one of the first to be finished, and you're right, M&M didn't sell it until 1978."

"Why?" Cole asked.

"Well, I can't say for certain, but my guess is that your house was probably used as a model, a show house for prospective buyers."

"For three years? Seems like a long time to hold a property," Cole said.

The clerk thought a moment. "Yes, that's true," she said. "Maybe there was some problem with your place. Something about it made it hard to sell."

Cole thanked her. *Yeah,* he thought to himself, *and I bet I know what that problem was.*

He went back to the terminal and scribbled down the few details about M&M in the property filing. There wasn't much. The partners had an office over in Roseville, which was a suburb of Sacramento but just over the county line in Placer. He clicked forward. M&M sold his house in 1978 to a Ryan and Phyllis Danner. The Danners sold it to William and Donna Fredrick in 1990. Cole found the settlement agreement when he and his ex, Anne, bought the place from the Fredricks in 2008.

He felt a rush of sadness looking at the paper, seeing Anne's signature. *A lot of water under the bridge since then,* he thought. *Good times, bad ones. Look at the price we paid: one-ninety! Damn, I'd be sitting on a goldmine now if I didn't have to refinance and give half the profit to Anne.*

Life goes on.

Next, Cole looked for any of his neighbors that might have been around back then. Curtis Court wasn't a long street. There were fifty-seven neighbors in all. It didn't take too long to run through the list. He downloaded records for each of the current owners onto a USB drive, just in case he'd need to talk to one of them. When he finished the list, he found only one on the block who owned his house back in the mid-1970s, a man named Wallace. His house was about halfway to the end of the cul-de-sac from Cole's place. Cole tried to think if he knew the house or the man. He'd be pretty old by now.

***

Cole was almost home when Abe called.

"Have you talked to Billy?" he said with slight irritation.

"No, why?"

"Criminy, do I have to do everything around here?" Abe said. "I'm glad I caught you. I got something for you. Could be real money."

"Money is good. Who is the client?"

"She talked to Billy, but he said she's some sort of Hollywood media consultant working for a hedge fund."

"At least I know she can pay."

"Well, we didn't vet her."

"OK."

"Look, JJ, we haven't talked about this yet, but the firm has an interest in this work you'll be doing for us."

"Come on, Abe. You going to take a cut of my meager pay?"

"Nothing like that. We want first refusal for any litigation that might come out of your activities."

"If I cause a fight?"

"More or less," Abe answered. "We think you might generate some business."

"Fair enough."

"I've got some marketing materials I'm going to email. There's a contract, too. I want you to take all this to the meeting and get her to sign."

"I'll try."

"Thanks, Jamie," Abe said. "She wants you to meet her in the restaurant at the Sheraton in about twenty minutes. Can you make it?"

"I will," Cole said. "Name?"

"Evelyn Morris," Abe answered. "Lemme know how it goes."

The hotel diner faced L Street. Big picture windows followed the busy traffic outside. With the breakfast crowd gone and lunch still an hour away, it wasn't hard to find her. She was in her late twenties, attractive, and dressed in a dark business suit. Her trendy haircut was short and tinted a grayish blonde.

"Ms. Morris? I'm James Cole. I believe you contacted the Metzger firm and asked to meet me."

"I did." She smiled and gestured for Cole to sit. "Thanks for coming on such short notice."

"I understand you might have a job for me?"

"I do." She pulled her briefcase from the chair next to her and slid it up on the table. "I understand you're an investigative reporter. Or, rather, that you were."

"That's right; I used to work for the *Journal*."

She opened the briefcase, found a file, and opened it. "You were an editor or something? The I-team. Twice a finalist for the Pulitzer," she read. "Impressive. And now you work for Mr. Metzger's firm?"

"I'm doing legwork for them, yes."

"Research? Investigations?" She looked up. "And still writing, too, I assume?"

"All of that."

"Good. I need someone with your skills."

"Great," Cole said. "What's the assignment?"

"One thing first," she said. "I had my assistant do a little background check on you. There seems to be some mystery surrounding your separation from the *Journal*. I'd like to know what happened."

Cole's shirt was open at the collar; he pulled at it anyway. "I was fired," he said flatly. "I messed up a big story and caused a libel suit that cost the paper a lot of money to settle."

"How did that happen?"

"We chased down a pharmaceutical distributor selling inferior drugs he was getting off the black market," Cole said. "He was using grocery store pharmacies, mostly in the poor neighborhoods in the Central Valley and down in LA. He was putting lives at risk, and the authorities couldn't figure out where the bad drugs were coming from. We did."

Cole paused. "We had the whole scheme nailed down. All that was left was to give this guy a chance to respond, but he wouldn't talk to us. We camped out at his office, at his home, tried his attorney—we did everything. I figured he was just stonewalling, and I insisted the editors run the story without the guy's rebuttal."

She gasped slightly. "You got the wrong man?"

Cole clapped his hands. "Two guys about the same age with the same crazy-ass Ukrainian last name," Cole said. "Both lived in Fresno. Both named Robert. One was a con and soon-to-be felon. The other was just a taxpayer who didn't like the press."

"That's quite the mishap," she said. "I suspect that's not a mistake you'll ever make again."

"No." Cole tried to smile.

"Thank you for telling me the truth." She pointed to her file. "I already knew the details, of course. I needed to know if you'd own up to it. I need to trust you."

"You can."

"Good, because any work you do for us will have to be bulletproof, absolutely bulletproof." Cole noticed her lip gloss was a light pink, not translucent as he had first thought.

"I understand."

"Very well," she said, getting another file out of the briefcase. "I'm working with an investment firm that is interested in an almond grower north of here, a company called Stony Creek Farms."

She passed Cole a single sheet of paper, a brief that included a few basic facts about the company, its address, top executives, that sort of thing.

"They've recently become the largest exporter of almonds in California, which makes them one of the biggest in the world," she continued. "They are family-owned, but we believe they are preparing to take the company public. We are poised to make them an offer, a substantial partnership offer, and while we've performed routine due diligence, I feel like we need something more."

Cole took out a notepad and pen from his coat pocket. "Anything specific?"

"Not really. I want fresh eyes on them. I want the passion

that a reporter brings to a big story. I want that instinct. Do you understand?"

"I think so."

"At the end of your digging, I also want the option of having you write up your findings, journalism form."

"You mean as if it was a news story?" Cole asked, making a note.

"Exactly. Assuming you find something interesting."

"You mean scandalous, don't you?"

"Not necessarily, but sure." She played with a ring on her finger. "I could have hired a private investigator to perform this inquiry, but when I heard about you and your services, I thought, 'That's the man I need.' We think there's a business advantage to having a writer do this job."

"So, this would be something you'd want to publish?"

"Potentially," she answered. "You do still have contacts in the industry, right? If you brought a big story to one of them, you could get it published, couldn't you?"

"Depends, but yeah, I probably could," Cole said and then took a moment. "You want me to investigate this company and its executives and then freelance the story to a newspaper or magazine?"

"No." She put up a stalling hand. "Let me try again. I could have hired a PI firm. They would have given me a report. Maybe I could leak it to the press and then wait for the editors to decide what to do with it." She shook her head. "I don't want to do it that way. I want to be able to control the process. I want the people at Stony Creek to think that you're writing a story about them, but I want the option of holding it."

"A threat then," Cole said.

"Yes, it could be an advantage for us as we negotiate terms with them," she said, smiling. "Does any of this bother you? I know how you guys are about ethics."

Cole rubbed the hair on his chin. "I guess not," he said. "I'm no longer a practicing journalist. I'm something else now."

"Excellent."

Cole was ready to talk money, but before he could raise the question, she reached for an envelope in the briefcase and handed it to Cole. "That's five thousand dollars," she said. "If you have expenses, keep track of them, and we'll cover those too. When the time comes, and depending on what you find, we'll talk about an additional fee for the writing end of this job. I hope this is enough for the first step. I would think this won't take more than forty hours."

Cole did the math in his head. One-twenty-five an hour. This was too much, way too much. He left the envelope on the table but took another look at the digest paper she'd given him. On the second line, he spotted it.

"Lorraine Wilmer?" he put a finger on the name just above the listing for CEO. "Any relation to state Sen. Ted Wilmer?"

"His wife."

Cole rubbed the back of his neck. "Hmm."

"What's that mean?"

"It means, hmm. You want me to shake down one of the most powerful families in Northern California. I was thinking the money you were offering was too much, now I think it might not be enough."

"Why do you say that?"

"This could be trouble. The Wilmers are very rich and very powerful."

"Mr. Cole, you spent a career going up against the likes of the Wilmers."

Cole stared back at her a moment. "You expect me to find something, don't you? You suspect them of wrongdoing."

"As I said, we did our due diligence."

"You're not answering the question," Cole said.

"That's correct," she said, getting up. The meeting was over. "I'll be in touch." She turned back. "One more thing, you don't have much time. My sources tell me the Wilmers expect to bring the IPO forward in a month."

He picked up the envelope.

SEVEN

Cole knew a guy who covered California agriculture for Goldman Sachs. Trevor McCallum. He was a big country boy from Napa. Also, a Dodger fan. Cole met him at Top's the night Kershaw pitched a perfect game—or would have if the shortstop had handled a routine ground out in the top of the seventh.

McCallum's office was on the top floor of Esquire Tower, one of the newer buildings downtown. The lobby had a well-appointed waiting area. Trevor only had a few minutes.

"I've been hired to take a run at a firm called Stony Creek. You ever hear of them?"

"The country's biggest exporter of almonds? Yeah, Jamie, I've heard of them."

"Run by the Wilmers," Cole said. "Senator Ted Wilmer's wife."

"Correct."

"Tell me things I don't know."

"Theredore Wilmer inherited the farm when his father died maybe twenty years ago," Trevor said, slipping off a shoe and scratching furiously between his toes. "Ted wasn't much of a farmer and even less a businessman. He was running the operation into the ground when his creditors forced him to bring in a management consultant. That would be the former Lorraine Davidson. She worked for us for a while. A knockout back in the day."

Cole tried to ignore McCallum's business with his feet. "She's his wife now."

"Right. Second wife and she runs the place," Trevor explained, jamming the shoe back on. "Took it from a dead sleep to the mega-conglomerate it is today."

"How did she finance it? They're privately held, aren't they?"

"Borrowed it same as anyone, as far as I know."

"Who from?"

McCallum closed his eyes briefly and then shook his head. "I can't say. Or I won't—at least not until you tell me more about who hired you and what the hell you're doing."

"Some twenty-something media consultant who said she works for a hedge fund hired me," Cole answered.

"A hedge fund?" McCallum leaned forward. "Which one?"

Cole shook his head when he realized he'd never asked her. *That was a mistake.* "I don't know."

"You don't know?" he said harshly. "Lost a step or two, haven't you, Cole? She *said* she worked for a hedge fund and you believed her?"

"I know." Cole rubbed absently at his chin. He was right. *I should have asked more questions.* He wasn't sure why he hadn't. Abe had warned him she wasn't vetted.

"What's the mission?"

"Same old, same old—dig for dirt, find something ugly she can threaten to take public."

"Why?"

"Well, now maybe I've got something to help you," Cole said, leaning forward. "She said Stony Creek is going public. She wants me to find something that'll help her firm negotiate a taste."

"The IOP is an old rumor, but maybe they're finally serious about it," Trevor said. "Thanks, man. That could be valuable info."

"Now, what about finances? Who's backing them?"

"We think it's a Chinese bank."

"Chinese?

"Yep."

"I wonder how that plays with the senator's folks down-home."

"Probably not too well, I'd guess," Trevor said. "Which is why they've been careful. Their Chinese partners are well-cloaked."

"What about them personally?" Cole asked. "Anything in the closet?"

"Nothing unusual. Ted likes to drink and play golf. Rumor is he fools around with other women. The wife is Wharton School, a former Miss Vicksburg, or some damn thing."

"Kids?"

"I don't know." McCallum got to his feet. "I gotta go, Cole. But you hear anything more about the IPO, you give your old pal a call, right?"

"You got it."

The Central Library was just a few blocks away. Cole hoofed it. The research room was crowded with homeless men and high school kids. He had to wait before a terminal opened up. When Cole sat down, the guy next to him was looking at porn and quickly dropped the screen.

Cole spent the next two hours running the Wilmers and Stony Creek through every index they had.

Cole found Wilmer's disclosure forms online—the required annual filings all elected officials had to submit showing what they owned, what they earned, and where all of it came from. Nothing out of the ordinary. Ted and his wife owned a house in Shasta County. They had other stocks and investments, mostly blue chips. There was an apartment building in Chico, a house in Tahoe, another in Palm Springs. The only thing Cole spotted that gave him pause was an interest Wilmer had in a company, the Solon Group. Cole looked it up. Privately held, based in Eureka.

When he finished with the Wilmers, Cole took a run at Ms. Morris. She troubled him. Trevor's slap about Cole losing a step since he'd left the paper wasn't off target. He found a report from McCallum's unit at Goldman that identified several big Wall Street funds with interests in California agriculture. Dairy ranked first. Grapes third. Almonds were second.

Somehow, Cole didn't think Ms. Morris was out of New York. It wasn't just her clothes or her haircut. It was something else, something Abe said. He'd mentioned Hollywood.

Cole stepped out of the research room and into the library's open hallway, already ringing up Billy Porter, one of the partners in Abe's firm. He'd been the one who first spoke to Morris.

"Abe said she told you she worked for a hedge fund. Did she mention which one?"

"I don't know, Cole. Maybe."

"How did she know to call you?"

"We put out a press release on your behalf, sent it around to some other firms, people we know. I was listed as a contact."

Cole thought a minute. "She called the office, then."

"The main line, yeah."

"You have a record of her number in the system, right?"

"I guess. What's the deal, Jamie?"

"I need to know who she is. I need to know who I'm working for."

"I'll get Martha to check."

It took a few minutes, but Martha, the office manager, called him back with the number. It was the 626-area code, which he knew was somewhere in LA. He punched in the number and the call immediately picked up a fast-paced busy signal before it dropped completely. He tried it again. Could be he was blocked. Could be a dead line.

Cole went back to the computer room and had to wait again. He Googled around until he found a possible hit—Altadena Partners, based in Pasadena.

From the firm's website, Cole learned they managed nearly $50 billion in assets, including investments from the state's two largest public pensions. Cole noted that one. Their website was polished and slick, with flattering images of companies they were invested in and the smiling people who worked there. The only bio posted was for the head guy, a man named Steele Logan, who used to be chief of private wealth management at a bank in London. Cole found nothing on the site about Evelyn Morris.

He ran the firm through a news archive at the *LA Times*. Forty-six billion in assets wasn't that big, so the business press didn't pay a lot of attention to them. He did find one story from two years ago. It was a column originally in the *New York Business Times* that included

Altadena as one of twenty large hedge funds believed to have major investments from banks based in China—banks that may or may not have been government-owned. The article implied that the Chinese were trying to influence US business through such investments. A spokesperson for Altadena declined to comment.

Cole took note of that too.

He made copies of the senator's financial records and some of the news stories. He still didn't have a fix on Senator Wilmer. When Cole had been with the paper, Wilmer was new to the Capitol and played mostly as a back-bencher for the GOP. He'd jumped from local government to the Assembly and then to the Senate without attracting attention. And yet, according to McCallum, Wilmer liked to drink, play golf, and fool around.

Cole needed details, and he knew just the man to ask: Hal Davis, a political consultant who played friendly with both sides of the aisle.

Hal's office was about halfway between the library and the courthouse on the worn edge of the business district. A loosely organized homeless camp had taken over half the parking lot behind the building, and there was a stand-only bar on the ground floor. Latina B-girls walked the corners in short shorts. Meth runners hid in the shadows. Vice cops sat in unmarked cars.

Cole flashed his press credentials at the guard sitting in the lobby and then slipped into the elevator. The machine made a grinding noise, as if moving even one person from floor to floor might be too much for it. He knew the office door would be open and that no one would be staffing the reception gate. He snuck down the hall and entered an office without knocking.

"This is a stickup," Cole said, pointing a cocked finger and thumb at a startled black man sitting in front of a computer screen. "I want all your jelly doughnuts and the cold pizza in the fridge."

"Christ, Cole!" the man said, jumping to his feet and pushing the door closed. "What you about, man? Coming in here? You crazy?"

"How you been, Hal?"

Hal was a bear of a man; he reached out to offer Cole a fist bump.

"Haven't heard from you in a long time."

"I've been getting along. How's Thelma?"

"She cool. We got a granddaughter now. So, we all up in that, you know."

"That's great. I'm working again."

"And, as usual, you need help."

"What do you know about a state senator named Ted Wilmer?"

"He's from Redding, a safe Republican district with constituents who don't want much, don't need much." Hal leaned back in his chair, which howled under the pressure of the big man's slouch. "There's talk the boys from Wichita want him to run for US Senator."

"Not much hope for that, is there?"

"He'd be the front runner in the Republican primary if he'd say yes."

"He doesn't want to run?" Cole asked.

"No one really knows."

"How about the family business?"

"The nut farm?"

Cole laughed. "Yeah, the almond operation."

"I don't know much, except that I think they're doing pretty well."

"You hear anything about the Wilmers being in business with the Chinese?"

Hal shook his head with a small smile. "I don't think Ted Wilmer would be that stupid. It'd kill him nationally."

"What about something called the Solon Group?" Cole asked. "Out of Eureka?"

"Never heard of them," Hal got to his feet. "But Eureka and Chinese ring a bit of bell. Let me see here." He started to dig through a pile of paper on a table crowded with magazines and old newspaper clippings. "Here it is. Local paper up there on the coast ran a story about two months ago. Someone bought the old Klamath Railroad line and this reporter, whoever the hell he or she is, said the buyer was anonymous except *sources* say it's a Chinese bank."

"Trinity-Klamath Railroad?" Cole asked, looking at the headline and having no idea what it was or where it went.

"Trinity-Klamath line connects the North Coast to Redding," he said. "Used to anyway, long ago. It's been abandoned for probably twenty years. What a ride. Followed the river. Beautiful country. Except in winter when big rainstorms bring flash floods and debris slides down on the tracks. Maintaining that line was monster expensive."

"Why would a Chinese bank want to reopen it?"

"Dunno, fish." Hal took his seat again. "Except that Eureka is the largest deep-water port between San Francisco and Coos Bay. That's a stretch of about 500 miles."

Cole picked up the newspaper clipping and scribbled down the name of the reporter. "The Chinese want another place to offload their goods?"

"Maybe. Or maybe to send goods out."

"Like almonds?"

"Could be."

"That's a pretty good tip. Thanks, Hal."

"I don't know nothing. I'm just thinking."

Cole left believing he'd found what Ms. Morris was looking for—the Chinese buying into a man that might become a US Senator.

EIGHT

After parking his car in the garage, Cole came around to the front of the house to get his mail. As he did, a white Prius turned the corner. Susan was in the passenger seat, and a man Cole didn't recognize was driving. He was older, handsome, with a big head of gray hair. Susan leaned over and gave the guy a quick smooch on the lips before jumping out. The guy backed up, blew her a kiss, and drove off.

Instead of retreating immediately into her house, Susan remained across the street, looking at him. Cole waved and started for the front door. The scene he'd just witnessed gave him a tiny tug inside his chest.

"Wait!" She started toward him. "Cole," she said when she got closer. "Wait, I want to talk to you."

His hands were full; the briefcase, a six-pack of beer he'd bought on the way home, and now the mail. "Come on in."

She followed him inside. "I've been meaning to tell you."

"It's OK, Susan. You got a new boyfriend; that's cool. Good for you." He tossed the mail on a table in the hallway and dropped his briefcase on the floor. In the kitchen, he pulled a bottle of beer from the bag. "Want one? I think I've got some wine if you'd rather."

"A glass of red would be nice."

He found a glass and the wine. They stood in his kitchen, silent.

"I'm fine," Cole said, breaking the lull. "Fine, Susan. Really."

Susan's soft brown eyes drifted to the floor. She held her hands at her chest as if ready to pray. "It's just . . . you're important to me, and I want you to know about what's going on in my life. I guess I . . . well, I never found the right time to tell you."

"It's OK."

"You don't know all of it yet," she said, her body becoming rigid and still. "My friend. Daniel. He's asked me to marry him, and I said yes."

He was facing her. He swallowed hard and took a long pull on his beer. Their eyes locked and then Cole broke away, opened the fridge, and looked around for something. He reached for the cheese, and when he turned around, her eyes were still on him.

"So, it's like that," he finally said. "Guess I didn't realize how important you are to me. I'm surprised; seems sudden."

"It is." She caught his hand, giving it a squeeze. "We've only been going out for a month or so. But I'll be forty-five in the fall, and I don't want to wait too long."

"He's a good guy? Treats you right?"

"Yes." She put both her arms around Cole's neck, giving him a warm hug. "How about you? I worry about you being alone."

"I'm working on that," he said, breaking free and taking a seat at the breakfast table. "You should have seen this woman I was out with just last week. A schoolteacher."

"Was she nice?"

"No-ooo." Cole cackled. "She was awful. Accused me of being a deadbeat and walked out after about five minutes. An utterly amazing performance to live through."

"You are not a deadbeat," she said in a serious tone. "A puzzle sometimes, but not a deadbeat."

Cole got to his feet, retrieved a knife from the rack above the stove, and began cutting cubes from the cheese block. He got a box of crackers from the pantry.

"So, tell me about him," he said.

"He's a retired airline pilot," Susan said. "He's got a place in Healdsburg." She popped a piece of cheese into her mouth. "I'm going to go live with him."

"Man, you really do have news."

She took his hand a second time and put her face in front of him. "Are you OK?"

Cole pulled away and got up and went to the liquor cabinet. He found the tequila and a shot glass. "You want one?"

"Jamie?" Her voice pleading. "Talk to me."

"About what?"

"About you." She came close again. "Are you sleeping?"

"Yeah, enough."

"You should find someone to talk to."

"Talk to about what?"

"Your anger, the firing, all that's happened to you in the last six months."

Cole poured out two fingers into the glass and threw it back. He took a deep breath and then he took her hand. "I'm fine, really. I'm over it. I have some regrets, things I would have done differently, but what's done is done."

He smiled, grabbed a big wedge of cheese and two crackers, took them in one bite and then washed it down with a swig of beer. "I'm going to put on some music, any requests?"

She laughed. "You mean any requests as long as it was written two hundred years ago?"

"Maybe just a hundred years," he called back from the living room. Something upbeat, he was thinking as he flipped through the CDs. Paraguayan folk songs. Spanish guitar. *Madrigal Gavota* by Agustín Barrios. Yes.

"I've got a new gig going," he said, returning to the kitchen. "An investigative service for law firms. I've got a pretty good-paying client already."

"That's great. She cut a couple of slices more. Cole had another shot. She watched with wary eyes. "You're not going to get drunk now, are you?"

"No, I just had a good day. I deserve it." His head bounced in rhythm with the song.

"What about the other thing?" she asked. "Here in your house? You figure out who the mailman really is?"

"No. That's quite the cipher."

"How are you going to solve it?"

"Not sure. Still wondering if it's worth my time. There's only a downside to finding out."

"What? You mean disclosure?" She stepped forward and took possession of the liquor bottle. "That's so selfish, Jamie. I'm shocked you'd think that way."

"I said I haven't made up my mind. Could be a major pain in the ass to track down. I mean, it was forty years ago." He sat on a chair, kicked off his shoes, and slid his belt off too. "Why do you care?"

"Because maybe I'll be selling my house too," she answered.

"And you think it could have happened across the street? I get it."

"The thought crossed my mind."

"I found an old FBI map. Showed one of the attacks was around here someplace."

"Really?"

"Yeah, and I know my house was built by then. Not sure about yours." He grabbed a row of crackers and another beer. "Come with me. Let's go to work on it right now."

He led her to his office, sat down at the computer, and booted up his machine. She pulled a chair up behind him.

"Had an editor once tell me that every good story starts with *the first question.*" Cole punched words into the search box: *Golden State Killer and Curtis Court.* "And here is the answer."

The machine brought back 4.2 million results. Cole looked down the list. Almost all had to do with a guy named Curtis, who ran the genealogy DNA website that played some role in helping identify the killer, DeAngelo.

Cole tried again by adding the name of their town, *Rancho Cordova.* Once again, nothing relevant came up.

"Try Golden State Killer and map of crimes," Susan suggested.

Another twelve million results. Cole scanned them, finding the story that his friend Murray Downes did in 1978. He pulled it up and showed Susan the FBI map.

"I count six attacks that took place in Rancho," she said. "Only one on our side of the freeway."

"Doesn't mean it was here," Cole answered and set up another search. "Let's back up a step." This time, Cole removed the names of their street and town and added *timeline*.

Another long list of results. Toward the bottom of the page, he clicked on a site called E-A-RTerror.com. The page loaded under the heading Golden State Killer Timeline.

"My goodness," Susan said. "Look at that. These people found the killer's middle school yearbook."

"Folsom High baseball team photo." Cole pointed.

He clicked forward until he got to the end of the timeline. "Look at this. April 23, 2018. DeAngelo goes fishing with a friend the day before the arrest."

"Look underneath it," Susan said, pointing. "The next one. They have the arrest warrant."

"I've seen it," Cole answered. "No mention of Curtis Court."

He scanned the site. Susan went to the kitchen to refill her wine.

"This is amazing," he called out. "Whoever found all this did it quickly. What's it been since the arrest? Maybe three weeks? That's a pretty amazing job of reporting."

"You should find out who these people are," Susan said as she came back into the room. "I'll bet they'd know in a heartbeat if a murder happened here in your house."

"That's a really good idea." Cole returned to the site's homepage and scrolled down until he found an email link to the webmaster. He hesitated before beginning, trying to think of the right thing to say.

Hi, my name is James Cole. I'm a writer working on a book about the Golden State Killer. I'm hoping you might have time to chat. This site is amazing. The amount of detail is stunning. And that you got it all within just a few days of the arrest? Remarkable. Please contact me when convenient.

Cole added his cell number at the bottom.

She stood behind him and put a hand on his shoulder. "That's a good ploy, a book. It should get their attention."

He tapped the desk with his fingers. "Maybe it's not a ploy," he mused as the tequila kicked in and a germ of an idea blossomed in his mind. "Maybe there is a book here."

Cole sat back in his chair. She touched the curls on the back of his head. "You need a haircut. And the beard has got to go. Enough already, Jamie; it makes you look ten years older."

"I thought you liked it."

She leaned down and kissed his ear. "I never said that," she whispered.

"What are you doing?" He turned to look at her.

She leaned down again and kissed him warmly on the mouth. "Jamie, will you make love to me one last time?"

NINE

The editor, the inspiration, and the full-time webmaster of E-A-RTerror.com was sitting in the patio working on a gin and tonic, her laptop open on a newly refinished picnic table shaded by a big, striped-colored umbrella. A plump tabby sat on the table too, comfortable in the shade and indifferent to the sudden outbursts of Karmen's fingers dancing up and down on the keyboard.

She read Cole's email again. The book interested her. She'd seen his note the night before and almost called him right away. She was glad she'd waited. Karmen still wasn't sure about him. She'd Googled him. "Goddamn *Journal* reporter," she muttered.

They had been killing themselves—Karmen and her small army of cold-case evangelists. Pulling all-nighters. Scouring sources. Chasing leads all over the country. Anywhere the story of Joseph J. DeAngelo took them. She noticed right away that some reporters were stealing content from them. First, it was the local TV. Screenshots of images they'd dug up. Then, *Journal* reporters started to poach too, all without attribution. That burned her. Karmen called an editor the one night and left a bitch message, threatened a lawsuit, closed with a string of street curses.

She figured Cole was up to something too, planning some bigger rip-off.

A chime from the computer indicated a new email. The sound startled the cat; he rose quickly and jumped off the table, retreating into the house.

"I think I found DeAngelo's mother!" *pepperprincess* messaged the group. *Princess* was a nurse who lived in Portland. "We know her maiden name was DeGoat and that she was married in upstate New York. My brother lives in Ithaca and look what he sent me! An item from the *Elmira Heights Star-Gazette* from 1939! A Kathleen DeGoat. Got to be her!"

Karmen opened the attachment. May 18, 1939. Kathleen DeGoat, chair of the Sigma Phi Tau, a dinner-dance with Ernie Dobberstein's orchestra. There was a photo of her; she looked like the killer. Karmen was impressed.

"What's Sigma Phi Tau?" asked *saintthomasthebear*, an insurance broker from Salt Lake.

"An honor society for philosophers," *princess* answered. "Can you believe it? The killer was raised on Sartre and Nietzsche!"

"That could cause anyone to go off," quipped *mrbeachbum5*, an auditor for a big accounting firm in Los Angeles.

"How do we keep the newspapers from stealing this?" Karmen asked.

"Copyright it," *mrbeachbum5* said.

"You can't copyright something that's already been copyrighted," *saintthomasthebear* argued. "I'm looking at the *Star-Gazette* website right now. They're still publishing."

"Do it anyway," Karmen ordered.

A new member, *rosaritasurfcat*, who'd just joined the group and appeared to be a Southern California beach rat living in Baja, said, "Why does this guy have so many nicknames? I'm tired of writing them all out. Can't we just use one?"

"Michelle used EAR-ONS and let it go at that," said *giantsbeliving*, a tech worker from Marin.

"What's that?" *surfcat* asked.

"East Area Rapist and Original Night Stalker," *giants* answered.

"Who's Michelle?"

The chatter went dead. They were waiting for Karmen. Michelle was Michelle McNamara, the bestselling author not only credited with getting authorities to restart the investigation into the Golden State Killer but also convincing them to mine DNA data compiled by subscription genealogy websites. DNA from a distant relative of DeAngelo's eventually linked him with a number of the crime scenes.

Everyone knew Karmen was red jealous of the writer's success, even though she'd died before finishing the book. Michelle's husband, a famous TV comedian, hired a couple pros to complete it.

"Use all of them," Karmen wrote. "Everything he did while he was in Visalia, use Ransacker. For the Sacramento crimes, he's E-A-R. Bay Area, ONS; and SoCal, Golden State Killer."

Sylvia, the owner of the house and Karmen's partner, called to her from the living room. "Phone, Kar," she said. "Your phone."

Karmen ran inside to answer it.

"It's Brooke," a female voice said.

"What do you want?" Karmen asked gruffly.

"You did it again, Karmen. I found another totally false item. The sheriff saw it too. He wants it taken down."

"Screw that."

"No, Karmen, screw you. You want to be treated like real media? You got to act like real media. Unsubstantiated and incorrect reporting is not tolerated."

"Which item?"

"The second to last. You say we have an investigation into one of DeAngelo's family members. You're accusing someone of helping him. Totally false. No such investigation is going on or being contemplated."

"Well, my source inside the department says there is," Karmen said, moving back to her bedroom where her pile of notebooks, news clippings, and odd scraps of documents were scattered on a small folding table against a wall.

"Who?"

"I'm looking."

"It's bull, Karmen."

"We'll see."

"Take it down. You got until tomorrow morning. Otherwise, I'm cutting off your access to department personnel, press releases, news conferences, everything."

"You can't do that."

"I'm the sheriff's press deputy. I can."

Karmen snapped her phone shut. "Go to hell!" she shouted after the call ended.

Sylvia stood in the doorway wearing a disapproving expression. "Winning friends and influencing people?"

"That bitch is always on our ass. She doesn't do it to the papers or the dipshits on TV, just us."

"Shows how important you are, girl."

Karmen tossed around several notepads until she found the one that included her notes on the tip. The info came from a retired sheriff's deputy she met at a cop bar near the rail yard.

The guy's name was Fred Dixon. She read her notes and then returned to the patio to check what she'd posted to the website. She remembered it. She thought it was a big scoop, something the papers might follow. She'd wondered why they hadn't.

Karmen grabbed the keys to her pickup. "I've got to run up to Scotty's," she told Sylvia.

***

It wasn't yet six, and only about seven or eight guys were hanging around. She didn't see Dixon among them. She took a stool at the bar and said hello to Scotty, and he drew her a draft.

"What's up, kid?" he asked. Karmen told him about the run-in with the sheriff's flack. "You said one of our guys told you that? Who?"

"Fred Dixon."

Scotty sneered. "Dixon? Did he tell you he was part of our network?"

"Yeah."

"Well, he ain't. He's not well-liked, tends to be full of it."

Karmen hung her head. "You think he made it up?"

"I honestly don't know, but my guess is he was trying to get in your pants and was willing to say anything to get there."

"That sounds about right." She sighed. "I guess I should take that one down."

"Probably a good idea."

She sipped her beer. "Was he lying about working the case too?" she asked. "He said he'd been a deputy with Sacramento sheriff before becoming an investigator with the state prisons. He told me he was on the task force for a while."

"That part's true, I think," Scotty said. "He started with the sheriff's department. Joined up in the late eighties. I knew him from the academy. He got assigned as a stooge for the E-A-R task force. Just one or two investigators were still kicking the case then, looking for new leads. I knew the guy that ran it pretty well. Captain Donovan, good man."

"Dixon worked for him?"

"For a few months, just before Donovan retired. He didn't like the lad much either."

"Why?"

"Probably the same reason none of my guys like him. Not a real team player. Out for himself."

She sat in silence and then paid for her beer. As she got up to leave, she waved a finger in the air. "I almost forgot. You ever hear of a reporter with the *Journal* named James Cole?"

"Jamie? Sure, what's up with him? He was just in here the other day."

"He sent me a note. Said he's working on a book about the Golden State Killer, saw our website, wants to talk. Is he legit?"

"Yeah, sure. Although he ain't with the *Journal* no more. He's working with a law firm as an investigator."

"There's no book?"

"I don't know. Cole worked a long time as a news reporter; all those guys eventually try writing a book or two."

"He wouldn't be trying to scam me, would he? Those bastards at the *Journal* have been stealing our stuff since we went public."

"You might call Cole many things, but a lazy cheat wouldn't be one of them."

"You said he was here? What did he want?"

"Looking for intel on one of the E-A-R crimes," Scotty said. "He was looking for Skip. How is Skip, anyway?"

"Looking for Skip Harkin?" Karmen put a hand to her cheek. "Skip is OK, except, you know, old man stuff. This guy Cole found out about Skip? That's interesting."

"Cole was one helluva reporter."

TEN

I n Cole's home office, there were two growing files—one labeled DeAngelo and the other Wilmer. He figured he'd done as much legwork from Sacramento as possible on the Wilmer job, and it was probably time to carry on the dig up north.

The senator's district was the Shasta County seat in Redding. The corporate offices for the almond company were in a town called Red Bluff; Cole had to look that one up. Turned out it was the county seat of Tehama County. The town's population was 16,000, and it was about a half hour south of Redding.

The trip north to visit both towns would be a minimum three hours up and back from Sacramento. To make that drive, do the research he needed, and maybe try to jump the senator some place? That would be a very long day.

Tomorrow, he thought, *or maybe Thursday*. He'd need to be on the road before seven.

Cole pushed the Wilmer file aside and pulled the DeAngelo paperwork forward. He tapped on the computer keyboard and checked his email. Nothing yet from the people who ran E-A-RTerror.com.

He got his briefcase and found the thumb drive he'd used to download the property records on his visit to the assessor. He needed to find out about his house.

The original title to Cole's place showed the developer as M&M Partners. He opened a new browser and got to the home page for the state department of corporations. He plugged M&M into the search box.

No M&M Partners. He found businesses with close names, like M&M Group and M&M&T Partners, but M&M Partners no longer existed. He scanned the list again, looking for some version of M&M that was located somewhere close to Sacramento. He found one,

M&M Raddison. The agent for the company was a woman named Lynn K. Raddison, and her address was in Roseville.

Cole opened another browser and keyed in the state's department of real estate. He plugged Lynn K. Raddison into the agent search box. No Lynn K. Raddison from Roseville, but when he searched just Raddison, a Cynthia A. Raddison from Roseville popped up. He went back to the corporation's page that was still open on M&M Raddison, and he noted the address. It matched the address for Cynthia.

Next, he Googled Raddison and real estate and Roseville. At the top of the results was Raddison Realty, but it wasn't in Roseville, it was in Lincoln, a town just north. He found the company website. Cindy Raddison was the owner. There was a photo of her. She had the bright smile and the all too eager expression of a sales professional. She looked young, maybe mid-forties, probably too young to know much about all the chaos that took place in Rancho Cordova during the 1970s.

He tried calling but got the phone tree. He started to leave a message when another call interrupted.

"Is this James Cole?" a woman's voice. "The writer?"

"It is."

"My name is Karmen Mueller. I'm the one who runs E-A-RTerror. com. You messaged me a couple days ago."

"Thanks for calling back. I'm trying to run down some details about one of the crimes this Golden State Killer allegedly committed."

"Which one?"

"Well, one that I've been told was committed in my house," he said. "A rape and murder."

"Weird. Where's your place?"

"Rancho, on a little cul-de-sac, Curtis Court. Ever hear of it?"

"No. What part of town?"

"Northeast corner, not far from Costco."

"Close to Mather Airfield?"

"Yeah, sort of."

"Well, the E-A-R was active all over Rancho Cordova. But I've never heard of an attack on Curtis Court."

"Then there wasn't one?"

"Beats me, man. I'm just saying I've never heard of it."

"Can I come by and maybe look over your files?"

"Hell no. Me and my crew worked our butts off to get what we have. Some of your buddies at the *Journal* have already ripped us off."

"I'm not with the *Journal* anymore, and no one there is my buddy."

"Dude, the answer is no."

"Maybe we could work something out."

"Maybe," Karmen said. "Money isn't a big motivator for me. Tell me about this book deal."

"Well, it's just an idea for a book, so far, based on the murder."

"The murder you don't know anything about."

"Right," Cole said. Yes, he thought, *she's right about that.* "How about this? I buy you lunch someday soon, and we talk about it some more."

"How about today?"

Cole looked at the clock. It was twelve thirty. "OK."

"Meet me at two," she said. "The restaurant inside the Rancho Marriott."

***

Cole thought the Marriott an odd choice for lunch. Rancho Cordova didn't have a lot of fine dining; it was a town better known for its drive-thrus. And the Marriott? Seriously? A last resort for the weary salesman. A layover for the grandparents on their way to Portland. A place the husband retreats to when the wife kicks him out.

The restaurant was empty except for a young couple sharing a pizza. Cole didn't see anyone who might be Karmen. He pictured her as young, tattooed, and wearing some sort of grunge outfit. The hostess started to take Cole to a table in the middle of the room, but he asked to be seated farther from the young couple. He wanted more privacy.

He'd only just sat down when two women came into the room. One tall, one short. One Asian with a flowery dress and sandals. The other Latina, thin, stylish shades, and a row of tattoos on both arms.

"Mr. Cole," the tall one said. "I'm Sylvia Kim. This is Karmen Mueller."

"Thank you for coming." Cole put out a hand, giving the tall Asian woman a second glance.

"So, you're a writer?" Sylvia asked with a warm smile.

"Someone told me you got fired from the *Journal*," Karmen broke in. "Is that true?"

They sat. Cole rubbed the bottom of his beard. "True."

"How come?"

"I screwed up a big story, and it cost the paper a lot of money to settle a libel suit."

"Damn, man," Karmen said. "That's all messed up."

Sylvia threw the other woman a serious eye and then returned to Cole. "And now you want to write a book?"

Cole's head tilted. "To be honest, I'm not sure there's a book. I'm still at square one."

"Karmen said you think one of the E-A-R's murders took place inside your house," Sylvia said. "Is that what you want to write about?"

He waited, studying her. He reached for the water glass in front of him. "Who knows?" he said. "There could be a book. If it's true, I think there could be a story to tell. About the victim, about my neighborhood, maybe bringing all of it up to date, the arrest and everything."

"You'll need help," Sylvia observed. "You'll need to learn everything there is to know about the case and the accused."

"I suppose," Cole said. "Although that's what I've done professionally for more than twenty years, digging out the story."

"Karmen could help."

"What do you mean?"

"I want in," Karmen said. "In exchange for helping you with research, giving you access to my files, my sources, all that—I want a byline, maybe a bit of the book profits."

The sides of Cole's mouth drew up in amusement, and he slowly shook his head. "I don't think so," he said.

"Why not?" Sylvia asked. "You saw her website. You can see how good a researcher she is. She's an expert on the case."

"Maybe so, but that doesn't make her a reporter." Cole looked at Sylvia. "Who are you, anyway? You want a byline too? Or are you the attorney?"

"I'm Karmen's partner and a paralegal. I'm here to make sure she's treated fairly."

"I told Karmen I could probably come up with a few bucks for her time."

"And I told you, butthead, that I didn't want a few bucks." Karmen pulled off her glasses, her sharp brown eyes glaring.

Cole's head tipped to one side as he gave her a long up and down. The table went silent.

"Do either of you know what I did at the *Journal* before I was let go?" Neither woman answered. "I was the head of the investigative team. I'm pretty good at finding things out—especially things people don't want found—so I'm just not sure what you think Karmen would be bringing to the party. And, by the way, we are so far from having a book project with bylines and profits that you couldn't see it from here with a laser telescope."

"I told you," Karmen hissed. "Screw this guy." She got to her feet and abruptly walked out of the restaurant.

Sylvia stayed put, her hands folded in front of her. The server approached. Cole waved him off.

"Mr. Cole, you're a very mistrusting man."

"I think I might have heard that before."

"I apologize for whatever we've said today that's caused you to think we're trying to take advantage of you. It's not our intent."

"Look, writing a book isn't like opening a hot dog stand," he said. "It's an extremely intimate activity. For any writer to risk bringing in someone else, there needs to be an enormous amount of trust in that other individual's skills; otherwise, it's a big waste of time. I'm impressed with the website, but I don't know how much of it she did or someone else did. Clearly, it's the work of a group of people."

"She's the editor. She brought those people together, and she's the one sweating out the details each day."

"No," Cole said again. "I can't bring someone in that I don't even know."

Sylvia had a sip of water. "You want to know what happened in your house, correct?"

"Yes."

"If Karmen can answer that question, you take her on for a tryout. Say a month."

"Then something did happen in my house?" Cole's eyes focused on her. "You know, don't you?"

"I don't, no."

"Does Karmen?"

Sylvia held a poker face.

Cole scratched his head and then folded his arms. "OK fine, I'll bring her on for a tryout," he said abruptly. "But let's make one thing clear: I'm running the show. If she gets out of line or ends up being as big a pain in the ass as she appears to be, she's out."

"Understood."

"I decide if there's something to pursue here." He pointed a finger. "No questions asked."

"I'll make sure she gets the message."

"So, tell me. What happened in my house?"

Sylvia smiled. "I don't know."

"Karmen knows?"

"No."

Cole groaned and dropped his head. "I knew this was a dippy move."

"Karmen knows who does."

"And that is?"

"Skip."

ELEVEN

ole was out the door by 6:50. North on Interstate 5 bound for Redding and Red Bluff. Three hours with nothing but the moonscape of the northern Central Valley as a company. Music was a double album of Bach chamber music.

As a kid, Cole had seen the southern end of the Valley up close on long dull drives with his father, a state geologist who worked in the petroleum industry. The lower Tulare Basin and the oil fields of Bakersfield. Cotton and corn as far as the eye could see, broken only by see-saw pump jacks scattered between.

Often the trip extended north to the Capitol. The ag towns were stretched out by the hours—Fresno, Turlock, Manteca. More fruit. Tomatoes especially.

Cole thought about those trips. His dad would tell him about the land, the rock underneath, and how the two formed the economies of man. They never went north of Sacramento. This was his first visit to the upper Sacramento Valley.

It was still May, but summer was bearing down. The sun rose early and big and stayed late. Just as he'd done as a boy, he counted the hours and minutes between the towns. Dunnigan. Williams. Willows. Corning.

In the upper Valley, farmers grew alfalfa and rice. And indeed, nuts. Almonds.

He arrived in Redding about ten, and the air was already still with heat. Overhead, the sky was clear and brilliant blue, but closer to the ground, the dust from thousands of tractors working in the fields washed the air into a murky brown.

Cole found the senator's office on the third floor of the state building in the city's center. Although the sign on the door promised it would be open Monday through Friday, nine to three, the door was locked. It was Friday and Cole knew the Legislature wasn't in session; they'd already shut down for the weekend. Maybe Wilmer was on a golf course some place. Maybe he was home.

The Wilmer place was about eight miles east into the foothills, a place called Palo Cedro, the last home of country music legend Merle Haggard. Cole had noticed that when he looked up the town on Wikipedia.

He also knew particulars about the Wilmer mansion from Zillow. Five bedrooms and four baths; 5,800 square feet in all. There was a guest house behind the pool; nine acres for the horses; and a fenced-in driving range, 450 yards long. It was located about halfway up a steep one-lane road, tucked on the western edge of the Lassen National Forest.

The property was surrounded by tall concrete walls connected at the driveway by an iron gate. The gate was open, but two men sat in a golf cart just inside it. Cole spotted a shotgun standing in a rack between them. He drove past and then up the road another 500 yards before pulling into the driveway of a house directly above. He worked his way around another big wall and got to the edge of the neighbor's property. He could see a lot of activity in the Wilmers' backyard. Tables were being assembled. A man on a ladder pulled a string of red, white, and blue balloons through an archway. Several more workers were moving about with boxes and folding chairs. There was a woman in the middle of it all. She seemed to be directing things.

Cole noticed a service road at the bottom of the hill. It looked like he could access the property from down there, but he'd have to brave a thicket of untended brush, then the driving range, and another couple hundred yards before he could get to the pool area and then the patio. That would take too long, and he'd arrive a sweaty mess. It would also be easy for someone to spot him from above.

The pace of preparation for the festivity made Cole think the party was probably scheduled for later today. He didn't see Senator Wilmer around. Might be better to come back. He thought he'd just sneak in once the festivities were underway.

Cole rolled back down to Redding, got lunch near the civic center, and then went to the Recorder's Office to start the dig.

The Wilmers were a prominent family, and they owned a lot of property. He skimmed through a handful of records; most were old, and none were too interesting. He ran Stony Creek through the system and got better results. The company had completed more than a dozen land purchases in just the last two years. Hundreds, some even thousands of acres. He pulled several of them. On one of them, he found Altadena Partners listed as the lender. He made notes. Altadena, he suspected, was the hedge fund that employed his Evelyn Morris, the young media consultant who'd hired him to do the Wilmer dig.

The courthouse was just across the way. He didn't expect to find much. And indeed, the civil litigation against the senator was routine. A mechanics lien from two years back. A property dispute with a neighbor. A wrongful termination suit from a household employee. The family business, Stony Creek, had more. Much of it wasn't interesting either, although Cole took note of a series of suits filed within the last year by rival growers over water. That seemed significant. The state drought had ended at least two years ago.

In the criminal index, Cole was surprised. When he plugged in Wilmer, an entire screen of records came up. Not Ted, but a man named Callen. The cases were old, decades old. He scribbled down a few of the case numbers and went to the counter, handing the clerk his check-out slips.

"None of these would be here," the clerk said, returning the slips. "We don't keep cases that old."

"Where would I need to go to find them?" Cole asked.

The kid turned to a woman working behind him. "Hey, Barb? Where can this guy find old criminal files?"

She came to the desk and looked at the slips. "Callen Wilmer?" she asked, looking at Cole. "Why are you looking for his files?"

"I'm a reporter," Cole answered politely.

She looked at him blankly. "You know he's been dead at least ten years."

"I didn't."

"You'll have to go to the state to access his records," she told him. "Department of Justice."

Cole returned to the indexing terminal and clicked through the screens, making sure he didn't miss anything. At the end of the criminal records for Callen Wilmer was one more recent, a Dalton J. Wilmer. Cole filled out another request and returned to the counter.

"How about this one?" Cole said, giving the boy the slip.

"I don't know," the kid said, taking it back to his boss.

The big woman came forward again. "What's this about?" she asked.

"I told you, I'm a reporter working on a story."

"This file has been sealed."

Cole snatched the slip from her hand and waved it at her. "I can easily check," he said. "And if you're wrong and attempting to interfere with the public's right to view government records, you could face a year in state prison."

Her eyes deepened and sank further into her head. Cole tapped the countertop before returning once more to the index terminal. He got out his phone.

The woman got to her desk and picked up her phone too.

Cole sat tight, watching her with one eye. He called Karmen.

"It's Cole. Did you talk to Sylvia about my terms?"

"Yeah."

"You in?"

"Sure."

"OK, good. She said you could set me up with this old cop, the guy from the task force, Skip. When can you do that?"

"It might take a while," she said. "Skip isn't well, and even when he is, he's usually cranky. I'll need time."

"Meanwhile, can you do something else for me? I want you to find what you can on a man named Callen Allen Wilmer. And another named Dalton Johnson Wilmer."

"Who are they?"

"That's what I want you to find out."

"Is this for the book?"

"Damn, Karmen, you already forget what my terms are? I give directions, you follow them."

"All right, all right." She clicked off.

Cole hadn't noticed, but two Shasta County sheriff's deputies were approaching him.

"Let me see some ID," the older of the two deputies said.

"What's this about?"

"Gimme."

Cole handed him his press credentials.

"*Sacramento Journal*," the officer said. "Come with me."

"What for?" Cole tried to wring his arm out of the second cop's grasp. "What the hell is this?"

He was taken out of the courthouse lobby and down a private hallway to an empty room. The younger one took Cole's briefcase and patted his pockets and his torso and took his wallet and his phone, car keys.

"What's this about?" Cole asked.

"Never mind that," the older cop said, looking at Cole's driver's license and then inspecting the press pass. "Mr. Cole, you are going to have to wait here until I can sort things out. Jimmy, get him a chair."

"Sort what out?" Cole said. "What the hell is this?"

The older cop left and the younger deputy slid a plastic chair into the room. They locked the door.

At least an hour later, maybe more, the door unlocked, and the older deputy stepped inside. He returned Cole's things, minus the press credentials.

"Mr. Cole, we called down to Sacramento and you're no longer a working journalist, ain't that right?"

"That's not true. I'm writing a book," Cole argued. "I've got free-lance assignments too."

"Yeah, well, when you handed me these credentials, you committed criminal impersonation."

"Criminal impersonation?" Cole laughed and started to say something else but bit his lip and didn't.

"The county counsel said I have to give this back to you," the deputy said, holding out the press badge. "Criminal impersonation is a class six felony. If we hear you've flashed this thing anywhere else, I can assure you, mister, we'll drag your ass back here and you *will* be prosecuted. Now get on your horse."

***

No way was James J. Cole—Pulitzer finalist and a two-time winner of the University of Southern California's Selden Ring Award for investigative reporting—no way was *he* going to be chased out of town by a tin badge and a hick clerk. Cole checked the time, four-twenty. The party at the Wilmer mansion was probably just getting started.

***

The gates were open. Valet boys from the high school were running between the courtyard and a temporary parking lot down by the barn. There was a jubilee jazz band playing on the back patio. The murmur of the guests surrounded the bar, and the poolside tables were crowded.

Cole followed a line of cars into the open field near the barn and parked himself. He slipped into the party with a man and his wife decked out in cowboy boots and big Stenson hats. The event appeared to be a fundraiser for the county farm bureau. The headliner was a conservative radio host with a daily show on the same Sacramento station that launched Rush Limbaugh's career in the mid-1980s. He got in line for a beer and then dropped a twenty-dollar donation on raffle tickets.

He circulated but didn't see the senator. He got another beer and then found a quiet spot under an umbrella near the pool. A tall, attractive woman in her fifties approached him along with a broad-shouldered, square-headed man.

"Good afternoon," she said with a hint of a Southern accent. "I don't believe I've had the honor. I'm Lorraine Wilmer, I'm the hostess. And you are?"

"My name is Cole, James Cole."

"How do you do, Mr. Cole?" She smiled. "You know, I've lived here in the Redding area for almost ten years now, and we have these sorts of events all the time. Each and every time, the very same people attend. I've gotten to know almost all of my husband's friends and supporters. But I don't remember you. Sage, is there a James Cole on the guest list?"

"Nope."

Cole noticed that Sage didn't have a guest list to check. He didn't like the look in Sage's black, deep-set eyes.

"I didn't think so." Her expression turned serious. "I'd like you to come with me, Mr. Cole. Quietly please."

Sage took Cole's arm and led him beyond the pool, away from the party, and then out a gate to the street. There was a sheriff's patrol car waiting. Mrs. Wilmer waved to one of the officers.

"Trespassing," she said.

For the second time in the same afternoon, Cole was taken in custody by the Shasta County sheriff, this time in cuffs.

***

It was after two in the morning when they processed Cole through the gate. They gave him back his phone and wallet. Nothing else, no paperwork, no order to appear. He asked about his car.

"Down four blocks at the city yard," the deputy said. "The security guard has your keys. There's a hundred-and-fifty-dollar lock-up fee. He'll only take cash. You'll find an ATM at the bank, a block down on the right."

He found the ATM and fumbled with his wallet. It was dark and hard to read the blurry screen. From behind him came the sound of screeching tires. A pickup jumped the curb just a hundred yards away and headed right at him. It stopped just short. Two guys jumped out. Before Cole had a chance, one of them bull-rushed him and threw him back into the ATM stand. Cole's head snapped against the machine's hard metal shell. Cole fell to his knees. The other guy pulled Cole up by his collar and threw a hard punch into his gut. The other one held Cole from behind. The second guy took another shot in the ribs. Cole fell again, gasping for air.

"Just a little goodbye message, hotshot," the second guy said as he jumped back into the truck. "We don't like outsiders coming around poking their nose where it don't belong."

TWELVE

Robert F. 'Skip' Harkin remembered the silence the most. The silence and the darkness in the early morning hours before dawn. Cigarettes and coffee from a steel thermos. The scratchy call of the dispatcher signaling tragedy in another part of town.

There were the victims too. Their faces blurry and indistinct, as if he was passing a big crowd while sitting on a bus. He remembered the kids better. Sometimes a husband was there too; sometimes sobbing quietly in a corner. The sun would be up by then. It always seemed to be sunup when he reached them.

The arrest brought it back.

At first, when he heard the news, he had trouble remembering. It seemed foreign and far away. No tears or screams of joy. He'd told his daughter it was just another arrest, just another case that could be closed. One less to carry around.

Within a day or two, he couldn't stop thinking about it. Couldn't let it go. He thought about the mistakes. The missteps. He knew he wasn't the only one who carried the burden. Cops all over did; a fraternity of want. As the decades passed, no one would bring the case up when they gathered for a retirement party or a funeral.

He sat in the chair, smoking. The arrest warrant flipped open on the big table in front of him. The sheriff released only some of what the detectives had given the judge. Much of the complaint was redacted, entire pages. It didn't matter. The old man knew what had been blacked out. Moreover, he knew what was missing. The times the bastard got away.

His daughter was in the kitchen beginning dinner and his grandson sat at the big dining room table, doing his homework. Skip sat in front of the big windows staring out at the million-dollar view of the American River. Opposite from the house, on the other side of the canyon, were steep red cliffs that reached down from the thick pine forest to the ribbon of steel blue water that was still rushing cold with the winter snowmelt.

He wanted to smoke, to roll out on the deck and watch the sun go down. He wanted to forget what he knew. He wanted to silence the voices in his head.

He quietly rolled out of the living room to the hallway and down to the back den which had become both his hospital room and his office. Skip and another retired investigator had once wanted to write a book about the case, but his friend died a couple years ago. Everything they'd gathered, all the police reports, the witness statements and investigator notes, forensic analysis—all of it sat in three big file cabinets on the other side of the room from Skip's big desk.

Since the arrest, he'd been digging through the material. He'd pick up the warrant, dogeared and smudged, looking for something and then to the cabinets for something else. He'd been at it all afternoon.

Sally, his daughter, called from the hallway, "Dad, phone call." She brought him the remote extension. "It's Karmen."

He nodded and took the phone. "Hi, sweetheart," he said.

"Hey, Skipper, how you doing?"

"I'm OK. Hey, I saw the new post. DeAngelo's mom? Good stuff."

"Thanks. Listen, I met this guy, a writer."

"Yeah?" Skip's voice slow and cautious.

"He could be the one."

"For what?"

"Your Victim Eleven," Karmen said. "The theory of the second suspect."

"What are you talking about?"

"Why not? You said no one downtown gives a damn about it. That they got DeAngelo's DNA on enough of the attacks to put him away and close the case."

"I know, I know."

"Well, that means we can take a run at finding the accomplice. Free and clear."

"Who is this reporter? What makes you think he'd be the one?"

"He used to run the investigative team at the *Journal*," she said. "And he's on it, anyway. He thinks one of the attacks took place in his living room."

"That don't mean much; the crimes all had to happen someplace."

"His place is in Rancho, eastside, near Mather. Could be her, Victim Eleven."

"We don't know where she was killed. Lon never said."

"You've told me both you and Lon thought there had to be an accomplice, and you said Lon knew of one attack in particular. You said it was in Rancho near the airfield."

Skip put the phone on speaker and rolled to the cabinets. "Hang on, I'm going to look," he said. He got open one of the drawers, found a file, and rifled through some paperwork. "Not here."

"What?" Karmen called.

"I'm just looking," Skip said. "Looking for Lon's notes. I'm not sure where they are. Maybe in the garage."

"What do you think?"

He didn't answer right off. His attention went to the windows and the same stunning view of the river. A bottle of water on the desk. He rolled back and had a sip. Karmen waited politely.

"I don't know, sweetie. I don't like the idea of just giving what little evidence there is about the second suspect to some reporter."

"At least meet with him before you say no."

Skip's head was shaking, no. He turned off the speaker and brought the receiver close. "No, I can't. I won't, at least not until I get a hold of someone at the department. I can't in good conscience make an end run without at least talking to someone first."

"Come on Skip, this is the book, man. This is it."

"No, ma'am," he said definitively. "I've got to at least try."

"When?"

"Hell, right now."

"OK, and if they blow you off, will you promise to meet with this guy?"

"Sure."

"Let me know what happens."

"Roger that."

Skip noted the time. Almost five. The day shift would be wrapping up. He would have a better chance of getting someone in charge if he called in the morning.

The forty-eight-page warrant request didn't mention Victim Eleven. No reason to. The consensus was that the E-A-R had not killed her. There were similarities. Enough in fact that Lon, who was one of the primaries at the crime scene, initially wanted to mark her down as Number Eleven. But when the lab got done, and the team had time to consider all the evidence, everyone agreed this was the work of someone else.

Lon had told Skip about it. The murder bothered him. It wasn't a copy-cat. "Couldn't have been," Lon had said. "No one outside the department knew the M.O. at that time. It was still early in the rampage."

Later on, Skip recalled, everyone on the task force worried about it, about there being a second suspect, an accomplice. Everyone could see there was evidence to support the notion, but no one wanted to speak of it out loud.

It was bad enough that one rapist was running amok. No one wanted to raise the notion of a second suspect. But it was hard to ignore.

With the last of the summer sun coming through the bedroom windows, Skip knew he needed to say something. The guy could still be out there, perhaps still committing crimes. Or, worse, passing the techniques he'd learned from DeAngelo to others.

He got a pencil and a pad. He wanted to organize his thoughts. He didn't want to come across as some crazy old man. Skip knew he wouldn't get a second chance to explain it.

He tried to rehearse it in his head.

It's simple, he'd say. There's a second suspect in the Golden State Killer case, and I can prove it.

A second suspect?

Yes. Look at the arrest warrant, right there. Page Two. The Statement of Probable Cause. The very first charge. The key to the whole case against DeAngelo.

The Maggiore murders?

Yes. Feb. 2, 1978. Another murder no one on the task force believed the East Area Rapist was responsible for.

What was the other?

The Snelling killing down in Visalia. Page Eight of the warrant. September 11, 1975.

What's the point?

This guy DeAngelo was never what we thought he was. As the Visalia Ransacker, the police were looking for a break-in artist. In Sacramento, as the East Area Rapist, he was all about sexual assault. Down south, the Golden State Killer, he was a serial killer.

You're still missing it.

I don't follow.

You're looking at the case now as the product of just one criminal. There's another one out there, an accomplice. I can prove it.

Give me the short version.

Brian Maggiore was a sergeant in the Air Force, recently transferred from Mississippi to the Mather airbase in Sacramento. His wife, Katie, had just celebrated her twentieth birthday. They lived in Rancho Cordova, not far from the river where they sometimes walked their dog, a poodle named Thumper.

It was a Thursday, Groundhog Day. About seven in the evening, Brian put the dog on the leash, and they started for the river. They got close enough that Brian let Thumper free. Before he could stop him, the dog ran off into someone's backyard.

A kid sitting in his bedroom was the only witness. He heard one gunshot and then another. He saw Brian and Katie running through a neighbor's backyard, chased by a man with a gun. Brian fell dead on the brick patio; Katie got as far as the gate before she took one in the head.

For years, we thought he'd been killed because of his job. There was a lot of smack being smuggled into Mather on Air Force planes in those days. We thought Brian's job might have put him in jeopardy.

But decades later, after the DNA technology improved, we learned it was the E-A-R, that it was DeAngelo.

None of this is news.

Check the files. You'll find the statements of two witnesses walking in the same neighborhood just minutes before the shooting. Both saw two men. The suspects were both in their mid-twenties or early thirties. One was blond, clean-shaven, with a big round head like DeAngelo. The other was about the same height, but skinny, with a dark mustache. Both wore dark clothing and leather gloves.

It's the second guy, the skinny one you should be looking for.

We got DeAngelo's DNA off the weapon used to kill the Maggiores. No other DNA was found.

Check the file. There was a rape and murder somewhere in Rancho. Pretty sure it was in 1976. The lead investigator on the attack was later the head of the E-A-R task force. He thought the accomplice committed this one.

Who?

Captain Lon Donovan.

Don't know of him.

Look him up.

You say somewhere in Rancho? And maybe seventy-six? Can't you be more exact?

You'll have to do some of the work, Sergeant.

Who are you again?

Skip Harkin. I worked for the US General Services Administration, head of investigations, from 1978 to 1986. We helped protect federal workers and installations up and down the Central Valley. That mission brought us close to the East Area Rapist more than a couple of times.

General Services? OK, sir. Got it. I'll pass this upstairs. Thanks for calling.

THIRTEEN

The doc told Cole to take it easy for a couple of days. He didn't see any signs of a concussion but blows to the head were tricky. The ribs were bruised. Nothing to worry about.

Cole spent part of the afternoon in the spa at the gym, soaking his ribs and nursing his wounded pride. He got home only a few minutes before Kim called, inviting him to dinner.

"I need someone to run interference between Brit and me," she said. "Every day brings a new challenge."

"She's sixteen, Kimmy. What do you expect?"

"I know, but it's so difficult without Frank. She misses him."

"When does he come home?"

"August. But he's one of only two radiologists at the hospital, so really, who knows."

"You're doing a great job."

"Did I tell you about the boyfriend? He's nineteen. I'm just terrified they're having sex."

"Part of life, sis. She's got a good head. Sometimes all you can do is trust."

"I'm not sure I can. Anyway—steak, fresh corn on the cob, mushrooms the way you like them, carrot cake for dessert."

"Wonderful. Can I bring anything?"

"Maybe some red wine."

"Sounds great."

"Oh, by the way, Jamie. I heard from the Kimbels' agent; they put an offer on another place. I don't think they liked your neighborhood."

"As opposed to just the murder in my house."

"So it's true?"

"I don't know. I'm still working on it."

There was a knock on the door and a familiar voice called out from the hallway. Susan. "Jamie, it's me. Can I come in?"

"I got to go, sis. See you tonight." To Susan, he called, "In the office." She entered a minute later, looking morose. "What's up?"

"I need a hug," she said, holding her arms out. Cole sat at his desk but didn't get up. She moved in and embraced him. Cole remained in the chair, stiff.

"What's all this?" he asked.

"Daniel and I had our first serious fight," she said, tearing up. "I think we broke up."

"What were you fighting about?"

"You."

Cole scratched his head, annoyed that she was dragging him into another drama. "How so?"

"I don't want to talk about it," she said, resting her head against his shoulder and putting her arms around his chest.

Cole hunched his shoulders and tried to move away. "Susan, honey, we can't. I can't."

"Why not? It's just sex."

"No, it's not. Sex is never just sex."

She pulled away, took a chair, and let the tears rain down. Cole found a box of tissues.

"Why do you say we're not right for each other?" she cried, softer now. "Why not?"

Cole smiled. "You don't remember?" he asked. "I was self-centered. I was aloof. I was childish. And I still am, Suzie. I'm still that same man."

"You could be sweet. I remember that too."

"I drove you crazy."

"You did, but that's just your way of saying I'm needy." She blew her nose and went to the bathroom. When she returned, she had collected herself. "I think I still want to sell my house. Maybe I'll move to Alaska, where the ratio of men to women would be more in my favor."

"You're gorgeous, you're smart, you've got money. I think you can do all right down here."

She sank into the chair again. "What are you working on? What's going on with the case?"

"Not much," he said. "I've been busy with another job." Cole reached for his DeAngelo file and opened it. "Do you know an old guy that lives on our street about halfway down on your side? His last name is Wallace."

"Teddy? Sure. He's a widower. His wife was the one that used to go all out on Christmas displays."

"OK, yeah. I know that house."

"What do you want with him?"

"He's the only one that might have been around when our victim was killed," Cole said. "I was just about to take a walk down the street to see if the old guy is home. Would you like to come with me?"

"You want me to help?"

"Sure. I could use a pretty woman by my side."

She gave him a half-smile. "Lead on," she said, taking his arm.

The lawn was green and well-tended. An American flag hung on the porch and a white pickup was parked in the driveway.

Cole rang the doorbell. "Mr. Wallace?" Susan called. A small voice replied before an even smaller man opened the door.

"Hello," he said with a bright smile.

Susan introduced herself and Cole as neighbors. Cole further explained he was a writer working on a book about the Golden State Killer. The old guy's eyes lit up at the mention of the criminal.

"Been reading about him," he said. "Glad they finally caught up to that sonofabitch."

"Me too," Cole agreed. "You've lived on our street for a long time. Do you remember anything happening here on Curtis Court?"

"Here? No," he replied quickly.

"How long have you lived here?" Susan asked.

"Well, we bought the place new," he said. "Which was in 1974, but we rented it out at first."

"You haven't actually lived here all that time then?" Cole asked.

"I was with the state transportation department, and they wanted me to take a job in LA," he said. "It was supposed to be temporary, but we were there six years. We moved back in 1980, or thereabouts."

"So, you weren't around during the height of rampage," Cole said with some disappointment.

"No, I wasn't." Wallace thought for a moment. "Why are you asking about this street? You think something happened here?"

"Our mailman said one of the victims was murdered in Jamie's house," Susan said.

"My goodness." Wallace put a hand to his mouth. "I don't know anything about that, although I would think one of the neighbors would have said something to us, you know, after we moved back. Right next door to me was a city policeman. You'd think a story like that would make the rounds."

"What about your renters?" Susan asked. "Any chance you know where they are?"

Wallace shook his head. "We used an agency. There were several. I'm sorry I can't help more."

"Do you think anyone else from our street might remember something?" Susan asked.

He thought a moment. "Bill Gallagher's widow might still be in the area. I think she remarried. Not sure what her last name is now," Wallace said, shooing a fly away. "The Hendersons were the only other ones. The developers didn't finish building out this street until the early eighties, you know."

"Bill Gallagher's widow." Cole scribbled in his notebook. "Where did they live?"

"The red-roofed house at the very end," Wallace replied. "With the big pine tree."

"And the Hendersons?"

"The yellow house with the brick driveway just two doors down."

"You mentioned a city policeman lived here, what was his name?"

"Powell, Art Powell. But he's been dead for years now.

Cole thanked him and then jogged down the block far enough to see the address on the Gallaghers' place. He took it down. On the way home, he got the Hendersons' address.

They walked slowly. Susan didn't take his arm this time. She seemed distracted. As they got closer to his house, the white Prius came around the corner and stopped in Susan's driveway.

"Looks like someone wants to apologize," Cole said.

"I should hope so," Susan said. She picked up Cole's hand. "You're right, Jamie, about us. You did drive me nuts and I'm sure I did the same to you. Daniel's right for me. I'm going to marry him."

"It's OK, Suzie. I'll be fine."

"I still care about you."

"And I you. Go head. Go to him."

FOURTEEN

Karmen's cryptic message told Cole to meet her at a Park-N-Ride in Folsom's historic district. She'd explain later.

It was pleasant, mid-morning. Not hot yet. He crossed the river at Rainbow Bridge, a century-old truss that magically delivered its traffic from the frenzy of life in the third millennium to the lemonade summer of grandma's backyard. Three full blocks still clinging to Gold Rush California. Brick and iron. Redwood. Spanish domes. Shutters on the second floor. Antique shops crowded with tourists on the weekends and covered plank sidewalks between the honky-tonks, sweet shops, and fine-linen bistros.

Cole often met his dates here. He kept his eye out for his almost-friend Shari. He wanted to see how she made out with her 'financially self-sufficient' partner. Or maybe she was back with the ex-con.

"Get in," Karmen said, pulling up.

"Where are we going?"

"You asked Sylvia about Skip."

"I did."

"Well, I know him pretty well. He's been a source of ours for the website. Anyway, I told him about you, and he wants to meet. He might have answers."

"About the murder in my house?"

"Yeah, what the hell else?"

Karmen's pickup was heavy with the odor of cigarettes or reefer; Cole couldn't decide which. He kept his window down. They took the freeway up into the hills to Placerville and then north as the semi-urban neighborhoods gave way to big rural parcels dotted with big animals grazing—not just cows and horses but also sheep, llamas, and even a few ostriches.

She seemed to be in a good mood, or at least talkative. She told Cole the story of how she and Sylvia had met. Karmen had been working for a landscape architect, running the tractor and other heavy equipment, and Sylvia had hired them to redo her backyard. They'd been dating a while when Karmen broke her ankle and Sylvia invited her to stay at her place during recovery.

"What about your website?" Cole asked. "When did you get interested in the Golden State Killer?"

"High school," she said. "I'm a sucker for all those true-crime TV shows. I saw one about the case and I've been hooked ever since."

"What about this cop?" Cole asked.

"Skip Harkins. He'd been an investigator for a federal police agency," she said. "Not the FBI, one of the other ones. He'll explain."

After a few more miles, Karmen slowed down, and they turned into the driveway of a ranchette, where a pair of German shepherds stood guard at the gate. Karmen punched a code into the lockbox and the gate opened.

"Roll up your window," she said. "Ike and Mike are not exactly friendly to new visitors."

Cole did as he was told. Both dogs ran along his side of the car, excited and menacing. A modest house was partly hidden behind a ring of big pines. A slim, dark-haired woman in her late forties stood at the door as they pulled up. She shouted at the dogs to stand down. They obeyed instantly.

"Hi, Karmen." She waved.

"Hi, sweetheart," Karmen said. "How is he today?"

"Usual."

"Oh, great."

Karmen introduced Cole. "This is Sally. It's her father I've brought you here to meet."

Cole followed them into the house to a big living room dominated by a wall of windows facing west and a spectacular view of the river.

A small man in a wheelchair sat at a table outside, under an umbrella.

"Dad, Karmen's here with her friend," Sally said, opening the glass doors.

Karmen moved ahead and gave him a hug.

"How you doing, honey?" The old man extended a hand to Cole. "I'm Skip." The grip was strong and his voice clear. He had deep brown eyes, and a face etched by more than a few of life's skirmishes. "You're the writer I've been hearing about."

"I am," Cole answered with a smile.

"And now you want to tackle the case of the Golden State Killer?"

"Thinking about it."

"What has Karmen told you? About Victim Eleven and the second suspect?"

Cole shook his head. "Nothing."

"Victim Eleven might have been the one killed in your house, and it could be the second suspect who did it."

"OK," Cole said, taking a quick glance at Karmen. "I'm interested. Why do you say 'could be'?"

"The last few years of my career in law enforcement, I was head of security for a big federal agency, the General Services Administration. This was in the mid-seventies," Skip said. "Our office was responsible for the Central Valley. I was based in Sacramento. As such, I had a seat at the table with the task force trying to track down the East Area Rapist. Even ran into him once."

A leather pouch was tied to one of the arms of Skip's chair. He reached in and brought out a folder. Then he poked through it, looking for something.

"I don't have a date, I don't have a name, and I don't have a location," the old man said, sliding a single sheet toward Cole. "But I have this."

Cole took a quick scan. "Press release?"

"A draft release that was never sent," Skip explained. "A good friend became head of the task force at one point, Lon Donovan. One night, he got a call. A young woman had been attacked in her home. Raped and murdered. He told me it was in Rancho Cordova; he never said exactly where."

Skip reached into the pouch again, brought out a pack of cigarettes, and left them in front of him.

"Lon said that he was certain that the E-A-R had done it," Skip said. "Had all the characteristics. No signs of a forced entry. The woman had been tied with shoelaces. The bedroom, the underwear tossed."

Skip shook a cigarette out of the packet, tapping it a few times on the tabletop.

"Lon said he called the boss and told them they needed to put out a press release. Our serial rapist was now a killer, he said, and the public needed to know. The boss agreed. And then someone upstairs put a boot on it. Lon figured the sheriff himself didn't want to set off alarm bells just yet."

He held the cigarette and pointed it at Cole.

"After the tech guys got done, they all decided that the sheriff was probably right, that the E-A-R couldn't have done this one."

"Why?" Cole asked.

"Lon said there was a problem with the timing. Another attack the same night in another part of town made it unlikely that the same man could have done both. Apparently, the investigators were confident in the ID from the other victim. It matched what they knew about E-A-R."

Cole read the release more carefully. There wasn't much to it. The victim wasn't named, pending notification of next of kin. They said the crime occurred in Rancho, but that was all. It was mostly a warning that a man known as the East Area Rapist was now suspected of murder and considered extremely dangerous.

"That's it?" Cole asked.

"No, son, that's not all. My friend Lon, he and I started working on a book about the case after we both retired. This was seven, eight years ago. We talked about this murder a couple of times along with the notion of an accomplice. He told me once that Victim Eleven, that's what he called this young woman, was the key to finding the second suspect."

He lit the cigarette and blew the smoke away from the table.

"Why the certainty about a second suspect?" Cole asked.

Skip drew up one shoulder and dropped it. "No certainty. Just suspicions. The signs were there with Victim Eleven. Things the press didn't know about, so Lon knew it wasn't a copycat. He told me he ran into the same thing a couple of times. He thought other women were attacked by a second man."

"What about now?" Cole asked. "Do you know if the sheriff's department is looking for this other guy?"

"I don't know," Skip answered. "Maybe."

"Shouldn't you tell them what you've just told me?" Cole asked.

"Tried to," he replied. "I'm sure the guy I talked to thought I was some crazy old man. That's when I agreed to talk with you. I asked Scotty Walsh about you. Maybe Karmen is right. Maybe you're the guy that could find this bird."

"The sheriff and the DA, they don't want to find him," Karmen interjected. "They got a nice, neat case all squared away on DeAngelo. If you throw a second suspect into the mix, they'd have a mess. Last thing those bastards want is a complication. They already got a lot of that."

"She's right," Skip said, taking another drag.

Cole leaned back and put his hands behind his head. "You said it couldn't have been a copycat. Why not?"

Skip ran his hand over his chin. "Lon's stuff is here someplace. I just can't find it. Though we talked about it enough that I remember most of what he said."

Skip broke into a coughing spell and had to take a sip of water. His daughter came outside to check on him. "I'm not sure this is good for him," she told Karmen. "Dad, you may need to pick this up another time."

Skip waved both hands, dismissing the notion. He cleared his throat and continued.

"Like I said, I don't have a date, but I'm pretty sure the attack on Victim Eleven took place in seventy-six, still early in the case," he said. "The press didn't get wind of the rapist until November that same year. Therefore, no one but the detectives knew the rapist's MO—the shoelaces and the vandalizing and whatnot. Copycats don't usually show up until the press has sensationalized the hell out of something."

Cole stood and went to the rail to gaze down at the river's relentless churning against the canyon's granite rocks. He came back to the table.

"This is all very interesting, but I haven't a clue where to start," he said. "And I still don't know if something happened in my house."

"Start there," Skip said.

"I have." Cole sat. "A mailman told my neighbor about the crime. I know my house was built in seventy-five, so it was there about the time of the murder. I found an old guy down the block who's owned his place since seventy-four, but he doesn't know anything."

"Who owned your house in seventy-five?"

"I'm working on it," Cole answered. "I also got leads on a couple other families that lived in the neighborhood back then."

"Sounds like a starting place to me," the old man said. "I'll keep looking around for Lon's notes. I know he had a file on this Victim Eleven."

"What do you think, Cole?" Karmen asked. "Is this enough for a book?"

Cole pulled on his ear. "It would be if we found the guy. That's a story that would sell a lot of books."

Skip patted the table, bringing the attention back to him. "There's something else to think about," he said. "Hunting a killer is a dangerous damn business. Neither of you knows anything about it."

"I thought you were on my side," Karmen objected.

"You both need to know what you're up against going in," Skip said, crushing the butt into an ashtray. "I sure as hell won't be out there with you."

"I think I have a general understanding," Cole said.

"Do you?" Skip said. "Let's say there *is* another guy, and he's alive and living someplace like Alaska or Memphis or even right here in

Sacramento County. To make this thing work, you'll have to get close enough that he'll know you're there, on his doorstep. And once you are, he's liable to do anything. You'd be putting yourselves in the path of an extremely dangerous animal."

"Damn, Skip, we're not going to have to arrest him," Karmen said.

"No, but it could be eyeball to eyeball. You just don't know what someone might do." Skip shook his head.

Cole got to his feet again and went to the edge of the deck. "You're right," he said. "We need to think about this."

"Are you saying that you've never been face-to-face with someone dangerous?" Karmen asked Cole.

"Oh, I have, several times." He turned back with his hands up. "And I didn't like it. It's not the kind of situation you want to press your luck on. Lots of things can happen and none of them good."

Skip nodded.

"Here's more," Cole said. "Let's say we get close and we think we have a suspect, and we tell the cops. Then what? What if, as you say, the cops want no part of trying to bring a second suspect into their case against DeAngelo? We can't sell a book about a maybe-sorta-kinda suspect. But in the meantime, we've just become targets."

"Man," Karmen sneered. "You wussing out?"

"No," Cole said. "But we are damn well going to take this one very careful step at a time."

FIFTEEN

The city of Lincoln was the first in the state to approve an Indian casino. It was also a quintessential California boom town, recognized as the fastest-growing in the entire country in 2010. Cole had trouble finding a parking place downtown.

He recognized Cindy Raddison, the owner of the real estate agency, from the photo he'd seen on her website. The photo was old. Cindy Raddison was at least sixty.

"Can I help you?" she asked as he stepped inside.

"Are you Cindy?"

"I am."

"My name is Cole, James Cole. Are you any relation to Lynn K. Raddison?"

"She was my aunt. Why are you asking?"

"I'm trying to track down the chain of ownership of my house in Rancho Cordova. Did she ever work with or for an outfit called M&M Partners?"

"Why do you need to know? Is there some sort of problem?"

"No problem." Cole got out a card. "I'm a reporter working on a story related to the Golden State Killer."

Cindy's face went white. She put a hand to her chest and swallowed hard. "You want to know about Vivien," she whispered. "Jesus, that's all I've been thinking about since they got the guy."

Cindy stepped back, fumbled for the chair behind her, and fell into it. Cole came closer.

"You OK?" he asked.

"No, I'm not." She reached for her purse, got out an inhaler, and drew in a puff of medicine. She waved a hand in front of her face and then briefly closed her eyes. "What do you want?"

"To learn more about what happened."

"For a news story?"

"Actually, no. Probably a book," Cole said, pointing at his card on the desk in front of her. "I'm no longer working at the *Journal*. I've gone out on my own."

"Well, you'll have to find out about it from someone else." She got to her feet and picked up the card, handing it back to him. "This is not a topic I am interested in revisiting."

"Wait," Cole said. "Please, I'm working with a retired cop, a guy who was actually part of the investigation. He believes that your friend—Vivien? That she was murdered by an accomplice of this DeAngelo, the man the police believe is the Golden State Killer."

"DeAngelo didn't kill Vivien?"

"It's not one of the crimes he's been charged with," Cole replied. "This cop I'm working with says there's evidence of a second suspect in the case."

"I've never heard that, and I've talked to the police many, many times."

"How recently?" Cole asked. "When was the last time they contacted you?"

"Not in years, but before that I talked to them a lot."

"That's just it, Cindy. My guy says the authorities don't want to find this second suspect. They're afraid it'll muck up the case against DeAngelo."

Her eyes widened.

"They don't really want to find Vivien's killer," Cole continued. "I do. That's what the book would be about. Finding the second suspect."

She took another look at this business card. "You used to work at the *Journal*?"

"I did," he answered. "Twenty-two years in print news. I worked down in LA and in San Francisco before coming to Sacramento almost eight years ago."

"It says here you were associate editor of the I-team. What's that?"

"I was head of investigations," he told her. "We did those big projects that start on Sunday and run all week. We tried to win prizes.

You know, like the Pulitzer."

"OK, wait here." She left him in the outer office and went into a private room. Checking up on him, no doubt. She was gone about five minutes. "There's a wine bar around the corner. If you can wait a few minutes, I'll come down and we'll talk."

***

It was mid-afternoon, and the place was empty. A three-sided bar in the middle of the room. Stools and dinettes. Potted palms. Shiny hardwood floors. Cole asked if they had beer. They didn't. He got a glass of house red and waited. The wine was sweet; Cole didn't take a second sip.

There was a man with her when she got to the bar. She introduced him as Albert, her husband. Albert got a big glass of chardonnay for her, and one for himself, too.

Cole ran through the highlights of what he'd learned to date, including the general details of what they knew about the murder, some of what Skip had said, and why Vivien's murder might be the work of another criminal.

He then explained the interview process and that he would be using a recorder app on his phone. He said if they got an actual contract for a book, he'd probably want to sit down again.

"Before anything is published, you'll be able to look over your words and the context in which they are being used," Cole said. "This is something I promise."

"OK, let's get started," Cindy said. "I want to get this over with."

"What was Vivien's full name?"

"Vivien Bordeaux."

"How did you know her?"

"From Huntington High," she said. "We were in the same year and had some of the same classes as freshmen. We were best friends right away."

"When did you move to Sacramento?"

"When I was twenty, which was in 1975," Cindy answered. She was calm and collected. Having her husband there probably helped. Perhaps she'd had some time to think about things.

"What brought you north?"

"A job. The real estate business actually," she said. "My aunt started the agency and offered me a chance to learn from her. She paid my way through school and helped me get my license. When she retired in 1990, I took over. Now Albert and I run it."

"You came north in 1975." Cole had the recording going, but he took notes too. "And where was Vivien then?"

"She was going to school, USC. She was a junior, studying architecture."

"Ah, interesting."

"We had these big plans to create a development company together one day. She'd build and I'd sell."

"What was she like?"

Cindy put a hand toward Albert, and he gave her a photo album. "She was beautiful. Here's a picture. Blonde, brown-eyed, really smart, really pretty, one of the sweetest people I've ever known." She swallowed down a flash of emotion. "It was just such a loss."

"Tell me about that day."

"Well, I was living in the house on Curtis Court," she said. "Your house now, right? I was living there all alone. My aunt had taken possession of it in some sort of agreement with the builders, and she was planning on selling it later the next spring. That part of Rancho, she thought, was poised for a growth spurt. She was flipping houses before anyone called it that.

"I was working by then. Showing homes for clients and holding open houses. All the things a realtor does," she explained. "Vivien and I hadn't seen each other in months, and with the Christmas break coming, I invited her to come up. I knew these kids that were going to rent a big cabin in Tahoe for the holiday. The plan was to spend a few days with them the week before Christmas and then she would go home to be with her family for the holiday itself."

"Do you remember the day she arrived?" Cole interrupted.

"It was the same day as the murder," she said, her voice trailing off. "Saturday, the eighteenth."

"The eighteenth? You're sure?"

"Absolutely, December eighteenth, 1976."

"She drove up from SoCal that day?"

"Yes."

Cole thought for a moment. The timing was important. He'd learned enough about the East Area Rapist to know he usually chose his victims carefully, stalked them sometimes weeks ahead of an attack, and got to know their routines.

"Did anyone else know she was coming? Or that she would arrive that day?"

"Well, sure. Her parents, probably her boyfriend, my aunt, I think. That's about it. Her little sister."

"What's the sister's name?"

"Jana."

"Do you know where I might find Jana?"

"I don't."

"That's OK," Cole said, jotting down another note. "Did Vivien call you from the road that day?"

"Not from the road. We talked later, once she'd arrived." Cindy thought for a second. "No, we must have talked before because I had to tell her where to find the key. We were going to have dinner together, but I was caught up at the office. I had a client trying to close on a house. We had offers and counteroffers going back and forth. I didn't get out of there until after eleven."

"What time did she get to the house?"

"She called me around nine. I remember because I couldn't talk very long. She said she'd already stopped to have dinner, and she wanted to open a bottle of wine."

Albert got up, came around the table, and put his hands on her shoulders. Cindy clenched her teeth and looked past Cole as if she could see into the house on Curtis Court on the night of December 18, 1976, and the lifeless body of her friend on the floor.

Cindy started to cry. First just tears, and then sobbing, quiet and restrained.

"Don't you see?" she said, her face straining with emotion. "He was waiting for me. He couldn't have known Vivien would be there. He was waiting for me."

SIXTEEN

be's assistant didn't say why the meeting had been called or who would be there, only that Cole should arrive on time and that he should wear a suit. He was early, polished, and primed. The assistant ushered him into Abe's office.

"Hey, JJ, thanks for running down," Abe said, handing Cole a note with a phone number. "This here is a guy I know, an attorney in Stockton. He needs help with an arson investigation."

"Arson? What the hell do I know about arson?"

"Call him and find out what he wants. Maybe you know more than you think," Abe said. "What's going on with the Wilmer job?"

Cole touched the still sore bump on the back of his head. "I went up to Redding, poked around a little, and got arrested for trespassing."

"Christ, Cole."

"That's not all. A couple of goons jumped me, gave me a pretty good butt-kicking."

"My God, Jamie." Abe shook his head. "You think the good senator sent them?"

"Who else?"

"You get anything? Sounds like you struck a nerve."

"Not sure yet," Cole said, remembering he'd asked Karmen to run down the two members of the Wilmer clan who'd turned up in the criminal index two days ago. He made a note to ask her about them. "Is it OK if I run a dig using the firm's research services?"

"Of course."

It wasn't all he wanted. "Hey, Abe. There's this other thing I need to tell you about."

Cole fessed up about the house and the murder. "I would have said something sooner, but I was afraid you'd tell me I'd have to disclose it to a buyer of my house, and I wasn't sure that's what I wanted to do."

"You'd probably need to," he said. "The Legislature recently tightened up the real estate law surrounding disclosure of crimes."

"It's not as much an issue now," Cole said. "I'm thinking of taking it off the market."

"Glad to hear it. I didn't like the idea of you running off to Idaho or wherever to write a book."

"I think there's one here," Cole said. "This murder in my house. I met an old cop who said the murder might have been done by an accomplice of DeAngelo."

"An accomplice?"

"Yeah, that's the other thing that's been taking up some of my time. I got this kid working with me and the cop."

"You're looking for this other guy?"

"Sure, why not?"

"Nothing. In fact, it's the kind of thing you should be doing more of. Do you carry?"

"What? As in a gun? Shit, no."

"Maybe you should."

"Really? Why? The Russian mob suddenly in town?"

"Jamie, this is where the money is," Abe answered. "You've been great with the jobs you've done for us, but to be honest, I can send an intern down to the courthouse or out to interview a plaintiff. You're a talented investigator with loads of experience working in unfriendly settings. You put that together with the hard tools of the street, and you're worth something to me and a lot of other attorneys."

"Hard tools of the street?" Cole said breezily. "What is that? An AK?"

"More like a Beretta. I know a guy that runs a training center up near the airport. He owes me a favor. I can give him a call. You'll be permitted in no time."

Cole's ribs ached at the memory of the two hoods jumping him in Redding. "Maybe you're right."

"I know I am."

"Hey, one thing more. I'm thinking about papering the county sheriff on my murder. Get everything I can on it."

"A public record request?" Abe asked. "I'd think anything they had in the file having to do with DeAngelo would be strictly off-limits."

"He's not charged with it," Cole said. "I checked."

"Yeah, I get that. Still."

"I was hoping I could use the firm's letterhead. Might make an impression coming from you."

"Not sure how that helps," Abe said. "I run a political firm. Media law isn't something we know much about."

"Connie does," Cole said. "I had to deal with her when she was a deputy DA in San Francisco. She knows First Amendment law as well as anyone. The state's public records act too."

"I'll talk to her."

"Thanks."

Someone outside Abe's glass doors caught his attention. Cole turned. An older woman, stooped, walking with a cane. Abe's assistant and a guy in a chauffeur's uniform were helping her navigate the way. Abe jumped up to greet her.

"Marian," Abe called. "So good to see you."

"Abraham," she said, twisting her head slightly. They helped her to a chair, the assistant and the chauffeur exited the office. Abe closed the door.

"Marian, I'd like you to meet the man I told you about, James Cole. Our new investigator," Abe said. "Jamie, this is Marian Hodges. She's the widow of Judge Hodges. You might have heard of him. State court of appeal and the co-founder of the firm."

She offered two fingers that he pressed lightly.

"Pleased to meet you," Cole said.

"I've got a job for you," she said. "Doesn't pay much and it won't be easy."

"This will be off the books, Marian," Abe said. "I wouldn't dream of billing you."

"I can still decide how I spend my money, thank you, Mr. Metzger," she said in a clipped tone and then turned to Cole. "I'm willing to spend five thousand dollars, Mr. Cole, for information about the death of my granddaughter."

Cole glanced at Abe. "I can do that," he answered. "What happened?"

"The police said it was an overdose, but I just can't believe that Emily was taking drugs. She was twenty-four. The very flame of youth and expectancy. Found dead in her apartment two months ago."

"Was there an autopsy?"

"Yes. Don't get me wrong; drugs were found in her system, enough to have caused the asphyxiation that killed her. I just can't believe Emily would do such a thing."

"You think foul play?" Cole asked.

She shook her head. "I don't know what to think."

"You were close?"

"I raised her," Marian said. "Her father, my son, died in an auto accident when she was still a little girl. Her mother, she was the addict. Alcohol. Cocaine. Pills. An undiagnosed bipolar, I believe. My late husband and I took custody of Emily when she was eight."

"From then on Emily's life was stable?"

Marian adjusted her glasses. "Catholic school, soccer teams, sailing in the summer, proms, and boys. She attended Mills College and graduated in three years."

"Well-adjusted then."

"As well as you could expect."

"Was she working at the time of her death?"

"She was attending law school at Davis and she had a part-time job in the Capitol with one of the legislative committees. She was interested in environmental law."

"She wasn't living with you, then?"

"No, she had a roommate, a loft downtown."

"I assume you kept in close contact."

"She would come by the house every once in a while for dinner or just to say hello. We'd walk sometimes on the weekends. She was very happy."

"Forgive me for asking this, but did she drink?"

The old woman winked at Abe. "I like this one. He gets to the point," she said and then looked back at Cole. "To answer your question, she drank sparingly around me."

"Ever think she might be doing more?"

"Not really. Emily was an athlete as a young girl. She still ran in the morning, every morning. But you know kids today. She liked to have fun."

"Did she have anyone in her life? A boyfriend?"

"I don't know. No one she ever mentioned to me."

Cole stroked the hair on his chin. He didn't want to say it, but this seemed like a dead-end, tragic as it might have been. She read his expression.

"Abe says you're a top investigator. I want you to investigate. The authorities tell me Emily died of an overdose; I want to know how that happened. I want to understand."

"I'll need access to her place. Her personal possessions, bank accounts, all that sort of thing."

"I'm her only living relative. I can get you anything."

"Very well, I'll need her full name, her address, and I'll want to look through her things."

She handed Cole a piece of paper. "Here's the basics: her full name and contacts for her friends that I knew of; her address is there too, phone number."

"OK, I'll get started."

Abe waved his assistant back into the office, and Mrs. Hodges and the chauffeur were on their way.

"Sorry I didn't get a chance to explain about all that," Abe said. "Judge Hodges sold me his stake in the firm. I'm still paying on that note, so you be real careful with this."

"In a way, I'm taking your five grand on this," Cole kidded.

"Get out of here. I've got work to do."

Cole retreated to one of the empty cubicles in the office. He would leave the Hodges case for tomorrow. Right now, he had something more pressing: Victim Eleven, Vivien Bordeaux. He ran the name through a vital records database that Abe's firm subscribed to and found her death certificate.

Mystery solved.

There it was, the place of death: 3631 Curtis Court, Rancho Cordova, Ca. The cause of death was a cervical fracture, C1. She was listed as twenty-one years old; five foot three, 107 pounds; blonde hair, brown eyes. She was identified as a student. It gave her residence as 141 Dolphin Avenue, Seal Beach. Her parents' names were Andre and Lois Bordeaux; her sister was named Jana.

Maybe Mom is still around, Cole thought. *Someone needs to go down there and find out.*

SEVENTEEN

A Diablo wind gathered in the afternoon along the edge of Nevada's Great Basin. As the summer heat baked the plain, the air swirled and rose up-slope along the northern Sierra and the southern Cascades. Something offshore, a vacuum hundreds of miles west, beckoned the wind up and over the mountaintops. Once free, it drove down the other side, its fury intensifying, wild and explosive as it raced across the Valley at hurricane speeds.

Lorraine felt the hot gusts as soon as she opened the front door. Each day she rose at five, had a cup of tea and a slice of dry wheat toast, and then she and the dog, a four-year-old collie named Ace, would walk through the woods for an hour, taking the same trail every day. The wind gave her pause. The Diablo brought the threat of fire.

She cut the walk short, worried about the dry trees and the many rotten limbs weakened from years of drought. Already some debris had fallen on the trail. Perhaps the wind would die down, she thought, and they could walk after sundown.

When she reached home, she noticed a familiar black Lincoln sedan idling in the driveway. It was a company limo. There were three of them.

At this hour, the car in her driveway signaled bad news, a message that needed to be delivered in person. Maybe one of the bankers working on the stock deal ran into a snag. Maybe a big problem at orchards, a labor issue, or an accident. Maybe it was the Chinese.

Maybe her stepson.

When she got to the car, she recognized the driver. Rick, the company pilot. He dropped the window.

"Morning, ma'am," he said.

"Good morning. You here to collect Ted?"

"I am."

"Where to?"

"Monterey. I think he said there's a fundraiser."

"Of course there is," she said, and then called for the dog. She headed for the kitchen door, anticipating which exit her husband would try to use to avoid her. Things had reached that point. They were living in separate bedrooms, and because of their work schedules, she often didn't know where he spent the night. Sadly, she didn't care.

She found him upstairs, still packing.

"You're flying out this morning?" she asked. "Even with this wind?"

"You worried about me?"

"As well as the million-dollar aircraft and to say nothing of our pilot."

"Rick says we're good."

"Who approved the flight?"

"What do you mean?"

"I mean, who is paying for it? The company is not."

"Don't worry, Raine," he said. "I'll take care of it out of campaign funds. There's an event at Pebble Beach, the tribes are putting it on. All perfectly legitimate."

"An event?" she muttered and left the room.

She showered and dressed for the day. At fifty-one, she still carried enough of the teenage beauty queen and college cheerleader to attract attention in almost any room. She was modest with her dress and yet aware enough of the fashions to remain stylish.

Sage, her driver and the firm's head of security, had another of the company's limos waiting for her in the driveway. Her assistant Polly came to the door.

"Ready, Raine?"

"Almost, I've got a stack of papers in the TV room. Can you grab them while I brush my teeth?"

They had a thirty-minute drive down to the corporate offices of Stony Creek Farms. The ride was barely underway before Lorraine called their operations manager, who among other things oversaw the use of company equipment, including the Cessna jet.

"Did you know Ted was taking the plane today?" she asked bluntly, a rare departure from her usual Southern civility.

"I did."

"You approved it then."

"He's the owner, Raine. He has authority."

"He's *one* of the owners," she snapped. "Next time, I want to know about it ahead of time. You understand? And you get in Rick's face and make damn sure he knows too."

"Yes, ma'am."

"I want you and Denny to take a look at all administrative expenses for the past two years—no, go back five. If Ted has taken a joyride without reimbursing the company, I want to know about it. Look for any other misuse of company property by my dear husband too."

"You got it."

She took a breath. "What else is going on? How's the fruit?"

"I don't like this wind drying things out. It's been even hotter down south, so we're using more water than I'd like, but I think we're OK."

"Good. Let me know when you've finished your audit into Ted's spending."

Next, she called a project manager in Eureka working on the rail line. She didn't reach him and left him a message.

"OK, Polly, what have we got today?"

Polly ran down the list. Lorraine would be meeting at nine thirty with the IPO team. Noon, a working lunch with the CFO. At two, marketing. At four, there was a board meeting at the hospital.

Lorraine was looking at the calendar she kept on her tablet computer. "Wasn't there a meeting with Dalton's doctor? I have that at one."

"Mr. Wilmer canceled it," Polly said.

Lorraine waved a hand. "Perfect," she whispered. *It's his son,* she thought, *who cares if he goes off again?*

She studied the computer screen. "What about our visitor last week? What do we know about him?"

"His name is James Cole. He was an investigative reporter at the *Journal*," Polly said, finding her notes. "He was out of work for about six months and now appears to be working as an investigator for a Sacramento law firm."

"My goodness, I knew he was trouble. Do we know anything about why he came to the house?"

"I don't. But Mr. Milic, I believe, might have further details."

Lorraine keyed the limo's intercom. "Sage? What do you know about this man James Cole, our uninvited guest from the fundraiser?"

"He's a reporter. Don't know what he's working on, but he was at the courthouse earlier in the day and got into a jam with the clerk. They put him in stir for a bit."

"Do we know what he was looking for?"

"Files on the family. He found something on Dalton."

"Lord," she gasped. "Someone is setting us up. Polly says he's working for a law firm. Do you know about that?"

"No," he said, then chortled. "I wouldn't worry. I'm pretty sure he won't bother you again."

"Why?"

"The senator had me send Pat and Mike to see him off before he left town," Sage said.

"What exactly does that mean?"

"Nothing serious. Bruised ribs, probably. Maybe a shiner. Just a little message to stay away. He didn't fight back."

"I don't believe it," Lorraine said, shutting off the intercom. *Of all the boneheaded moves,* she thought. Ted again. He couldn't care less about the arduous day-to-day challenges she faced protecting the family and the farm. *Beating a reporter! Stupid!*

"Polly, I need you to find this James Cole and get me a phone number or email or something."

"Certainly."

***

The student center was crowded and rowdy, with kids working through the cafeteria line or eating at long tables. Mostly underclassmen, they attended a top academic school with Nobel laureates on the faculty and Olympic athletes in the gyms. But kids were still kids, and as the end of the spring session approached, they had long ago sorted themselves into an unbreakable caste system.

In the middle of the big room was the biggest and loudest of the clicks. Many of the boys were athletes. Some played football. The girls were the prettiest on campus. Some of them played sports too. Volleyball and tennis. Scattered about were smaller groups. Some consisting of just two or three students huddled in a corner.

The boy was alone.

He sat on the other side from the Jock Club, as he'd come to call them. He wasn't bad looking himself and reasonably self-assured, but he didn't fit in and he knew he didn't. Never mind, he understood. He took refuge in new feelings of freedom, being finally out of the house at age nineteen, away from his father and stepmother and all the doctors.

His lunch plate included fresh fruit, roast chicken, and dry wheat toast. Only a few bites of the toast had been eaten along with a couple of slices of an orange. His backpack, swollen and heavy, sat on the table next to him. He had a pad in front of him, and he jotted down notes every few seconds.

Just off the center, in the middle of the Jock Club, was a girl. She had curly red hair and a blooming smile with sweet dimples and turquoise blue eyes.

The boy studied her. He knew things about her already. She was a sophomore and didn't have a steady boyfriend. She lived in the dorm nearest the concert hall. She came from a suburb in eastern San Diego. She didn't have a car. She worked part-time at a deli in town on the weekends. And she lived on a tight budget.

Her girlfriends surrounded her at the lunch table and a gaggle of boys too. Everyone seemed to be her friend. She was the Queen; anyone could see that.

The boy noticed she had the same chemistry book as he, Chem 20-A. He hadn't known that before. That was interesting. Advanced Chem. He knew she wasn't in his class. He scribbled a reminder to check the schedule.

He would need such details if she were to be the one.

The boy spotted something else. Unlike most days, the redhead didn't buy her lunch from the line. She'd brought a Tupperware of food that she warmed up at the microwave at the far end of the center. The boy noted the date, near the end of the month. Maybe she was running low on funds.

That could be important, he thought. She might be more susceptible to an offer. The boy's father was wealthy, and he'd used money in exchange for sexual favors before.

The term was coming to an end. He might have to move quickly. He cautioned himself. *We are not ready, not yet.*

He got the idea months before, after joining a matching service for men with money and attractive girls with none. He met one and exchanged messages. They met at a hotel room in the East Bay and he gave her what she wanted.

Afterward, he followed her. She lived in Richmond, a rented room in an old house. It wasn't hard to get inside the house or inside her room. He examined her things using gloves and was careful not to disturb them. Once he spent an entire afternoon, standing and then sitting in her closet, holding the knife and shoelaces. When she finally came home, her boyfriend was with her and he watched them make love. Painful. Suffocating.

The couple fell asleep and he quietly left the room and ran, carelessly, out of the house to his car, found an empty underpass, and masturbated.

He knew then that his plan would work. He could take her anytime, even let her see his face. It wouldn't matter. They'd had consensual sex before. The cops could never make a case.

The boy wouldn't waste this approach on the girl from Richmond.

The urge was all about the redhead, the Queen. She was the one who needed it. She was the one who believed she had all the power.

She did not.

He watched her gather her things. Lunch was over. She dismissed the boys, and her girlfriends assembled around her, forming a protective cocoon.

The boy knew he had work to do. He needed time. Time to train. Train the body and the mind.

If we are going to do this, he told himself, *we need to be smart.*

We need to be cautious. No, that's not the right word. We need to be deliberate. We need to be calculating.

I must learn to stand, without moving, without breathing. I must stand for an hour in one place. I am a block, I am a tree trunk, I am a wall.

Are you sure you want to do this?

I am not. I'm not sure, but I have no choice. The need, the yearning, the draw is too strong.

You must fully commit, or else you will fail.

I have. I'm committed. That's why all the work.

EIGHTEEN

The gun center was under a flight path maybe a mile north of the airport. A simple setup. A trailer. An outdoor target range protected from the sun and rain by a tin overhang. The instructor's name was Buck, and he stood about five foot six and weighed over 300. A former Marine who chewed a big wad of bubble gum wrapped in snuff. He kept it to one side of his mouth when he spoke and spit black rivulets to the side every few sentences.

Buck told Cole he could take the gun test the next day if he did both the morning and afternoon sessions.

"None of my students have ever failed the test," he promised.

The basics took up most of the morning. Stance. Posture. How to grip the gun. How to aim. How to breathe. The guy finally let Cole take a few shots around noon. In the afternoon, there were a handful more students. They spent time at the range. When they finished for the day, the big Marine took Cole aside.

"I'm not so sure you're ready to take the test tomorrow," Buck said. "You might need more time."

"That bad?" Cole asked.

"Pretty bad."

"That's OK. I wouldn't think the gun would be anything more than for show."

"That would be best."

On the way home, Cole heard from Abe's friend in Stockton, the attorney with the arson problem.

"Abe says you're a good man working in tight corners. Is that right?"

"Depends on the corners, I guess," Cole answered, putting a hand on the back of his head, still very sore from the incident in Redding. "Why don't you tell me about your problem?"

Parker explained he had a client who had invested in a pizza parlor in downtown Stockton. Just a couple weeks after the money changed hands, there was an after-hours kitchen fire and the place burned down. There was supposed to be insurance but there wasn't, and now the client was out a couple hundred thousand.

"We suspected his partner of fraud," Parker said. "We've taken a pretty deep look at him and can't find any hard evidence, but the guy has a checkered past. I also had a forensic fire expert take a look at the arson report that the city issued, and he said the analysis was sloppy enough to disguise the real origin of the fire. He thinks that the arson investigator might be in on it."

"How can I help?" Cole asked.

"This is going to sound a little out of left field, but I need someone with a brain to plant a couple tracking devices."

"Bugs?"

"More like beacons. They got these tiny transmitters these days that can work off a phone app," he said. "Very high tech."

"Where do you want them planted?"

"One needs to be placed somewhere on the arson investigator's car and one on the pizza partner's car," he said. "I can trigger them from here and if one of them comes within twenty yards of the other, I'll get an alert and I'll know something's up."

Cole thought about it, picturing himself sneaking into someone's garage and slipping the transmitter under the bumper. Very Tom Cruise on a Mission Impossible. It sounded both goofy and illegal.

"You're right, this would be something way outside my comfort zone. What if I get caught?"

"I have another client that's in auto repossession and I can get him to say you're working for him and that you just got the wrong car," Parker said. "That's where the idea came from, to use the transmitters. He plants them all the time to plan the best opportunity for a repo."

"I don't like it," Cole said. "If I were engaged in a fraud scheme, the last thing I'd ever do is go visit my co-conspirator. Why would I? Easier and safer ways to communicate."

"You are exactly right," Parker said. "That's why there's a second shoe to drop on you."

"Yeah?"

"I need you to spook them into a meeting."

"How am I going to do that?"

"Abe said you were a reporter. What if you were to confront one of them, say you had an investigative piece going about arson in Stockton, tell him you want to interview them."

"Did Abe suggest that too?" Cole asked. "You're the second client to want me to play fake newsman."

"No, it just seemed like a natural approach. Well, what do you think?"

"Depends."

"On what?"

"The pay."

"I can get you two grand. It won't take more than a few hours spread over a couple of days."

"I'm going to need three," Cole said. "This job will require another pair of hands. I've got an associate I'll need to cut in on this."

"All right, but I need this taken care of pronto."

"What about the transmitters? Where do I get them?"

"I can overnight them to you."

Cole hung up and called Karmen and told her about the job.

"A quick grand," he said.

"Sounds good."

"What about the dig I told you to do?" Cole asked. "Those two guys named Wilmer?"

"I did it," she said defensively. "There wasn't much. Nothing at all on the guy named Dalton. The other one is dead. Some sort of sex fiend."

"When were you going to tell me about it?"

"I sent you an email, dog. Yesterday morning."

"I didn't get it. Send it again."

"Yeah, sure."

"One more thing," Cole said. "Dress nicely tomorrow. I need you to blend in."

"I'll dress any damn way I want."

***

Marian Hodges lived in a three-bedroom Tudor on 46th Street, around the corner from where Ronnie and Nancy Reagan kept house while he was governor. The neighborhood was called the Fabulous Forties and it was crowded with old money, almost all of it wrung out of the taxpayers somewhere along the way.

A maid answered the door and led Cole to the parlor. Marian arrived, followed by the maid with a tea set and homemade macaroons.

"What do you have for me?" the old woman asked.

"Nothing yet," Cole answered. "I have a meeting with the roommate in an hour. I want to first examine Emily's personal items."

Marian twisted slightly and froze Cole with a stern face. "I expect to receive regular updates, Mr. Cole."

"Yes, ma'am."

She rang a small bell on the table next to her. The chauffeur appeared and took Cole to the garage.

He found only the usual things: clothes, cooking utensils, decorative items, a few books. He took her phone and her laptop. No calendar. No letters. Not even any bills or bank statements. Cole asked the chauffeur to remind Mrs. Hodges about getting copies of her granddaughter's financial records.

The phone was a Samsung, and Cole figured there was little chance of hacking in. The computer was an HP. He knew a guy, Aldo, who did that sort of thing and dropped in on his way to see the roommate.

"What's the backstory?"

"The owner was a twenty-something girl that OD'd a few weeks ago," Cole said. "I'm working for the family."

"What did she do?" Aldo asked.

"Law student. Busy. Comes from money. Grandma doesn't believe she was taking drugs."

Aldo picked up the phone. "What's the number?"

"Good question, hold on." Cole ran back to his car to retrieve the sheet of contacts Mrs. Hodges had given him. Aldo called the number.

The ringtone was a tune, something familiar and bluesy, but Cole couldn't place it.

"OK, give me a couple of days," Aldo said.

Cole met Emily Walker's roommate for coffee in a joint just downstairs from the loft near the river that she'd shared with the deceased. The roommate worked in the Capitol too, and she was as surprised as the grandmother that Emily had taken drugs.

"Did you find her?" Cole asked.

"The building super did. We had a leaky pipe in the kitchen, and he'd come by to look at it."

"How long did you know Emily?"

"A few months. We were in a Legislature-sponsored graduate program at UC Davis."

"Graduate program? I thought she was going to law school."

"No, not that I knew of. She was working full-time in the building."

Cole made a note. "Her grandmother described Emily as very happy," he said. "Would you agree?"

"No," she said rubbing her fingers. "Emily wasn't all that happy, especially toward the end."

"Do you know what was bothering her?"

"Not really. We lived together, but it's a big apartment, and we were both busy with work and social lives."

"Emily have a boyfriend?"

"She did. Alex. He works for an environmental group in town. I don't know his last name, but I could probably find out."

"Anything else that might be useful?"

"I'm pretty sure Emily was talking to a therapist. She said

something once about missing her appointment to have her 'head shrunk.' She joked."

"Do you know who?"

"I'm sorry, no."

NINETEEN

Karmen didn't exactly dress up, but a long-sleeved blouse covered the tattoos on her forearms. She wore blue jeans, running shoes, and a Giants hat. She sank into the passenger seat without a word. Cole didn't ask. The destination was Fairfield, which was about a half hour away without traffic. They ran into some outside Davis.

Cole's playlist jumped around. Khachaturian. Puccini. Sibelius. He waited for her to say something about it. She didn't.

When they got closer to the first stop, Cole explained his plan and exactly what he needed her to do.

The target was a retired fire captain in the San Joaquin County Fire Department who lived in Fairfield. He had a forensic business that did fire and explosion analysis. The city hired him to look into the pizza fire, and it was he that Cole's client suspected of fraud.

The guy's house was big, surrounded by a vanity vineyard. A wire fence marked the perimeter, and an electric gate protected the driveway. Cole drove past and found a dirt road on a hill above the property where he could monitor the comings and goings.

They sat for more than an hour.

"This is stupid," Karmen said, finally coming to life. "Why didn't we take two cars?"

"Too complicated," Cole answered. "I just need you to keep watch while I'm doing the deed."

"Sitting around like this is crazy. We could be here all night. And you got another dude to track down, too."

Cole remembered Sylvia's suggestion to give her twenty-something partner 'her room.' "How would you have done it?" he asked.

"Like I said, two cars. You do one mope and I'd do the other."

"And risk getting caught?"

"Slipping a bug under a car bumper don't take much talent."

Cole kept his eyes on the house. Maybe she was right. What did he know? After all, he'd only been in this sleuthing business a few weeks.

There was movement. A black SUV was backing out of the garage. Cole followed them to a big box outlet and parked about a hundred yards away.

The couple got out of the SUV and headed into the store. The man was wearing a blue tee-shirt with the insignia of a fire company on the back.

"Take your phone and call me if they start coming back," Cole said. "I'll text you when I'm done."

"Brilliant."

When he was sure the fireman and his wife were inside the store, Cole got to the side of their SUV and placed the button-size trans-mitter inside the well of the right rear wheel.

One down, one to go.

Stockton was an hour away. Karmen took a nap. Cole put a sports talk show on the radio. As they got closer, she woke and started quizzing Cole on how he wanted to approach the pizza investor.

"The guy's name is Petrov, and we have his home address," Cole said. "We wait around until we get a fix on him, his family, and the neighborhood."

"He's got a family?"

"I think so."

"Kids?"

"I don't know."

"Well, this time, we're doing it my way," she said. "Drop me at the corner. I'll knock on the door. Find out what I can."

"No."

She folded her arms in protest.

He parked the car in front of the house and both he and Karmen went to the door. A kid about ten years old answered. Cole asked if either his mom or dad were home. The kid said he was alone with his brother, who was sick.

That was it. "OK," Cole said and started to back away. There were some lines he was not ready to cross, and taking advantage of a ten-year-old was one of them.

Karmen recognized no such restriction. "We need to see your dad today," she said aggressively. "It's about his insurance on his car. There's a problem." She waved her phone in front of him as if it contained proof. "He drives a Mustang, right?"

"What's a Mustang?"

"A muscle car," she said.

The kid was trying. "I don't know. He's got a truck."

Karmen looked at her phone. "That's right, red Chevy."

"No, it's black."

"Oh right. Black?" Cole said, shaking his head. "You sure?"

"Yes."

"Well, I'll have to fix that," Cole said, looking at Karmen. "Where can we find him?"

The kid said his parents would be at the vacuum shop they ran in the business district a few miles away. Cole noticed a family photo on the table just inside the door. Mother had a mop of brown hair dyed blue and pink at the ends. Petrov, the dad, looked large and had a dark beard.

The kid didn't have an address for the store, but it wasn't hard to find. Karmen suggested that she go inside the store and occupy the owners while Cole scouted for the black pickup. He found it in parked in the alley out back. Cole rolled slowly by, studying the layout.

He parked a few yards further up and adjusted the mirrors so he had a clear view of the back of the building and the rest of the alley. The rear of the apartment building faced the store and the truck. The other buildings all seemed to be commercial with little activity. Cole noticed that Petrov's store had two security cameras aimed at the back door and the alley.

He got out of the car and walked casually toward the truck, scanning the building and the rest of the alley for movement. He ducked under one side of the pickup. Plastic wheel guards made it hard to find a place where the magnets would work. It was taking too long. He heard a dog barking but wasn't sure where it was. Cole considered pulling out. He finally got the device planted.

"What the hell?" a man's voice shouted into Cole's ear. A big hand gripped his shoulder and jerked him back from the vehicle. "What the hell are you doing?"

Cole wrestled free and got to his feet. In person, Petrov was about the size of a grizzly bear behind his long black beard and menacing red eyes.

"Nothing, nothing, man." Cole put up his hands and backed away a step or two. "I was looking at the wheel guards. Those are custom, right?"

"What the hell, man?"

"I've got the same truck at home," Cole said. "I'm sorry. I was driving by and noticed them. I've been thinking about getting guards."

"What the hell?" Petrov said and bent down to take a closer look at his back tire.

"Honey!" Karmen shouted from the back door of the store. "Honey, what are you doing back here?!"

Petrov looked toward her. Confusion replaced the anger in his face. Karmen ran out and put a hand on Petrov's shoulder.

"My husband," she said calmly. "I asked him to park the car and come inside to help me pick a vacuum." She stepped closer to the big man. "The poor man fell off a ladder painting our house a couple of months ago. He's working on it."

Petrov gave Cole a long stare. "Really?" he said to Karmen. She gave him a phony smile and then reached for Cole.

"Come on, honey." She took his arm. "Where's the car?"

Cole pointed up the alley where his car sat, still running. "Honestly, John, leaving the car like that?" She turned back to Petrov. "Can you take him inside? I've got to go park the car in a proper spot. Show him the bagless Hoover I was looking at. I'll be right back."

Petrov gestured with his hand for Cole to come into the store. Cole played along, acting a little off-center. Inside, the dog, a big

Rott, was still barking and had to be put into the office. When Karmen returned, she was calm and folksy. Cole would never have guessed she had it in her. She charmed them into forgetting the whole incident. She also insisted that Cole buy the bagless Hoover. Cost him a hundred and thirty-three bucks. They walked out arm in arm.

"It was the dog, right?" Cole said as they reached the car.

"Cameras," she said. "You didn't see them? They fuckin' had them all over the place. Hard to miss, pendejo."

A wave of irritation twisted Cole's face. He started to respond, but reluctantly let it go.

TWENTY

The rush-hour traffic was snarled. He heard on the radio that the I-5 was choked just south of Elk Grove by a big rig mishap. Cole wasn't looking forward to sitting for two hours in traffic with the ever-turbulent Karmen. Cole knew of a good Mexican cantina in Lodi. That way, they could avoid I-5 and take Highway 99 home. He suggested they sit out the traffic, get a beer and a taco. For the first time all day, Karmen seemed to approve of a decision Cole had made.

She ordered a carnitas burrito; Cole got fish tacos and a pitcher of beer. He waited until they had chips and the cerveza. He wanted to try a new tactic with her.

"You're not half bad at this detective stuff," he said, pouring beer into her mug. She eyed him suspiciously. "Really. I'm still trying to unlearn the way we had to do things in the newsroom. We had to be above reproach in how you teased information out of people. You could get fired for being even slightly disingenuous."

"You saying I'm disingenuous? Whatever the hell that means."

Cole grimaced. "Will you relax?" he said. "I'm trying to give you a damn compliment. What's the matter with you?"

She sipped her beer.

"This game takes a little moxie," he tried again. "I'm just saying you did good today."

"OK," she allowed a small grin. "Thanks, boss."

"Anything bothering you beyond the normal shitload of things you carry around in that crazy damn head of yours?"

She tossed her hair and smiled broadly. "Not really. I was sort of scared about today. Working with you. You being this big-league investigative reporter and writer. I didn't want to mess up."

That made Cole laugh out loud. "You're something. You're nervous about working with me, so your answer's to be a major pain in the ass?"

She was still grinning. "That's how I approach things."

Cole burst out again. "I'll remember that."

"What's next?"

"We wait a few days and then spring phase two on them," Cole said. "I'm just going to walk into the vacuum shop, flash my press credentials, and tell them they're in the middle of a major expose on arson."

"Sounds like a plan," she said. "What about after that? What about Victim Eleven, now that we know that it happened?"

"Well, we need to find the family. We got the parents' address in Seal Beach at the time of the murder. Do you think you can run that down?"

"Sure."

"Then someone needs to go interview them. You want that job too?"

"OK, over the phone?"

"Naw, this one needs to be in person."

"You sending me on the road? Cool."

"Well, remember this is the other side of our little partnership—the journalism side," Cole said. "The approach is completely different. You don't want to put people on edge if you don't have to. And in this case, the family is key. We want them to open up. Understand?"

"Yeah, I can do that."

The food arrived. She ate like a farmhand.

***

While they were inside, Aldo, Cole's hacker buddy, left him a message. He couldn't break into the phone, but he did the laptop. Cole owed him two bills.

"Got a stop to make on the way home," he told Karmen. "Another job."

On the way, Chopin. Cole quietly whistled along.

"What is this?" Karmen pointed at the dash and Cole's iTune setup.

"You don't like it?"

"No, it's fucking beautiful, what is it?"

"Polonaise in A-flat by Frederic Chopin," he answered.

"How do you know that? What's the deal with this dead man music?"

"Something my father left me."

Aldo's apartment was jammed with computers, music equipment, and video components. There was barely room for Cole and Karmen to step inside.

"You open the computer?" Cole asked.

"I did," Aldo said with a proud smile.

Cole fished out two bills and waited. "Well? Can I have it?"

"Don't you want to know how?"

"Sure."

"Well, remember the ringtone on the phone?" Aldo said, and then he punched in the number on his own cell, and the same bluesy tune came on from Emily's phone. Cole still didn't recognize it.

Aldo waited and then looked to Karmen.

"Amy Winehouse," she said softly. "'Back to Black.'"

"You go to the head of the class, girl," Aldo said.

Cole shook his head in disbelief. He knew just enough about Amy Winehouse to know she'd died of an overdose when Karmen was probably still in middle school.

"Did she use a line from the song as a password?" Karmen asked.

"No." Aldo picked the laptop up off a cart in his kitchen. "That's where my true genius took over. You said she was mid-twenties and a law student. Thus smart, young, hip. And yet she's taking life cues from one of the pop world's seriously bad ass ladies. Where do you go with that? Who do you also honor if you this sort of person?"

"Taylor Swift," Karmen said, softly again.

"Bingo," Aldo snapped his fingers. "Good thing you've got her around. So, little girl, where would you look for a line or message from Taylor Swift that could be used for a password?"

"I'd say, 'Call It What You Want,'" Karmen answered.

"Exactly, from there it was just a matter of playing around with some lyrics until I broke in."

"Bona fide genius," Cole said.

Back in the car Cole needed to know. "How do you know the work of Amy Winehouse?"

"Sylvia turned me on to her. I was a total freak about her music for a while."

"And how do you put her with Taylor Swift?"

"I think they knew each other," she said. "I know Winehouse came to some of Swift's studio sessions in London, the old Beatles studio. And Swift covered some Winehouse songs. Can't you see the influence?"

"The shit I don't know."

They got to Sylvia's house in Carmichael and Karmen paused before getting out. "How did she die?"

"Who?"

"The law student."

"OD."

Karmen's expression was serious. "Like Winehouse."

"Yes, like Winehouse."

"How old was she?"

"I don't know, maybe twenty-six or twenty-seven."

"I'm twenty-six," Karmen said, pulling on a strand of her hair. "She sounds a little like me."

"Yeah?"

"Yeah, I got a little attached to painkillers, the opioids, after I broke my ankle. That was one reason Sylvia brought me here. She found me one night. I'd gone to a pretty dark place."

***

Cole got home, poured a drink, and began an inventory of the files he could access on Emily's laptop. The first thing he found was the boyfriend. There were dozens of emails between them going back months. The most recent exposed some tensions. He had questioned her commitment several times.

His name was Alex Ruffin, and he worked as a project manager for an environmental consulting firm. There was an office number; Cole called and left a message.

Cole also found a weekly appointment labeled simply DR. The first entry was almost a year ago. There was a phone number. He called and left another message, knowing the doc wouldn't be able to tell him much.

That was about it. No wild journal entries. No smoking guns. Cole went into the kitchen, got a splash more bourbon, and then sank into one of the soft leather chairs in his living room. He punched on a ball game.

The Amy Winehouse thing, it kept bouncing around in his mind and what Karmen had said. She'd opened up to him tonight, he thought. Maybe for the first time, he saw her true self. That was cool. And Cole agreed with her. Karmen and Emily Hodges probably weren't that different.

Could have been suicide, Cole thought. *Emily might have committed suicide.* He went into his office and made a note on the whiteboard to call the coroner the next day.

When he got back to his chair and his drink, he noticed he'd missed a call. There was a message from the 503-area code. Redding.

"Mr. Cole, my name is Lorraine Wilmer. We met the other day at an event at my home. I believe I made a terrible mistake that afternoon, and I'd very much like the opportunity to apologize. Please call me back when convenient. There's also a business opportunity I'd like to discuss."

TWENTY-ONE

Brooke was worried. The boss's message came late in the night. He was curt and his tone weary. He didn't say why the meeting had been called, just that she was required. The time was precise, seven-fifteen, which suggested that Sheriff Horace Henley had called it himself.

Even before seven the traffic between her place in Davis and downtown was slow but her route from the freeway to the admin building was clear. In an hour, everything would be bustling. She parked in the underground lot and took the executive elevator to the top floor. The wide hallways, the marble floors shoe-shine clean, the yellow lighting. The doors to the sheriff's suite were knotty alder and glass. No one was tending the reception station.

She was early but the lights in the conference room were already burning. Another bad sign. They were having a pre-meeting.

Inside she saw the sheriff, at the head of the table, his big round gut pressing against his belt. Brooke's boss was on one side—Undersheriff Steve Bell, who oversaw administration and finance. He was in a dark suit, red tie. Next to him was Brian Stanton, head of operations. He was in uniform. Black mustache. Shaved head, shiny in the light. On the other side of the table from the sheriff officers was Lou Fournell. Brooke knew him. He was chief of staff to the Sacramento DA.

This was as high a level meeting as it got.

She stood outside the door. Henley waved. Brooke closed the door behind her. The faces she met were grim and serious.

"I received an email last night," the sheriff said, looking at her. "A public record request. Came from a law firm in town, Hodges Rivas & Metzger. Signed by one of their partners, a Connie Ying, and another guy, James Cole. Do you know Cole?"

"I do," Brooke answered. "He was a top reporter at the Journal.

I heard he left suddenly last fall. Haven't seen his byline anywhere since. He's working with Metzger?"

There was a coffee set on the table. A platter with bagels, cheese, pastries. She'd like a cup of coffee.

"What about this Ms. Ying?" the sheriff asked her. He was dressed in a suit. His tie was red, white, and blue.

"I don't know her."

Henley pushed a single sheet of paper down the table toward her. "Why in blazes would the Metzger firm be interested in a rape and murder that took place forty-two years ago?"

Henley rarely cussed but she could see the tension in his face. There were dots of perspiration on his forehead. He wiped them away with a cloth napkin.

Brooke didn't have an answer. She scanned the records request. "Looks like a pretty big fishing net," she said, and then she read out loud. "Any and all reports and associated documents related to any crime committed on Curtis Court in Rancho Cordova between 1973 and 1981."

"That's why we can just deny it," Fournell said with a finger tapping the table.

"No," Bell said. "That's foolish. We need to know why they want the records."

"Who cares?" Fournell argued. "I don't give a shit. Abe Metzger never tried a criminal case in his life. It couldn't possible matter what he's up to."

"Stupid," Bell snapped.

Henley put up a hand and looked at Brooke.

"What about it?" she asked. "Do we know if a crime was committed on this street during that timeframe?"

Henley's eyes narrowed and his lips drew tight. Brooke looked across the table at Stanton.

"There was," he said. "A rape and murder of a young woman in December 1976."

Brooke's head jerked slightly. "The East Area Rapist? DeAngelo?"

"We don't think so," Stanton said. "At the time, some thought it might be him, but later on, after all the forensic work was done—for what it was worth back then—the investigators decided it wasn't."

"It doesn't matter," Fournell jumped in. "I say we deny it, lord knows we have grounds."

Bell leaned in. "You're missing the point here, Lou. Metzger knows something. You want to fuck up this case, well, blowing off a guy like Metzger would be a good way to do it."

"What the hell do you know about trying a case?" Fournell's voice raised. "Last thing my boss wants is complications. And this here records request has complication written all over it, in big red flashing lights."

Brooke waited until the room settled before speaking up again. She looked at Stanton. "You just said that you didn't think DeAngelo committed this crime. You aren't sure?"

Stanton shook his head but didn't answer.

"The fact is that we don't know," Henley said. "That was such a messy time. From what the old-timers say, there were attacks six and seven times a month all over the county. The department's best men couldn't get a line on this guy. He called the hot-line once and told the dispatcher he was going to hit one night in a particular part of the county, and we still couldn't stop him. Messy, messy damn time."

"Is DeAngelo charged with this one?" Brooke asked.

"No," Fournell answered.

"Why not?" she asked. "It was a murder."

Again, the room went quiet.

"Here's the thing," Henley said. "When I got the request from Metzger, I sent it down to records and asked them to bring up the file so that I could look at it before deciding what to do. Captain Riggers comes into my office instead and says there's nothing in the file."

"I wonder how that happened?" Stanton said, nodding at Bell.

"Go to hell," Bell said. "Do you know how many God damn investigators have been through our files on this case the past forty fucking years?"

"Nonetheless," Stanton said.

"There's a murder file with nothing in it?" Brooke looked at the sheriff.

Henley nodded.

"How does that happen?" she asked.

"Who the hell knows?" the sheriff bellowed, his round face reddening.

No one spoke. Brooke looked over the letter again and then put a hand to her chin. "Then how do we know there even was a murder?"

"There's a coroner's report," Bell said. "We know how she died and when and where. After that, don't know anything. No police report. No investigator's file. Nothing."

"And now, Abe dadgum Metzger is sending us a records request!" the sheriff shouted. "Jiminy-Christmas!"

Brooke shook her head, waiting for the sheriff to compose himself. Bell gave her a nod. "What do you think Alverez?" he said. "This subtle stuff is your department. What's your counsel?"

"Well," she was looking at the sheriff. "I agree with Steve. We need to at least try to find out what they're up to first."

"How do we do that?" Henley asked.

"I know Cole a little. I'll just ask him," she said.

Stanton cleared his throat, shaking his head. "What? You'll just ask him. Nonsense."

Brooke waited, her eyes flaring back.

"This is my department, officer. I trade information all day long, every day. Tips are the currency of this town."

"It's worth a shot," Bell said.

Brooke turned back to Henley. "What's the alternative? Deny this request and then look up some afternoon to see Metzger holding a press conference outside the courthouse, trotting out a witness or some evidence of God knows what that turns your prosecution of DeAngelo upside down?"

"You think this is about DeAngelo?" Henley asked.

"Absolutely," Bell said.

"I do too," Brooke added.

"Damn blast it," the sheriff shouted, slapping a palm on the table. He got to his feet, stepped away and put his hands on his hips before turning. "You say you know him? This Cole?"

"Well, more by reputation," she said. "My first job out of college was in the press office for Schwarzenegger. I talked to Cole a few times. I was in on some of the meetings dealing with Cole and his team."

"What if he doesn't play ball?" Fournell asked.

"Let's cross that bridge when we get there," Brooke answered.

"All right," Henley said. "I don't have to remind any of you that this all stays between us. Lou, I know you've got to brief your boss, but I don't want this getting out. Hear me?"

***

"James Cole for Mrs. Wilmer," Cole told the operator.

It took a moment before she came on the line. "Mr. Cole, thank you for returning my call."

"Of course."

"I'm afraid I made a serious misjudgment when you were here."

"You did."

"Yes, but this has been a very trying time for us. Because of my husband's work, we get threats from time to time. In recent months, we've had to be especially careful."

"Your husband's work or yours?"

"Both, of course. You are no doubt referring to the expansion of the family farm. Not all of our neighbors are happy about it."

"Lowball acquisitions during the recession," Cole said with an air of authority. "Then hardball during the drought. No, I don't think you've got a lot of friends these days."

"Tell me, Mr. Cole, what was it you were trying to accomplish, coming to the house like that?"

"I was hoping to hit up your husband. Ask him about the rumors he's running for the US Senate."

She scoffed. "My, my, what an imagination some people have."

"So, it's not true?"

"Let's just say that it's highly unlikely."

Cole grunted, not sure if he believed her.

"Why were you at the courthouse?" she asked. "I understand you were attempting to get access to old criminal files involving my husband's family. What does that have to do with the Senate race?"

"I tend to be thorough in my research. I began that morning looking at you and your husband. When I didn't find anything, well, I worked my way down the list until I found something."

"What did you find?"

"I don't know yet."

"Who are you working for, Mr. Cole?"

"I'm not with the *Journal* anymore if that's what you mean."

"That's not what I mean."

Cole let the conversation die a moment. She clearly knew more than she was letting on. Cole wanted to tread slowly.

"Here's what I think. I think you didn't come up here as a reporter, but rather as an investigator. I think you went to the courthouse looking for dirt on my family. I think you came to the house to set off alarm bells so that you could watch what we'd do."

"If that's true, you pretty much failed the test," Cole said. "Ran me into jail on a trumped-up charge and then had Moof and Goof jump me in an alley. If you think that's going to scare me off, you'd better think again."

"Moof and Goof." She laughed, lilting and sweet. "That wasn't me. That was the product of our overly protective head of security. I hope you weren't hurt?"

Cole didn't answer right away. "What are we doing here, Mrs. Wilmer? You said something about a business opportunity."

"I did. Please, call me Lorraine."

"What's it about?"

"I'd rather speak in person."

"You'll keep the hired help on a leash?"

"You have my word."

"When?"

"How about tomorrow for lunch?"

"Tomorrow's no good. That's a long drive up and back."

"I'll send a plane. A twenty-minute flight from the executive airport in Sacramento. Meet my pilot at eleven thirty. You'll be back before three."

"How about Friday?"

"Friday it is."

TWENTY-TWO

Before Karmen's flight left for Orange County, she logged into BE-A-RTerror.com. It had been weeks since she checked in with the crew. She'd received email from most of them, all wondering where she was, why she'd abandoned them. She decided just to post a short message on the site itself. She said she had taken a job assisting an investigator working on the DeAngelo case. "Could be there's more to come, could be there's a second suspect. More to come, later."

She closed her laptop with a grin. *That ought to rile them up some,* she thought.

***

Karmen found the Bordeaux residence, about two blocks from the water on the south side of Seal Beach. A woman in her forties was sitting on the porch, smoking, when she arrived.

"Are you Karmen? I'm Jana," she said. "Mom's inside. I think you and I should talk first. Can we walk?"

Jana put on glasses and they strolled first toward the ocean and then along the main street closest to the beach.

"Mom's not well. She's been battling leukemia for quite a while. We're not sure how long she has."

"I'm sorry to hear that."

"Her attention wanes sometimes too. She can be sharp as a tack one minute and then lost in some memory the next."

"Dementia?"

"I suppose." Jana tried to smile. "She's eighty-four. You can be whatever you want at that age."

A kid on a bike with a surfboard passed them and a couple with a dog came the other way. "I guess I want you to be prepared. She might have trouble remembering things; some of her answers may not make sense."

"I understand."

"You said you have leads on a second suspect," she asked. "Can you tell me anything?"

"We don't have much yet. It's just as you said. We have leads." Karmen thought it best not to share much. "My boss and I are working with a retired cop who was part of the original investigation into the E-A-R case. He has strong opinions but not a lot of real evidence yet."

"The investigators told us that Vivien was almost certainly not one of the E-A-R victims, that it was a copycat."

"We think that it was more than that. We think there's evidence that whoever attacked your sister was working with the E-A-R."

She nodded and thought about it for a moment or two. "I'm grateful that you're looking into it. Vivien's death left an enormous hole in my life."

"Why was she in Sacramento?"

"She went up there to visit her friend. They'd planned to go skiing over the holidays."

"She made the drive alone, is that right?"

"Yes."

"Did she have a boyfriend?"

"She had been dating this one boy. We didn't know about him until later; we met him at the funeral."

"Any chance he might have had a reason to hurt her?"

She thought too for a moment. "Sure, anything is possible, but I don't think so. They'd only been out a couple of times. If it had been more than that, we—my parents and I—well, Vivien would have told us about him."

"Do you remember much about what the sheriff's department said happened?"

She nodded and took a breath. "Yes, a pair of detectives came to the house one afternoon. It was probably six months after Vivien's funeral. I insisted on sitting in."

Her voice trailed off. Karmen remembered Cole's directions and gave her time. They crossed the street and found a bench facing the water and the scattering of people enjoying the sand and sun.

"As I said, they told us the East Area Rapist wasn't a suspect. They said it was a copycat and they didn't have any suspects."

"Can you remember anything they might have said about why they believed the East Area Rapist didn't commit this attack?"

"I think they believed the E-A-R stalked each of his victims," Jana said. "And since there was no way he could have known Vivien would be in that house, that night, then it probably wasn't him."

Karmen took a note. "That's all?"

She nodded. "That's what got us," she said. "They only met with us for about fifteen minutes; they barely told us anything."

Karmen could see that she was having trouble. She waited.

"My parents, my mom, all of us, fell apart over Vivien's death," Jana said. "There were just so many unanswered questions, the attack just seemed so random. It hit my dad hardest. He became terribly depressed and he already had something of a drinking problem, which got worse. It was the beginning of the end for him."

"What questions did you have? What questions have gone unanswered?"

"I don't know—everything." She stopped and put a hand on Karmen's arm. "I became fully obsessed with the E-A-R for a while. I thought I could solve the case." She shook her head. "I saved practically every newspaper article ever written on the crimes starting right after my sister's death. I kept a notepad next to the TV so that I could jot down something important I saw on the news or one of the cold case programs. Before the internet, there was a gang of us. Some of us were relatives of survivors, like me. Some were just true-crime junkies. We had chain letters that were sent back and forth. It wasn't until I was almost out of high school in the late 1980s that I finally gave it up. I was frustrated. I hadn't really learned anything."

Jana got up from the bench and they began walking back to the house.

"I still have the notebook; you can take it with you—there's a report you might be interested in."

"A report?"

"Yes, my mom prevailed on Daddy maybe five years after Viv's death to hire a private detective," she said. "We thought it might help my dad, maybe give him closure. I don't think you'll find much that you don't already know, but you're welcome to it."

When they got to the house, there was a priest there. He was introduced to Karmen as Father McGee. The priest called out, into the back of the house and a dark-haired medical aide wheeled the old woman into the living room.

"Mother," Jana said in a loud voice. "This is Karmen Mueller. She's the woman working with the reporter, investigating Vivien's death."

"Good morning, ma'am." Karmen bent down and gave the woman's hand a soft stroke.

"You need to see her room," Lois said in a frail voice. "She was a cheerleader in high school. Come."

The aide pushed the wheelchair, and everyone followed. The room was bright from the light glistening off the ocean. There was a double bed in the middle and a desk to one side. On one wall were posters: Chris Evert and Jimmy Connor; Stevie Wonder in another. A bookcase held a series of Nancy Drew mysteries along the bottom two rows. On the bed was a Hello Kitty pillow.

"We never changed a thing," Lois said. "I wouldn't dare." She turned to look at Karmen and laughed, her eyes wide. "You know, she hadn't lived in this room for years. She was away at college. That's why it looks like a little girl lived here. That's how I think of her."

She waited until Karmen had a chance to take it all in. "That's enough. Let's go into the parlor," she told the group. "There's a photo I want her to see."

Jana brought an album from off a coffee table. "Not that one, honey," she said. "Get the one off the mantle. Bring that over."

Jana handed it to Karmen. The girl in the photo looked about ten or eleven. She wore a sweatshirt that was too big for her and a smile that lit up the room.

"My little pixie," Lois said. "That's how I think of her. Just a slip of a girl." The old woman's shaky hand reached for Karmen and put a hard grip on her wrist. "She was all alone that night. She died all alone, terrified. She couldn't fight back. Even then, fully grown, she didn't weigh much more than a hundred pounds. My baby. Ms. Mueller, find out who did this to her. Please."

Karmen's heart raced. The mother's pain was palpable. She thought of the girl. Her last moments. Karmen could feel it, in her chest and down her arms and her legs. Anger. Fright. A chill.

"I will, Mrs. Bordeaux. I promise I will," she said.

***

Karmen had a beer in the airport lounge. She checked her phone once or twice, looking for new email. When she found nothing, she started for the gate, stopping to get a magazine on the way. She found an empty row and took a seat. She started to flip through the magazine and thought back to the interview. What could she tell Cole? Was there anything new? Just the sadness of it. A brutal crime and family ruined.

She remembered the overstuffed notebook Jana had given her. She got it out of her backpack and started to leaf through it. Jana's clippings were filled with little notes off to the side. The thoughts of a teenage girl, heartbroken over her sister's death. There were pages and pages of letters printed on old dot-matrix computer paper. Photos too, brown and faded, cut from newspapers and magazines.

Buried deep in the book, Karmen found the private detective's report.

She read it over quickly. Jana was right; it didn't add much. There were some details from the autopsy and references to investigator interviews. The bottom line didn't change anything—she was most likely killed by someone other than the E-A-R, and the cops didn't have a clue who that other man was.

At the bottom of the second page, under the heading CONCLUSIONS—that's where she found something new.

The existence of a copycat assailant had been a frequent point of contention among task force personnel. The sheer number of attacks the E-A-R was believed responsible for gave credibility to the theory. In fact, one of the key members of the team told me directly that he strongly suspected that as many as ten of the rapes that took place between 1976 and 1978 were the work of at least one other attacker. Three in particular:

   • *December 18, 1976. Rancho Cordova.*

   • *May 15, 1977. Orangevale.*

   • *June 6, 1978. Rocklin.*

TWENTY-THREE

ole read Karmen's note and then went to the whiteboard in his office and copied the dates and places of the two new attacks in big letters. He logged into the *Journal's* archive and looked to see if the paper had covered either of them. They hadn't. Next, he looked up the PI who'd done the report of the Bordeaux family. His name was Jack Perry. He still had a shield. Cole scribbled down his number.

Cole logged on to E-A-RTerror.com to check for anything related to the attacks in Orangevale and Rocklin. He found nothing and started to write a note to Karmen, asking her to start looking through Skip's files on the two cases. He stopped writing in mid-sentence. Cole saw the note that Karmen had posted the day before, alerting her web colleagues that she was working with Cole and intimating that they were chasing for the second suspect.

It was early, too early to call. Cole rewrote the email to Karmen, demanding she take it down. "We'll have a conversation about this."

He got back to work, finding his notes from his conversation with his neighbor, Mr. Wallace. He got the USB drive out of his briefcase, which held the real estate records on all the neighbors that lived on Curtis Court that he'd downloaded from the assessor's database. Wallace had mentioned two families that might still be in the area, the Hendersons and the Gallaghers.

He crossed checked the home address for both families with the assessor's property records. Both homes had been bought and sold several times since the families lived on Curtis Court.

He logged into the computer system at Abe's office and opened the research menu. Using one of the firm's identity databases, Cole found that Bill Gallagher died in 2002 and that his widow was named Colleen. She remarried in 2010, but the trail went cold after that. It looked like she had a son still in the area; Cole found a local number for him from an online phone book. The line was disconnected.

He ran the same search for the Henderson children. He knew the names of the parents—David and Margret—and found out that both had died more than five years earlier. The three children, however, still jointly owned another piece of property in another part of Sacramento County. Cole caught a break because the tax collector had the current city where each resided: Sean, a son, was in Oregon; Patti, a daughter, lived somewhere in Los Angeles; and Lucy, another daughter, was in Toronto.

He used the online phone book to find a Sean David Henderson in the little seaside town of Tillamook, Oregon. A man answered, but hung up as soon as Cole said he was a reporter.

Patti Henderson was also a problem. Sixteen women with the same name lived in the Los Angeles area. He decided it would take too long to sort out where Patti was, and he moved on to the oldest daughter, Lucy.

Lucy's married named was Devere. He searched Facebook and was certain he found her. She was a grandmother living in the Bedford Park neighborhood of Toronto.

"That's me," Lucy politely answered when Cole called. He explained why he was intruding. "My, yes. I saw the arrest on the news. That was an awful period. I was just out of high school."

"And your family, were you all living on Curtis Court in Rancho Cordova?"

"Not exactly," she explained. "When I was living at home—I'm the oldest—my parents were still renting. We lived on Pinecrest Street, which isn't far from Curtis Court. After I left for college, several years later actually, that's when they bought the home on Curtis Court."

"But you were in the general area during the mid-seventies."

"Yes."

"Do you remember if there was an attack anywhere close to you?"

"No," she said. "I'm sorry, I don't. I would think I would have remembered that, had there been one."

"Anyone else I can contact that might know something? How about your brother or sister?"

"The twins were very young then. You know, nine years younger than I, which would have put them in grade school. I doubt they'd know anything."

"Well, if you think of something, you've got my number."

"Wait," she said. "There is someone. Funny I didn't think of her. She was on the swim team with me when we were in high school. I didn't know her well, but she lived on Curtis Court at the time. Her name is Julia. Her maiden name was Mears, but I'm pretty sure she got married, and I don't remember her married name."

"What high school? Cordova?"

"Yes."

"What year would this have been?"

"I was a senior in seventy-five."

"Great, thanks."

Cole returned to the USB file and the property records of all his neighbors. He looked to see if Julia Mears or someone in her family still lived on Curtis Court.

Nothing.

Next, he used Facebook and found an alumni group for the high school. There was an image of a pretty girl in her early twenties who was the administrator. Cole sent her a note asking to join. He turned to LinkedIn next, and then he just Googled 'Julia Mears'.

Sometimes the most obvious options paid off.

A Julia Mears-Carney had a pediatric counseling practice in Fair Oaks. Cole went back to the assessor's property records and found a Mr. and Mrs. Fred Carney who owned a house located at 3654 Curtis Court.

Cole stepped outside and looked up the block. Julia Carney's house was on the same side of the street as his, only a few doors down. He walked closer, noticing that hers was a big lot, just like his place. From the outside, it looked like it might have the same design, floor plan, and landscape layout.

He went to the door and knocked. No one answered.

When he returned to his study, he found a new email from some-one named Brooke Alverez at the sheriff's department.

Ms. Alverez was responding to the records request Cole had made. He'd nearly forgotten about it. It seemed pointless now. He knew all he needed about the crime, including the victim's name and family. Hell, he had a photo of her. Still, Cole wasn't ready to jettison the message. There still might be some valuable details about the crime among the documents the sheriff's office would have.

The name was familiar. Cole found her bio on the department website. He remembered her. She was one of the sweethearts that worked for Schwarzenegger in the press office. Fox News cute.

Too young for him, probably. She looked barely thirty. A graduate of the University of Washington. The gig with the governor was her first job out of college, Arnold's last year in office. After that, she went to work for the Secretary of State, and earlier this year, Sheriff Henley named her his communications director. She was also a lecturer at UC Davis. Busy girl.

Brooke's message asked him to call. He had the phone in his hand when it lit up with one incoming. Ms. Evelyn Morris, the hedge fund lady interested in the Wilmers.

"What have you got for me?"

"I've got a few things, but what's the story on all the smoke and mirrors?" Cole said. "I tried calling you the other day on the number you used to contact my office. Got a dead line."

"I told you I'll contact you."

"Right. And today you're on a blocked number."

"That's the way I want it."

"Why?"

"Mr. Cole, you don't need to know. I've hired you to do a job. Now tell me what you've got so far."

Cole pulled the Wilmer file off the shelf behind him and opened it. "How about a Chinese bank, likely government-owned, financing the Wilmers' farming expansion?"

"Go on."

"Well, Ted Wilmer owns stock in a company based in Eureka, called the Solon Group. And there's a Chinese investor I haven't yet identified who bought up an old rail line that runs between the port in Eureka and the Valley."

"OK."

"The state Senate is contemplating an award of ten million dollars to help dredge the Eureka port," Cole said. "Wilmer is vice-chair of the appropriations committee."

"That's it?"

"Wilmer's on a shortlist of candidates that the Koch brothers are looking to back for US Senator next time around."

"That's in 2022," she said. "Anything could happen by then. I don't see it."

"You're not interested in Wilmer using his office to benefit the family business? That a foreign actor might have strings to pull on a US Senator?"

"And you don't think the Koch brothers know about this Chinese bank? Or don't care? I doubt that very much. Besides, it's not what I'm looking for. A conflict of interest would take forever to prove. I've only got a couple of weeks."

Cole's mouth tightened. It irritated him that she didn't see it. The loose strings surrounding Senator Wilmer were too good to pass up. Any good reporter could see that.

"Since you already know what I'm looking for, why not just tell me?"

"I have my reasons."

"This is some goofy game you got going, lady. You hire me to find something you already know about and you're making me dig around like a blind man."

"That's the way it's got to be," she said, her voice bristling. "Isn't it obvious? If I just told you, they'd know I was the source. It can't come that way. You've got to find it yourself. It must be organic. They have to believe you'll write about it, too."

"Organic, is it?" Cole tossed a pen against the wall. "Fine, I'll keep looking."

***

The sweet smile of Ms. Brooke Alverez still sat on the screen in front of Cole. He rang her back.

"You got time for a beer?" she asked straight off.

"A beer? Why?" *Another dippy deal*, he thought.

"I need to explain a few things. Best if it was in person."

"What's there to explain? If you have documents related to my request, you've got to give them to me."

"It's not that easy. Can you meet me in an hour at the bar in the Sheraton? I'm buying."

Cole stared at her photo. "Sure."

The reason Ms. Alverez wanted to meet at the Sheraton and not the Hyatt wasn't lost on him. Both hotel bars would be reasonably quiet on a weekday afternoon. The Sheraton was the Democrats' hotel; it was unionized. The Hyatt, a block closer to the Capitol, was GOP territory. It was where Arnold had lived when he was in Sacramento as governor.

Brooke Alverez didn't want any of her friends to see her meeting with Cole.

He was early and she was late. The cold IPA he'd ordered was half gone when she arrived. A bright yellow summer dress, lots of bling, high heels. Not exactly an outfit for the office. She looked as though she'd run home to change.

"I'm so-o sorry I'm late."

"Sure." Cole accepted her small hand in greeting and caught the light, fresh scent of perfume.

"I see you've started without me." She ordered a daiquiri. "Thank you for coming."

"Seemed like I didn't have a choice."

"Well, I do need to ask a few questions, which I think will help you get what you're after."

"Shoot."

"The nature of the request, we found troubling," she said. "Making such a broad sweep. Normally we'd reject it just because it was so wide—I mean, all crimes committed in Rancho Cordova over an eight-year period? My goodness, Mr. Cole."

"You can call me Jamie, and it wasn't for all of Rancho. Just one street."

"Right. What was it? Curt Street?"

"Curtis Court."

"Right. Why that street?"

Cole was playing with house money. No reason to lie to her. "I live there," he said. "Curtis Court is a little cul-de-sac on the east side of town. There's maybe fifty homes on it. Shouldn't be too hard for your people to see what's happened there over the years."

"You live there?"

"I own a house there. I'm trying to sell it."

She chuckled. "That's what this is all about? You're worried about disclosure?"

"I am."

"Well, that's just silly." She waved her hand. "I can't imagine a buyer would care about anything that might have happened forty years ago."

"Unless a notorious criminal committed the crime."

The smile faded. She took out her phone. "Can I make a note or two?"

"I thought you said this was off the record."

"I did, for you. I need to make sure I get this right when I brief my boss or the sheriff." She had an electronic pen and some kind of fancy device that was half phone, half computer. "What makes you think something happened in your house?"

"The mailman told me," Cole said dryly.

"The mailman?" She broke into a big smile, her eyes searching his. Cole liked it.

"Yes."

She put the pen down. "OK, here's the situation. Anything that happened anywhere in what was unincorporated Sacramento County back in the seventies is automatically under the jurisdiction of the team of investigators and prosecutors working the DeAngelo case. Doesn't matter what the crime was, those guys have total control over the files, the records, witness transcripts, whatever we've got."

"What does that mean?"

"It means not even Sheriff Henley can approve your request. The DeAngelo team must concur."

"But as far as I know, DeAngelo hasn't been charged with anything that took place on Curtis Court."

"Doesn't matter. New charges are being considered every day."

Cole finished his beer and waved the bartender for another. Since they were on her.

"Now who's casting a wide net?" he said. "*Everything* that happened *anywhere* in the county is under their rule?"

"It's a very important case."

"Really? You don't say."

She closed her tablet. "This is really why you're interested in this crime? To sell your house?"

"Why would I lie? Easy enough for you to check." Cole got his refill and took a sip. "What about you, Ms. Alverez? What do you know about what happened in my house?"

"Honestly, I don't know anything."

"I don't believe you," Cole said. "You wouldn't have gone to all this trouble if something in the files wasn't bothering the sheriff."

"What trouble?"

"This here," he said, adjusting his back, a muscle in the middle had been bothering him since his dust-up with the two goons in Redding. "This little charade. You wanted to know why I asked for the documents. OK. I've told you."

"I appreciate your candor." She fingered her drink. "To be honest, I wanted to meet you."

"Really?"

She tossed her hair. "We've spoken before. When I was in the governor's press office. You were rude."

"People have said that about me before. What was the beef?"

"Same sort of thing. You wanted documents; we didn't have them ready."

"Sounds like a pattern."

"My boss was scared to death of you. The top staff hated when you showed up to press conferences, always asking the governor something he either didn't know or wouldn't want to answer."

"That was the job." He was starting to like her. She was good, disarming. He could see why she'd advanced so quickly through the ranks. "Well, Ms. Alverez—"

"Call me Brooke."

"Well, Brooke, what are we going to do here?"

"I'm going to take this up with my boss, who will likely take it up with the sheriff. I'm going to recommend that at least we confirm if a crime did or did not take place. I think that's fair."

"No," Cole said. "You'll recommend they release everything you've got. I've already got an attorney on this. A very good one."

"That's such a bluff."

He left his eyes on hers.

"Something else?" she asked.

"Yeah," he said, keeping eye contact, noticing her green irises were golden brown near the pupil. "To be honest, I remember you too. Prettiest girl in the room. Any room."

Her hand covered her throat; her eyes widened.

"You dating anyone?" Cole asked. "Want to get dinner sometime?"

She had to think. He could see the wheels turning. What could disqualify him? A working reporter covering the cop beat? A married man, for sure. Maybe his age? She couldn't say no.

"I'd like that, Jamie."

"My best friends call me JJ."

She winked.

TWENTY-FOUR

At one end of Main Street in Fair Oaks Village was a tiny hardware store jammed with everything from under the sun. It was run by brothers, both retired contractors, who knew everything there was to know about home fix-it projects. At the other end was a grandmother bakery famous for its sourdough bread and fruit pies. In between was the village square, where a wild flock of chickens lived.

Julia Carney's office was just off the square. She shared space with another therapist. He was the one who greeted Cole when he came through the door.

"My name's Cole. I'm a reporter." Cole handed him an old card from the *Journal*. "I'm working on a story about the Golden State Killer, and I was hoping to speak with Dr. Carney."

"Of course. You mean Julia," he said. "I'm a Doctor Carney too. Fred Carney. Julia's husband."

He put a hand on Cole's shoulder and led him outside. "She's with a patient right now," he said. "Why don't I buy you a cup of coffee? I'll need to know more about what you're doing."

They found a table outside the bakery. No shade. Cole peeled out of his sport coat and explained about the murder in his house, about Skip and the second suspect, and how he was fairly certain the county authorities weren't interested in finding the other guy. Fred Carney listened without interrupting and then shook his head when Cole finished his pitch.

"Julia grew up in the Curtis Court house," he said. "Her father's place. One of her nephews lives there now. I'm not sure she'll want to relive any of it with you."

"Did something happen?"

The older man nodded and took a sip of his coffee. "I can't say much. It's not my place," he explained. "Since the arrest of the accused, this man DeAngelo, Julia's been on edge."

"If it helps, we could do the interview on background for now," Cole suggested. "That means I can't use anything from the conversation without her approval. Could be we won't need any of it for the record when the time comes."

"That might help," he said. "Would this be for a news story?"

"No. I'm sorry I didn't explain. I'm no longer with the *Journal*; I'm working on a book. I still use the cards because my cell phone number is on it."

"I'll talk to her," he said. "I'll let you know in a day or two."

***

The old city morgue was off Stockton Avenue in a hardscrabble neighborhood called Florin. Between a big Asian grocery store and aging apartments was a flourishing, open-air sex market that began business around two each afternoon.

Cole needed to get a copy of the autopsy report on Emily Hodges, and he wanted to talk to the physician who'd conducted the review. He wondered what the doc might think of his theory that Emily had committed suicide.

He found the guy's office; the door was open. It was a cramped space. A wood table, a couple of filing cabinets. No windows. A fan sat in the middle, humming softly. He was having lunch, a greasy cheeseburger wrapped in yellow paper. The *Journal* sports page was open in front of him.

"Dr. Tran? My name's Cole. I'm an investigator hired by the family of a young woman who died of an overdose a couple months ago. Her name was Emily Hodges."

Tran wiped his mouth and used the straw to take a quick drink from a soda can. "Don't recognize the name," he said. "What do you want?"

"A copy of the coroner's report."

"You need to go to the public counter at the main office," he said. "I don't have it here."

"Right, but I was interested in the cause of death," Cole said. "You listed it as an accidental OD. I've come across a few things that suggest it might have been suicide."

The doctor shook his head. "If we found evidence of suicide, we would have said so."

"Can you just take a peek at your notes?"

The guy shook his head again. "I don't have time."

Cole closed the door and put up a hand. "The family," he said. "They are very well connected. The deceased's grandfather was a state judge. Her grandmother could stir things up if she's unhappy with my work. Please, I promise not to take too much time."

The doctor stood. He was tall, maybe forty. He pulled his laptop from the other side of his desk and opened it. "What's her full name?"

Cole answered.

"OK, I found the file. Let's see." The doctor read his notes. "She had a synthetic fentanyl in her blood."

"That's very bad shit."

"It is." He looked up. "Nothing we found suggested she took her own life. Nothing."

"People occasionally overdose on that stuff, right?"

Tran took one last bite of the burger and tossed it in the trash. "Sometimes."

"And sometimes maybe the overdose is intentional?"

"We didn't find any evidence of suicide. But it does happen."

"OK. Thanks, doc."

***

Five o'clock loomed. Cole headed across town to the courthouse. Jack Perry, the old PI who'd worked on the Bordeaux murder, had a one-room office upstairs from a dime laundromat. Cole tried the old glass door. No one home.

As it happened, Top's bar was just around the corner. Cole thought he deserved a cold one. It was a quiet afternoon. Topper was on the customer side of the bar, drinking coffee.

"You got a secretary now?" he asked Cole.

"Me? Hell no."

"Well, someone named Betsy called looking for you," Topper said. "She thought you might be here."

"I don't know a Betsy."

"Abe Metzger's firm?"

"Right. I'm working for Abe these days."

"I guess she knows you." Topper grinned, revealing two shiny gold teeth on one side. "And she sent those two over there here. Your next appointment, sire."

A young man with shoulder-length hair and wire-rimmed glasses sat at a booth next to an older man, bald, dress shirt open at the collar, expensive suit and shoes.

"What do they want?" Cole asked.

"Beats me. Go on over and find out."

The girl behind the bar served Cole a draft, and he took a sip before walking to the two men.

"My name's Cole. Topper said Abe sent you?"

The older man got to his feet and waved the younger one up too. "Not Abe, my attorney is Dwayne Reston. He said you sometimes work out of this bar," he said. "My name is Dennis Sheppard. This is my son, Clark."

Dennis, who had a highball glass in front of him, took a seat next to his son, currently nursing a double shot of something brown.

"What's the trouble?" Cole asked.

"I just had my life threatened," Clark answered, turning the shot glass in his fingers.

"I hate it when bankers do that," Cole tried to joke, but no one laughed.

"This dude ain't no banker," Clark said. "He's connected. He's going to take everything I have or kill me."

Cole looked him over and then to the dad. Neither face suggested any of it was make-believe. "Tell me what's going on," Cole said.

Clark began. His father owned a chain of upscale grocery stores, mostly in the Bay Area. Cole knew the brand. Clark wanted to strike out on his own and opened a brewpub near the new Kings Arena. It didn't do too well. The kid exhausted his credit from mainstream lenders and had to borrow money off the street. To keep up with the juice, the kid put up his shares in Dad's company. Then the loan shark upped the vig. They had just met with him in hopes of paying off the loan. The old man didn't want a new partner.

"I want to pay off the note, but the lender refused," Mr. Sheppard said. "He wants to get his mitts on the shares in the grocery chain. He implied violence in a meeting we had just an hour ago."

Cole sat up and ran his fingers over his beard. "What is it you think I can do?"

"You're muscle for hire, aren't you?" Clark asked. "I heard about you from my attorney. We want you to meet with my lender, set him straight."

Cole took a pull on his beer. He was counting. The Wilmer dig. The job for the old woman, Mrs. Hodges. The arson thing.

And, of course, there was the DeAngelo case and the second suspect.

For a guy who'd spent the last four months sitting around the house, Cole had become a very busy man.

"If it's a matter of money, Mr. Cole, I assure you we can pay," Dennis pleaded.

"It's not that. I'm spread a little thin."

"Please, we really don't have options," the old man said.

"Have you talked to the police?"

"You know we can't do that," Clark said.

"Tell you what, send me this guy's contacts and I'll look into it," Cole said. "If I do this, I get a five-thousand-dollar non-refundable retainer and a thousand dollars a day. If I need help, my associate gets a two-grand retainer and five hundred a day."

"Done," the old man said.

TWENTY-FIVE

The flight to Redding wasn't until eleven thirty. Before he met with Mrs. Wilmer, Cole needed to review everything he had on the family, including the two men with criminal records—Callen and Dalton.

He left the house around nine and got to Abe's place a half hour later. He found an empty cubicle and got to work. Karmen had sent him two emails containing what she'd found. Not much.

She'd found court filings tied to a 1998 trial where Callen was convicted of sexual assault and sentenced to twenty-five years. There was also an obit the Redding paper had run in 2007.

Callen R. Wilmer, a scion of a wealthy northern Sacramento Valley farming family, died Wednesday in the infirmary at the Soledad State Prison in Salinas, California. Authorities did not release any details about the circumstances of his death, pending an investigation. Wilmer, 67, was nine years into a 25-year sentence for aggravated sexual assault. Callen Wilmer is survived by a younger brother, Ted Wilmer, who is a Shasta County Supervisor and the president of Stony Creek Farms based in Red Bluff, Ca.

Karmen found nothing on the younger family member, Dalton. Cole gave her a call.

"What's up boss?"

"For one, what the hell were you thinking with that post on your site about our working together? You even mentioned the second suspect."

"No biggie. I had to tell the troops something. I've been off-line for a couple weeks. Anything wrong with the truth?"

"It's a damn public site, Karmen. Anyone can see it, including, possibly, the guy we're after. Stupid move."

She didn't answer.

"Take it down immediately."

Cole moved on. "I'm looking at your mail on the two Wilmers with criminal records. You found nothing on the younger one?"

"Nothing."

"Where did you look?"

"I used the data base at the state law library."

"OK. I'm heading up to Redding this afternoon. I'll call when I'm back around three."

"Gotcha boss."

Cole ran Dalton Wilmer through a database Abe's firm subscribed to. Dalton Wilmer was twenty-five. His home address was in Palo Cedro. Cole recognized the street number. Dalton was Ted's son and Lorraine's stepson.

He wondered about the sealed file on Dalton he'd found in the index up at Redding. A young woman interrupted him.

"Are you Jamie?" she asked. She had a round face with freckles and short red hair.

"I am."

"I'm Betsy," she said. "Abe asked me to look in on you now and then."

Cole got up and shook her hand. "You found me the other day at Top's."

"Yes, well, there's a call for you. Jack Perry? A private investigator?"

"Send him through."

Perry's voice was raspy and shallow. "Cole? You the reporter? I thought I'd call you back, but I've got to warn you, I don't talk on the record."

"That's OK, I'm not longer reporting," Cole explained. "I've sort of moved to your side of the street."

"Working as a PI?"

"Yes."

Perry snorted. "Why would you do that?"

"I need a job."

"Well don't think this is going to be any fun," he said. "You think you know the streets because you've been a reporter. You don't."

"I'll be OK."

"I have a cousin, lives in Philly. He was one of the top crime reporters on the East Coast and he came to work for me for a year. Thought he'd learn a little, maybe write a book. He lasted three months, went back to the paper."

"Well, I can't go back. I can't go to any other paper either."

"Black-balled?"

"Something like that."

"Well, good luck to you. I hope you have the stomach for it. The difference is that as a reporter, you arrive at the scene of the crime, after the body is taken away. You talk to the people who were there, but you weren't. Doing my job means you can be standing there when the hit is made. Sometimes the blood spatters on you."

"Yeah, well, I've seen blood before. Listen man, I appreciate the heads up, but can we get back to the reason I called?"

"Sure kid, sorry, sometimes I rant."

"No worries," Cole said. "I'm working on a case involving the Golden State Killer."

"Been wondering if someone was going to remember that kid in Rancho. It's all I've been thinking about since the arrest."

"Right, we're working with the Bordeaux family and they gave us the report you did back in, what, eighty-two? Any chance you still have your file?"

"I was just looking at it, hang on."

"Thanks."

"What do you need to know?"

"I'm interested in the reference to the copycat attacks at the end."

"That's what the task force decided. That the Bordeaux girl had been killed by someone else."

"Any details about why?"

"Well, let's see." He put the phone down and Cole could hear him shuffling papers. "I got some notes here about talking with a captain."

"Name?"

"Lon Donovan."

"Donovan? Shoot, then I've probably got everything you have. I'm working with a retired investigator who was Donovan's friend, another man on the task force."

"Oh yeah? Who's that?"

"Skip Harkin."

"Damn. I know Skip. Salt of the earth."

"Is that it?"

"I don't think so." Cole could hear him again digging through the file. "Here's something, but I have no idea what or why. A business card from a cop. Olimpo Police Department, a Sergeant Harold Remy. This must be something that fell into the file by mistake. Where the hell is Olimpo, anyway?"

"I don't know," Cole said, dismissing it. "Did you happen to talk to Donovan about why they believed the Bordeaux killing wasn't the E-A-R?"

"Yeah. He said there was another attack that same night and they decided the E-A-R couldn't have done both."

"Do you have anything more on that other attack?"

"Sure. She was thirteen years old, the youngest of the E-A-R's victims," Perry said. "The MacFarlane kid. She's been on the news since the arrest. Donovan said she gave a good ID on the perp that fit the East Area Rapist perfectly."

"Where was she attacked?"

"In Carmichael," Perry said. "The MacFarlane kid's call for help came to dispatch about nine. The victim said the attack began around seven thirty."

"I think the Bordeaux girl was found around midnight," Cole said.

"The lab fixed Bordeaux's time of death around ten forty-five," Perry said.

Cole did the time equation in his head. "Is Carmichael really that far from Rancho?"

"It's on the other side of the river," Perry said. "You got to go over one of the bridges. It's easily ten miles."

"I don't know," Cole said. "The MacFarlane kid called for help around nine, which meant her attacker was long gone by then, maybe half an hour? Probably more. Let's say he leaves the MacFarlane place by eight thirty. Twenty minutes to Rancho. Attacks Bordeaux around ten. Why couldn't the same guy do both crimes?"

"Maybe they got this one wrong," Perry said. "But if they did, there would have been DNA. Which there apparently wasn't. I'm sure if they could've thrown another capital crime on DeAngelo, they would have."

"Yeah, I know. Thanks for your time." Cole got off the phone, less certain about Skip's second suspect theory. *If Victim Eleven is key*, he thought, *what am I missing?*

***

The private plane to Redding wasn't what Cole expected. The cabin was tight, almost claustrophobic. An almost overwhelming odor came from the new vinyl interior, the carpets, and the plastic fittings. The ride was bumpy too. There was a lot of wind.

Cole couldn't tell where they were when the plane began its descent. There was a small town out one side of the plane and a lot of well-tended farmland. A pickup was waiting for him. The driver, dark and rugged, didn't say much on the short drive to the company headquarters. They approached from the back, which was busy with farm equipment, trucks, workers in cowboy hats and bright-colored long-sleeved tee-shirts. Cole was dropped around the front and he entered through the glass doors where the setting was far more corporate.

A young woman with oval glasses and sharp brown eyes met Cole in the lobby. She said she was "Raine's assistant" and escorted him up a flight of stairs to the executive suite. He didn't wait long.

Lorraine came from the hallway, trailed by a gaggle of people. She was, as Cole remembered her, regal and elegant. She greeted him and he followed her to her office. He noticed the modern art on the walls; most of it looked original. There were small displays of plants and real flowers. Muted piano music was playing. Mozart maybe.

"I thought we'd just dine here," she said, pointing to the large conference table toward one end of the room. There were two table settings; a glass pitcher filled with water, lemons, and ice; and a menu card. She took a seat.

"You've got a choice between steelhead trout in cranberry Dijon sauce or bavette steak in a mushroom sauce."

Cole sat down. "Don't tell me you cook, too?"

She laughed. "No, we have a cafeteria downstairs," she said. "And I asked them to prepare something nice for everyone today."

"The trout sounds good."

"Excellent."

Polly the assistant popped in and took the orders.

"Tell me, Mr. Cole, do you know much about almonds—or as they call them around here, a-monds?"

"Nothing."

"I didn't either," she said. "Almonds are considered one of our great superfoods. There's growing evidence that almonds are, nutritionally, among the best single things a person could eat."

"Why aren't they on the menu?"

She smiled. "I'll make sure you get a snack packet to take with you for the ride home." She poured them both water from the pitcher.

"You mentioned our expansion during our phone conversation," she said. "It's true. We have orchards here in Red Bluff and in Glenn County and thousands more acres down in the Bakersfield area. We are three times larger than our closest competitor."

"Probably even bigger once you go public."

"Yes," she said without hesitation. "We are a for-profit business, and we aspire to make money at the end of the day, but I have strong feelings about the good we are doing along the way."

"What do you mean?"

"We've got plans for a nonprofit spinoff that will take the millions of pounds of product deemed unfit for the consumer market and turn it into protein powders for national distribution to needy families. We're also looking to partner with UNESCO on a program to help identify potential orchards in Africa and South America."

"While still protecting the big slice the Chinese will take off the top."

Lorraine sat up a bit. "Are you always so cynical, Mr. Cole?"

"Yes."

The doors to the office opened and Polly, along with another woman, pushed a lunch cart into the room. Lorraine only had a salad. He dug into the trout anyway. He hadn't eaten much breakfast.

She left him alone for a few bites and then asked about his work as a journalist. He waited for the question, the circumstances for his leaving the *Journal*, but she didn't go there. Cole figured she already knew.

When lunch was done, she invited Cole to the soft chairs on the other side of the big office near the floor-to-ceiling windows and their view of the orchards, blooming white and cloudlike.

She sat still and straight, ready to talk business. "I asked you before, Mr. Cole, who you are working for. I'd like an honest answer now."

"To be very honest, I'm not sure." Cole rolled his shoulders, relieving a bit of the tension that had been building since he got on the plane.

"Good," she said. "You are conceding that someone sent you here, at least. We're making progress."

"Who is Callen Wilmer?" Cole asked, studying her face. Her expression didn't change.

She drew in a breath. "My husband's older brother. As I understand it, he died in prison. Not a good person."

"Aggravated sexual assault," Cole said. "He got twenty-five years and was stabbed to death in his cell. Do you know why?"

She shook her head.

"What about Dalton?"

"What about him?"

"He's your stepson."

"He is."

"He's got a criminal record too."

"I don't know about that," she answered, pushing her hands against her dress at the knees. "He's a college student, a math major. I know that he had some troubles as an adolescent. An emotional breakdown of some sort. It happened before I came here and before Ted and I married. If some sort of crime was associated with it, I don't know what it was. You'll have to ask Ted."

"I will."

She sighed again. "Mr. Cole, as you know, we are on the verge of completing a massive business transaction, a move worth hundreds of millions of dollars. Some people don't want this transaction to take place. Our corporate competitors, rival growers, Wall Street pirates—the list is long. One of them has obviously hired you to come and threaten us. To find dirt. To try to intimidate us." She paused. "How am I doing so far?"

"It's your dime."

"It's safe to say, Mr. Cole, that you're nothing more than a hired gun. And as such, I'd like to offer you an alternative business arrangement."

Cole relaxed. *Here it comes.*

"You have a house for sale, correct? What's the list price?"

Cole cracked a small smile. He hadn't anticipated this one. "Three fifty."

"What if I offered four? If I bought your house for four hundred thousand, would you walk away from all this business here with my family?"

He rubbed his beard absently. Fifty thousand dollars over list was a mighty attractive offer. He'd known she might do something like this, but it was a lot more than he'd been expecting. Cole walked his way around the offer.

What did he actually owe Ms. Morris? Lorraine was right; Cole was a hired gun, and he was free to take whatever offer came his way. *Why not?*

Abe.

Abe wouldn't like it. At least not without being consulted. Evelyn Morris had hired Cole at least in part because of Abe and the Metzger firm. He certainly owed allegiance to Abe. It wouldn't look good for Cole, right out of the chute, to dump one client in favor of another. He could see that might damage Abe's rep. Nope.

"That's a very interesting offer," Cole said, leaning forward and putting his hands on his knees. "But I can't do it."

"Really?"

"I'm thinking of taking it off the market anyway."

Lorraine got to her feet and went to her desk. She put on a pair of reading glasses and picked up a folder before returning to the chair facing Cole.

"Very well, I've got another idea," she said. "Were you being honest when you told me earlier that you don't know who hired you to come here?"

"More or less."

"Well, I'd like to hire you to find out conclusively," she said. "I'll match whatever you're getting from the other side."

"You want me to investigate my client, who's paying me to investigate you? Seems like a bit of a conflict of interest."

"I don't see it that way," she answered. "You want to investigate our firm, our family—go right ahead. I promise I'll cooperate. You want to talk to Ted? I'll set it up. Haven't I answered your questions today?"

Cole ran his hand through his beard again.

"You're in the big pool now, Mr. Cole, and you are no longer bound by the ethics of a journalist," she argued. "You turn me down, and I can assure you your job investigating us just got a lot more difficult. Remember your friends—What did you call them? Moof and Goof?"

Cole nodded. "I'm getting fifteen from the other side."

"Half now, half when you deliver your employer's identity."
"OK, Mrs. Wilmer, you got a deal."
"I'll need this done quickly."
He smiled. "Everyone says that. I understand."

TWENTY-SIX

Lorraine was right. Cole was back in Sacramento by three. While he was in the air, Fred Carney left a message. He wondered if Cole could come by the Fair Oaks child counseling office at five. His wife was ready to talk. Cole agreed and then called Karmen to ask her to join him.

Julia's inner office was a playroom containing a big wooden dollhouse, a cabinet crowded with picture books, and a row of play trucks and tractors—some big enough for a small child to sit on. Julia was rigid on the couch, her husband beside her. Two wooden chairs faced her.

Cole showed her the tape recorder and explained the interview process. He assured her that nothing she said would be used without her consent.

Julia took a sip of water and began.

Her story started a few months before the attack in Cole's house. She had just finished up a degree in education at Sac State and was student teaching at a middle school near the university. She had a boyfriend, and they planned to marry in the spring.

"I hadn't heard anything about the East Area Rapist attacks; I was just too focused on my own life." She stopped talking, swallowed hard, and took a breath.

Her husband put an arm around her shoulders.

"I broke down over this," she whispered. "I ended up quitting my job and breaking it off with Bob, my boyfriend. The events of that fall almost destroyed me. Even now, it's hard to talk about it, so bear with me."

"Take your time," Cole urged.

"In October, we had a break-in at the house. Some small items were taken. My dad was a track coach, and the thief took a fancy whistle and gold lanyard one of his teams had given him. He took my dad's starter pistol." She paused. "The burglar also rummaged through my bedroom dresser and tossed some of my underwear on the floor."

She paused again.

"He had masturbated on them."

"God damn," Karmen whispered.

"We called the sheriff, and they came out," Julia continued. "They told us there had been some other burglaries in the area and to call them if we saw anyone suspicious."

She pulled another tissue from the box.

"A few weeks later, I had an interview for a teaching job in Auburn. My father drove me up in the morning, but I had to take the bus back. On the way home, I noticed a young man watching me. At first, I just dismissed it, but after I changed buses in Rocklin, I saw him again on the same bus. When I got home to Rancho, it was getting dark and I was afraid this guy would follow me, so I called Bob from a payphone and then waited for him at the Denny's on Sunrise.

"The man following me was tall. He had bad skin and was about my age," she said. "I had just turned twenty-two.

"Anyway, I sat at the counter talking to the waitress; she was a friend of mine. And then I saw the man again. He poked his head inside the diner, looking around. My friend saw how frightened I became; she got the manager and a busboy. They ran after him, but he got away."

She opened the water bottle sitting on the desk next to her and took a sip.

"A week later, the night before Thanksgiving, I drove to the store to get some things. I had about three or four bags of groceries. I was putting the bags in our car and I saw something out of the corner of my eye. I remember thinking it was just a shadow, but then a car came up with its lights on, and there he was, in the parking lot. Lord, it scared me."

Tears welled in her eyes, and she put her hand to her mouth.

"I got in my car and locked the doors. When I got home, I called the sheriff, and they took a report." Julia ran a hand through her hair.

"Both Bob and my dad went crazy. They wanted me to stay home with one of them all day and all night, but that wasn't practical. By then, I'd heard about the attacks on the news and how the police couldn't catch this criminal. It was truly terrifying.

"Two weeks passed. And then there was the murder in your house." She stared at Cole with blank eyes.

"I'm as sure now as I was then," she said, "that the killer intended to attack me. He mistakenly chose the wrong house." She patted her tears away. "That poor girl."

"Did you know the victim?" Karmen asked.

"No. In fact, I was shocked to learn anyone lived there," she said. "It was a model house for the developers and sat vacant for more than a year after it was built."

"Were you around on the night of the attack?" Cole asked.

"Bob and I had been out that night. I think it was a Saturday, and we'd gone to the movies or something," she explained. "It was about midnight when he drove me home. We came around the corner and here were all these police cars. Maybe a dozen of them.

"Bob took me home before walking over to see what he could find out," she said. "The sheriff's deputies wouldn't answer any questions, but one of our neighbors was a city policeman. A few days later, he told my dad what had happened."

"Did the police ever come back to interview you?" Cole asked.

"No." Julia took another sip of water and composed herself. "Not until many years later." She motioned toward her husband. "Hand me the envelope, honey."

Her hands still shook. "It was 2005. A detective from Auburn came to see me. He brought me this photo."

She handed it to Cole. A black and white mugshot. Just a man. Bald. Late thirties, maybe younger. Cole turned the photo over. It was stamped 'Auburn PD, August 17, 2005,' and beneath that, a handwritten name: C. Barrett.

"Is this his name?" Cole asked.

"I believe so, yes."

Cole studied the photo. The man stood against a wall with height measures. He wasn't tall, maybe five-five. "You said the guy who stalked you was tall. This guy isn't tall."

"No," Julia answered. "He looks nothing like the man who followed me. It's someone else."

"What did the police say about Barrett?"

"That there had been a similar crime in their town; they wanted to know if I recognized him."

"Did they mention the East Area Rapist?"

"No. I would remember that."

"I need a copy of this photo," Cole said.

"I can scan it right now," Fred said, getting to his feet.

Karmen leaned in. "Did you say the detective was from Auburn?"

"Yes."

Fred came back with a copy of the mugshot. Cole got to his feet. "This has been very helpful," he said. "One last thing. Is there anyone else from the neighborhood back then that we might talk to?"

"Tommy Hughes," she said. "His mom passed away last summer, and he recently sold their house. They lived next door to us."

"Do you know where I might find him?"

"He's a day manager at Safeway."

Cole and Karmen didn't speak until they were back in the car.

"OK, so this stalker was tall and thin," Cole said. "DeAngelo is heavy set."

"What about the other guy? Barrett?"

"I'm thinking he might be my mailman."

"Really?"

Cole rubbed his chin and got the car going.

"I got one too, boss."

"Yeah?"

"It was the Auburn police who brought her the photo of Barrett," Karmen said. "DeAngelo used to live in Auburn. He was a city police officer there for a while too."

"Was he? Good work."

TWENTY-SEVEN

Back at the house, Cole logged into the research network at Abe's office and looked for men in their sixties who lived in Northern California and had the last name Barrett, first initial 'C.' There were twenty-seven of them. Cole printed out the list and gave a copy to Karmen.

"You start at the bottom; I'll start at the top."

"What? You want to just Google around until we find something?" she said caustically.

"You got a better way?"

"Go on Facebook," she said.

"Facebook? You crazy? That's about the dumbest thing I've ever heard. A Facebook profile is about the last thing that our guy would have."

"I know, dumbshit," Karmen snapped back at him. "We can eliminate all the C. Barretts who do."

Cole blinked. "Hmm."

It took her five minutes to trace a likely subject; his first name was Charles. He appeared to live somewhere in Sacramento. Cole opened a browser on his computer and called up the federal registry of sex offenders. He tapped the name 'Charles Barrett' into the search box. There were nineteen nationally. He picked through the list for ones living in California. He found a Charles A. Barrett, last known address as 910 K Street, Sacramento. There was a photo of the man. Neither he nor Karmen thought he looked much like the man in the mugshot.

"I know who might know," Cole said. "Wait here. I'll be right back."

He grabbed the mugshot and ran out the door and across the street. He noticed the white Prius in the driveway but knocked on the door anyway. Susan answered and her fiancé Daniel stood behind her, looming over her shoulder.

"Jamie? What a surprise. I want you to meet someone. This is Daniel. Danny, this is Jamie."

"Nice to meet you," Cole said, extending his hand.

"Likewise," Dan said. "You're right, babe. He does look like James Garner, except for the beard."

Cole showed Susan the mugshot as Daniel disappeared into the house. "Could this have been your mailman?" he asked. "He's younger here. This photo was taken in 2005."

"Could be. I don't know." She studied it. "The eyes. It would be better if this was a color photo. The man I met in your driveway had these weird sort of gray eyes. I can't be sure."

"He's short, though," Cole pointed out. "He's in a lineup. See? He's about five-five."

"I'm five-five, Jamie, and I told you I was taller. Might be him."

"You were probably wearing heels," Cole said. "But it could be him?"

Susan nodded. He thanked her, wished them well, returned to his driveway, and got into his car, honking the horn. They were going downtown.

Barrett's address was an older apartment building with a drug-store and a coffee shop on the ground floor. The outside door was on a code lock. To get inside, they had to wait until a tenant exited. They didn't have an apartment number. The hallway was dark and smelled of an unholy combination of cat urine, rotting fruit, and bleach. They wandered around some before a large woman with a set of keys, pushing a custodial cart, confronted them.

"Who are you?" she demanded.

"I'm looking for a friend of mine," Cole blurted. "Charles Barrett. I can't remember his apartment number."

She eyed the two of them suspiciously. "You don't belong here," she said.

"OK, so he's not a friend of mine. I'm a reporter."

"A reporter?"

"Which apartment is Barrett's?"

"What are you doing here?"

"Working a story."

"You got no permission to be here. I'm going to call the police."

Cole got out the mugshot. "Have you seen this man?"

She pushed her cart to one side of the hallway and took out a mop, holding it like a baseball bat. "You go on now!" she shouted. "Get!"

"Does Barrett live here?" Cole asked as he and Karmen backed away.

"Get!"

Out on the street, Cole scanned the area. Maybe their guy was having coffee or a drink nearby. They wandered around some before returning to the car. The afternoon traffic was getting thick and slow around downtown.

"What now, boss?"

"I don't know," Cole answered.

"What about Auburn? Shouldn't we go up there and see if anyone recognizes this guy Barrett?"

"Yeah," Cole said, distracted. His mind was elsewhere. The dirty apartment building. The dim lights. The stink. He wanted out. He was tiring of this ugly sex attacker business.

He was thinking of something clean and bright, pretty and sweet. *Brooke*.

After Karmen left, Cole got a beer and settled into a chair near his pool. After a second cold one, he called Brooke, if only to hear her voice.

"There she is," he opened "How are you today?"

"OK, I guess, what's up?

"Just checking on my records request, anything new?" he asked.

"Nothing."

"The sheriff's not blowing me off, is he? Big mistake."

"I didn't say that. He hasn't made a decision."

"You tell him about my house and all?"

"I told my boss, and I believe he spoke to the sheriff."

"So why doesn't he grant the request?" Cole picked up a baseball signed by Don Drysdale he kept on his desk.

"I don't know, Jamie. He doesn't tell me everything."

He thought she sounded annoyed. "Are you angry about something?"

"You've waited too long."

"Too long for what?"

"To ask me out and then when you finally do call, you start with this shit about your records."

Cole put the ball back on the shelf and shifted the phone to his other ear. "Well, I didn't mean to wait too long. I apologize. What are you doing tomorrow night?"

"Are you asking me out?"

"I am."

"I'm not sure about you. You're sort of old for me."

"Too old? Forty is the new thirty. Besides, I'm more accomplished than any of the boys you usually date. Probably better-looking, too."

"And so modest."

"How about seven? I know a cool place in Carmichael. I'll text you the address."

She sighed. "I don't know. Something better might come along."

"Like a *Friends* marathon."

"*Friends*?" She laughed. "See, you are so-oo old."

"Seven, then?"

"I suppose. Please don't bring your walker."

***

Saturday. Cole decided he deserved a day off and purposefully left all the detective work in the office. He made reservations at a new bistro that had been featured in the Sunday paper. He wouldn't know trendy from a lamppost, but Brooke seemed like the type to know about it. Maybe she'd be pleased with his choice.

It was warm, not hot. Cole decided on a bike ride all the way up to Folsom Lake. After the ride, he mowed his lawn and swept up the backyard. He jumped into the pool for a bit and then fell fast asleep in the shade.

Cole took care getting ready. He followed a long, hot shower with slathering lotion on dry skin. He decided to shave—Kim would be happy—using a trimmer to get down to the bristles and a sharp razor to do the rest.

Music was Steve Reich, *Duet for Two Solo Violins.*

He paired his favorite blue Hawaiian shirt with khakis and, since summer wasn't far off, his Birkenstock sandals.

SoCal summertime comfortable.

Brooke sparkled through the restaurant door, waving. She wore a white dress with a red and blue shawl. He got up and she let him give her a friendly hug. No kissy kiss on the cheeks; that wasn't him.

"This place is cute," she said. "I told my girlfriend we were going here. She was jealous. I guess the chef ran a fancy place over in Napa."

"You look great."

"Thank you." She did a little double take when she realized the beard was gone. "And look at you. You clean up nice."

"How was your day?"

"Nothing special. I went to yoga this morning. Had lunch with a friend. Put in a couple of hours at the office. What's new with you?"

"I bought a gun."

"You? Whatever for?"

"Hey, man, I'm a gumshoe now. Hadn't you heard?"

"A gumshoe."

"You know, a shamus, a dick, a PI."

"Oh my. Did you say dick?"

Cole broke up. "Yeah, sorry. We don't want to get ahead of ourselves."

A small grin lingered as the waiter approached. She ordered a Manhattan. Cole liked that. He ordered Jack on the rocks.

"Seriously, I've just been hired to roust a loan shark," Cole said.

"Last week, we made a run at a couple of guys suspected of arson. And earlier this month, I was tossed in jail for trespassing at a state Senator's house."

"You're being paid for this?"

"I am."

"That sounds scary," she said with concern. "I'm not sure how I feel about that."

"Hence the gun training."

"I know I don't like that."

"Don't worry. The trainer said I should never take the weapon out of its holster." Cole grinned. "Said I'd hurt myself."

"You be careful," she said sincerely. "I'd like to give us a chance."

Cole bit his lip. "Me too, Brooke."

The server returned. Brooke ordered the special: seared scallops with English peas and herb-roasted Yukons. Cole had the fresh salmon.

They worked on their drinks as she told him a bit about herself. Never married, but twice engaged. Father was an aerospace engineer for Boeing in Seattle. Mother taught school. One sister, two brothers.

"Why politics?" Cole asked.

"Politics is fun," she said. "I love my job. I like working on campaigns—even with the long hours and bad pay. Good candidates are interesting people."

Cole knew going in she'd only worked for Republicans. He hesitated to bring up the man in the White House.

"Like Sheriff Henley?"

"He's all right," she answered. "Not too ambitious. I'm sort of looking to jump elsewhere."

"National?"

"You mean to Trump? God, no. Now there's a bad candidate."

Cole nodded in relieved agreement. *Good,* he thought, *got that out of the way.*

"What about you?" she asked. "You ever been married?"

"Yep. It lasted almost ten years," he said.

"What happened?"

"We grew apart. Wanted different things."

"Such as?"

"I wanted kids. She didn't."

Brooke was quiet for a moment. "Are you at all interested in getting remarried?"

"Sure, if the right partner comes along."

"You are looking, then?"

"I'm usually working on something."

"Now I get a turn?"

"Too soon to tell."

"What are you waiting for?"

"To see what you're like after a second Manhattan. You're out if you go sloppy on me."

She giggled. "One's my limit, then."

Dinner was served. He told her more about his trip to Redding. He gave her an honest account of how he lost his job at the *Journal* and his ambitions regarding a book-writing career. He was self-effacing, but still confident. Time seemed to slow. The jitters of a first date faded.

"I spoke to the sheriff this morning," she said. "I think he's going to confirm if a crime took place in your house back when, at least."

"I guess that's good news."

"He split a gut laughing," she said, smiling. "He couldn't believe all this was because you're trying to sell your house. You threw quite a scare into him."

"I did?"

"He thought you had something big in your back pocket. Something that could upset the DeAngelo case."

"Something big, huh? Like what?"

Brooke's smile vanished. "What are you asking?"

"Nothing."

She studied him. "Bullshit. You *are* working on this, aren't you?"

"Wait," Cole said, on the defensive. "No."

"What is this, Jamie? Did you ask me out just to pump me for intel?"

"No." He tried to reach for her hand, but she pulled back.

"What's going on, then? And it had better be the truth, or I'll never go out with you again."

She got up quickly and asked for directions to the ladies' room.

Cole sighed and waved. "Bring me a beer. The lady will have a glass of white wine."

The drinks arrived ahead of her, and Cole took a healthy belt.

When Brooke returned, she cast a sideways look at the wine. "I'm going to need more alcohol for this?"

"Maybe." Cole searched her eyes, inhaled deeply, and began. The whole truth and nothing but the truth. She needed the wine. They each had another round.

"This is just great, Jamie. Put me in the middle, damn you."

"Listen, I like you very much. I don't want this to end things. It doesn't have to."

"No, sure, I can see this working out just great. And when the sheriff finds out—because when you bag this second suspect he obviously will—I'll lose my job and probably won't be able to get another one."

"You like me."

She shook her head and looked away. "I do."

"Then let's just keep this under wraps for now. We don't talk about it, ever. Church and State."

"That doesn't help me, Jamie."

"You have plausible deniability," he told her. "The sheriff asked you to meet with me about this. When you told him what I was doing— and selling my house was the only thing I had going, then—he gave you permission to confirm the crime to me. After that, you know nothing."

"Except we're dating."

"Exactly. I know of a dozen couples with mixed political allegiance.

You can tell Henley that we agreed not to talk shop. Done."

This time, Cole needed to visit the men's room. Brooke was still there when he got back.

The restaurant was in a trendy part of town with bookstores, antique shops, and art galleries. He asked if she had time for a walk. When they found an ice cream vendor on the street, they shared a cup of handmade strawberry. They traded berry-flavored kisses and held hands as he walked her to her car. Then they kissed again.

TWENTY-EIGHT

This time, Cole and Karmen took two cars. Karmen was headed to the bluff overlooking the firefighter's place in Fairfield while Cole went straight to the vacuum shop in Stockton. Phase two of the pizza job was ready to unfold.

"All you got to do is stay with him when he bolts," Cole said. "I'll be with Petrov. I'm betting they meet somewhere near Rio Vista."

"OK, boss," she said.

Karmen got into place a few minutes ahead of Cole. He parked outside the vacuum shop. Petrov's wife recognized him right away and called for her husband.

"What do you want now?" the big man said as Cole came to the counter.

"I want to talk about arson."

"Arson?"

"Yeah, a pizza place you owned with another guy. It burned down two months ago."

"So?"

"Well, it was arson. You either did it yourself or you had it done."

"Get out of here."

Cole handed the wife one of his old business cards from the *Journal.* "That little song and dance we played for you the other day was just that. I'm actually a reporter. I was getting an imprint of your truck tires. Now I have proof you were there when the place went up in flames."

The wife wore an I-told-you-so expression and handed the card to her husband.

"I've got the report from the city," Petrov said. "It was electrical."

Cole shook his head. "Arson. Got anything to say?" He held up his phone. "No? Well, the story's going to run this Sunday. If you change your mind, my number's on the card."

Cole quickly got out of the shop and into his car. He drove into the alley behind the store and up the block. Nothing for half an hour. Then Karmen called.

"A garage door is opening," she said. "A white sedan coming—wait, the SUV too. Damn, they're using two cars."

Cole watched the back door of the store. Petrov emerged, got into his truck, and started for the freeway.

"I know where they're going to meet," Cole said. "Rio Vista. It's halfway. Stay with whichever vehicle heads east on Highway 12."

A few minutes later, Karmen called back. "Both vehicles are taking the 12."

"I still say it's going to be Rio Vista. It's OK; I've got Petrov."

Petrov got off on the first exit for Rio Vista. Karmen called and said the white sedan was getting off the highway. The SUV was still going east. "I'm coming up to the bridge," she said. "What do you want me to do?"

"Stay with the sedan," Cole said. "If the SUV's on the bridge, there's no exit until the other side of the delta. I'm pretty sure they're meeting somewhere on my side, probably near the waterfront."

"OK, chief."

This time, Cole was wrong. Petrov turned north when he got off the highway. They drove another twenty minutes on a small, two-lane road until they reached a crossroads called Ryer. Petrov turned into a parking lot. Ahead were three cars waiting in line. Cole saw the sign. They were waiting for a ferry. The meeting was going to be on board. Cole called Karmen.

"Where are you?"

"Hell if I know. Some wild-ass backwater road."

Cole tapped his location into his phone. "You see a sign or anything? Ryer Island?"

"Two miles ahead."

"OK. You'll be coming to a ferry," Cole said. "Looks like a little boat, probably only carries a couple of cars at a time. If there's a line, park your car and go on foot."

"Got it."

The ferry docked on Cole's side of the river. Petrov got out of his car and walked down the ramp. Cole called Karmen again.

"OK, my guy is onboard. He's on foot. You there yet?"

"Yeah. There's no line. The SUV is the only other car. I'm going to park."

"No," Cole said. "The firefighter's never seen you. Stay in your car and pull in behind him. You'll be able to duck down once Petrov is there. If we get lucky, you'll be able to take the shot we need. They'll be meeting in the SUV."

Fifteen minutes later, wearing a smug grin, Karmen handed Cole the camera. She'd got the photos they needed.

***

On his drive back to Sacramento, Cole called Karmen and gave her instructions for her visit to Auburn in the morning. He told her how he'd gone to the assessor's office and researched all the neighbors on his block, looking for any of them that might have been around in the 1970s. He told her to do the same thing.

"I want you to start by getting the title to the house DeAngelo owns," he said. "The one where he was arrested over in Citrus Heights."

"Why?"

"It might have his previous address in Auburn," Cole said. "And that would make your day easier."

"OK."

"Once you have DeAngelo's Auburn address, I want you to walk the old neighborhood. Knock on some doors. Talk people up."

"Got it. What about Barrett? Should I show his photo around?"

"Sure, but after our little snafu at his building, I'm thinking Barrett is in the wind," Cole said. "He knows we're on to him."

"You think he's the mailman?"

"Don't know," Cole said. "You got a tape recorder?"

"No, what for?"

"In case you find someone worth interviewing, pendejo."

Karmen laughed. "Good one, boss."

"On your way up the hill to Auburn, stop by my place and I'll give you one of mine to use," Cole said. "If I'm not there, it will be in a box on my porch."

There were still a couple hours left in the workday, so Cole stopped in Abe's office, found an empty cubicle, and logged into his email. He opened the note from Sheppard, the grocer's son. Enclosed was the name of the loan shark, Vincent Darna, and the address over in West Sacramento where Darna kept his book.

Cole called an old source at the Attorney General's office. Dean Slatkin was an investigator who worked organized crime. Cole asked if Darna was on their radar.

"I don't recognize the name," Slatkin said. "Let me check around and call you back."

Abe appeared at the cubicle. "Mrs. Hodges's chauffeur left a packet of stuff for you this morning," Abe said, taking the only other seat in the office nook. "How's that going?"

"Unbeknownst to Mrs. Hodges, her granddaughter wasn't doing that well," Cole said. "She'd dropped out of law school and she was seeing a shrink."

"Hmm," Abe said.

"It gets worse," Cole said. "They found synthetic fentanyl in her blood."

"Fentanyl? Christ. Marian told me it was a sedative."

"It was. Just a really strong one."

"Get your stuff," Abe said, getting up. "I've got a little surprise for you."

Cole followed Abe through the maze of cubicles, copiers, and fish tanks of the main office floor until they got to a side office with glass doors and a window facing the parking lot. Next to the door was a nameplate: James J. Cole.

"Wha-at?" Cole cried. "My own digs?"

"We're doing some restructuring, and we thought it best to make you more formally part of the team."

Cole danced inside, dropping his briefcase on a side table and falling into the fancy office chair. "This is great, Abe. Thanks."

A girl appeared at the door. Betsy.

"Cole, this is Betsy," Abe said, waving her into the room.

"Yeah." Cole smiled. "We've met."

"She's going to be your liaison to the rest of the firm," Abe explained. "Help you keep track of things. Keep your calendar and your accounts. More importantly, she's going to help me stay in the loop. Right now, I have no idea what you're doing."

Cole nodded.

"She's also another pair of hands," Abe said. "She's got other responsibilities around here, too, but she's a resource if you need it."

"Works for me."

"The deal here, JJ, is that I need to keep track of what you're doing, in case there's a business opportunity for us," Abe said. "Like this Wilmer thing. I don't know what's going on there. Let's take a minute right now to bring me up to speed."

Cole started with the Wilmer dig. He filled in the details about going up to Redding, finding criminal records on two family members, and going out to Wilmer's place and getting arrested. He also owned up to getting jumped by the two goons.

"Have you started the gun training?" Abe asked.

"For what it's worth."

Cole told them about his lunch with Mrs. Wilmer and how she tried to sugar him off the case, offering to buy his house. He told Abe he'd agreed to accept fifteen grand for finding out exactly who Evelyn Morris was.

"Who?" Abe asked.

"The hedge fund lady who hired me to dig into the Wilmers in the first place."

"Wait." Abe put up a hand. "This Morris person hired you to investigate the Wilmers, and now Mrs. Wilmer has hired you to look into Morris?"

Cole shrugged. "Evelyn Morris is cagey. She knows what I'm supposed to find, but she won't tell me. It's some sort of cat-and-mouse thing."

Abe furrowed his brow.

From here, Cole explained his work with Karmen. The arson case. The new job for the grocery store owner and the loan shark. Betsy was taking careful notes.

"What about the murder thing?" Abe asked. "At your house?"

"It happened, probably in my living room," Cole said.

"Really?"

"Yep."

"Let's huddle again before you say anything to Mrs. Hodges about her granddaughter and suicide. I have a meeting."

Cole saw Dwayne Reston coming through the office. "Wait," Cole called to him.

Reston had an armful of files. His tie was off-center and he was sweating. "I don't have time, Cole."

"I just wanted to thank you," Cole said. "For the Sheppard job. They told me you recommended me."

Reston's small eyes grew soft. "Yeah, no problem. I talked to Abe's friend over in Stockton, he said you did a good job on the arson case."

Cole nodded. "You need help carrying those things?"

He pushed out his bottom lip. "It was just a referral, Cole. I don't want to go steady with you."

TWENTY-NINE

Abe left for a meeting. Betsy took Cole's cell phone to the firm's IT crew to have an app installed that would allow her to help with his calls. When she returned to his office—and damn, he liked the sound of that, again—with his phone, she brought him the package Mrs. Hodges's chauffeur had dropped off.

Cole was digging around, looking for intel on the loan shark. He asked Betsy to find an inside phone number for the head of communications at Altadena Partners, which was where he believed Evelyn Morris worked.

Slatkin called back on the business line.

Cole picked up. "What have you got, Dean?"

"OK, Vincent Kazimir Darna. Age: twenty-eight. Five-foot-seven; 160 pounds. No criminal priors, although a domestic restraining order was issued on him back in February. Married. No kids. Wait. Nope, not married; divorce pending. Hence, the restraining order."

"Who does he work for?"

"Armenian family out of Fresno," he said. "We have them on our radar. We suspect the boss is one Adam Grigoryan."

"The big contractor?"

"That's the one."

"They've got money on the street?"

"They've got a lot of things going. Tell me, Cole, are you working up a story on them?"

"I'm out of the news business. I'm sort of running interference for a client who's getting jammed."

"These are serious people, JJ. The kind that don't let you take them to court. I hope you're being careful. Call me if you need help."

"Thanks, pal."

Betsy returned with the name of the man who ran the communications unit at Altadena.

"Mr. Holcum's office," the woman answered.

"Hi, my name's Booth. I work on the copy desk at the *Times*," Cole said. "We're on a deadline to close out the business section, and we just noticed a hairy-ass typo in your ad copy. I need someone's permission to fix it."

"Hold, please."

"This is Holcum. What's this about an ad?"

"Public service, climate change, and whatnot," Cole said. "Big typo in the subhead. We got *gard-ner*. Should be *gar-den-er*. Can I fix it?"

"I don't know of any ad. You say it's ours?"

"Yep, my paperwork says it was placed by an Evelyn Morris. Is she around?"

"Evelyn Morris isn't on staff, and she certainly doesn't work in communications."

"Well, who is she? I don't imagine she's a Russian hacker."

"She's a consultant working on the investment side. She has no authorization to place an ad for us, that's for sure."

"Huh. OK. Do you know how I can reach her?"

"She's got an office in Santa Monica. I don't have a number. E&M Securities or something like that."

"OK. Thanks, pal. Sorry about the confusion."

Cole buzzed Betsy. "I need you to track down whatever you can on my client, Evelyn Morris. She's probably got a broker's license with the Securities Exchange Commission, start there. OK?"

"Yes, sir."

It was close to six. Cole packed up his things. He had one more stop to make.

Safeway was jammed with shoppers hunting down dinner. Cole scouted between the aisles until he found a harried, middle-aged man helping a young woman move a load of milk from the storeroom to the dairy section.

"Mr. Hughes?" Cole asked.

"That's me. You Cole? The writer guy?

"Yes."

"Julia called. Said you'd probably be by." He got the cart positioned and he and the woman started to unload the cartons. "I got this and one other thing to do, and then I'm done. Why don't you get a cup of coffee or something at the café? I'll be along in about fifteen."

A cold beer would have been better, but Cole settled for an iced tea and a newspaper and found an empty table. The front-page article was about the DeAngelo trial.

There had been a court appearance where his defense team requested a "long delay," and the judge was considering it. Sacramento County's Supervising Public Defender Diane Howard had told reporters outside court at Sacramento County Main Jail that they were working through "volumes of discovery," and they'd need at least six months to get through it all.

DeAngelo had lost a lot of weight in the month or so he'd been in custody; the reporter described the inmate as looking 'gaunt.' Ms. Howard wouldn't comment about her client's health.

Tommy wasn't long. He settled in the chair opposite Cole and explained that he was in middle school when the rage started. A paperboy for the *Journal*.

"We had a vigilante patrol in the neighborhood," he said. "Some of the men organized it. Back then, Mr. Powell, who was a city police officer, lived on the block."

All the papers were delivered to this one house at four each morning. The distribution manager wanted the kids to start their routes before six. "That meant we were out in the neighborhood really early, which was also when the police thought this rapist was prowling around. Mr. Powell, the cop, came by now and then to make sure we kept our eyes open and were ready to report anything suspicious. It was sort of fun," he said. "Scary, too, but as a kid, you know, it was exciting to feel you were part of it."

"Did you see anything?"

"I didn't, but one of my pals probably came face to face with

DeAngelo one morning. He was riding a bike near the park."

"You think it was actually him?"

"I've seen some photos taken about that time. A big guy. Large oval head. That's how my buddy described the man he saw."

"What about this man Julia said was stalking her?"

He shook his head. "I remember hearing about it, but no, I didn't see anyone like that." He thought about it for a moment longer. "My dad chased some guy up the alley one night. He didn't get a good look at him, but he said he was fast as hell. Now that I think about it, this DeAngelo probably wasn't a track star."

"What about the murder? Were you around that night?"

"You bet. It was huge."

"Anything jump out at you now? Knowing what you do about DeAngelo?"

"Not really. It was just really scary, really surreal. You know, something like that happening just a couple houses down the block."

"Yeah, well, now I live there." Cole shook his head.

Tommy chuckled. "I guess it's not funny." He tapped the table with the knuckles of one hand. "One thing made a big impression on me. This is silly. You'll laugh because it's just the kind of thing only a twelve-year-old would focus on."

"I won't laugh."

"Weeks, maybe months later, I heard about how the murderer had taken some things from the house," he said. "I guess it was part of his MO. Little things, right? Apparently, he took two medallions, bronze medallions. This kid told me he heard on the news that the medallions commemorated Disneyland opening. One had Mickey Mouse on the back; the other had Daffy Duck. Isn't that bizarre? When I think about the murder, that's what comes into my head before anything else. A Mickey Mouse medallion."

THIRTY

Cole got takeout from a little Greek place near his house. A lamb gyro sandwich with tiropita, spanakopita, dolma, and orzo. He stopped at the liquor store and picked up a fifth of Jack and a 12-pack. It had been a long day, and he wanted to spend a quiet evening watching a ball game and letting the alcohol ease his troubled mind.

Turned out his mind needed a lot of easing. Cole overdid it and fell asleep in the leather chair. It was close to one when he woke. The TV was still on. Plastic plates and beer cans crowded the side table. He stumbled around the room, collecting what discards he could and turning off lights and the TV. He stripped down to his skivvies, dropped hard on his mattress, and was out again before his head hit the pillow.

***

Movement on the bed woke him. A body, close. Small. Lightweight. A bright light. "Susan?" Cole turned. The light, dart-like and intense, blinded him. A wet cloth across his nose and mouth. Sweet smelling. *Bleach?* Cole swung an arm wildly against the other person in bed with him and tried to sit up. He couldn't.

***

"Cole, wake up."

The voice was a mile away. A light shone in his face, close enough that he could feel its warmth.

"Wake up, Cole."

A man's voice. Not much more than a whisper.

Cole was on his stomach. Blood rushed to his temples, pounding and painful. He tried to sit. Couldn't move. He blinked, trying to understand. His hands were behind his back, bound. His legs too. The light was too bright. Couldn't get enough breath.

Completely immobilized.

Terror. Blind rage. A masculine outburst against his bindings. They bit into his wrists and ankles.

He was going to die. A warrior's eruption. Everything he had.

"It's no use, Cole."

Again, every fiber of muscle and will was enlisted in the fight for freedom.

God, no, Cole thought. *Not gonna be killed. Not gonna be raped.*

He rolled off the bed and hit the floor hard. He brought his knees to his chest. Another violent, furious attempt. Cole screamed for help. The light came close and some hard, metal object snapped him on the bridge of the nose. Faint. Out of breath. Panic still rode him hard, but the body, weak now.

"Be quiet, and we'll get along just fine," the voice said.

Something trickled down his nose; he tasted blood. "Whaddaya want?"

"I'm not here for sexual gratification. I just need to control our conversation."

"Who're you?" Cole coughed. More blood. The world around him was foggy, dreamlike. *Who'd do something like this? Why?*

"Guess."

"I can't breathe." He'd landed face down. The intruder flipped Cole over and put a pillow under his head.

"You're all right."

The light went off. Darkness. No, more than that. Blackness, as if all the curtains had been drawn. Even in the empty pitch, his surroundings became more familiar. The bedside dresser. His shoes. The throw rug near the door. His shoulders ached from his efforts to break free. His nose throbbed. The pain sharpened his senses.

"Who are you?" Cole asked again.

"You know."

"Barrett?"

"Good guess."

"What do you want?"

"Just to set you straight on a few things."

The voice came from across the room. He was probably sitting in the chair he kept by the glass doors leading out to the patio. He couldn't hear a damn thing. The glass doors were probably closed.

"Like what?"

No answer.

"Barrett? You still here?"

"Yes, Jamie, I'm here." He'd moved closer to the bed on the other side. Cole heard a dresser drawer close and then another open. "No more women's undies. Just guy stuff. Hmm."

Barrett moved back toward the glass doors. "I was sorry to see you and Anne break up."

"What did you just fuckin' say?"

"Yes, I've been inside before."

"Why?"

"Because I can. And because of the crime you're trying to solve."

Barrett was a small man; Cole had at least thirty pounds on him and was probably fifteen years younger. All he had to do was get to his feet. Cole could take him down with a head butt. He'd need to roll back on his stomach. He waited.

"You were there?" Cole asked. "You killed her. The Bordeaux girl."

"Not me, kitty cat. I'm not the one you're after. I didn't kill her. That was a man named Dale. I only watched."

Cole thought it might be better to go for the hallway. Smaller confines. He'd have a better chance. If he could get to his stomach, he could leapfrog into the hall and then hit Barrett as he followed.

"Why are you doing this? Why tell me?"

"Because Dale's planning to kill me. Now that DeAngelo's in custody, he'll try, anyway. I'm a loose end. A link to his many crimes."

"Who's Dale?"

"A friend of Joe's. I met him years ago. I watched him. I watched Joe work too."

"What do you mean, watched them?"

"I'm a voyeur," he said in an impassive tone, as if clarifying his zodiac sign or the color of his hair. "Some guys like to force themselves on women. I like watching."

"You watch guys raping women?"

"Sometimes, but any act of intimacy will suffice," he replied.

This guy is truly crazy. Anything could happen. Cole tried to move again. He lifted his head first, followed by torso. The pain in his left shoulder sheared through him like he'd been stabbed. He had to relax.

"A voyeur?" Cole repeated. "Christ. Why should I believe you? Why should I believe any damn thing you say?"

"Mr. Cole, I've been aware of you since you bought this place. As I said, I've been inside. I've watched you with your ex-wife and with some of your other partners. I knew this day would come. I knew I'd need your help."

Cole took a deep breath. Somehow this was all starting to make sense. The pretense of a mail carrier. The elaborate break-in. Cole could visualize Barrett, tiny and old and scared.

Cole was suddenly weary. Colors flashed behind his lids when he closed his eyes.

"Help you?" Cole said weakly. "How the hell do you expect me to do that? You don't even have this guy Dale's last name."

"He's a sex offender with a record," Barrett said. "And I know he served time. He's in his mid-sixties. Tall, lean. You'll find him."

"If you know him, why don't you have a last name?"

"This is the social circuit he and DeAngelo and I shared. It's not exactly the Rotary Club. We don't hand out business cards," Barrett said. "Years ago, Dale caught me in a closet when he was working. I escaped. Later, he went to prison. He found me when he got out about two years ago. He said he's going to kill me. I knew Joe from

Visalia. Joe and Dale were partners. Joe wouldn't let him touch me, I think because Joe worried it would draw attention. There's someone else involved, too. Someone with money."

"You knew Joe from Visalia?"

No answer.

"What do you mean, someone else?"

No answer.

The wind-chime in the yard tinkled outside, and a breeze pushed at the black curtains. The glass doors were open.

Barrett was gone.

***

Cole lay on the floor for half an hour before trying to move again. His shoulder aching. He wiggled to the kitchen like an inchworm and got to his feet by pushing himself up a wall. He hopped to the knife drawer. He spent an hour trying to manipulate a blade from behind his back. He cut a finger. Blood dripped on the floor.

The clock in the den said it was four thirty. It would be hours before anyone would think to look for him. Cole tried to relax; maybe he could slip out if he could just loosen up. He focused on his ankles, using his leg muscles to push and release, push and release, push and release.

***

It was almost nine thirty when Cole heard Karmen calling him from the door. He was sitting in the front hallway. He called back, telling her to go across the street.

"Susan has a key!" he shouted.

"What's going on?"

"Just do it."

Susan cried out in shock when she opened the door and fell to her knees, putting a hand to Cole's cheek. Karmen burst out laughing.

"What in God's name happened?" Susan said, putting a hand to her lips.

"I had a visitor last night," Cole said. "Someone get a knife and cut these damn things off me. My hands are about to fall off from the loss of circulation."

Susan ran to the kitchen and got a pair of scissors and cut him free. Cole told them about Barrett, how he knew about Victim Eleven, and the new target he knew almost nothing about except for the name Dale.

"You think Barrett's for real?" Karmen asked.

"Hard to find a reason he wouldn't be." Cole finally got to his feet, massaging his wrists. "First, he sets the thing in motion by telling Susan about the murder, knowing she'd tell me."

He looked at Susan for a moment. "He knew you and I were together once," Cole said.

"What do you mean?" she said with a gasp.

"I mean, he'd broken in before. He said he liked to watch."

"That is the creepiest thing I've ever heard," Susan said, waving a hand.

"That's pretty weird shit, boss."

"That's the world we're venturing into," Cole said. "Why would Barrett go to all the trouble if it *weren't* because he was worried about this other guy? I can't think of any other explanation. And I had a long time to do nothing but think."

"A first name isn't much to go on," Karmen said.

"It's not."

"You still want me to go up to Auburn today?"

"Yeah," Cole said. "Did you get the title for DeAngelo's Citrus Heights house?"

"No, I came here first."

"OK, get a copy of that title and head up the hill." Cole found one of his digital tape devices and gave it to her. "Take notes. Ask lots of questions, get people talking. Don't be an asshole."

"I'll do my best, boss," she said smiling. "Don't get taken down by any more midget sex maniacs while I'm away."

He shoved her playfully out the door. "Just go."

THIRTY-ONE

Karmen pulled the deed for the three-bedroom, two-bath home in Citrus Heights owned by Joe DeAngelo. He and his then-wife had bought the place in April 1980, almost exactly a month after Lyman Smith and his wife Charlene were bludgeoned to death in their bedroom on an upscale street overlooking the beach in Ventura.

Karmen knew the Smith case. The double homicide was probably the highest-profile crime ever committed by the Golden State Killer. Lyman Smith was an attorney in private practice but had started his career as a deputy DA. At the time of his death, the governor was vetting him for an appointment as a Ventura County judge. The gruesome crime scene drew a massive response from law enforcement and media coverage from all over the nation. The case was messy with suspects. Lyman's years as a prosecutor and tangled business relationships offered an almost limitless pool. The case had gone cold as investigators chased one bad lead after another.

Lyman Smith had grown up in Citrus Heights, the same Sacramento County town where DeAngelo lived. He was younger than DeAngelo, but maybe there was a connection. The forensic evidence showed that man and wife had been intimate during the night of the attack. And that the killer was likely hiding in the bedroom at the time, watching.

Karmen got the clerk to print out a copy of the title. Driving up to Auburn, she kept thinking about it. DeAngelo killed the Smiths, then returned to his own wife and went house hunting.

***

The place that the DeAngelos had owned in Auburn was at the end of Hard Rock Lane, a small street with just six other houses. After looking through the property records of each, Karmen didn't find any owners who had been around more than ten or twelve years. She widened her search to include two other nearby streets. From there, she came up with a list of seven families that had been around the same time as the DeAngelos.

Karmen found the house DeAngelo and his wife had lived in and knocked on the door. No answer. Two doors up, a guy was working in his yard. She asked him about the house and who was living there now. She explained that she was working with a writer and that the Golden State Killer had lived there during the 1970s. He wasn't much older than Karmen, but he waved his hand dismissively. "Go on, get out of here. I got nothing to say."

She tried another house on the list. This time, a man who looked to be in his twenties opened the door with a smile. Karmen explained who she was and why she was bothering him. She braced for another brush-off, but the man invited her inside.

"This isn't my property," he said. "I'm just a boarder, but I'll get the owner. He's here."

A moment later, another man entered the den. He was closer to sixty, bald, and sporting a big round belly. Karmen went into her spiel again.

"Yeah, I've been seeing that guy on the news," the man said. "Creepy shit, isn't it?"

"Do you remember him?"

"A little, but the man you want to talk to is my buddy, Jacob. Jacob Shulman. He lived right next door, and he was over there a lot."

"How can I get in touch with him?"

"He owns the deli downtown. You can't miss it; it's just a few steps from the courthouse on Maple Street."

Karmen thanked him and went on her way. She found the deli

and, since it was close to lunchtime, ordered an avocado sandwich with jack cheese. Three people were working behind the counter, but none were old enough to be Jacob. She decided to eat her sandwich and wait for him. It didn't take long.

Jacob was thin and had long gray hair pulled into a ponytail. Karmen waited until the lunch crowd thinned before introducing herself. She told him about Cole and the book project.

Jacob didn't care who she was or what she was doing. He was just busting to talk to someone, anyone, about Joe DeAngelo.

"Since the arrest, I've been telling everyone that I knew him," Jacob said. "It's so trippy. I mean, I lived next to the Golden State Killer for five years."

"Can you tell me about him? Can I take notes?"

"Sure, hon." Jacob took a chair. "I remember when they moved in. Me and my brother were shooting hoops in our driveway and here comes a U-Haul van. He was still with the Auburn PD then."

"How did you meet him?"

"He pulled into the driveway, jumped out, and called us over," Jacob said. "He was real friendly. Loud, too. Asked us if we wanted to make some money helping him unload."

"It was just him in the truck?"

"Yeah. I didn't meet the wife until later. She wasn't always around; I think she was going to school or something."

"He was friendly?"

"Yeah, the Joe I knew had a sort of East-Coast personality, if you know what I mean," Jacob said. "The neighbors didn't like him—the adults, anyway. My parents, too. They called him Crazy Joe or GD Joe because of how often he said goddamnit. But he was always nice to me. Well, nice isn't the right word. He paid attention. He was one of the few adults I knew that treated us as equals. Plus, he dropped the f-bomb all the time; we thought he was sort of cool. He let us hang around."

"Hang around?"

"When he wasn't working, he was always tinkering with something in his garage. He built stuff, like model ships in bottles, stuff like that."

"How old were you?"

"They moved in when I was in the sixth grade," Jacob said. "So, twelve. That would have been 1975."

"Did he ever say or do anything that concerned you? I mean, knowing what you know now?"

"Not really," Jacob answered. "He was a peculiar guy. Everything with Joe was an exaggeration. He'd talk louder than he needed. Sometimes he talked to himself. You'd be walking by and he'd be doing stuff, like in his garage or out in the yard, and he'd say something, like, 'Ah, that's what I should have done first.' You know? Just things that might have floated from his brain right to his mouth."

"But you were never afraid in his company?"

"Did I feel threatened? No. No, I don't remember ever feeling that way." Jacob looked toward the store windows and the street beyond as if remembering something. "A guy stayed with Joe a few times. He was older, like in high school older. He was sorta scary."

"How so?"

"He didn't like me for some reason. Acted angry anytime I was around." Jacob drew his hand through his hair. "I surprised him once. We'd kicked a ball over our fence and into Joe's backyard. I ran over to get it and here was this guy, I forget his name. He was like, sharpening a knife, and I surprised him. He jumped up and waved the knife around, yelling at me to get out."

"Why did you think of him?"

"I dunno. You asked the question."

"Who was he? A relative or something?"

"Naw, I don't think so. He came around now and then. Sometimes stayed with Joe. Ugly mother."

Karmen pressed for more details. "Do you remember anything else about him? We're trying to find as many people that knew Joe as we can."

"He was older, like I said, in high school or even older, maybe. Tall, skinny. He had terrible skin, pimples; it was almost like he'd been burned or something."

"He would spend the night at Joe's?"

"Yeah. I think he wanted to become a police officer, maybe. Joe would take him to the shooting range. They'd go off together sometimes."

"You don't remember a name?"

"No."

"Could it have been Dale?"

"I don't know."

"Anything else you think I should know?"

"Not really. When Joe got arrested trying to steal stuff, that was a big deal," he said. "It was in the local paper here. After that, Joe kept to himself more. My parents didn't want me over there anyway, and honestly, I was OK with that. It was weird, him stealing stuff at the Pay N' Save. He got caught trying to steal a hammer and dog repellant. I heard he was crying like a baby when the cops came. The store owner and his son or someone had Joe tied up in a chair. He got fired from the police department not much later, and they moved. Over to Citrus Heights, I guess."

Karmen thought she had what she needed. She thanked him and sent Cole a text, asking him to call. *I found a guy who knew DeAngelo!*

THIRTY-TWO

I f the run-in with the thugs in Redding hadn't completely convinced him, the midnight visit from Barrett certainly had—Cole needed to be armed. He'd seen Karmen's message the night before but put off calling her. First thing in the morning, he drove up to the gun range and worked with new intensity. Buck, the instructor, said he saw improvement but remained skeptical that Cole would ever become a truly competent shooter.

Nonetheless, Cole finished the program, passed the test, and picked out a gun. His choice was a used Glock 43, which cost him $400. The instructor threw in a shoulder holster. "You should spend the two-week waiting period practicing," he said. "Even then, you should keep it strapped."

Cole planned on driving down to Lodi in the afternoon. Betsy had discovered that Emily Hodges's boyfriend was working day and night at a job site in a tiny burg called Daytown, about fifteen miles east of Lodi. When Cole finished at the gun center, he got a burrito from a lunch truck, got on the road, and quickly came to a halt. The freeway was backed up from downtown all the way to the airport. There was a wreck in Natomas.

Cole checked the GPS app on his phone. He got off the I-5 and tried to go around the accident by taking Highway 80 through West Sacramento.

He saw a sign for the street that Darna, the loan shark, had his shop on. It was only about one; plenty of time to check out Darna's place and still get down to Lodi.

The shop was in a sad-looking strip mall. There was an accountant's office at one end, which was where Darna was set up. At the other end was a liquor store and, in between, a laundromat, a pawn shop, and some sort of martial arts studio that looked like it had been closed for years. Only the laundromat was open. A banged-up sedan pulled into the parking lot ahead of Cole and then stopped. A kid, maybe in high school, ran from the laundry and made an exchange. Then the banged-up sedan drove off.

Cole parked at the far end of the lot, got out, and opened his car hood. From where he stood, he had a clear line of sight to the accountant's office. There didn't appear to be anyone inside. The same kid that had done the exchange came back outside the laundromat, peeked at Cole, and disappeared inside again.

An older guy appeared. Latino. Tats on his arms. Dirty, white, sleeveless tee-shirt. He wasn't tall. Potbellied.

"What you want, man?" the guy called out to Cole.

"Nothing. No problema." Cole slammed the hood down.

"What you want?"

"Engine overheated," Cole said. "Just waiting for it to cool down."

The guy looked up the block and then down the other way. He gave Cole one last stare-down before returning to the laundromat. This time, two kids came to the doorway to keep watch.

Cole was about to shut down his little stakeout when a black Mercedes spun into the lot and screeched to a stop in front of the accountant's office. A small man in his twenties got out. He was dark and well-dressed. *This has to be Darna. He's not so intimidating.*

Cole knocked as he came through the door to the accountant's office.

Darna glanced away from the coffee he was making. "Who are you?"

"Friend of a friend," Cole said.

"What friend?"

"The Sheppards," Cole said.

"Who?"

"Clark Sheppard. He owns a brewpub over near the new Kings Arena, and he borrowed some money from you."

"Ah." Darna finished putting the coffee on. He took a seat behind a big desk and gave Cole a long look. "You a cop?"

Cole shook his head. "Just a friend hoping to help."

Cole stood in the doorway, calm and cool. He wasn't nervous. He was falling into character. Something new, something he didn't know he'd had inside him.

Without being invited, Cole took the chair that faced the gangster.

"What's the play here, man?" Darna demanded.

"I've been asked to deliver a message," Cole answered.

"It's like that, huh? You know who I am?"

"I do. You work for Adam Grigoryan."

Darna measured him. Cole was poised if something more than conversation happened next. A moment passed. Then another. Cole didn't blink.

"What's the message, friend?"

"The Sheppards want to settle," Cole said. "The old man will pay off the note, the interest, and maybe toss a cherry on top for your trouble."

"What if I want to keep the kid on my book? Maybe that's better for me."

Cole shook his head. "Ain't going to happen."

"Is that right?" Darna's eyes went dark and intense. The gangster jumped to his feet and slammed his palms down on the desk. "Do you know who I am?!" he shouted.

Cole didn't flinch, but he kept his eyes on Darna's hands. Darna stood over the desk for a moment before breaking into a grin and sitting down again. "What sort of cherry we talking about, man?"

"Something small but sweet."

"How quick can I get my money?"

"I'd have to talk to Mr. Sheppard, but I think a case could be made for swift payment."

"OK, you got a deal, cowboy," Darna said. "The loan, the ten points over prime, and whatever this fucking cherry shit turns out to be. And you owe me one, pal."

"I'll get on it." Cole stood.

"What's your name?" Darna asked. "I've never seen you around."

"My name's Cole, James Cole."

Darna snapped his fingers. "Not JJ Cole? The reporter?" He whooped and punched the air with a fist. "I'm a big fan, man. You're the one who took out that prick Cirillo a couple years ago. The developer. That was a damn punch! I know Cirillo, man, and that sonofabitch ain't no bandleader."

Cole nodded cautiously.

"What's all this you're doing? What's this gunsel shit? You got a side job?"

"I'm no longer employed by the *Journal*," Cole replied. "I'm doing consulting work for a couple of law firms."

"Consulting work?" Darna whistled. "Is that what you call it? You strapped, man? I need to know."

Cole shook his head. Darna grinned again. "Damn, man. That was a cool play. You had me. You had me all the way."

Cole shrugged and gave Darna a two-finger salute. "Thanks, I guess I'll be shoving off."

"Wait, dude." Darna got up. "Give me a card, man. I might need a guy like you. Here, take one of mine. You never know."

Cole fished a card from his wallet and handed it over.

"JJ Cole." Darna laughed as Cole left. "Damn."

***

The animal shelter was miles out of town, next to a concrete mill and a heavy equipment rental yard. The boy could hear the yelping of the dogs when he got out of the car.

He asked the clerk if he could see an older dog, small to medium. The color and the breed didn't matter. There were half a dozen dogs he could look at, the young lady said. The first one seemed accept-able. He filled out the paperwork. There were expenses he'd have to pay, the clerk said: a vet exam, shots, and the neutering procedure. The bill came to $412.52. The boy had cash.

It was a lot to spend for just a week or two, but he couldn't think of another way.

For this next one, the boy decided against working on campus. There were just too many people, too much unpredictability. He took long bike rides on the tree-lined streets surrounding the college. He found a part of town where most of the residents commuted to the Bay Area, leaving for work early and coming back late. That left a lot of unprotected bedrooms.

The dog's name was Dolly. She was ten years old, about thirty pounds, and had a brown coat. Docile and attentive, she would work just fine.

He had a second apartment his parents didn't know about. He kept some of his things there, things that were part of *the game.* He practiced often. Worked on improving his skills.

The first night, he took the dog to the apartment. He fed her and let her run around in the grass in front of the building. She had water and a blanket on the floor. She would be fine. He went back to the dorm.

The next day, after morning classes, he got the dog and drove to the east side of town near the country club, where the big homes were. He and Dolly walked along Macero Drive, all the way around the golf course. Then again. A third time.

He was tired, but he needed to study the houses. Two particularly interested him. Or two women did.

He thought each lived alone, but he wasn't sure. One was a student, but the other was a little older, maybe a lecturer or even an adjunct professor. He'd followed both around campus several times and then back to the houses near the golf course. Both had night classes. He liked the older one better. On Tuesdays, she didn't go to class. Thursdays she was at school until ten.

He wanted to know everything about her block. He wanted to study it during the daylight. He made note of the alley access to her building and the fence between her yard and the golf course. He could leave a bike on the other side of the fence and then ride through the course. He could leave his car in the lot.

He wondered if he should buy another vehicle, just for this, just for *the game.*

After the walk, he took the dog back to the apartment in West Sac. They repeated the route on Wednesday and again on Friday. He had what he needed.

When the time came, he chose the younger one. Her condo was easier to get into, and it backed onto a storm channel thick with overgrown trees and shrubs. He slipped into the bedroom and waited until she got home.

He satisfied *the urge* and left through the bathroom window.

That same night, he got the dog and drove until he found some quiet, flat farmland. He took a dirt road until the darkness lay like a blanket over the land. He sprinkled poison into Dolly's meal. After she finished, he watched as the poison kicked in and the dog writhed in agony while white soapy foam flowed from her mouth and bright red blood ran from her nose.

THIRTY-THREE

All Daytown lacked was the town. It comprised two roads, empty, with a large olive grove on one side and a dry brown pasture on the other, the cows or sheep or horses elsewhere. Half a mile down a dirt road, Cole found the job site where Emily's former boyfriend was working.

His employer was an environmental consulting firm. Most of their clients were real estate developers who'd run into groundwater problems. Contamination from old gas tanks, ruptured sewer lines, toxic waste. It was hard to tell what they were pumping out of the ground in Daytown. Couldn't be good.

Cole picked the kid out right away. Tall and angular. He wore mud-splattered overalls, goggles, and an A's hat turned backward.

At the gate, Cole told the guard he was from the home office. The sleepy-eyed man waved him through.

Ruffin took one look at Cole and started for the trailer, slamming the door after getting inside. Cole tried the handle. Ruffin had locked it.

"I'm Cole, the investigator looking into Emily's death. You've been ducking me. What gives?"

Cole pounded on the thin metal door. "Open up."

The door opened. A burly man with Popeye forearms stood in front of him. "Get out of here," the guy said. "This is private property."

Cole was taller. He called inside: "Ruffin, I'm working for the family. I just want to talk."

Popeye pushed Cole. Another day, Cole would have gone with the push. Not today. Not after the visit from Barrett. Not after his encounter with Darna. Cole had become a different man.

The guy pushed Cole again, harder. Cole snatched the man's right hand and took control of his fingers and wrist, bending his hand back until the guy squealed with pain.

"OK!" he cried. "Jesus, OK."

Cole released him and pushed him off the steps. He jumped into the trailer, closing and locking the door behind him.

"Why the dodge?" Cole said before he realized Ruffin had a pistol trained on him. "Whoa. Hold on."

Cole put his hands up.

"Let me see some ID," Ruffin said. Cole tossed him his wallet. Ruffin glanced inside. "If you work for the family, you'd know who Emily's grandfather is."

"Was," Cole said. "A judge."

"Where do they live?"

"Midtown. Grandma has a chauffeur. I work for her attorney, Abe Metzger. And I know that Emily liked Amy Winehouse and Taylor Swift. A lot."

Ruffin nodded and dropped the gun. "OK, I believe you."

"What's the story? Why so jumpy?"

"Just before Emily died, she told me something. A warning. She said people might want to hurt her."

"Yeah?"

"That's it."

"Did she tell you who?"

"No. But I'm being careful."

"OK, let's back up. You two had been together how long?"

"A year. Maybe a little more."

"I've got access to her laptop. Found some emails. There was some tension between you two toward the end. Can you tell me about it?"

"There was always tension. Emily wasn't easy."

"How do you mean?"

"I was someone she passed time, had sex, maybe watched a movie with. What she wanted when she wanted it."

"Did you know she was seeing a therapist?"

"Yeah, something was going on. She'd suffered some sort of trauma a while back."

"Physical? Emotional?"

"I don't know. Both, probably."

"What about drug use?"

"Nothing I ever saw."

"Drinking?"

"Sure, she liked to drink sometimes."

"What did she say about someone wanting to hurt her?"

"Just that. It was a couple weeks before she died."

"Do you think she could have taken her own life?"

Ruffin took his cap off and ran a hand through hair sweaty and in need of a trim. "Yes," he said in a soft voice. "That's what I thought when I heard the news. Something was eating at her."

"Besides the therapist, do you know of anyone else she might have confided in?"

"There's her grandmother, but I'm guessing you've already talked to her."

"I have."

Ruffin played with the cap. "Have you looked at her money?"

"What about the money?"

"She was weird about it. She used to say she could retire if she wanted to. One night, when she'd been drinking, she asked me if I wanted to run off someplace, a Greek island or something."

"Her family's got money, I guess."

"Yeah, but she made it sound like it was something else, a secret. I asked about it the next day and she blew me off. She said something like, 'I can't talk about it.'"

"Like, I can't? Or I don't want to?"

Ruffin stared past the trailer walls. "This was maybe a month before she died," he said. "I wondered if she really wanted to run away. I would have gone with her. I could have loved her."

The office phone rang. Cole picked it up only to hang up and leave the receiver disengaged. "Tell me the rest of it."

"I asked her if she was serious. She started to answer me. I could see she wanted to. She was scared, crying. I put my arms around her and pleaded with her to tell me what was going on. She pushed me away, went into the bathroom. When she came out, she was just—"

"Just what?"

"Stone rigid." He looked up. "Check the money. There's something there."

"I will."

As soon as Cole got to his car, he rang Betsy at the office. He asked about the package Mrs. Hodges had sent him a couple days earlier.

"It's on your desk," she said.

"Open it. I'm thinking it's Emily's bank records."

When she returned a minute later, she confirmed the contents.

Cole nodded. "OK, listen. I want you to break it down for me. I'm looking for outside income. Anything other than her normal salary. Could be a lump sum or it could show up incrementally. I'm on my way in."

"Got it," she said. "I took a call for you about twenty minutes ago. A Sally Rodgers? She said Skip found something and wants you and Karmen to come to the house ASAP."

Cole chuckled. "OK, so maybe I'm not coming straight in. I'll let you know."

Cole called Sally. Skip had found Lon's files on Victim Eleven.

"I'm on my way," he said. "Have you told Karmen?"

"She's already here."

***

When Cole arrived, everyone was gathered in Skip's room in the back, listening to a recording from an old mini-cassette device.

"*The strongest evidence of a second suspect came from the victims themselves,*" said a man's voice, robust but scratchy. At times, it disappeared altogether.

"*One victim claimed his hands were small and soft as a baby's.*" Cole thought this was Lon speaking. "*Another was sure the assailant's hands were big and calloused. Those were details we heard again and again.*"

Another man's voice. Cole recognized it as a much-younger Skip. *"There were discrepancies about his build, too. One woman who worked at the Armory said he had a large belly and felt very heavy. Just two weeks later, another victim—her husband was a contractor at Aerojet—said he was skinny and his stomach was hard and flat."*

Lon's voice added, *"You can't go from a potbelly one week to a hard, muscled stomach two weeks later. Or cowhand one day and small soft hands the next. There's no question that two different men committed some of the crimes we've always solely associated with the East Area Rapist."*

The tape ended.

"That's it?" Cole asked.

"There's more," Karmen said, popping the mini-cassette out of the recording device and replacing it with another.

"We found about seven or eight tapes that Lon and I made while we were working on the book," Skip said. "I'd forgotten all about them."

"OK, the next one is queued-up," Karmen said, hitting the play button.

"And the voices," Skip said.

"Right," Lon replied. *"Several victims said they heard another voice in the house during the attack. One said she was lying there, all tied up in the bedroom, when she heard someone open a window. She could hear the assailant talking to someone in the backyard. Another victim reported how the rapist had gone into the garage at one point and someone else was there.*

"The prevailing thought on the task force was that this guy was trying to throw us off. Using a high voice to make it seem like he wasn't alone.

"I didn't buy it, but with this bird, who knows? I thought another person could be involved. For one, there was the report of a car horn. There was a victim in South Sacramento. The husband, tied up in the next room, reported hearing the car horn blaring like a signal—one,

two, three times. And then the attacker said something like, "Here, we'll go out the backyard." The husband said he heard another voice, higher, younger maybe. Then knocks on the door and some whispering at the window."

"Who did you think it was?" Skip asked.

"I don't know," Lon answered. "I don't know. Someone else."

The tape ended.

"Interesting," Cole said. "But it doesn't move the dig along much. We're already assuming there's a second suspect. Anything more?"

"Ease up, man." Karmen handed him a file. "There's this."

The file contained several documents.

The first was a police report from an attack in Orangevale, 1977. Cole skimmed it quickly.

At 11:14 PM on May 15, 1977, Dispatch notified Reporting Investigators (R/Is) Detectives P. Armstrong and J. Murphy to respond to the location of a reported home invasion/rape at 1721 Central Avenue, Orangevale. R/Is arrived at 11:39 PM and found SCSD Officers Wynston and Vitteli had secured the area.

Victim: Caroline Mason, female, age 57, white, 5'8", approximately 210 lbs.; brown hair, brown eyes.

She was alone in the house and reported being asleep when awakened by an intruder in her bedroom. He rushed her and put a knife to her throat. Intruder inserted a thick piece of cloth into her mouth and then produced a roll of duct tape, tearing off pieces to seal her mouth and then bind her hands. He turned her on her stomach and tied her legs with tape, binding each, spread, to the leg posts under the bed. The intruder raped the victim. She estimated that the sex act took about five minutes. She said he left immediately afterward.

He never spoke. He wore gloves and a ski mask. She couldn't describe the assailant except that he was a white male, not tall, with a slender build. He wore a long-sleeved tee-shirt, gray or black.

A canvass of the neighborhood revealed no evidence of other incidents of prowlers or break-ins.

A memo had been attached to the report.

North Orangevale had been active for a couple of weeks. Reports of crank phone calls. Strangers passing through. Attempted break-ins. I walked a few blocks between Elm Street, west of Hazel, which appeared to be the center of activity. We found a footprint, size eleven, outside a bedroom window and approached the homeowner. A young mother. She'd left an outdoor key under the doormat. I warned her and reminded her to keep her doors and windows locked.

Right across the street, open space, a neighborhood park that crossed a vernal pool and a small stream. We set up surveillance.

On the second night, three thirty AM, one of my guys intercepted a man on a bicycle riding in the park. He made contact. No ID. Nothing to hold him on. While still on contact, we got the call: assault on Central, two streets over. My officer disengaged and we responded to the house on Central.

The victim described her assailant as tall and lean, with a beard under his mask. A neighbor, coming home after working graveyard restocking a nearby grocery store, reported seeing a man dressed in black running from the victim's house. Heavy build; five-eleven to six-foot. [EAR?]

The man my officer stopped on the bike in the park was small, five-two or three, bald, thin.

Could the three men be connected? Could there have been coordination?

Skip and Karmen waited to see Cole's reaction.

"Wow," Cole said. "This is good. This is interesting."

"There's more," Skip said. "Keep reading."

Next was a news article related to the attack in Rocklin. It was short and the publisher wasn't clear, although someone had scribbled a date above the headline: June 1, 1978.

EAST AREA RAPIST
HITS ROCKLIN?

A housewife was attacked and raped early today at her home near Pacific and Pine Streets. The woman, in her early 30s, told police that a man entered her home shortly after her husband left for work around 6:45 AM. He bound her hands and feet with strips of cloth and raped her. He left the house at about 8:00 AM. Officers said the woman, still bound, crawled out of the house, where a neighbor heard her screams and came to help. Police arrived at about 8:30 AM. A spokesman for the Rocklin Police Department declined to comment on whether the attack could be the work of the East Area Rapist, who is believed to have committed at least 30 rapes in Sacramento County since October 1975.

Next, a note on a single sheet torn from a pocket-pad. The smudged writing was in pencil, and the letters were rushed and hard to decipher.

Rocklin?
Face, beard? Rough.
Tape not cloth
No ransack, no purpose breakage
Speed
Misdirection again

Then a scrap of paper dated Sept. 20, 2008.

Visited Placer County evidence room at 1400. Checking witness statements from Rocklin attack, 6–71. Rape kit missing. Last checked out to FD, 8–6.

Cole rolled his eyes and whistled.

"Lon's account in Orangevale is excellent," he said. "We got IDs on a man who fits DeAngelo; the guy that stalked Julia, who might be named Dale; and my mailman friend, Barrett."

"We got a book," Karmen sang out. "We got a book, don't we?"

Skip and Sally looked to Cole expectantly.

"Yeah," Cole said slowly. "It's looking pretty good."

"I've got a question," Sally said. "How does the mailman fit in with DeAngelo?"

"We're not sure." With a sigh, Cole filled them in on the details of Barrett's middle-of-the-night visit.

Karmen started laughing all over again. "We found him sitting on his ass in his hallway. His face was a bloody mess."

"Barrett knew DeAngelo?" Sally asked.

"That's what he said."

"Is Barrett tall and skinny, like Lon's description of the second suspect?"

"No," Cole said. "He's short with a small frame."

"Then who's tall and skinny?"

"Maybe this guy Dale?"

"I see," Sally said. "And we know DeAngelo is a big man. He's the one with the potbelly?"

"That's right," Skip said.

"OK," said Sally, nodding. "I think I'm following now."

"What about the book?" Karmen asked. "We need an agreement. How's it going to work? I get a byline, remember."

Cole put up a hand. "Let's not get ahead of ourselves. There are still miles to go here."

Skip cleared his throat and threw a quick glance at Sally. "All due respect, son, I agree with Karmen. Tomorrow is promised to no one."

Cole sighed. "Let's type something up right now. Three-way split. Any objections?"

Skip shook his head. "That doesn't seem fair to you, Cole. You'll be doing all the writing."

"I'll also be receiving the lion's share of the credit as the primary author," Cole said. "It'll lead to other books."

"I can help write—or edit, at least," Sally said. "I've got a degree in English lit."

"Sylvia, too," Karmen chimed in. "She's a great writer."

"Good," Cole said. He got an envelope out of his briefcase and tossed it to Karmen. "We got paid on the arson case. Here's your cut."

"About time," Karmen said. "What's next?"

"I'm going up to Auburn," Cole said. "I want to talk to your deli owner."

"Jacob? How come?"

"DeAngelo's friend. The one Jacob described as being spooky."

"He could be Dale!"

"Maybe." Cole stroked his face, not used to his clean-shaven skin. "He said he and DeAngelo went shooting sometimes. That he wanted to be a cop. I want to know more about that."

THIRTY-FOUR

Betsy's note was clear—borderline terse—but it did the job. She'd broken down Emily Hodges's expenses and income and found three suspicious deposits all for $33,333: one in June of last year, another in December, and a third just a few weeks before her death in February.

"My husband's an accountant. I hope you won't mind, but I asked him to take a look," Betsy wrote. "He said the routing number from where the funds were transferred wasn't a regular bank. He thought it might be foreign."

Cole wrote back: "Tell Abe. Ask him to get Mrs. Hodges to goose Emily's bankers. I want to know where the money was coming from."

Betsy also noted a $20,000 donation Emily had made to the women's center just a week before her death. Cole sent a message to Karmen, asking her to see what Sylvia could find out about the contribution.

***

Subs 'n Such, Jacob's place, was tucked in an alley off one of the main drags in downtown Auburn. It was the kind of place only locals would know about. Big and airy, probably once a Gold Rush-era saloon. The wood floors were worn and weathered by hard-soled shoes and decades of daily wet mops. A railroad stove in one corner would stave off the chill of winter, and big ceiling fans create a breeze in summer. They served eggs and bagels for breakfast and a dozen types of New York deli sandwiches until four.

Cole liked it. If he lived nearby, he could see himself being a regular. He was ready to like Jacob too, even before he spotted him coming out from the storeroom with bottles of IPA that he buried under shaved ice in a big wooden barrel.

"I'm Cole," he said. "You spoke to my associate the other day about Joe DeAngelo."

"Yeah." His eyes came awake. "The writer guy."

"You got another minute or two?"

Jacob led him to a small office in the rear and closed the door. There was a vintage teacher's desk in the middle of the room, covered in paperwork. Jacob took a bundle of things off the only other chair in the room so that Cole had a place to sit.

"I told her pretty much all there is," Jacob said. "But I'm happy to help."

"Thank you." Cole sat down and took out his notebook. "Just a couple of things. You mentioned a friend of DeAngelo's, a guy older than you but still in high school."

"Yeah, Scarface."

"Yes, you told Karmen something about him going shooting with Joe. What made you think of that?"

He shook his head and then adjusted a rainbow-colored bandana that held back his long black-and-gray hair.

"I don't know. I guess maybe that's how I remember his connection to Joe. That it involved guns."

Cole scribbled on his pad. "Did Joe have guns?" Jacob didn't answer. "Do you remember seeing him with his service pistol?" Cole pressed.

"No. I don't remember ever seeing Joe with his cop gun. In fact, I remember he kept it locked up."

"He was careful."

"Yes."

"Meticulous?"

"Yeah, Joe was meticulous about almost everything. The tools in the garage all had a place."

"OK," Cole said. "This other neighbor that liked hanging around with DeAngelo. Who was he? Why did you think of him?"

"I don't know. I just remembered the time I kicked the ball over the fence."

"Right, but I want you to concentrate," Cole said softly. "Close your eyes a second, take me back there. What do you see? Concentrate on it. Don't answer right away. What is this guy doing when you came into the yard?"

Jacob grinned and played along, closing his eyes in silence for a moment or two.

"He's crouched over," Jacob said. "He's on his knees, on the grass, and he's got a knife and he's cutting something or cleaning the knife."

"Cutting something?"

"Yeah." Jacob opened his eyes and put his arms out in front of him. "Yeah, I think it was a fish."

"Then what?"

"He jumps because I've startled the hell out of him. Then he gets mad. He gets this angry look on his face and he points the knife at me."

"Go on."

"He's tall and a lot older, but I was always big for my age and I knew my older brother was just on the other side of the fence and he's way bigger." Jacob grinned. "This guy, I think his name was Dan. Yeah. Dan. He's looking like he might come at me."

"What happened?"

"I'm thinking screw the ball and I ran like hell."

Cole picked up the pen and then took a note. "Let's go back to the guns," he said. "Why would you connect this guy Dan with Joe and guns? You said you never saw Joe with a gun. You said Joe kept his service weapon under lock and key. What about this guy Dan that brings guns to mind?"

Jacob considered that for a moment.

"I just remember hanging out with one of my big brother's friends," he said. "Gary."

"Gary is your brother?"

"No, my brother is Isaac. Gary was his friend."

"Tell me about Gary."

"He lived next door, on the other side of our place from Joe's. He was my brother's best buddy. His dad used to take them on hunting trips, fishing up in the woods. Gary was an eagle scout. He was totally into guns and hunting. They had deer heads and mountain goats and stuff like that on the walls in their garage."

"How does this guy Dan fit in?"

"I remember sitting around one afternoon and Gary starts talking about pistols. His dad only owned hunting rifles, and Gary wanted to shoot pistols," Jacob explained. "He said something about Joe and this guy Dan going to shoot together. Target practice. Gary said he asked Joe if he could go too, but Joe said, 'Not this time.' Something like that."

"Karmen said you remembered something about Dan wanting to be a cop?"

"I did?" Jacob pinched at his chin and his beard. "I don't know. You know who could answer better is Isaac."

"Can you put me in touch?"

"Sure, I'll call him right now. He works up the hill some, town called Colfax."

***

Fifteen minutes later, Cole was back on I-80, heading higher into the Sierra. Isaac worked as a biologist for the forest service. Jacob told Cole he couldn't miss him; his brother was about six-five and probably 350 pounds. He agreed to meet, but only after Cole offered to buy lunch at a diner just off the freeway.

"Do you remember a friend of yours named Gary?" Cole asked once they'd found a table.

"Sure, Gary Olsen. We were best friends. I still see him. He lives in Idaho; we go hunting together sometimes. Two years ago, we each got a black bear at a place he knew in Montana."

"Jacob said Gary and his dad were also hunters."

"Yeah. That's how I got interested in it."

"You're how much older than Jacob?"

"Four years."

"So, when Joe DeAngelo was living next door, you would have been in high school?"

"That sounds right."

"Did you have a gun?"

"I had an old Remington that Gary's dad let me use. My folks wouldn't allow a gun in the house."

"OK. Do you remember this friend of Joe's named Dan? Jacob told me a story about this guy. He was in his late teens or early twenties. Tall and skinny. He had bad skin."

"No," he said.

"No?" Cole asked, but before Isaac could respond, the waitress appeared to take orders. Isaac wanted the pulled pork sandwich and iced tea; Cole wasn't hungry and just got coffee. Once the orders were in, Cole resumed. "You don't remember this guy Dan?"

"Didn't say that," Isaac said. "I remember him, but his name wasn't Dan; it was Dale."

"Dale?" Cole made a note. "What about a last name?"

Isaac shook his head. "Naw, I never knew him too well. He was a piece of crap. He was involved in a rape once. I helped break it up."

"A rape?" Cole made another note. "What about him? How did he know Joe?"

"I don't know. Like I said, I wasn't around that much. I had a job and a girlfriend. Last place I wanted to be was sitting around with my folks."

The food arrived quickly. Isaac tore into his sandwich and then gave it a rest before starting again.

"I think Dale lived on the other side of town. He'd ride his bike over to see Joe."

"Dale was local? He lived in Auburn?"

"Yeah."

"He would have gone to Auburn High?"

"It's called Placer High, but yeah, I guess so. I don't know. He wasn't there when I was."

"Jacob told me about a time when you two were playing ball and one of you lost it over in Joe's yard."

"Yeah? I don't know."

"What do you remember about Dale?"

"I worked at the A&W, and he and Joe came in once or twice," he said. "One time, me and Gary and Gary's dad ran into Dale and Joe at the shooting range. Gary's dad was a really great guy, very experienced hunter, expert marksman."

"What happened at the shooting range?"

"Nothing, I just remember it. Gary's dad was super polite, a really nice guy. And Joe, as I recall, was sort of loud and kind of a jerk. He was still a cop then, and when he was on the range, he tried to show off. He really wasn't that good, but Gary's dad was real polite about it. They talked some. Joe was impressed with how well Mr. Olsen could shoot. Joe told us he was teaching Dale the ropes. When we got in the car to come home, Mr. Olsen made a joke. I remember it because he hardly ever said anything sarcastic. But he starts the engine and says to Gary and me, 'I hope Dale gets a better teacher at some point.'" Isaac cracked himself up while stuffing the rest of the onion rings into his mouth.

Cole didn't want to stop the flow of his memory but had a key point to come back to. "OK. What about the rape?"

"Oh, yeah. This was later, way later. Joe had moved on by then. You know he got fired from the Auburn PD for shoplifting, the dick."

Isaac took a gulp of his drink and searched his plate for anything he'd missed. "Me and the wife had just moved back to Auburn. This was about 2005. I'd been transferred a few times and finally had enough seniority with the service to come home."

"OK."

"Well, it was summer. I was playing in a softball league, and after the games, we'd go get a few beers at a bar downtown. I lived downtown, so it was within walking distance.

"Anyway, this one night, it's late, maybe one. I'm walking home, and I pass this car parked up the block from my house. I see the driver and I'm thinking, I know that guy," Isaac recalled. "I keep going because I can't place him. We were renting an apartment upstairs from the landlady, then. When I turned into our yard and opened the gate, the guy in the car starts honking. Three quick ones. So I stop. Like, what the hell?"

Cole took a note.

"Before I know it, this other guy comes running from the backside of my landlord's house and pushes into me. I had my back turned because of the horn; otherwise, I would have flattened this dude."

"It was Dale?"

"No, some other guy," he said. "But I think it was Dale in the car."

"Hmm," Cole said. "What was going on?"

"Well, I chase after this guy, but he jumps into the car and they drive off. I'm yelling my head off, waking up the neighborhood, and then my wife comes out and we go check on the landlady."

Cole gave up trying to get the story down on paper.

"I went in and turned on the light, and we found her tied up on her bed." Isaac's face drew tight. "I'm freaked. We call the cops. We found out later that the guy didn't actually rape her. Dale was the lookout; he probably honked to tell his buddy someone was coming."

"Wow, so you saved her."

"I guess so, although she ended up going a little nuts. She ended up selling us her place."

"What about the suspects? The cops catch them?"

"The cops called us maybe a month later to come in and look at a lineup," Isaac said. "It wasn't Dale they had. It was a different guy. He was short. I didn't think he looked like the guy I ran into either, but I wasn't sure."

"They let him go?"

"I guess so. Never heard from the cops about it again."

"You think this was about 2005?"

"I think so."

"Hang on." Cole opened his phone, tapped his photo app, and called up the mugshot of Barrett. "Does this look like the guy they had in the lineup?"

"Yeah, that's him. Who is he?"

"Charles Barrett," Cole replied. "Some sort of sex weirdo criminal. Maybe linked to DeAngelo."

THIRTY-FIVE

On the way down the hill, Cole stopped at the public library in Auburn and had the clerk bring out yearbooks from the high school. Jacob said that DeAngelo moved into the neighborhood about 1975. If this guy Dale was twenty years old and if he went to Placer High, he likely would have been a senior in 1973. Cole got the clerk to bring out all the yearbooks between 1969 and 1979.

There was just one young man named Dale during that period. Michael Dale Preston. He graduated in 1969. On the page where his senior photo should have been, Cole found an empty box.

Cole flipped through the 1969 yearbook, looking for any pictures or references to Michael Dale Preston. Nothing. Cole leafed through the book again. He went back two more years and again came up dry.

At least he had a name.

The courthouse was only a few blocks from the library. Cole walked over and ran Michael Dale Preston through the criminal case index. Nothing again. He called Karmen.

"We got a name now," Cole said. "Michael Dale Preston. Age sixty-six or sixty-seven. I need you to run him through the federal sex offender index. Go down to the Sacramento courthouse and run him through the criminal database, and if you don't find anything, take a hike over to Yolo County. There's got to be something on his guy someplace around here."

"I knew it," she said.

"Yeah, good work." Remembering the surprise jump they'd tried at Barrett's apartment, he warned her: "Do not for any reason try to confront this guy on your own. You hear me, Karmen?"

"Yeah, yeah."

"Also, call Abe's office and ask for Betsy and then fill her in on where we are on this."

As he drove, Cole had a thought. This Preston wasn't a player among his high school classmates. No sports. No clubs. Not even a senior photo. A loner. That could point toward criminal tendencies, maybe. But he didn't have a record. Jacob's description of this guy cutting up a kitten would argue he definitely had issues. Yet no criminal record—at least not in Placer County. There could be another explanation. Maybe this guy was a boy scout on the surface and a monster underneath. Could be he never got caught because he was trained by DeAngelo.

Both Jacob and Isaac had alluded to Preston wanting to become a cop.

Maybe he was.

From the road, Cole called Scotty.

"Can you put something out on your wire for me?" he asked.

"Minimum charge is one bill," Scotty said.

"That's fine. I'm looking for a guy named Michael Dale Preston. Lived in Auburn during the seventies, a known associate of Joe DeAngelo. He'd be in his mid-to-late sixties by now."

"Got it," Scotty said.

"He might also be an ex-cop."

"Like DeAngelo." Scotty whistled. "Gotta love the symmetry of the criminal mind."

"When will I hear something?"

"Maybe a few hours, maybe a few days."

"Thanks."

Cole had an incoming call.

"Dude," a man's voice said. "It's your new best friend, Vince."

Cole had to think. "Darna?"

"Yeah, where you at?"

"Few minutes south of Auburn, heading toward Sac."

"Good," he said. "You know the Go-Go Club? Rancho A-Go-Go?"

"Sure, it's just a few miles from my house."

"You got your piece with you?"

"No."

"Well, get it. I need you to babysit a deal. Meet me outside the club at seven, OK?"

"Babysit?"

"It will take like, fifteen minutes. I'll pay you two hundred bucks."

"What's the mission, Darna?"

"It's a save," he said. "This is your sort of thing. We're rescuing a girl from the clutches of evil."

"Sure we are," Cole said.

The gun range was on the way. He stopped in and tried to convince Buck, the ex-Marine trainer, to let him have the Glock, even though there was still a week to go on his waiting period.

"No way," Buck said, spitting into the dirt near the training course. "I could lose my license."

"Not if there's no ammo in it," Cole said. "I just need it as a showpiece."

Buck finally gave in. *Crazy*, Cole thought, walking out with the gun in a paper bag. Crazy where his new employment was taking him.

***

Rancho A-Go-Go was just off the freeway between Costco and Home Depot. The club was quirky and affordable, and over a generation, it established a cult following. By tradition, every bachelor party that began in any of three neighboring counties ended at the Go-Go.

Cole had spent an entire afternoon inside during the 2003 recall election that Schwarzenegger won. That campaign was littered with funky candidates: Gary Coleman, the child TV star; Larry Flynt, publisher of the adult magazine, *Hustler*; and Gallagher, the watermelon-smashing comedian. Also on the ballot was Mary Carey, a well-known adult film star who famously held a press conference at the Go-Go club during the campaign. Cole was working for the wire service in SF then, and his bosses sent him out to cover the event. Cole arrived early. Mary was late. He ended up sitting around watching skank dancers for over two hours before Mary finally showed. Cole got to know the inside of the Go-Go Club pretty well.

Darna's Mercedes whipped into the lot and the young gangster leaped from the car. There was another guy with him, a large black man. Darna waved Cole over and they huddled.

"Cole, this is Jack. Jack, this is Cole," Darna said. "The mission is a girl, the granddaughter of my boss's cousin. She's got mixed up with some pricks that want her to do porn. She's going on stage in about ten minutes."

Darna reached inside the car and drew a gun from the glove box and put one in the chamber. "We go in hard, push right past security at the door, and we grab the girl," he said. "I go first. Jack, you stay with me. Cole, your job is to cover Jack. Questions?"

"Yeah," Cole said. "You ever been inside this place? I have. You're not going to get anywhere close to the stage. There's like an orchestra pit surrounding it."

"You know this?" Darna was shocked. "You go here?"

"No, just been inside before," Cole said. "Pushing at the door is a bad idea. Removes the one thing you got going for you, the element of surprise."

"You got a better idea?"

"I do."

Cole's plan was for him to go in first, pay the cover, and find a table. Jack would come ten minutes later and sit at the back of the main room near a hallway Cole knew about. When the girl finished her routine, Cole would wave over a handler and offer a hundred bucks for a private lap dance. The hallway led to the rooms where dancers and guests could be alone. At the end of the hall was an exit door, which was kept unlocked so the girls could go outside and smoke.

Cole said he would try to get the room closest to the outside door. "Jack, you wait about five minutes and then come hard," he said. "Darna, have the car waiting."

"What if you ain't in that room?" Jack asked.

Cole shrugged. "Try the next one," he said. "Keep knocking down doors until you find us."

"How you gonna get out?" Darna asked.

"Me? I'm just a John whose girl got snatched and I'm out a C-note," Cole said. "I'll demand a refund and walk out the front door."

Darna broke into a grin wide enough to show his gold fillings on the bottom row of his teeth.

"You've been wasting your time working in the news business, man. You should have been a street general or some shit."

It worked just as planned, and the Glock stayed safe in its paper bag in the trunk of Cole's car.

***

Cole hit the neighborhood bar on the way home. He was feeling pretty good about himself. He had a second round and chatted up the pretty bartender. Cole considered having a third but decided against it and drove home. As he pulled into his driveway, two men jumped out of a sedan parked in front of Susan's place and started toward him.

Had to be Darna's rivals. Cole wished to hell he had the Glock loaded and in his pocket. The two men stood on the driveway only a couple yards away.

"You Cole?" one asked.

Cole stood motionless. "Who wants to know?"

"I'm Sergeant Johnson, Sacramento PD, Homicide," he said, waving his badge. "This is my partner, Detective Vargas. We'd like you to come with us."

Vargas opened his coat, showing Cole his service weapon. Cole put up his hands. Johnson came close and turned Cole around, pushing him up against his car to pat him down.

"You got anything on you I should know about?"

"Nope."

They cuffed him and took him to the unmarked car. Cole didn't say a word. God knows what was waiting for him. Relieved momentarily that they were cops and not mobsters, he was reasonably sure they had come for him because of Darna and anything he said could and would be used against him. *Damn stupid,* he thought. *Playing high school games with a thug like Darna. Real damn smart, Cole. Real smart.*

They drove him to the big shop, the city PD headquarters, which Cole had passed many times on his way to and from Scotty's. They took him upstairs and put in him an interview room, cuffing him to a chair bolted into the floor. Twenty minutes, maybe half an hour later, another cop came in.

"Mr. Cole, I'm Detective Hansen. I want to ask you a few questions about a man named Charles Barrett."

"Barrett?" Cole drew in another sigh of relief. "What's going on with him?"

"How do you know him?"

Cole caught himself. "What's the name again?"

The detective frowned. "Charles Barrett," he repeated. "You know him. How? Why was your address in his list of phone contacts?"

"I have no idea."

"Did he hit your place?"

"I don't know what you're talking about."

"Barrett attacked your wife, didn't he?"

"I'm not married."

"He did your girlfriend then, and you tracked him down and paid him back, didn't you?"

"No. That's nuts."

"Where's your gun?"

"What gun?"

"We know you've got a gun. You've got a conceal permit. Where is it?"

"I'm in the waiting period. I haven't taken possession yet."

"Where is it, Cole? We're going to find it."

"I just told you, I don't have it yet."

"What were you doing at Barrett's apartment last week? We talked to the building manager. You were looking for Barrett's apartment. Don't lie."

"I'm thinking I might need to talk to my lawyer."

Hansen shook his head. "That's up to you, easier if you didn't."

"Easier for you," Cole answered. He lifted his arm and rattled the handcuffs. "If I'm suspected of something, I'd like to know what that is. And I'd like my attorney present for any questioning."

Hansen looked at the one-way window and then stood up and came closer. "You're a goddamn person of interest in a murder investigation, Cole. Don't fuck around here. Tell me what you know. Tell me now."

"I'm working a story," Cole said defiantly. "I decline to answer questions without my attorney present. I further evoke my rights not to disclose any unpublished material as defined under the California Shield Law."

The steel door to the room banged open and a large black man in a rumbled suit came into the room. Cole recognized him. Captain Trey Miller. *This isn't good.*

Miller took the other chair and, with a jerk of his head, sent the other detective out of the room.

"James J. Cole," Miller said. "All alone, cuffed in a sealed room at police headquarters. Last known visitor to a man shot twice in the face. We call that murder with malice. A stone-cold hate crime."

"I don't know anything about it."

"Working a story, you say?" Miller said. "We talked to your neighbor, the pretty blonde. She said someone broke into your place the other night, tied your ass up, and then ran off."

"I'm not talking, Trey."

"He buttfuck you?"

"Shut up."

"Did he?"

"No."

"Why was Barrett at your place?"

"I'm working a story, Trey."

"Damn it, Cole!" he shouted. "You're not working a story. You got some half-ass investigator game going with Abe Metzger. You don't have the protection of the shield law. I could throw your ass into lockup right now."

"Lawyer."

"We'll get to that. What's the deal with the gun? Why do you need to carry?"

"Haven't you heard? All the fashionable PIs in town are carrying."

Miller hissed. "Playboy shit. You'd sooner shoot yourself."

Cole allowed a small smile. "That's what my instructor says. I'm too anxious with the trigger."

"It's a Glock? What caliber?"

"Beats the hell out of me. It's not big."

Miller's eyes narrowed and Cole caught the hint of frustration. The captain waved at the window.

"Not the right size bullet is it, Trey?" Cole said, grinning. "Our boy got hit with something bigger didn't he?"

A uniform cop came into the room with Cole's things – his phone, his wallet and his car keys.

"You'll have to Uber home," Miller said. "Get with Abe, figure something out. I want to know what the hell you're working on. You got twenty-four hours."

"Or what?" Cole said, standing.

"Get out of here."

THIRTY-SIX

Lorraine was looking over a troubling memo she'd received from her chief financial officer. Ted's raids on the company accounts. They found a lot more than just joy rides on the company pane. Millions of dollars had been siphoned off in just the last five years. Some of it Ted had in California and New York banks, some was offshore.

She exhaled and looked out her windows that faced the orchard. Summer had begun and the tree limbs were heavy with clusters of nuts, some with shells hardening. It would be useless to confront Ted. This was his family's company. Of course he had a right to skim some of the profit.

She slammed her hand onto the table. The fact was, her job wasn't just keeping the trees growing. Her job was to grow this company, increase profits, and position Stony Creek for a public offering. Ted's recklessness jeopardized that work.

The audit found a series of LLCs tucked into the expense accounts from before Lorraine took the reins. Each month, tens of thousands of dollars went payable to all of them. One of them received $2 million a little over two years ago. Another $1.5 million went to a bank in Panama a year later.

Why?

She knew Ted had other women. He had a condo in Sacramento and his houses in Palm Springs and Tahoe. Had to be another woman. Someone expensive. Lorraine's plan hadn't changed. She'd see the IPO through, take her share, and file for divorce. She was done cleaning up after him.

Polly appeared at her door. Lorraine waved her in.

"Raine," she said. "There's a police officer from UC Davis on the line."

Lorraine froze. "What's happened?"

"I don't know."

"My God, is Dalton hurt?"

"I don't think so."

Lorraine picked up the line. The officer was the chief of campus security. "I'm sorry to have interrupted your day, ma'am," he said. "It's just that we couldn't get in touch with your husband, who we usually deal with."

"What's happened?"

"Your stepson, Dalton, was arrested early this morning by the city police," he said. "He's suspected of breaking and entering a local residence. We have an agreement with them. I recognized the name, and I arranged for him to be held here on campus."

"Thank you, but I'm a bit confused. Has Dalton been charged? Is there bail?"

"No, ma'am."

"But he's being held?"

"Yes, ma'am."

"What are you asking me to do?"

"This isn't the first time he's been picked up," the officer said.

"Good Lord."

"Like I said, ma'am, I recognized the name and I'm aware of your family's generosity to our university." He paused. "I spoke to the dean earlier today. We think it would be best if Dalton left campus for now."

"You're expelling him?"

"Let's just say he needs to take a break, maybe spend time with his family. I understand he's been under a doctor's care—maybe time for some of that, too. Perhaps he's been given too much freedom all at once. It happens to a lot of underclassmen."

"I see."

"Someone will need to come down here and get him. Today. Right away."

"Of course."

"And, ma'am, we never had this conversation."

"Understood."

Lorraine quickly dialed her husband's cell. It went to voice mail. She fumbled through the company directory, looking for Rick's number. When he answered, she said simply, "Put him on the line."

"What is it, Raine? I'm right in the middle of a round. Can't it wait?"

"Dalton has been arrested. I just spoke to the campus police chief, who says they're kicking him out of school. You need to drop the damn golf clubs and go take care of your son."

"Damn," Ted said. There were other voices and loud laughter. Ted's line went quiet for a moment. "You talked to Rettington?"

"He didn't say. I don't want Dalton here, Ted. I don't want him staying at the house."

"What am I supposed to do with him?"

"The best thing," she said with a sigh. "The best thing is to take him back to the center. Dr. Swanson said he wasn't ready."

"You're right," Ted said. "OK, I'll take care of it."

"When will you be back?" she asked. "We need to talk about something else."

"What is it now?"

"Spending," she said. "I want an accounting of about four million in company funds."

"I don't know what you're talking about."

"When will you be home?"

"I don't know. Couple days, I guess, assuming there's room for Dalton at the center."

"We'll talk then," she said. "By the way, I met with the reporter you had Sage rough up. That was a seriously bad move. We've got a real problem there."

"That wasn't my fault."

"No, Ted, nothing is ever your fault."

***

Ted considered calling the center, getting Dalton admitted, cleaning up the kid's mess, and making amends with Lorraine. He knew he wouldn't. Things had fallen apart. Things were spinning out of his control. Her admonition about the reporter troubled him. Ted was well aware of who Cole was; he had a reputation around the Capitol. He knew Abe, too. The combination was alarming.

Too late to settle things, he thought. *I have to up my game.* He gave Sage a call.

"I need you to get a hold of our new friend, the former cop."

"Dixon?"

"Tell him about Cole. Ask him to do something about him."

"What about the kid?"

"Go get him, smooth things over with the university people, and bring him to the condo in Sac," Ted said. "If Lorraine asks, Dalton is going to the center."

"What do I tell Dixon?"

"He'll know what to do."

***

Karmen looked for Michael Dale Preston in the federal sex offenders database. There were two men with the same name, neither of them old enough to be their guy. She drove to the Sacramento courthouse and looked him up there. Nothing. She moved on to Yolo County court in Woodland, a town about twenty minutes northwest of Sacramento. Still nothing. She called Betsy.

"I've found a few things," Betsy said. "Birth certificate. A 2003 conviction for rape. And a prison record. Nothing after 2010."

"Yeah, I've been all over and I can't find anything."

"Strange."

Karmen hung up, stopped at a coffee shop and opened her laptop.

She sent a help message to her web crew, her team from E-A-RTerror.com. "Looking to find a man named Michael Dale Preston, most likely someplace in California. Would be in his sixties by now."

Before she had a chance to finish her latte, she got an answer from a member who'd hardly ever helped with the work of building the website, *bigdataman*. He sent her an address. Right there in Woodland.

Karmen knew Cole would be angry, but she couldn't stop herself. She tapped Preston's address into her phone and got directions to the place.

She got off the freeway at Main Street and headed west toward the industrial end of town. She passed the rail yard and the county bus depot. There was a big vegetable canning operation at the corner of Main and E Street. Preston's place was on D Street, which only had a couple of residential houses and ended abruptly at the edge of an empty field.

A couple of young men were sitting on the porch smoking. They eyed Karmen suspiciously as she drove past. *Screw it*, she thought, and parked the car and boldly walked up to them, carrying a notepad and pen.

"Do you know if a Dale Preston lives here?"

"Who are you?" one of them asked.

"Reporter."

"Yeah?" the guy sounded interested. "Which paper?"

"The *Journal*," she told him. "What about it? You know Preston?"

"What's it to you, sweet-face?" the other man asked.

"We're working on a story tied to the Golden State Killer," she answered. "Do you?"

"Maybe," a third man said, coming through the screen door. "What do I get out of it?"

"How about a twenty?"

The man put out a dirty hand. "Make it forty."

Karmen got her wallet out of her back pocket. She had a ten and three ones. She gave him the ten. "That's all I have."

The man snatched it. "Dale's dead," he said. "Cancer or something. Died in prison."

"Dead?"

"Yep. Couple years back."

"How do you know?"

"I was there, in Soledad. He was on my row."

THIRTY-SEVEN

Skip was resting. He'd had an awful night. The shakes, difficulty breathing. His daughter had almost called an ambulance for a run to the ER.

Around dawn, he finally got some sleep. He woke at noon and Sally brought him some soup. He felt better and was considering getting out of bed when Sally returned with the cordless extension, handing it to him.

"Some old friend of Lon's," she said. "Fred Dixon. Do you feel up to talking?"

"Dixon?" Suddenly the energy drained from him. This would be work. Skip didn't know Dixon that well, but he remembered Lon complaining about him. Always looking for an angle.

Skip motioned for the phone.

"Dix, what's up?"

"You old hoot," Dixon said. "I hear you're looking for some ex-cop from Auburn linked to DeAngelo. Are you working on the book again?"

"Naw," Skip answered. "Just trying to put the pieces together like everyone else."

"Yeah, it's quite a case."

"It is."

"Well, I heard through Scotty's grapevine that you're working with some reporter and looking for a guy named Preston."

"A reporter came by, but I'm not really working with him. Just chasing an old lead."

"OK, I won't press, but I think I could make a pretty good guess what you're after and he's not an ex-cop."

"Tell me."

"It's obvious, Skipper, you're looking for DeAngelo's accomplice."

"What do you know about it?"

"I know that Lon always thought there was one," Dixon said.

"Go on."

"The guy you're looking for isn't an ex-cop."

"No?"

"Nope."

"Do tell."

"I don't have it, but an old buddy of mine does. I could put your reporter in touch with him."

"I'd need more."

"Well, from what I remember, the guy you're looking for served with DeAngelo in the Navy. The two of them did some damage down in Pacific Beach back in the day."

"San Diego? Can you give me his number? I'll pass it on to this reporter."

"Why not give me his? I lost my phone the other day. I'm calling on my girlfriend's phone."

Skip hesitated. Lon had never liked Dixon. Hadn't trusted him, though he'd never said exactly why. But the draw of the chase prevailed on the old cop—chase down every lead. He gave Dixon Cole's number.

***

Dixon didn't want to talk over the phone and suggested Cole meet him at a coffee joint in Natomas the following afternoon. Dixon was taller than Cole, and even though he was a few years older, he looked to be in better shape, what with the lean hard biceps gunning from under a tight tee-shirt. He wore gym shorts and tennis shoes and a pair of mirrored sunglasses.

"Thanks for meeting me," Dixon said, sitting down with a plastic cup of something. "I wanted to talk in person for a couple of reasons. First, what exactly are you and Skip working on? I don't want to get officially sideways with the DA in any way, shape, or form."

"We're looking for DeAngelo's accomplice. Didn't Skip tell you?"

"Yeah, but I want to impress on you that we are not having this conversation and nothing I say will ever end up in any damn book." Dixon ran up a disingenuous smile.

The mirrored glasses kept Cole from getting a read on him.

Cole nodded and took out his notebook. "You are on deep background, but I'm going to need to take some of this down."

"Go ahead," he said. "I think we understand each other."

"We do."

"The guy you're looking for is a man named Phil Westly," Dixon said. "Westly was a suspect in a handful of sexual assaults and burglaries in El Dorado County about fifteen years ago. El Dorado contacted us because the attacks were enough like the East Area Rapist that investigators up there were worried the same dude was back at work."

"They thought Westly might be the E-A-R?"

"That's right. The MO and other characteristics of the crimes were very similar."

"Such as?"

"Doesn't matter," Dixon said.

"Why is that?"

"Because Westly went to Folsom High School in the 1960s," he said. "The same time that DeAngelo was there. We didn't know that until DeAngelo was arrested."

"They knew each other?"

"Could be. My source also said this Westly bird joined the Navy in 1963. DeAngelo enlisted in 1964, also the Navy."

"That's what Skip said." Cole scribbled down a note. "Any chance they were shipmates?"

"Dunno. My buddy doesn't have anything on where Westly served," Dixon said. "But get this, my buddy said there was a string of residential burglaries in Pacific Beach around sixty-six. Then a rape and then another one. The break-ins all happened within a day or two of each other, and the San Diego PD didn't have a clue. Then it stopped. And about three months later, another string, this time near the state university."

"Huh." Cole put his pen down. "How the hell did your buddy remember all that?"

"They thought he might be the E-A-R. Had a file on him two feet thick. You don't forget stuff like that."

"Any chance Westly's still around?"

"Who knows, but my buddy said that back when they were running at him, Westly had a brother or some other relatives over in Newcastle."

"Great," Cole said. "Are the cops chasing this guy now?"

"I don't think so," Dixon said. "Not much sense in it. The statute of limitations has probably run out on anything he did."

"OK, thanks again."

"And we never spoke," Dixon said, jabbing a stiff finger into Cole's chest.

Cole ran Westly through the research system at Abe's office. He found a Phillip Westly Jr., owner of an auto shop on Indian Hills Road in Newcastle, and a Jan Westly, on 191 Peach Road.

*****

Newcastle sat just a lick under a thousand feet and, therefore, missed out on the fun part of winter snow. Unlike most of its neighbors in the foothills, Newcastle had never been trendy or chic. It was a town of secondhand stores, trailer parks, and rusty farm equipment.

On the way, Cole stopped at the gun range and bought some ammo. Buck, the trainer wasn't around. The guy at the counter didn't check his permit. He'd seen Cole around enough; he didn't bother.

Cole felt a little strange having a loaded weapon in the car. He'd thought it would make him feel invincible, but mostly he was uncomfortable, as if something alive lurked in the glove box.

Phil Westly's auto shop was ten miles east of the freeway. Cole chose to look at the Peach Road address first; it was closer to the highway. The owner was a woman named Jan Westly, who could be a sister or the wife.

There were a couple of pretty houses on the street, but the Westly place wasn't one of them. The part of the yard that was green was overgrown and weedy; the rest of it was mostly dead brown. A three-step staircase led to the porch, and a broken rail. The front windows were blind behind dark red sheets. No one answered his knock. Cole heard an engine revving around the side, and he found a guy in the garage, working on a big chopper.

"What do you want?" the guy said, looking up.

"Looking for a Jan Westly."

"No one here by that name. Get lost."

He was tall, mid-twenties, and wore a tee-shirt stained with spots of oil and engine grime. His hands were greasy black. He held an unlit cigarette between his lips. He revved the engine again.

"I'm in real estate. I might want to make an offer on this place," Cole said when the engine died down.

"No one wants to sell," he said without looking at Cole. "Now beat it."

"She might be pissed if she found out I was here and you didn't tell her."

He got out from behind the bike and wiped his hands on a rag. He had been working with a wrench, and he held the tool in an out-stretched hand.

"You'd better go now, mister," he said in a menacing tone.

Cole had left the Glock in his car. He was starting to think that had been a big mistake.

Cole put up his hands in surrender and retreated. "Can I at least leave my number? Maybe she'll want to call."

Another guy came up from behind him. Cole gave him a quick up and down. Same age, about the same size. He wore leathers like a biker, dark glasses, and big boots.

"What's you got here, Chet?" the new guy asked, stopping a few feet behind Cole.

"This fool said he was looking for Jan Westly."

"Jan?"

"Yeah, says he's a real estate man, wants to buy the house."

"What the hell?" The second guy came closer, pulling a long-bladed knife from a belt sheath and brandishing it at Cole's face. The other man took hold of Cole's arms by locking them behind his shoulders. "Get his ID."

Cole didn't struggle. They were playing a hand, and Cole wasn't holding any cards. "Look at this. James J. Cole. He's a reporter with the *Journal*. Why the snow job? What's the game?"

"I'm on a story. I'm looking for Phil Westly."

"Now it's Phil, is it?" the second guy said.

"Let's fuck him up," the first guy suggested.

"No," the second guy said, taking charge. "Put him in a chair inside the garage. I'll make a call."

Five minutes later, he was back. "Hazel wants to see him."

The boys pushed Cole into a pickup parked on the street outside. Cole sat between them and, without a word, they took off. An overpass led them out of town. Cole noticed they were on Indian Hill Road. After a couple miles, the pine forest thickened, getting deep and dark enough to hide almost anything. They pulled into a driveway and drove another minute or two. At the end was a tall gate made of corrugated metal; it was wide open. Walls, also made of aluminum siding, surrounded the compound. The boys parked outside and then pushed Cole through the gate. A cabin with a Confederate flag in the window. Seven, eight, nine big bikes parked along one side. A couple of guys with long hair and long beards exited the cabin. They wore leather vests and chains on their belts. A crude sign stenciled in black block letters hung over the cabin door: *Placer White Knights MC*.

Inside, the cabin was more of a bar. There were stools in front of a counter and bottles on a shelf behind it. A pit bull chained to the side of the cabin barked wildly as Cole stepped by. Inside, a dozen or so men were drinking at tables and at the bar. Two or three women, too. The boys pushed Cole until he stood in front of a big woman with a face that had run squarely into life more than once.

"You're looking for Phil?" she said, spinning on the bar stool. "What for?"

"I'm a reporter. I'm working on the Golden State Killer story."

"That shit? What about him? What's Phillip got to do with it?"

"Maybe nothing."

She measured him and then turned back to her drink. "You want something?"

"Water," he said. She waved at the bartender and a plastic cup with ice quickly arrived on the counter.

"You can sit," she said, and Cole took the stool next to her, easing the tension in the room. The boys from Peach Road got beers and took chairs at a table nearby.

"Don't lie to me," she said, putting up a finger. "You got something on my boy? You tell me. What it is?"

"Your son?"

She squinted. "Oh damn, you're looking for Senior? My ex?"

"Yeah, that's probably right."

"Why?"

"I got a source, a retired cop. We're chasing a second suspect in the Golden State Killer case," Cole told her the truth. "Phil Senior could be that guy."

Her eyes widened. "Him?"

"Phil lived in Rancho about the same time the guy they've accused of the crimes, a man named DeAngelo? They both went to Folsom High. And they were both in the Navy about the same time."

"Well fuck me," she said.

"And, as I understand it, Phil did time for sexual assault and probably had a few other scraps with the law."

She stared at him with her mouth ajar. "We met at Folsom," she said. "Phil served in 'Nam. Everything you've said is true. But he can't be the guy you're looking for."

"No?"

"We got divorced in 1969 when Phil Junior was a baby," she said. "He was my first husband—a real piece of work, that one. No respect for anything or anyone. We lived in Long Beach; that's where he was stationed. I came back here after the divorce, and I remember those attacks. The East Area Rapist. Phil was in Oklahoma all that time. He worked in the oilfields, remarried, and had other kids. That's where he went to jail, too. In Tulsa. Some sort of bar fight."

All this info could be checked. Cole wondered what the upside would be for her to lie to him.

"But he came back here to El Dorado County, right?"

"Yeah, when he got out. He heard I'd done pretty well without him. I'd remarried, and my second husband—he's dead now—well, we bought this place. I got the bowling alley too and a couple of houses. Phil came back when he got out of prison, tried to put the bite on me."

"Where is he now?"

"Dead." She picked up the glass and took a pull on the straw. "Cancer, two years ago."

***

The two bikers drove Cole back to his car. The first one, the guy who was working on the bike when Cole arrived, surprised Cole as he got out of the truck. Slugged him in the mouth, knocking him hard to the ground.

"Been wanting to do that all afternoon," he said. "See you around, slick."

THIRTY-EIGHT

Cole got to his feet and into his car. He considered pulling the Glock out of the glove box and shooting up the garage, including the prized bike on the rack. Instead, he meekly withdrew. He stopped at a convenience store and got a bottle of water and a bag of frozen peas for his lip. He sat in the parking lot. *Damn it*, he thought. *Tired of getting hit in the face. Never leaving the gun again. Don't leave home without it.*

There was a text from Karmen.

Don't get mad, but I tracked down Preston and went to his place, a group home. One of the housemates told me Preston's dead.

Don't get mad? Seething, Cole punched in her number.

"What the hell?" he barked. "Didn't I specifically tell you not to go to Preston's place? I used English and I was very clear."

"Easy, man," Karmen said. "I know, but I got the dope we needed."

"I don't give a shit! You disobeyed my order!"

"What the hell, man? What's eating you?"

Cole stopped, cleared his throat, and took a breath. "Just do what I ask, will you?"

"Sure, dude."

"I'm sorry, I've just had a rough damn day. Skip sent me on a god-damn cluster fuck up in Newcastle where some Hell's Angels took my head off."

"I get it. Cool down, man."

"Screw that. I hate this damn story. We got nothing. We got nothing. No leads. Nothing."

"Chill, man."

"I've had it. I'm done with this."

"I got something."

"What?"

"Betsy at your office," Karmen said. "I had her look. There's no death certificate on Preston."

"What the hell does that mean?"

"She did a nationwide scan. There's no death certificate."

"Preston is still alive?"

"Beats me, dude."

"OK, swing by the office and pick up Betsy. Call Skip. We all need to talk. I'm about half an hour out."

"Will do."

Cole punched in Abe's cell. "You got a minute?"

"Not much more than that. What's up?"

"Well, first off, my mailman, remember him?"

"This is the DeAngelo case?"

"Right. He came by the house the other night. We had a conversation, and he told me about another guy, a friend of DeAngelo's. He said this other guy killed the girl in my house."

"OK."

"The mailman said this other guy wanted to kill him. And now the mailman's been murdered. I got picked up last night by Sacramento PD. Captain Miller."

"Christ, Cole."

"Yeah, they want me to spill everything I got on the DeAngelo case."

"Did Miller ask you about the second suspect?"

"No, but he knows we were tracking the mailman. I got his name, found his apartment. They knew he'd come to see me. How long can I stall them?"

"Not too long, Jamie. Miller runs homicide, if I recall. That's serious police."

"Can you call him? Maybe buy me a day or two?"

"Sure. Anything else?"

"Nope. Thanks."

***

The receptionist wouldn't let Karmen pass. Betsy was in a meeting. When Karmen asked to see Abe, the woman politely smiled and asked her to take a seat. After about fifteen minutes, Karmen lost her patience. She waited until the woman was on the phone and then brazenly stormed through the inner sanctum to the boss's office.

Abe was alone, working at the computer.

"What's the deal?" Karmen demanded of him. "Didn't she tell you I was waiting?"

"Who are you?"

"Karmen Mueller. I work with Cole. He sent me down here to help with some of his stuff, and your bitch receptionist left me cooling out there like I'm selling magazines."

"I see." Abe pointed to the chair in front of his desk. "You're here now. What does Cole want you to do?"

"I'm supposed to get with Betsy. We got a meeting to go to."

Betsy and the receptionist arrived at Abe's door. "I'm so sorry, sir," the receptionist said. "I was on a call."

Abe waved at her. "It's fine." He got up and brought Betsy inside. "This is Karmen. She's working with Cole too. You need to go with her."

Betsy smiled briefly at Karmen. "We've been exchanging emails."

"We got a meeting with this old cop," Karmen said. "Cole's meeting us there."

"I get to meet Skip?" Betsy sounded excited. "I'll get my things."

Karmen lingered a moment, giving Abe a once-over. "You and Cole go back?"

"We do."

"He can be kind of a jerk, can't he?"

Abe laughed. "Yes, he can."

"A hair-trigger, too, like he's always afraid of something."

Abe cocked his head in puzzlement. "I wouldn't say that. He carries the burden of responsibility. It was his years in high-stakes journalism. No room for error."

"Yeah, except when he made one and they canned his ass."

"True." Abe stood and put a hand on Karmen's shoulder as he walked her into the hallway. "You probably don't know the whole story about how Cole lost his job, lost his entire career."

"I do. He told me. He said he messed up a big story and there was a libel suit, cost the paper big time."

"Jamie didn't mess it up," Abe said. "He was the head of the investigative team. It was one of his reporters. Cole didn't find out until it was too late."

"He took the hit even though it wasn't his fault? Man, that's old school."

"That's Cole."

***

The four of them—Skip, Sally, Karmen, and Betsy—were waiting when Cole arrived. His lip was split and still bleeding some. Sally went to get him an ice compress.

"Son, you look like you've been ridden hard and put away wet," Skip said.

"That Newcastle tip was a load of crap. That damn friend of yours."

"I was a little worried about that," Skip said. "But it sounded strong—the thing with the Navy and DeAngelo."

"Well, it was a setup. What's the deal with this guy, what's his name, Dixon?"

"I told you," Skip said. "He used to work with Lon."

"Dixon!" Karmen shouted. "That sonofabitch gave me bad dope, too. He told me the sheriff was investigating a member of DeAngelo's family as a possible accomplice. Total bullshit."

"When did that happen?" Cole asked.

"Just after DeAngelo's arrest. Like, the day after," Karmen said. "Complete bullshit. I got busted by the sheriff's press office. No such investigation."

"He made it up," Cole said, thinking it through. "He gave Karmen a bum steer on an item for her website. Sends me on a wild goose chase up to Newcastle, where I get rousted by a biker gang. What's he up to?"

Skip snapped his fingers and rolled quickly out of the room. "Be right back."

Sally returned with a towel wrapped in ice. "Don't worry about staining it," she said. "Just keep it on the lip."

Skip was back with a sheet of paper. It was the half note from Lon on the attack in Rocklin back in the seventies.

"Look," he said, waving it. "I'd wondered what bothered Lon about a missing rape kit. Those damn things were turning up all over hell when we were working the case. Lost more than a dozen of them. I wondered why Lon was so worried about this one."

Skip handed the sheet to Cole. "Look, he's got a note on who checked it out last." Skip pointed to the initials FD. "I bet that's Fred Dixon."

"What the hell does that mean?" Karmen asked.

"Dixon is in on it," Cole said in a soft voice. "He's somehow tied-in with our second suspect, this guy Preston."

Cole stood and went to the big window. "Maybe the item he fed Karmen was intended to play inside the department. Something to distract investigators, get them to actually consider a family member as an accomplice."

"Then, as we're closing in on Preston, he sends you on a dead end," Karmen said. "Hoping you'd get the hell beat out of you."

"It's as if he's protecting Preston," Skip said.

"Yeah," Cole said, turning back to the group. "There's something else you don't know, Skip. Barrett's dead. Murdered two days ago."

"Your mailman?" Skip asked.

"The cops picked me up last night and tried to sweat me on it," Cole explained. "He took two in the face, apparently."

"Well, that certainly fits with what Barrett thought might happen to him," Skip said. "But I have a hard time imagining a former sheriff's officer and state investigator like Dixon could have anything to do with murder."

"But the evidence points that way." Betsy had her laptop open and her fingers flew across the keyboard. "I think you've got to assume that Preston is still alive, that he's your second suspect, and that Dixon is helping him somehow."

"That's quite an assumption," Cole said.

"I think she's got something." Skip pointed at Betsy's screen.

"We know a Michael Dale Preston was convicted of sexual assault and sent to prison," Betsy said. "We have court records. What if he changed his name at some point? Or something like that?"

"Witness protection?" Skip offered. "Karmen, when did your source say Preston died?"

"He thought it was 2010 or 11."

"And where was he?"

"Prison."

"Well, let's start there," Skip said. "Maybe he was in on a case, a snitch. Maybe he's out running around under a different name."

"The key is Dixon," Skip said. "You should talk to Scotty about all this. Maybe one of his guys knows something more."

Cole suddenly wasn't feeling good. Very suddenly. The living room started to circle. He felt faint, found a chair, and put his head between his legs.

When he came to, Betsy was leaning over him, holding an ice compress to his forehead. "Shit," he said and started to get up.

"Hold on, Cole." She put a hand on his chest. "Stay still, take your time."

"How long was I out?"

"A minute or so," she said.

Karmen came back into the room, eating with a spoon out of a cup. "You guys want to stay for dinner? Sally invited us. This spaghetti sauce is crazy good."

"I can't," Betsy said. "I got to pick up my kid."

Cole got his feet on the floor.

"How you doing, boss?" Karmen edged closer. "I'll bet you didn't eat anything today. That's when crazy stuff happens to me."

"I don't think I did."

She offered him the cup. "Want some?"

Cole pushed it away. "No, I got to get going too. What time is it?"

"Almost six," Betsy replied.

"Come on, boss. I'll drive you home. Let Betsy take your car."

"No, I've got a date."

"A date? The same one? Who is she?"

"You wouldn't know her. She works at the sheriff's department."

"You're dating a cop?"

"No, she's a political appointee, runs the press office."

"No way!" Karmen burst out. "You're dating Brooke Ball-Buster Alverez?"

"You know her?"

"Giant pain in my ass," Karmen said. "She's damn cute, though. Good for you."

THIRTY-NINE

Cole let Betsy drive him back to the office. They talked about the case. She asked about Dixon. Cole realized how little he knew about him, and then he told Betsy to do a backgrounder on him.

"That reminds me," she said, getting out of the car. "I've got some material on your other client, Evelyn Morris. I'll email it to you tonight."

"Anything interesting?"

"Not really. Born in Modesto. Graduated from UC Santa Barbara with an economics degree. Worked at Wells Fargo before opening her own investment shop."

"OK, thanks."

***

Brooke was teaching her class until eight. The plan was to meet at a place near the campus. He had time to go home, shower, change, maybe catch a quick nap. He was dead tired. He checked his face in the rear-view mirror. His split lip was ugly and growing more swollen. *Great*, he thought, *Brooke will love seeing this*. He was rolling down Curtis Court, almost home, when he got a call.

"Are you the reporter friend of Scotty's?" a man asked.

"Yeah, I'm Cole."

"My name is Lee Hampton. I'm a retired sheriff's deputy. Scotty says you're looking for intel on a rape in Orangevale, 1977."

"I am."

"I'm at the saloon now. We should talk."

Cole turned around and got back into freeway traffic.

Scotty wasn't working. Cole asked the guy running the bar if he knew a man named Lee Hampton. He pointed to an older man shooting pool alone. Cole asked what he was drinking and got two.

"Lee Hampton?" Cole said, approaching him, holding out a fresh gin gimlet. "I'm Cole."

"Yeah," he said, putting down the cue and taking the drink.

"You got something for me on this Orangevale attack?" Cole asked.

"Not much, just that you're the second person to ask me about it since DeAngelo got busted."

"Really? Who else?"

"This dickhead I used to work with, another retired cop. We were both rookies assigned gofer duties for the task force on the East Area Rapist back in the eighties."

"Dixon?"

"Yeah, you know Fred?"

"In a way." Cole rubbed the back of his head. "He asked about Orangevale?"

"We got talking about it, yes. He had a photo of some bird. Asked if I recognized him."

Cole had Barrett's mugshot on his phone and he quickly called it up. "Was it this guy?"

"Yeah. Who is he?"

"Someone who knew DeAngelo and might have run with him," Cole said. "Now he's dead. Murdered two days ago."

Hampton thought for a minute. "That damned Dixon. He claimed he had a line on some big payday. Said he was working with an old CI of his. He said this guy in the photo was in the way."

"Dixon was trying to find the guy in the photo?"

"Yeah."

"Why would he ask you?"

"Who knows?"

"What did he say about Orangevale? Is there a connection?"

"Beats me. I guess Dixon thought there might be."

"What about an address? Where does Dixon live?"

"I don't know, man. All I wanted to tell you is that Dixon was asking about Orangevale too."

"OK, thanks."

Brooke wasn't amused to see Cole's fat lip. She scolded him and, instead of going out to dinner, took him back to her place, made some soup, and tended to his wound. She also sent him home right after dinner, telling him to get a full night's rest. Cole liked it.

***

He got to the office early. He wanted to double-team the research into Dixon. Before he could start, the receptionist buzzed him from the front desk.

"Someone here to see you, Mr. Cole. A Sylvia Kim."

"OK," Cole said. "I'll be right out."

"What happened to you?" Sylvia asked as Cole came closer.

"Ran into a guy's fist."

"Looks sore," she said. "Let's walk. I took a chance just coming here."

They got out to the street. She pointed toward the park. Cole went along with it.

"I checked around on the donation you told me about," she said. "I don't have much for you there, but I found out what happened to Emily. I got a source in the Assembly who says she was attacked in the building three years ago."

"Emily was attacked by an Assemblyman?"

"I didn't say that. All I know is that she was attacked one night in the Capitol, and that a member, not necessarily an Assemblyman, was involved."

"What sort of attack?"

She looked back at him blankly. "What else? Sexual."

"God, every time I turn around, that's all I hear about."

There was a bench. A mother and two young kids were playing on the swings. An older man was throwing a ball for his dog. A younger man was jogging. Cole took a seat and ran his fingers through his hair. Sylvia stood.

"I don't suppose your source would talk to me?"

"No way. You can't even tell Abe or anyone else I tipped you. It could come back on my source."

"A sexual assault," Cole said. "I guess that explains why she gave money to the shelter. She had a lot of money at the time of her death. Additional income outside her state salary. You didn't hear anything about a settlement, did you?"

"I wouldn't be surprised," she said. "Although you can be sure the state didn't pay for it. I seem to remember a certain investigative journalist who busted the hell out of the Speaker's office for secretly spending a couple million on confidentiality agreements."

Cole grinned. "That was a good story. One of my best."

"My car is over there in the parking lot. I've got to get going."

Cole remained seated. He watched the two little girls on the swings; the chocolate lab chasing the ball, grinning and resolute; the jogger standing at the corner, striding in place, waiting for a light to change. The sun was out. It would be warm later. Cole wished he and Brooke had the day off. That they had packed a lunch and driven up to Tahoe. He didn't want to go back to the office. It was barely nine thirty, and he'd already had enough ugliness to fill the entire week.

He realized he didn't have his cell with him. More ugly business was probably already waiting for him back at the office.

He wasn't wrong about that.

As soon as he stepped inside, Betsy waved to him. "You missed a call," she said. "It got routed to me. Sounds important. A woman, she wouldn't give her name. She has information on Emily Hodges. Wants you to come to the Cathedral at ten. Someone will meet you at the confessional with instructions."

"Cathedral? Confessional? Are you serious?" Cole looked at the clock. "Where's Abe? I need to talk to him."

Abe was with a client. Cole waved from outside the glass wall, put up five fingers, and mouthed the word *important.* Abe excused himself and came into the hallway.

"Jamie, I haven't had a chance to talk to Captain Miller, sorry."

"That's not it," Cole said. "I'm on the Hodges case. I've got a source inside the building who claims Emily was sexually assaulted and that a member was involved."

"Christ. A member attacked her?"

"I don't think so. Could be a cover-up. She was getting money, outside money. Could be the member arranged for a settlement. I don't know."

"OK. What's next?"

"I've got about ten minutes to get to the Cathedral. Someone who knew Emily."

"Go. We'll talk when you get back."

***

It took Cole nearly all ten minutes to get across town and find a parking place. He took the Glock out of the glove box and stuffed it into his waistband. He was at least five minutes late by the time he sat down in a pew near the confessional, as ordered.

A nun came to meet Cole. She said nothing but signaled for him to follow her through the rear entrance of the church. She pointed at a car waiting across 12th Street. Just the driver was inside, a man.

They got on the freeway, US 50, and went north. The driver got off at the first exit in Folsom. They drove west until they reached the I-80 and then headed back downtown. Somehow satisfied he wasn't being followed, the driver got off close to where they'd started and dropped Cole at a Starbucks about a mile from the Capitol. The same nun was waiting for him. She took him to a booth where a young woman sat with a shawl over her head and big sunglasses obscuring her face.

"This is James Cole," the nun said, taking a seat next to the younger woman. "Mr. Cole, this is Rosa. Don't ask for her last name."

"I'm listening," said Cole. "How did you know Emily?"

"We were in a support group together," Rosa started. "Survivors of rape. The sisters run it."

"Rape?" Cole repeated. "She tell you how it happened?"

"She wasn't big on sharing. But she liked to drink, and, for a while, so did I."

"You told my associate you have some information? What do you want me to know?"

"I didn't even know she was dead until yesterday. Alex called me. He told me about you. He asked if I thought her death could have been suicide."

"The coroner ruled it an accidental overdose."

"I don't think it was an accident and I don't think it was suicide," she said, her voice catching. "I think she was murdered."

"What?"

"The last time I saw her was a couple of weeks before she died, I guess. We got drunk at a bar across from the Capitol one afternoon. She told me she'd been paid off. She got a lot of money. Signed some agreement."

Cole took out his notepad. "Mind if I take some of this down?"

Rosa looked at the nun. The nun nodded.

"Go on," Cole said.

"We got pretty drunk, and she went off," Rosa explained. "She said she'd heard that this same guy had attacked another girl, that he'd done the same thing again. She said she'd met with an attorney. She was going to give back all the money, tear up the settlement, and go public with her case, go to the cops, the whole deal."

Cole put his pen down. "Who else have you told?"

"No one," she said. "I want to be left out of this."

"The child would be a target if the wrong people found out what she knows," the nun said. "You must protect her."

"You can trust me. I promise."

The driver came in from outside. "Time to go," he said. He looked at Cole. "You stay here for ten minutes."

Cole put up both hands in agreement.

FORTY

The lunchtime crowd poured out of the office buildings and scattered downtown. It was nearly July. The Legislature was in session. They were fighting over the budget. They only had a few days before the end of the fiscal year—the deadline for passing the spending plan—or the lawmakers wouldn't be paid. Cole's car was on the other side of the Capitol, and it took him a while to weave his way upstream of the staffers, lobbyists, and who knew who else. He got through the Capitol's security check and then out the other side of the building.

A taco truck was parked near his car. He got in line to get a burrito when Brooke texted him with a better offer: *Meet me at the Galley in an hour? I've got great news!!*

He sent back: *I'd like that. I need some good news.*

Cole got in his car and went back to the office. The place was empty. He closed the door to his quarters and tossed his notepad and phone on the desk. He drew the blinds, turned off the lights, and laid on the floor. He just needed a minute.

His door opened. Betsy and Karmen. Cole peeked up at them and closed his eyes again.

"Have a second, boss?" Karmen stepped in, disregarding his choice of placement. "We got something big on Dixon."

"Yeah?" Cole kept his hands folded on his chest, his eyes still closed.

Betsy laid a thick legal brief on his belly with half a dozen post-it notes attached. "A couple of prison guards at Soledad were accused of running drugs and other contraband in 2010," she said. "Fred Dixon was one of the investigators on the case. And there's a reference in the file about a witness for the prosecution, an inmate known only by his initials: MDP."

Cole sat up and opened the brief. "Where did you find this?"

"One of Karmen's friends," Betsy answered.

Karmen took Cole's big chair behind the desk and put her feet up. "The crew," she said. "My dot-com team. They've been all over me to help with the case. I told them about Dixon. One of them knew about this court case."

Cole shot her a scowl. "I thought I was clear about that," he said, taking a deeper look at the brief.

"I talked to the defense attorney on the case," Karmen continued. "He said the inmate's name was Michael Dale Preston and that he'd been a longtime CI of Dixon's going back to Dixon's days as a deputy in Sacramento. Preston got paroled early because he cooperated in the case."

"All right," Cole got to his feet. "I give up. This is outstanding work. Do we know where Preston is?"

"No," Betsy answered.

"What about Dixon?" Cole asked. "Where is he? How do we find him?"

"We're working on it, boss," Karmen said. "I got Scotty's network going and my team too."

Cole's cell lit up with a 626-area code. The mysterious Evelyn Morris.

"I got to take this," he said, ushering them outside his office and closing the door. "Ms. Morris, I'm glad you called. We've got some things to discuss."

"You find something?"

"Not really. The fact is, Ms. Morris, I spoke to Mrs. Wilmer, and it took her all of five minutes to call my bluff. I don't think there's much sense in carrying your plan forward."

"Of course there is," she snapped at him. "You haven't found what you need yet. Once you do, you'll understand."

"No, listen, I'm done. If you need me to reimburse some of my retainer, just tell me how much."

"And I said no. What have you found? You said a moment ago that you found something. What was it?”

“A deviant family member who died in prison about fifteen years ago.”

“You’re finally on the right track,” Evelyn said.

“I said fifteen years ago, Ms. Morris. No one cares. The Wilmers don’t care. I can’t imagine anyone on Wall Street would, either.”

“Not attacks that Callen committed,” she said sharply. “It’s the son. Dalton.”

“What?”

“That’s right. Dalton.”

“How do you know?”

“I just do.”

“Tell me.”

She was quiet for a minute. “My mother was a victim of Callen’s,” she said. “For all I know I might be his daughter. I’ve kept a very close eye on the Wilmers for years.”

“Jee-sus.”

“I never knew her, my mother. She gave me up for adoption, and about four years later, she died. I tracked down my birth family. Found an aunt who told me everything.”

“This is about restitution, then?” Cole asked. “Why not just come through the front door, hit them with a lawsuit?”

“I tried back when Ted was still running things,” Evelyn said. “The court kicked it out. The Wilmers have much better attorneys than I do.”

“Does Lorraine know about any of this?”

“I don’t know.”

“Can I tell her?”

“Absolutely not,” she said. “They’ve got a freaking restraining order on me. Been renewed like, six times.”

Cole had the Wilmer file open in front of him. Callen Wilmer’s obit was on top. He peered at it, wondering if Evelyn’s story was credible. He was looking at the dates. Callen was murdered in 2007. He’d served nine years of a twenty-five-year sentence. That meant he was convicted in 1998 or thereabouts.

Cole figured Evelyn to be in her late twenties. *Could be*, he thought. *Could be she's telling the truth.*

Something else caught his attention. *What was it Betsy just said?* He reached for the legal brief she and Karmen had found about the prison guard drug case.

Soledad.

"Are you still there?" Evelyn's voice was louder and agitated. "Did you hear me?"

"What? Yes. Sorry. No. What did you say?"

"I said look closely at the son."

"I have. There's just one sealed file on him from when he was a juvenile."

"Talk to the farmworkers. There's more."

Cole noticed the time. He was running late for his lunch with Brooke. "Why not cut to the chase and tell me everything? I'm getting pretty tired of this mystery game."

"That is everything. Talk to the farmworkers. There's a civil suit in the works."

"OK, I got to run."

Cole grabbed the brief on the prison drug case and Callen Wilmer's obit. He dropped them both in front of Karmen, sitting in a cubicle outside his office.

"Soledad," he said. "Senator Wilmer's brother served time at Soledad. Check to see if our Dale Preston was there at the same time. And let's get a damn line on Dixon. We've got to find him."

Karmen put up a hand. "Can I call in the troops?"

"Who?"

"My dot.com crew. Some of them have skills, man."

Cole waved. "Sure, whatever works."

***

Brooke had a glass of wine in front of her as Cole arrived at the restaurant. "Are we celebrating something?" Cole asked.

"I am," she said as he leaned in for a kiss. "Join me?"

"I wish. I got a load of stuff going on."

"Tell me."

He looked at her with a strained face. "Church and state, don't you remember? You wouldn't believe my morning, anyway. Damn, I lived it and I don't believe it."

She took his hand. "We won't have that problem much longer," she said with a smile. "I gave the sheriff my notice."

"You did?"

"Yes, I got approached by an old friend who works for an international PR firm. They made me an offer, a fantastic one."

"International? You leaving Sac?"

She leaned into him and kissed him. "No, honey, I'm not. They want me to open a shop here. I get to hire a staff, run the show. It's a huge opportunity."

"That's great. How did your news go over with the sheriff?"

"Not good, but I don't care. He and my boss, they've been leading me around about all sorts of things. One was your records request."

"My request?"

"Yes. First, they told me there were no records in the file about your murder. And then I found something."

"Wait," Cole said. "They don't have anything on the Bordeaux murder?"

"You know about it? You know the victim's name?"

"Yeah."

"Since when?" Brooke said, sounding offended.

Cole waved. "Pretty much since I made the request. We tracked it down."

"Jamie, why? You can't imagine the trouble you've caused me."

"I had to know what was in the sheriff's files." He turned over his palms and raised his shoulders. "Please. Let it go, Brooke. Please?"

She frowned at him.

"Getting back to the issue," he said. "The file is empty? On a capital case?"

She folded her arms. "You can be so annoying."

"What about the case file?"

"Yes, it's empty. There's no police report, no investigator notes, none of that sort of thing."

"It's a murder. Where did it go?"

"It was forty years ago, Jamie," she said. "Paperwork can get lost, even on a murder case."

"Nothing?"

"Not a thing on the murder. That's what freaked out the sheriff so much when we got your request. I'm glad I won't be there when he finds out what you're really up to."

"You said they lied to you about it. You found the records?"

"I found a record," she said. "Another request to look at our file on the case made about three years ago."

"Another request? On my murder?"

"Yes."

"Who was it from?"

"It was an inter-agency thing. Another police department. Some tiny city someplace up north."

"Really? Where? That could be important."

"Olimpo?" she said. "A detective from the Olimpo police department."

"Olimpo?" Cole repeated. He remembered the town, remembered driving by it on the way to Redding. He was trying to remember. There was something else about the place, but he couldn't place it. "Weird."

"Now what about you?"

"What do you mean?"

"Your house? The baseball book in Iowa? What about you, James J. Cole? Are you staying in Sacramento with me?"

He put his arms around her and pulled her close. "I am."

The server came by. Cole ordered a glass of wine too. They finished a bottle and then took Brooke's car. They didn't go to Tahoe. Her place. Cole sent a text to Betsy. He took the rest of the afternoon off.

FORTY-ONE

The boy and the old man sat on a bench halfway between the soccer field and the zoo. It was a weekday afternoon. No one was around.

The old man was tall and wore a heavy wool coat, even though it was warm. He had a beard and dark glasses. A baseball cap was drawn down over his brow. The kid didn't care if someone recognized him. He wore shorts and flip-flops and a baggy, long-sleeved tee-shirt.

The old man had called the meeting. "How many now?" he asked the boy.

"Two."

"Is that enough?"

"I don't know. I don't think so."

"Best to quit while you're ahead."

"You never did."

"I didn't."

"How did he stop?"

"Joe? He just did. Something happened. He was done with it."

"He got scared."

"Maybe."

"I'm not."

"Don't go arrogant on me, Dalton. Hear? You haven't done shit yet."

"What else do I need to know?"

"Location."

"What do you mean?"

"You ever heard the saying 'Don't shit where you eat?'"

"Sure."

"Well, it's the opposite in this here game. You want to practice where you live. You want to be intimate with your surroundings and your prey."

"He say that?"

"Hell, he lived it. He hit close to home. Citrus Heights. Rancho Cordova, Orangevale. He hit there because he knew the neighborhoods."

"He moved on, though."

"Sure, you try it sometime, kid. You hit forty, fifty times in the same county, heat gets on you. You got to move on."

The kid listened.

"You got any more questions?" the old man asked.

"Yes," the boy said. "Dogs."

"Got to learn to deal with them. Chemicals are best."

"They sometimes hear me."

"Once again, know your surroundings. Know which homes have dogs and the times they get put outside. People are creatures of habit."

The boy listened.

"You feeling anything more? Like this ain't enough?"

The boy shook his head. "I think I'm OK there."

"Good. Keep it controlled. Keep it steady."

"Does he know about me?"

"Who? Joe? Hell, no. He's not talking to anyone, least of all me."

"I still can't believe they got him after all those years."

"His downfall was the murders. You could see it coming. The taste was in his mouth."

"They've written books about him, about his attacks."

The old man nodded.

"There's this website too," the boy said. "I've been reading about him, his life. I'm thinking of reaching out to them, maybe they'd be interested in me."

"Never mind that." The old man had a slip of paper with three addresses on it. "I need you to do something," he said. "I want you to visit each of these homes. Take a picture of the bedrooms, send the photos to me. Can you do that?"

"Yes."

FORTY-TWO

A breeze drew up the delta through the Valley after sundown. The curtains danced before an open window at the far end of the bedroom. She was wrapped in his arms, her face close. He caressed her cheek.

"Looks like your lip might start bleeding again, tough guy."

He licked it and sat up. "Someone's rough kisses." He rose and went to the bathroom. She put on a robe and headed to the kitchen. She came back with a glass of wine and a cold beer.

"Now," she said. "Tell me about your day. Tell me why you were so glum."

He lay down next to her. "I don't know if I can keep this up," he said. "At first it was sort of fun, this gumshoe thing. But it's horrible."

"I've heard some new deputies can go into a form of shock," she said. "The department has a fairly active counseling bureau. Maybe you should try talking to someone."

Cole sipped the beer. "This old guy—he's been a PI forever—he warned me about this. He said that just because I'd seen the streets as a reporter, I might not be ready to see them up close like this. I got rape cases. I got a murder. A kid pulled a gun on me the other day."

She put her arms around him. "It's hard when you care about people."

"Yeah."

They could hear Cole's cell ringing from the kitchen. He went and got it.

"What the hell, man?" Karmen snapped at him. "Where have you been?"

"What's up?" Cole said, opening the beer.

"Well, for one, Scotty's guys found Dixon. He lives in Eureka."

"You still in the office?"

"I am, damn you."

"OK, on the shelf behind my desk is a file marked Wilmer. Go get it and look for a document; it's the senator's economic disclosure statement."

"Hang on." She was gone a moment. "Looking. By the way, Preston and your boy Callen Wilmer were both at Soledad from 2002 until Callen got stabbed."

"I thought so. Good."

"OK, I got the form."

"On the second or third page, look for an investment he has in a company called Solo or something; it's based in Eureka."

"Solon Group."

"Right. What's the address?"

"It's 463 Front Street."

"Does it match the address Scotty's guy gave you?"

"No. It's weird. The address for the company is 463 *First* Street."

"That sounds like an intentional typo," Cole said. "Someone may need to go up there and sort it out."

"You want me to go?"

"I don't know yet. It's a hell of a drive."

"Abe was looking for you too. Sort of pissed. You'd better call him."

"I will. Listen, does anything about the town of Olimpo ring a bell? This afternoon, I found out a detective from up there wanted to see the sheriff's records on the Bordeaux file."

"Olimpo," she said. "No. Although I think maybe DeAngelo has family there?"

"That's not it. There's something else. I think I'm coming into the office."

"Well, I'm not staying. Movie night at home."

Cole got dressed and gave Brooke a careful kiss goodnight. The traffic was light. A practically perfect warm summer evening. There was a ballgame under the lights at the stadium. Bugs buzzing through the air. He made it over the causeway from Davis to Abe's place in ten minutes.

He found his DeAngelo file and started leafing through it. He paused, looking at the report Jack Perry had written on the murder of Vivien Bordeaux.

No, Cole said to himself, *it wasn't in the report. It was something Perry said.* Cole found his notes from their conversation. The business card from a cop the old detective thought might have been mistakenly in the file. Perry said he'd email the contacts, anyway. Cole opened his mail file and found Perry's message.

> *I remembered now, Perry wrote, I got a call from this cop in Olimpo. This was in 2015. He wanted to talk to me about the Bordeaux case. I had a heavy load on me then. My wife was dying of cancer, so I didn't exactly send back an invite. He even came by the office once when I wasn't here. Left his card. Maybe you should call him. I have no idea what he wanted to talk about. Here's his info: Det. Sgt. Harold Remy, Olimpo Police Department.*

Cole picked up the phone and dialed Remy's number.

"Sergeant's desk, Officer Williams speaking."

"My name's James Cole. I'm a reporter from Sacramento. I'm looking for Harold Remy. I think he's a sergeant with your department, although that was a couple years ago."

"Harold Remy?" the officer said. "Yeah, he used to be with the department. What's this about?"

"Do you know where I could find him?"

"You didn't answer my question."

"It's related to the Golden State Killer case."

"You say you're a reporter? What's your name again?"

"James Cole. Can you get in touch with Remy? It's very important that I speak to him."

"Sergeant Remy is dead. Shot to death three years ago after making a traffic stop."

"I see."

"Anything else?"

"No, thank you."

Cole sat for a moment before tapping out a note to Karmen and Betsy:

I'm heading up to Olimpo tomorrow. I'll call from the road. Thanks for everything you did today. I think we're getting close.

He called Abe.

"What the hell happened to you?"

"I think I'm in love."

"Seriously?"

"I think so. You know her, too. She's the communications director for Sheriff Henley. Brooke Alverez."

"Ooo-ee," Abe laughed. "You are forgiven. I understand completely. Good for you, young man."

"Plus, I just needed a break. The shit I'm dealing with, man."

"What happened at the Cathedral?"

"Met this kid who knew Emily from a support group. She said Emily told her she got a settlement payment and had to sign a non-disclosure agreement. Shortly before Emily died, they had drinks and Emily told her she'd been to an attorney. She wanted to tear the agreement up, give back the money. She was ready to go public with what happened to her."

"You're thinking her overdose wasn't accidental?"

"That's what the kid said. She's scared. She thought murder when she heard about Emily. I spoke to Emily's boyfriend too. He pulled a gun on me; thought I was coming to threaten him. He said Emily was worried about that, too."

"Holy hell."

"We looked at her financial records," Cole said. "Emily was getting outside income beyond her state salary. Big money, close to a hundred grand. We need Mrs. Hodges to goose the bankers to find out where that money was coming from."

"I'll look into it."

"Good."

FORTY-THREE

Cole smelled the smoke as soon as he stepped outside to grab the paper. A friendly scent. The smell of camping with his dad. Pine needles. The hushed quiet of the forest. It didn't occur to him to wonder where the smoke might be coming from.

He made a quick egg sandwich and poured two cups of scalding coffee into a thermos. He threw an overnight bag in the trunk packed with a change of clothes. Cole poked through his box of camping equipment looking for a small flashlight. He made sure it was working before putting the box into the trunk. He tossed the newspaper in his backpack and was on the road by seven. He hadn't decided on a plan of action once he reached his destination, but he knew he needed to find out more about the dead cop from Olimpo.

About halfway up, he stopped for gas at a town called Maxwell. When he got out of the car, the smoke was stronger, stinging his eyes and leaving an acrid taste in his mouth. There was a guy at the pump next to him with his family in the car and a dog in the back. He said they'd barely escaped. He pointed to a black smudge on his hood where a softball-size ember had exploded. "Pretty sure our house is gone," he said. "The whole neighborhood, probably. Maybe the whole town."

Cole wished him well.

Fires were burning all along the northern Sierra and the southern Cascades. The wind picked up. Radio stations warned of pending evacuations. Cole passed a line of firetrucks coming from Las Vegas.

It was midmorning when he reached Olimpo. The sun was out, hot and dry, but the thick smoke left the sky dark and gray. *And miles to go before I sleep. And miles to go before I sleep.*

Cole started at the city library. He figured the local paper had to have covered the shooting of a city police officer. The library wasn't much. A group of toddlers was crowded around an older woman reading them a story in the main room. There was a table with two computers that two older men were fully engaged with; three more men waited behind them. The kid at the checkout desk shook his head; they didn't keep news clips. They kept the whole paper, but only going back a year; every month they threw out the oldest copy.

He said Cole should try directly at the paper, *The Olimpo Compass*. The offices were just down the street.

The door was unlocked, but it seemed no one was home. Cole called out and waited and then tried a second time. A woman in her thirties came out of an inner office wearing an annoyed expression.

"Can I help you?"

Cole told her he wanted to look through their archives. She explained they only published once a month and had long ago given up on trying to keep any orderly files on what they'd written. He told her about the cop shooting from 2015. She said she'd only been working at the paper for a year.

"You should try the historical society," she said. "Ask for Craig Martin. He used to be our editor. They have tours today at the Oxford House; it's over on Main past the barbershop and the Olimpo Market."

There wasn't a line to get in. Cole stuffed a five into the donation box and waited until someone came to fetch him.

"You here for the tour?" asked a tall, lean man who looked to be in his eighties.

"Not exactly. Are you Craig Martin?"

"I am."

"My name's Cole. I'm a reporter working on something having to do with this Golden State Killer. You hear about it?"

Martin put his hands on his hips and stooped some to get a better look at Cole through his thick glasses. "I think I might have heard a little something about that. How can I help you?"

"You were editor of the *Compass*?"

"I was."

"Do you remember an officer getting shot, killed, maybe three or four years ago? A man named Remy?"

He nodded. "Summer of 2015. Harold Remy. Very sad story."

"What happened?"

"I don't think the police ever solved it," he explained. "Remy was found shot to death at the side of a back road." The old man pushed his glasses up on his nose. "Why you are interested?"

Cole told him about the Bordeaux killing and the second suspect.

"What's Remy got to do with all that?"

"That's the question," Cole said. "I know that Remy was interested enough in the Bordeaux case to come down to Sacramento not long before he was killed. He tried talking to a private investigator who had worked on the case."

"He thought there was a connection between this girl getting killed and someone up here?"

"That's my working assumption."

"I see," Martin said, taking a chair.

"Remy have family here?" Cole asked.

"His widow. I think she's in Chico."

"What about the guy accused of being the Golden State Killer, Joe DeAngelo? Would you know if he's got relatives around here?"

The old man shook his head. "No. I don't. That would be big news."

"What about a man named Callen Wilmer?"

"Oh, sure. He used to live in a cottage near the farmworkers' camp," the old editor said. "He was a wicked sonofabitch. Preyed on the weak and used his family's money to get away with it until they finally got him. He got his just desserts in prison. Someone knifed him."

"Yeah, I read about that. What about Ted?"

"The state senator? What about him?"

"You ever hear any wild stories about him?"

"Some," Martin said. "Our publisher was close to the Wilmers, so we weren't allowed to be interested in anything concerning the family. Especially Ted."

"What would you have chased?"

"I'd talk to the farmworkers' union," he said. "They got an office in Red Bluff."

"What about?"

"I don't think they liked Mr. Wilmer too much."

The farmworkers again.

Cole stopped at the city clerk's office and found an address for Remy's widow. He used Abe's system to find a phone number and called to ask if he could come by. She said she was busy all morning but would have time in the afternoon.

He looked up the farmworkers' union on his phone and got directions. Red Bluff was half an hour north. Their website listed the general manager as a woman named Lorena Gonzalez.

When he arrived, Cole flashed his press pass at the receptionist, and she retreated deeper into the suite. A stout woman in her forties came forward. She wore a turquoise necklace and bifocals and introduced herself as Lorena.

Cole explained he was a writer working on a story about the Wilmers. "I've heard about some trouble your people may have been having over in Olimpo."

She nodded solemnly and then waved for him to follow her into her office. "Who told you we have troubles in Olimpo?" she closed the door. "Take a seat."

"I can't say. She's a source."

"She?" Lorena said. "I ask because the subject is sensitive. I don't want anything going public just yet."

"We can speak off the record."

She nodded, obviously relieved. "Then what would you like to know?"

"What's going on with the workers in Olimpo? I hear there's trouble."

"What have you heard?"

"That your union is preparing to sue Stony Creek."

"You have an excellent source. I think I know who it is." She took off her glasses. "We're going to federal court, a civil rights suit. That's strictly confidential. We're still in talks with Stony Creek management."

"What's the action?"

"Failure to provide a safe work environment," she said. "The workers' camp."

"What's that?"

"We got about thirty families living there," she said. "The company rents out a few homes, there's an apartment building of sorts, a half dozen or so trailers, a couple truck campers. The city police don't normally patrol inside the camp. And people have taken advantage of that. Years ago, it was the Senator's older brother. Now, I don't know, someone else."

"Attacks on women?"

She nodded. "Break-ins, burglaries, and yes, a thirteen-year-old girl was assaulted in March. The men in the camp organized a watch, which brought out the cops because some of these guys were armed."

"The company won't help?"

"I think Mrs. Wilmer is trying. The Senator's the problem. He's always been hostile to the workers. So, we're going to court. I'm hoping it goes public just about the time they launch their big stock offering."

"The girl," Cole asked. "The thirteen-year-old, did the police investigate?"

"You could call it that."

"I take it no one was arrested?"

She frowned and shook her head.

"What are you asking for?" Cole asked.

"Better security. Housing upgrades. An actual patrol. And we want an arrest."

"You have a suspect?"

"A man's living in Callen's old place. His name is Berg. We suspect him."

"Have you told the police?"

"Berg is a family friend. Someone Ted knows. The cops won't do nothing."

"What about the Wilmers' son?"

Lorena squeezed her eyes shut. "What about him?"

"Do you suspect him?"

"There's been some talk. His car was seen in the area at the time of the attack."

"There's a sealed criminal case against Dalton. Do you know anything about that?"

"Two summers ago he was found with a couple of naked kids."

"Kids?"

"Boys, like eight or nine."

"Rape?"

"Naw, just weird games."

"What about a local officer who was shot three or four years ago, a man named Remy?"

"I remember it, but I don't know that there's any connection to the Wilmers."

"You ever hear of a man named Dixon, an ex-cop?"

"No."

"How do I get out to the camp? I'd like to look around, maybe interview one of the families. I'd also like to get a look at Berg and this cottage."

"There's a diner on Main Street. Olimpo's only got the one," she said. "Meet me in the morning. Around ten. I can take you."

FORTY-FOUR

The corporate offices of Stony Creek Farms were only a mile away from the union building. Cole had to wait; Lorraine Wilmer was busy.

Ten minutes passed before the pretty young woman with the big oval glasses Cole remembered as Lorraine's assistant came to greet him.

"You're Polly, right?" Cole said. "I just need a minute or two of her time. Tell her it's important."

"She's pretty booked but let me go ask."

Cole took a seat and checked his messages on his phone. He looked up as a bald, square-shouldered man passed through the lobby, followed by a younger guy with a short, military-style haircut. Cole recognized them both. The bald man worked for the Wilmers. He'd escorted Cole out of the fundraiser a few weeks back, which led to him spending most of the night in the county jail. The younger man, Cole remembered too, from later that same night. He was one of the two guys who had jumped him.

The bald man stopped short when he noticed Cole. "What do you want?" he asked, coming closer.

"I'm here to see Mrs. Wilmer."

The bald man flexed a fist and then rubbed his hands. "Well, she's busy."

"I can wait."

"You don't understand, pal. She isn't seeing anyone today." He crowded in close. The other guy, too.

Polly was back, holding open the reception door. "Mr. Cole? She's got a few minutes right now."

Cole stood.

"Sage," Polly said. "It's OK."

"What do you know?" Sage said, still sneering. "Her schedule just opened up."

The younger man was too close. Cole had to push him gently to get past.

Lorraine was on a conference call. She pointed to a chair and put the speakerphone on mute.

"Mr. Cole, I'm surprised to see you in person. Why have you come all this way?"

"I wanted to tell you face to face that I've dropped the job involving your family," Cole said, still standing.

"I'm glad to hear it."

"I don't think it changes things for you," Cole said. "My former client, I'm afraid, is highly motivated. She has no intention of backing off. My guess is that she'd do almost anything to waylay your stock deal if you don't pay her off as she believes you should."

She frowned and then punched the telephone box a second time. "Gentlemen, this is Lorraine. I'm going to have to jump off now. Gerald, can you handle things for me from here? Thank you all."

She pointed at the chair again.

"That's all I wanted to say."

"Who is this person? Remember, I paid you to find out."

"She's in investment banking and has some sort of tie to one of the firms working on your IPO. She wants to get in on it. She says your husband's family owes her."

"In what way?"

"She claims her mother was one of Callen Wilmer's victims."

"What?" She dropped her hands to her sides.

"That's what she told me. She also said your stepson is active and that she'd go public with it if she has to."

Lorraine picked up the phone. "Polly, have Sage come in, please."

She stood with her back to Cole, gazing out the big windows at the almond grove. She was silent. Sage and the younger man entered.

"Where's Dalton?" she demanded. "Did you and Ted take him back to the center?"

"I didn't, no."

"Do you know where Dalton is?"

"With the mister, in Sacramento."

"Damn him!" Lorraine shouted, waving a quick backhand. "Go on, get out! Both of you!"

Cole gave her a moment. "What's that about?"

"Dalton was expelled from school," she said. "He was arrested for burglary. Not for the first time. Is this what your client is talking about?"

Cole shook his head. "I think there's more. I think the farmworkers might be part of it."

Lorraine fell hard into her chair, grimacing. "The farmworkers," she muttered. "Something else that Ted thoroughly fouled up."

"Listen, I've got another appointment over in Chico," Cole said. "I've got to get going. I think we're square at this point."

"I don't," she said. "I'd like you to do one more thing. I want to meet your client. I want to know what she knows about Dalton. And about Ted."

"I'm not sure she'll go for that."

"You can ask?"

"Sure."

Cole left through the big glass doors in front. Sage and the other man were waiting for him in the parking lot, both leaning against the driver's side of Cole's car.

"I thought I told you to stay away," the younger man said as Cole approached.

"Try telling me again," Cole said, standing tall, but once again cursing himself for leaving the Glock locked in the trunk.

"Take it easy, Mick." Sage put a hand on his partner's shoulder. To Cole, he said, "What's your game, soldier?"

"Is that any of your business?"

"I could make it my business."

"You wouldn't like it," Cole replied, opening the back door and tossing his briefcase inside. "Pay's lousy."

"Smart guy, eh?" Sage gave Mick a slight nod and the younger man leaped, throwing a big right hand at Cole's face.

Cole was ready this time, and ducked enough that the shot glanced off the side of his head. It put Cole back on his heels but didn't hurt him. Instead, it ignited a rage that had been smoldering inside him for weeks. The Biblical quotation on his grandfather's wall flashed through his head: "Do *justice and righteousness.*"

Cole rose on his toes, staying loose and keeping one eye on Sage as the other man circled and then lunged at him with another big swing. Cole stepped back, slapping Mick's punch away before dropping a hammer of his own to the side of the other man's head. Cole's right fist didn't miss. Mick staggered and fell.

Sage went for a lunge of his own. This time, Cole stepped in ahead of the man's punch and landed a solid jab, smashing Sage square in the nose and upper lip. Sage dropped to his knees like a sack of potatoes and didn't get up.

"Not so easy, is it?" Cole asked, standing over both of them. "I don't slap around so good when I can see it coming."

"Get out of here," Sage said, spitting blood from his mouth. "We'll pick this up another time."

"Yeah, we will," Cole said.

***

The ride to Chico was just long enough for Cole to calm down. He hadn't been in a real fight since high school. It felt good. Payback always did. It was also satisfying knowing he was on the right side of things.

It was close to three when Cole came to a stop in front of an upscale two-story family home on the northwest side of town. There was a new minivan in the driveway and a couple of kids riding skateboards on the sidewalk. A Latino woman in her mid-thirties was watering the garden when he approached.

"Hi, I'm looking for Lana Fitzgerald," Cole said.

"I'm she," the woman replied.

Cole blinked in surprise. He'd taken her for the nanny and hoped he hadn't shown it. He introduced himself, showed her his press credentials, and told her he was investigating the death of her husband. The mention of her husband drew tension across her face.

She didn't say anything for a moment. Then she called the kids to come inside. "The smoke just isn't good for them," she said, waving for Cole to follow. "But we've all been cooped up for days."

She brought Cole into her living room. "What is it you want to know?"

Cole told her about Victim Eleven and how her husband had come to Sacramento shortly before his death while investigating Vivien Bordeaux's murder.

"I remember that trip," she said. "I'm afraid I don't know anything about the case. Harry didn't like to bring work home with him."

"Why do you remember his visit to Sacramento?" Cole asked.

"We were supposed to go with him, the whole family."

"Was that unusual?"

"Yes," she said. "Olimpo has a very small police department, and Harry was one of just three detectives. He worked a lot of hours, lots of weekends, holidays, overnights, but most of it was in town or somewhere in Glenn County. He went to the prison in Susanville once every couple of months."

"Why didn't you go with him to Sacramento?"

"Kids got sick," she said. "It was supposed to be a stop on the way down to Monterey. We were going to take the kids to the aquarium. The department was paying for the trip, anyway. A free hotel room. It was a big treat for us. He had business down there, too."

Cole pulled absently on his car. "At a prison?"

"I think so."

"The prison?" he asked. "Could it have been Soledad?"

She nodded. "That's it."

Cole had what he needed. He got to his feet but had one last question.

"The farmworkers' camp in Olimpo," he said. "Do you remember your husband saying anything about it? Do you recall if he was ever interested in it?"

"Sure," she said. "There was trouble out there from time to time. I remember him getting into a fight with his commander. They didn't want him to go in. It was hands-off."

"Was there a specific crime?"

"I don't know. But he'd complain about it sometimes."

Cole thanked her and returned to his car. He called Karmen.

"Hey, I need you to check a date for me," he said. "That drug case Dixon worked on involving the prison guards at Soledad. When was that?"

"I got it right here," she said. "Filed in 2010. Overturned on appeal in 2013."

"Hmm," Cole said. "Remy was shot to death in 2015."

"Remy's the cop from Olimpo?"

"Yeah. Not sure what to make of it, yet, but he visited Soledad a few months before he was killed."

"Maybe he knew about Preston."

"Maybe."

Karmen's voice faded. "Abe's here. He wants to talk to you."

"Wait, before you hand me off—I need you to get on your horse in the morning. I want you to come up here. I think I need another pair of eyes. I need Karmen's special talents."

"Cool."

"I'll get a room someplace and text you the address."

"OK, boss. Here's Abe."

"JJ, couple of things. We found out Emily's additional income was coming from a bank in Panama. Does that mean anything to you?"

"Nope."

"Impossible to trace back any further. Who's your source inside the Assembly? The one who said a member was involved in the attack of Emily."

"I didn't talk to the source directly," Cole said. "Sylvia Kim told me.

Sylvia is Karmen's partner. She's a victim advocate with the women's shelter."

"I know Sylvia. We're going to need to talk to the source."

"Tell Karmen."

"When are you coming back?"

"I don't know. A couple of days, probably."

"That's a problem," Abe said. "I talked to Captain Miller this afternoon. He's mad as hell that you haven't come in."

"Can't be helped," Cole said. "I don't know what the hell I've got anymore. This thing is a jumbled mess. I think there might even be a connection between Senator Wilmer and our second suspect in the DeAngelo case."

"Come on, seriously?"

"Wilmer's older brother was a con, served time at Soledad, which was also where this guy Preston, who looks like the second suspect, served."

"Sounds like a coincidence."

"Yeah, except that this cop from up here, Olimpo, the one interested in the murder at my place—he was also sniffing around Soledad. Just before he got shot."

"Wild."

"It is. I'll check in tomorrow."

"Okay. But, Cole? You need to talk to Miller. He knows you didn't kill Barrett. But he thinks maybe you know who did, and you're not telling. Withholding information on a homicide, Cole. The cops don't like it."

"I'll get to him, Abe. That's a promise. But not today."

"He doesn't give a toss about your gun, either. He knows you're mixing with some dangerous people. And so do I. Take care of yourself. Okay?"

****

Dixon sat in a tan sedan, far enough down the block that Cole couldn't see him. He watched as Cole left the house and got into his car. Dixon called Ted.

"He's made it to Chico, found Remy's widow," Dixon said. "Won't be long before he finds Preston. What do you want me to do?"

"Stay with him. Let me know if he shows up in Olimpo."

"Then what?"

"I don't know yet. I've got another play working that might turn him around. Keep me posted."

FORTY-FIVE

About a mile outside of Chico, the highway linking the mountain villages to the safety of the Valley swarmed with traffic. A Biblical exodus from the fire. An accident cut the flow to a trickle and Cole had to fight his way into the line. Twenty minutes to move just a few hundred yards.

Once free of the accident, the road opened up. Cole stopped at a motel. It was booked up. He stopped at another. No vacancies. He remembered seeing a billboard for an Indian casino ten miles northwest of Chico. He called and got the last room. He had to turn around and drive all the way back before taking a two-lane road twenty minutes out to the place.

He picked up the tail after turning around. A tan sedan. He noticed the big tires. Cop-like. It stayed with him all the way.

He parked in the casino lot and slipped the Glock into his coat pocket when he got his bag out of the trunk.

All they had was the bridal suite. It cost him five hundred for two nights.

Cole took the elevator to the third floor. He swung the hotel room door open, tossing in his overnight bag and his leather attaché and then ran down the hallway to the stairs, and then dashed back to the lobby. The place was crowded. Tuckers sat in the diner sipping coffee. Retirees worked the penny slots. Fire refugees waited. Cole couldn't pick out a face that might be interested in him. He slipped out a side door and snuck between the cars, pickups, and big rigs parked in the lot.

It didn't take long to find the big tan sedan. A man sat in the driver's seat with the window down. Cole got close enough to see his face.

Dixon.

How long has he been on me? Maybe all day? His suspicion about the link between Wilmer and DeAngelo's accomplice just got a lot stronger. He considered jumping Dixon right there in the parking lot. Cole fingered the gun. Then he heard the unmistakable sounds of a police scanner coming from the sedan.

Dixon opened his phone and made a call. Cole couldn't hear it, but a moment later, Dixon started the engine and drove out of the lot.

Cole retraced his steps to the room and called Brooke. She was chatty and sweet. He told her all about his day, excluding the most dangerous elements. He told her about the farm workers' camp and the possibility that the second suspect was nearby. She'd seen the news coverage of the fire and knew he wasn't far from the front line. He promised her he was keeping safe.

He took a shower and changed and then went downstairs for a burger and a beer. He played a few hands of video poker. He bought a half-pint of Jack and returned to the room.

He was out like a light before ten.

***

The morning sky reminded him of early summer on the beach, gray and dark. The wind had died down. He made coffee in the room and did his stretching. Music was Chinese folk songs: *Autumn Moon Over a Calm Lake* by Lü Wencheng. He put on a pair of shorts for a jog through the golf course next door. As soon as he stepped outside, he turned around. The overcast wasn't clouds, it was smoke. Too much to go running in.

He had a forty-minute drive to Olimpo to make his appointment with Lorena at ten. He had about an hour to kill.

He went back to the room and opened his laptop. There was a note from Sylvia. She said her source on Emily's attack inside the Capitol was willing to talk. She wanted to know when to set it up. Cole wasn't sure.

He scanned the rest of the mail. There was a message from Abe's personal email; it had been sent in the middle of the night. Odd. He'd had never received mail from Abe's private account before. He opened it and found three images embedded in the note. Empty rooms, dark and nondescript. At the bottom was a note: *Back off or you won't like what happens next.*

Cole looked closer. The first image he recognized. Brooke's bedroom. The second was Susan's. The third he couldn't place until he saw a poster of Jay-Z on the wall— his niece Bridget's bedroom.

He reached out to his sister first. It went to voice mail. He caught Brooke in the car.

"Someone broke into your place," he said. "They sent me a photo of your bedroom with a message for me to back off."

"What?"

"Brooke, this is serious. I think you're in danger."

"From your second suspect guy?"

"I think so."

She didn't answer.

"Can you stay with someone for a few days? Preferably someone with a big dog, good locks, and maybe a gun."

"No," she said firmly. "No one is going to chase me out of my house."

"Brooke, please. Just for a few days, until I can get things under control."

There was another pause. "I guess I could go to my sister's place. Should I tell the sheriff?"

"I don't know. There isn't much they can do."

"This feels like a bluff."

"I know but we can't ignore it. Look they sent me two other photos. One was my niece's bedroom. I need to go."

Cole called Susan next, she didn't pick up either.

Kim's line was incoming. He told her about the photos and the dangerous person he was tracking. "Get Bridget and you two get out of there," Cole said. "This is serious."

"Oh God, Jamie! Bridget isn't here." Kim's voice quivered. "We had another fight last night. She took off and didn't come home. I've called the boyfriend; he claims she's not with him."

"Oh, Lord."

"Should I call the police?"

"Maybe. I don't know."

"Who are these people you're investigating?"

"A state senator, for one," Cole said. "There's another guy we know was once a friend of Joe DeAngelo, the Golden State Killer."

"Oh my God!" Kim cried. "I'm calling the police right now."

"Sure," Cole said. "Do it."

"What do I tell them?"

"Everything," Cole said. "Have them call me if they need to. Making sure Bridget is safe is my only concern right now."

Cole's line lit up. Susan. Once again, he explained the situation. "Where are you?"

"I'm with Daniel. We're in Santa Cruz for the music festival."

"OK, perfect. Stay there until you hear from me."

Cole called Abe, too.

"This might be getting too crazy, JJ," Abe said. "You want me to reach out to the police? To Captain Miller?"

"And tell him what? That I got photos of three empty bedrooms? That I have no idea who sent them?"

"How about Wilmer? You said yesterday there's a connection between him and your second suspect."

"And you reminded me how flimsy it sounded." Cole looked out the window that faced the parking lot. No tan sedan.

Incoming call from Kim.

"I gotta go, sis is calling."

"Bridget just walked in," Kim said.

"Thank goodness. Now get out of there. Where can you go?"

"Vikki's."

"That's good. I'll call."

***

The freeway on both sides was nearly empty, a strange and unsettling contrast to the night before. On the way down, the wind picked up again, swirling and blasting sudden gusts from the mountains. Even big rigs were being pushed around. The fire wasn't far away. The smoke was heavy as fog in places. Firetrucks and emergency vans appeared and then whizzed past, red lights fuzzy in the haze.

Still no sign of the big sedan.

The diner was on the west side of town, away from the danger zone. Restless anxiety hummed in the air, even with barely a soul around. Cole parked his car and went inside. Lorena was waiting. The waitress came by and said the owner wanted to shut down because of the fire; if they wanted something, they had to order right now and get it to go. They opted just to leave. Cole had the Glock in his coat pocket. They took Lorena's car.

The almond orchard stretched several hundred acres beyond the east side of the freeway. The workers' camp was on the north end, closer to town. Closer to the fire as well. A red glow limned the hills; the flames were less than five miles away. Rings of smoke pulsed above the treetops, raining bits of white ash on the pavement.

A guardhouse and a gate marked the entrance of the camp. No one was tending it. A one-lane road connected the camp to the town. They passed a small store with laundry services and a gas terminal. Then a row of worn, clapboard houses; a dozen trailers, double-wide; and finally, a two-story building at the end. The place was a ghost town. Lorena parked in front of the building and pointed to one of the apartment doors.

"My cousin lives here," she said. "She knows the family of the little one that got attacked."

Lorena got out and she knocked. A woman answered and then pointed up the lane, toward one of the houses. Lorena got back into the car.

"Pepe's working in the field someplace. The rest of the family has taken off. My brother's one of the foremen. If I can reach him, maybe he'll know where Pepe is."

She got out her cell. Her brother didn't answer. They returned to the little lane and then drove until the pavement petered out into hard dirt. They drove a mile or two until they found a group of men working on the pump housing. Lorena got out and talked to one of the men.

They drove slowly back down the dirt road between the fence line and the almond trees. Cole noticed a pickup kicking up dust on the other side of the grove. Then, between the trees, he saw the truck stop in front of a small house. A tall man got out.

"Is that the cottage I keep hearing about?" he asked. "Where Callen lived?"

"Yes."

"Is that Berg?"

"I don't know."

"Do you mind if we take a look?"

"No, but why?"

"Just a hunch," he said. "This guy I told you about, Dale Preston, he served time with Callen in prison. He's tall, like the man I just saw. Maybe it's him."

Lorena backed up the car until she could turn around. They approached another trail that led to a driveway and the cottage. She pulled up next to the truck.

"Follow my lead," Cole said, getting out and calling. "Hello! Anyone home? Hello!"

The tall man stepped out the screen door. He looked to be in his sixties. Lean. An old Giants hat. Glasses. A thick white beard. A small dog barked at his feet.

"Hi, I'm sorry to bother you," Cole said. "But I'm interested in the cottage. I understand it's available to rent."

"I don't think so, friend. I got a deal with the owners. I'm here as long as I like."

"Oh, maybe I misunderstood. I'm with the property management company. We're inventorying Stony Creek's real estate assets."

"Well, I know the owners."

"My name is Johnson, by the way. And you are?"

"Gus," he said, opening the screen door and shooing the dog down inside the house. "My name's Gus Berg."

"Nice to meet you, Mr. Berg. Do you mind if I look around just a bit? I just need to see the condition of the house."

"Sure, go right ahead. It's not a big place, but it's sturdy."

There was a small garden near the side of the house. Cole stepped around it and looked in the back. Berg followed him. Lorena stayed in the car.

"You've done some work back here," Cole said, pointing to a patch of freshly trimmed bushes and grass. There was a barn or a garage. A culvert ran water from the state channel under the highway across the property to the orchard.

"Yeah, I'm a little worried about that fire. If we get a wind like we had the other day, wouldn't take much to send it this way."

Around front again, Cole pointed to the door. "Can I take a peek inside?"

"Let me get Peaches, first. She's very protective."

"Thanks. The company is being sold. You heard that, right?" Cole stepped onto the porch and followed Berg inside. "Chinese. There's going to be some changes."

"I heard."

The living room was small. A TV on a stand. A chair. A small couch. Things were neat, orderly. Cole looked in the kitchen. Pots and pans were put away, the countertop clean. He went down the hall. "Just the one bedroom?" he called back.

"Yes, sir," Berg said.

The bed was made. Clothes put away. Blankets carefully folded. A bookcase stood near the window, mostly without books. A row of odds and ends occupied one shelf—a couple of dusty shot glasses, a model airplane, a transistor radio, a black and white wedding photo in a frame. Something caught his eye. A large coin.

Before Cole could get closer, Berg was standing behind him. "My sister and her husband," he said, pointing to the photo.

"Ah, yes."

"You need to see anything else?"

"I don't think so. You've been generous. Thank you."

"Certainly."

Berg walked Cole to the door and shook his hand. Lorena was waiting in the car.

"You think that's him?" she asked.

"Could be," Cole said. "If so, he's one cool customer."

FORTY-SIX

Lorena dropped him at the diner. The day was shot. Karmen would arrive soon. He was about an hour away.

Gus Berg, he thought. *A common enough name. There can't be too many of them around here.* He thought about the big coin. It was too large to be real, even for a foreign issue. He didn't get a good look. He couldn't shake what Tommy Hughes had said about the Bordeaux killer taking two Disneyland medallions from the house as a trophy. The big coin might have been one of them.

The county seat, a town called Willow, was south of Olimpo. Just for the hell of it, Cole drove down to the clerk's office there and looked for records on a man named David or Gus Berg.

Not a thing.

He needed to get back inside the cottage, get a better look at the coin. He knew it wouldn't be enough to prove Berg was Preston and, therefore, also DeAngelo's accomplice. But if it was one of the medallions, it would probably be enough to turn up the heat, maybe get the cops interested.

Enough to make a compelling closing chapter in the book.

***

He spotted Karmen as he came through the lobby. She was at the blackjack table with a drink in her hand and a pile of chips in front of her.

"The bridal suite, eh, boss?" She motioned for the dealer to give her another card. "You know I'm taken, right?"

"All they had."

She closed her hand, tipped the dealer, and followed Cole upstairs.

He told her about the cottage, Gus Berg, and the interesting coin on the shelf.

"Let's go!" she crowed. "Let's bust him."

"I don't know. I've got to think about it."

"What do you want me to do?"

"Nothing for now. I'm going to take a nap. You can head back to the tables if you want."

He closed the door to the bedroom and laid down. He covered his face with a pillow and fell asleep.

He was out longer than he meant to be. It was almost seven. Karmen was in the living room, watching TV.

Cole got his phone out. "Let's talk to Skip," he said. He put the call on speaker and brought the old cop up to speed.

"You're right," Skip said. "It's not enough, even if that coin turns out to be what you think it might be. Disneyland? They had to have given out thousands of those things."

"Is there any way we could find out what the Olimpo cop was looking for down at Soledad?" Karmen asked.

Cole shrugged. "His widow told me he was worried about the farmworkers' camp," he said. "And the union boss told me a young girl was raped in the camp back in March. There were other troubles there too, burglaries."

"Sounds like our guy," Skip said.

"I don't know," Cole answered. "This guy Berg, he's in his mid-sixties at least. I don't see a guy his age breaking into houses, attacking women."

"What about the stepson?" Karmen asked. "Didn't you say the farmworkers suspected him?"

"Maybe Preston and the kid are working together," Skip said.

"That makes sense," Cole said. "The key is the camp, the cottage. I got to get back in there."

"That I wouldn't recommend," Skip said. "Far too dangerous. Is it time to call the pros?"

"You mean the sheriff?" Karmen said. "No way."

"There's the Barrett murder to consider." Cole rubbed his chin. "I know Preston had something to do with it."

"What about Dixon?" Skip asked. "You find him yet?"

"Yeah," Cole said. "He was tailing me yesterday. Not sure where he picked me up, but probably the widow's place in Chico."

"If you confront Preston, you'll need to get in his face," Skip said. "You'll need to press him. It's your only chance."

"Yeah, maybe. We'll talk soon."

Cole and Karmen had dinner at the casino buffet. She went back to the tables, and he went upstairs. He opened his laptop and started writing, news style. He tried to assemble what he knew so far. Two sentences. A third. He stopped. It was drivel.

He went downstairs to the bar. It was noisy. A live band playing on a stage at the far end of the casino. Cole didn't hear his phone. On his way back upstairs about an hour later, he realized there was a message.

"Cole, it's Lorraine Wilmer," she whispered. "Listen, everything's changed. I need you to go to the police in Davis. My stepson needs to be arrested. He's planning to attack a woman. I have proof that he's attacked others and that Ted—"

She stopped. There were sounds of a struggle. A scream. A sharp, hollow, terrified scream. The phone message ended.

***

The Hat Creek blaze had threatened the city of Redding and its 100,000 residents earlier in the week. In the last few hours, it had moved south, driven by the wind. While good news for Redding, the fast-moving inferno crossed over Highway 36 near the town of Paynes Creek and merged with the Butte Meadows conflagration, creating one of the largest mega-fires ever recorded—nearly 700,000 acres.

To get from Red Bluff to the Wilmer mansion in Palo Cedro, Cole and Karmen had to navigate about ten miles along the edge of the fire line. It was a slog of detours and cop stops. He used his press pass twice. On one winding stretch of mountain road, they were suddenly caught inside a roaring wall of flame exploding in the tree-tops above them, scattering bright limbs about the road. Cole could feel the white-hot air as he gunned the engine into safety.

When they reached Anderson, a town just outside Redding, the fire was no longer a threat. Everything within a mile of the road—the forest, the ranch houses, the roadside stores, everything—was already scorched or incinerated.

The sun was down, and the smoke and the darkness made the road up into the hills hard to follow. Cole had driven it once before, on his first trip to Redding more than a month earlier. He knew the turn to the Wilmer place and remembered the service road below the property. There was a golf range, some open space for the horses, and a couple hundred yards of brush. He could probably sneak in from below. He found the dirt road and then the edge of the Wilmer property. He checked the Glock and slipped an extra clip into his coat pocket. He fished around the trunk until he found the penlight. He gave Karmen the keys.

"I'll be coming out hot and the shit could be flying," he said. "Be ready to get us the hell out of there."

FORTY-SEVEN

Cole climbed over a loose barbed wire fence and made his way toward the house. It was all uphill. The horses were elsewhere. No one had used the range lately, and it was easy to spot the white golf balls. Cole had to scale a six-foot retaining wall to get onto the patio. Once he reached the pool, he stopped and crouched behind the outdoor kitchen.

He waited and watched. There had to be at least one sentry out back. Two, three, four minutes. Remarkably, no one seemed to be guarding the rear.

Closer to the house, he spotted a guy sitting just outside the glass doors of the main living room with a rifle in his lap. The weak buzzing sound of a golf cart sent Cole darting behind some shrubs.

"You awake, asshole?" a man's voice gruffly called out.

"Yeah."

"Stay alert."

Cole worked his way around the other side of the house. He found another set of glass doors. Locked. The lights came on inside. Cole hid against the wall. The door rattled open, and a man stepped out. Cole waited until he was behind the guy. He had the gun ready, and with one swift strike, pounded the back of the guy's head with the butt of the gun. The guard fell back into Cole's arms, and Cole dragged him noiselessly into a dark corner of the garden.

Inside, he silently pushed the glass doors closed and looked around. Probably the study, maybe Ted's office. Cole switched off the ceiling light, sparked his penlight, and rummaged through the big desk in the middle of the room. He opened a drawer. Business records. Legislative documents. There were voices in an adjacent room.

Cole stepped closer to the wall and put his ear to it. Three male voices. One he recognized as Sage's. Another he guessed was Ted because he was chewing out the third.

"It never should have come to this!" he shouted. "It's a goddamned mess. I've got to get her out of the country now. And how am I going to explain her absence to the bankers, the lawyers, my investors?"

"Say she's on vacation."

"Very funny, Dixon. Hilarious. You can laugh all you want. This isn't blowing up in your face."

"Take it easy, Ted. We got this."

"Sage, when will the plane be ready?"

"Eleven thirty."

"Who's flying?"

"Rick."

"OK, good."

Cole heard footsteps in the hallway. He moved to the wall next to the door and waited, holding his breath, until the footsteps faded. He opened the door a crack and peeked out. The hallway was empty. With the gun leading the way, Cole tiptoed toward the room the voices had come from. The door was slightly open. Cole stepped in. Ted was alone, his back to Cole. Cole kicked the door shut and Ted turned around. Cole had the Glock trained on him.

"It's over, Senator. Whatever the hell game you're running here, it's over."

"Hardly," Wilmer drawled, returning his attention to a liquor tray and a tumbler of ice. "Can I offer you one?"

"Hands up high," Cole said, coming close.

"I'm not armed," Wilmer said, but he complied. Cole patted him down with his free hand. Wilmer got his drink and took one of several armchairs in the room. "You're not seriously thinking you can shoot your way out of here, do you? I've got a dozen armed men."

"Only eleven are awake," Cole said. "And in a moment, you'll be down one or two more."

Lorraine's angry voice came from the hallway, and Cole slipped into the corner. The door opened and Lorraine was shoved into the room. She had her handbag on her arm. Sage followed. Cole came up behind Sage and put the muzzle of the Glock to his ear. "Don't move, tough guy, or I'll splatter your brains around the room like ripe tomatoes."

Sage put up his hands. Cole stood behind him, searching until he found Sage's pistol. He handed the gun to Lorraine.

"Keep your husband quiet," Cole said. He pushed Sage toward the windows on the other side of the room, jerked down the curtain cords, and tied Sage by his wrists and ankles.

Wilmer calmly sipped his drink. Cole checked on Lorraine. A bruise was rising under one eye and her split lip looked swollen and sore.

"Neither of you can prove a thing," Wilmer said.

"I can," Lorraine said, pointing the gun at him. "I can prove everything. The things Dalton has done. The things you *asked* Dalton to do. I got proof. I know about the murdered girl in the Capitol. You are all going to prison."

Ted jumped to his feet and threw his cocktail glass at his wife, just missing her. Cole stepped between them. He took the gun from Lorraine.

"You won't get two steps out of this room," Ted said. "All I have to do is whistle. They'll shoot whoever comes out that door."

Cole let a round go into the floor. "Now what, Senator? Now what are your boys going to think?" Cole fired a second and then grabbed Wilmer by the collar.

Cole used the gun to point at the opposite end of the room. "Where do those doors lead?" he asked Lorraine.

"The front drive," she said.

"Go, get out of here. There's a car waiting near the barn. Remember where you took me to meet the sheriff's deputies that day?"

"I do. What about you?"

"I'll be right behind you."

Lorraine had her purse in one hand and took off her heels with the other. She ran. Cole pushed Wilmer closer to the door.

"No!" Ted pleaded. "Don't!"

Cole took the handle of the door, keeping Wilmer in front of him.

"Stand down!" Wilmer shouted. "Everyone put your guns down! I'm ordering you to put them down!"

Cole kicked the door open and shoved Wilmer into the hallway. A series of shots rang out. Wilmer spun and fell. Cole returned fire and then dashed out the garden doors to the driveway, sprinted to the gate, and jumped into the car. Karmen laid rubber, careening down the hill.

"Where to, boss?" Karmen asked.

"Take the road into Redding," Cole ordered. "It's the long way, but I don't want to mess with that damn fire again."

"Then what? Home?"

"No, we're going after Preston tomorrow. First thing."

They didn't talk. The highway was nearly empty. Lorraine remained stiff and silent. In the back seat, Cole kept turning around, searching for a chase car. No one seemed to be following. That bothered him.

"Let me see your bag," Cole said, tapping Lorraine on the shoulder. She passed it back. Cole dug through it.

"What are you looking for?" she asked.

"A tracker," Cole said. "My guess is they've got a GPS device on you someplace and think they can come collect you whenever they want."

He emptied her purse but found nothing obvious. He got out her billfold; there were two fifties, a hundred, and a bunch of ones. He gave Lorraine all of it except for the hundred and her ID. "We're going to have to ditch this," Cole said. "Your phone, too." He put the phone and everything else back into the purse.

A heavy square object about the size of a drink coaster caught his attention. He fumbled with it, but in the dark, he couldn't figure out what it was.

"What is this?" he asked Lorraine, holding up the object.

"Something Ted holds as precious as life," she said. She took it from Cole and found a release button on the side. The object opened up. "A medallion," she said. "I stole it out of our safe at home this morning. I'm sure it means something."

She handed it back to him.

"Daffy Duck," Cole said. "Yes, it means something."

He put the medallion back in the container and set it aside, telling Karmen to get off at the next exit.

A half-mile up, Karmen pulled off. Cole had her stop a couple hundred feet from the service station. Cole got out and walked up to a kid filling his tank. His girlfriend sat in the passenger seat.

"Say, son, can you help me?" Cole held out the purse. "Are you heading back to Redding?" The kid nodded. "A lady friend of mine left this in my car this afternoon, and I'm on my way down to LA."

The girl rolled down her window.

"Any chance you guys could drop it off at her house?" Cole showed the purse to the girl. Her eyes widened at the luxury logo, and she reached for it, quickly examining its contents and checking the driver's license.

"She lives up in Palo Cedro," the girl said. "That's out of our way."

The couple exchanged sour expressions.

"Well, there's a hundred in the billfold. I can't imagine she would care if it went missing," Cole said. "I'd bet she'd add another just to be nice. The hassle of getting a new ID and canceling credit cards, you know how it is." Cole fished out another bill. "Here's a double sawbuck more."

"I guess we could do it, right, honey?" the girl said.

"Sure."

Cole ran back to the car. Fifteen minutes later, they were all safe and sound in the bridal suite. It was just after eleven, still early enough that Cole could order room service. He needed a drink, and he figured everyone else did too. A big pitcher of martinis, some appetizers, and a couple of cold beers were on their way.

Lorraine went into the bathroom. Karmen used the phone in the bedroom to call Sylvia. Cole stayed at the windows facing the parking lot and the freeway. He was wondering how badly Ted had been hurt and how soon the hometown cops would be on their tail.

He called Scotty.

"Hey, it's Cole. Any chance you can find me a friendly face driving south near Chico in the next few hours?"

"You don't want much."

"I got a witness on this DeAngelo case that I need safely delivered to Sacramento."

"If I can, someone will call. If not, well, you know."

Room service arrived. Cole grabbed a beer and took it down in two long pulls before pouring drinks for all three of them. Karmen served herself a shrimp cocktail and a martini, got comfortable in a recliner, and switched on the TV. Lorraine emerged from the bathroom and Cole handed her a drink.

"At the house," she said, "I heard gunshots. Did anyone get hurt?"

"Your husband."

"Bad?"

"Maybe." He watched her take a seat and choke back a sob. "I'm sorry," he said. "There didn't seem to be another way."

"He did it to himself. All of this, he did it."

Karmen found a box of tissues and handed it to Lorraine. Her face drained of expression. Eyes lost. Karmen put an arm around her.

Cole needed some questions answered. He wanted to ask Lorraine about what she'd said at the house. Could the murder in the Capitol she'd mentioned be Emily? What was Ted's involvement? The Disneyland medallion she'd taken from Ted's safe. What did she know about it? What about Preston? Did she know about him? Or Dixon?

The interrogation would have to wait. Karmen got Lorraine to her feet, walked her to the bedroom, and returned after closing the door.

"She's spent, man," Karmen said, refilling her drink and taking a seat at the small dining table. "What are we going to do with her?"

"I'm hoping to hear from Scotty," Cole said, still standing in front of the windows. "I'm hoping to find her a ride down to Sac." He drew the blinds shut and circled the room, turning off the lights.

"Why not just take her now?" Karmen asked. "I could drive."

"Maybe," he said. "But you'd have to take your pickup. They'll be looking for my car, and then what do I do tomorrow? Wilmer was wounded, not sure how bad. The local cops will be all over me. Let's wait and see what Scotty comes up with. I'll probably need your help getting inside the cottage."

Karmen downed her martini in one quick swig and then poured the last of the liquor into her glass. "Well, we did it, boss," she said. "We found the killer, saved the girl, and broke open the case, right? We should be celebrating."

Cole was back at the window, peering between the shades. "Yeah," he said listlessly. "Yeah, we should."

She made a razzing sound by blowing through her lips. "You sound convinced."

Cole checked the door and the lock before returning to the windows. "These guys aren't done," he said, staring out at the night. "Let's try to get some rest. You take the couch. I'll take the chair."

"Sure thing." She jumped on the sofa. "We got a story, though, don't we, boss? Some story."

Cole got comfortable. He put his phone on mute but left it on his lap in case one of Scotty's friends called. It buzzed around three.

"Is this JJ Cole?" a woman asked. "I'm Joanne Clevenger. I'm a probation officer with Alameda County. Scotty Walsh said you need some help."

Cole stepped into the hallway. "Where are you?"

"I'm just about to Redding on the I-5, heading for home."

"That's perfect. I got a witness who needs to get to Sacramento. Do you mind sliding east to Chico? There's a couple of C-notes in it for you."

"I guess so," she answered. "What's the backstory?"

"I'm a shamus on a hot case. She's a witness in a side event tied to the Golden State Killer prosecution. Could get bumpy."

"How bumpy?"

"The kind of bumpy that might require waving around that Roscoe they issued you. Does that give you pause?"

"Not at all. Just want to know what I'm up against."

"You're a good man, sister. See you in an hour."

Next, Cole called Darna. If things actually did get bumpy, he wasn't sure who else he could trust.

"Cole? What the fuck?" Darna groaned. "It's three in the morning."

"I'm sorry. I need your help."

"What is it?"

Cole explained the situation. "Do you have anywhere you can stash my witness for a day or two until I figure things out?"

"My sister. I'll make something up."

"Whatever works, man," Cole said. "They'll be coming into Sacramento around six. I'll text you the driver's number and you can make arrangements."

"OK, but now we're even, baby."

"No, I'll owe you. What did you call me, your new best friend?"

"That's right, Papi."

FORTY-EIGHT

Cole tucked Lorraine in for her ride south and then tried to get some rest. Karmen was dead asleep on the couch. He took the bedroom. Sunup was only a couple of hours away.

He was exhausted, but sleep wouldn't come. The mind kept playing out the wild night, all the dead-crazy things he'd been part of the last few days—hell, the last few weeks. What a ride. Cole was a different man than he was a few months ago. He was actually in a shootout. What did he tell the probation officer? *A shamus on a hot case?*

The wind was up again too. Battering against the hotel's walls. Thundering. Wailing. A tempest unleashed.

He was suddenly thirsty. Not for water. He needed some sugar. Cole found his wallet and crept out the door in search of the soda machine. He chose Squirt, two of them.

He went down to the lobby, to the casino floor. People were still playing. He watched a news channel on the TV. The fire. The broadcast was all about the fire scorching Northern California out of existence.

He returned to the room, laid down on the bed, kicked off his shoes, and finally drifted away.

***

Cole woke. Someone, Karmen, was shaking him.

"Shouldn't we get going?" she said. "It's almost ten."

"What?"

"Get up, man. Check out is in an hour."

Cole threw his feet on the floor. "OK, I'm awake."

He went to the bathroom, peeled out of his clothes, and took a shower. He changed and gathered his things. His phone had three messages. Two from Abe. One from Darna.

Abe's first call was at six. He said a detective from the state police had come to his house. "They're looking for you, JJ. What's up? Call me." The second call was about half an hour ago. "Goddamnit, JJ! Senator Wilmer was shot to death last night. They say you had something do to with it. Call me, damn it."

Darna's message confirmed he'd picked up Lorraine, and that she was safe at his sister's house.

Cole called Abe.

"What the hell, JJ? What the hell is going on?"

"Wilmer's dead?"

"That's what the police are saying. They say you had something to do with it. You need to turn yourself in."

Cole held his breath a moment. "Not yet."

"Where are you?"

"Up north. I got one more thing to do."

"Bad idea, Jamie. There's an all-points bulletin out on you. What happened?"

"Wilmer's wife is ready to testify against him," Cole said. "He was going to take her out of the country last night. I made sure he didn't."

"You shot Wilmer?"

"He caught friendly fire, but I was there."

"You've got to turn yourself in, Jamie. This has gotten out of hand."

"I will, as soon as I do this one last thing."

"Which is?"

"Preston. He's DeAngelo's accomplice. I've found him. I need to confront him."

"Where are you? Where's Preston?"

"Tell the cops that I'll turn myself in when I'm done, probably in an hour or so. Tell them I'll come to the CHP office in Willows."

"Jamie, I don't like this."

"Me neither," he said, waving to Karmen in the lobby. "Listen, I'm going to text you a friend's number. He's got Mrs. Wilmer stashed away. Wait a few hours. She was up all night. I need Betsy to interview her before the cops do. Tell Betsy to ask about a murder in the Capitol that Wilmer had something to do with."

"Emily Hodges?"

"I think so."

"Christ."

"She might know about Preston, too. Maybe Dixon. Get Betsy to wring whatever she can out of her and then call Miller."

"OK, I'll see what I can do."

Karmen got the pickup warmed up. Cole went to his car and got a new clip for the Glock and his box of camping equipment. They hit the road.

Cole tried Brooke's line but it went to voice mail.

"Baby, it's me. Listen, if you haven't heard already, I'm in the middle of a shit storm. I didn't do it, I didn't kill Wilmer. But I've found the accomplice. I'm on my way now to put my foot up his ass and when I'm done I'll be turning myself in. After that, well, we'll see. I'm calling—I'm calling, I guess just to say I love you. That's it."

Karmen gave Cole a knowing glance.

"Maybe you should call Sylvie," Cole said, offering her the phone.

Karmen shook her head. "She knows. I told her."

Overnight, the wind drove the fire within a mile of the interstate. A state trooper had blocked off the exit to Olimpo. A flashing road sign said the town was being evacuated. They drove about ten miles farther south before finding an exit.

It took more than an hour to navigate a way into town. They got to the gate of the workers' camp and drove in. The place was deserted. Cole pointed to the dirt lane and then to the driveway leading to the cottage. He told Karmen to stop.

"I'm going to work my way around the back of the house," he said. "Wait here a minute or two and then go straight up to the door. If he's still there, try talking to him. Say you're looking for someone, one of the workers. I'm going to try to get the jump on him."

Cole got out, Glock in one hand and a small ax in the other. A thick mix of stringing nettle, wisteria, and cordgrass shrubs walled off the driveway. Cole had to hack his way in. He crawled on his hands and knees until he found an opening and then headed to the culvert that fed water to the groves from the other side of the highway. The culvert cut through the back lot of the cottage. Cole waited in the bush until he heard Karmen calling from the front.

A man's voice responded. It was calm, even friendly. Preston. The dog barked.

Cole got to his feet and ran to the back door. Just as he did, a hot gust of wind threw a shower of tiny red embers across the yard. One bright knuckle of wood landed close to the house, singeing a spot of dry grass before flaming out. A finger of the fire was only a couple hundred yards away.

The backdoor was locked. Cole went around to the bedroom window and peeked inside. Empty. He broke the screen lock, pushed the window open, and then silently pulled himself inside. A suitcase sat open on the bed. Preston was getting ready to leave.

The medallion was still on the shelf. Cole grabbed it.

Mickey Mouse.

With the barrel of his gun leading the way, Cole snuck into the living room. Preston was at the door, talking to Karmen on the porch. The dog came at him, barking wildly.

Preston didn't look surprised.

"I thought you might be back." He reached down, scooping up the little dog. "You think you need that?" He nodded at the gun. "I'm sixty-seven and the docs say I probably won't see seventy. I won't give you no trouble."

"Nonetheless, sit down," Cole said, waving the barrel toward an armchair near the fireplace.

"What do you think I'm going to do? Confess?"

"Something like that," Cole replied. He opened the door and told Karmen to come inside. "Keep an eye out." She took a spot in the kitchen.

"Let's start with your name," Cole said. "It sure as hell isn't Gus Berg."

Preston was calm, collected, even smug.

"That medallion don't mean nothing," he said. "Doesn't prove a damn thing."

"Your DNA will," Cole said.

Preston held the dog close, stroking its back and head. "The statute of limitations on anything I've done ran out long ago, son. The cops can't lay a hand on me."

"They can for murder."

"I didn't kill her."

"You were there."

"Maybe, maybe not. You can't prove anything."

"You gunned Barrett."

A crash from behind the house was followed by the sound of tree branches breaking and the wind driving wood debris against the rear wall of the cottage. Cole stepped to a side window. Flames burst through a field of dry brown grass on the other side of the highway.

He called to Karmen. "My box of stuff in your truck—there should be some line. Go get it."

Preston smiled. "You don't think you can take me with you. That ain't going to happen."

Cole ignored him and watched Karmen get to the truck. The dog began barking again. Another big gust hit the back of the house. There was a sound behind him; a floorboard creaked. A sharp pinch on his neck. Cole turned.

Dixon. He held a gun in one hand and a syringe in the other. A chill ran the length of Cole's spine. Shadows crept in from the corners of his vision. He faded.

FORTY-NINE

Brooke listened to Cole's message a second time. He spoke too fast. His voice heavy and breathy. Not panic. Not fright. Something darker. Like death.

She checked the time. It was just after eleven. His call came in at ten-forty. She went quickly downstairs to the operations desk and asked one of the operators if there was anything on the wire about a state senator. The man pointed to his screen. A statewide alert for James J. Cole, 44, white, six foot, one ninety. She asked for a copy and then ran back to the executive suite, to her boss's office.

"I know where he is," she said handing Undersheriff Steve Bell the bulletin. "I know where Cole is right now."

"Where?"

"A farm workers' camp near the town of Olimpo."

"Olimpo? Where is that?"

"Glenn County."

"How do you know?"

She told him everything. She told him about the second suspect, the Barrett shooting, the murder in Cole's house, everything. Even the fact that she was in love with him.

"He could be next," she said. "These people he's chasing are killers. He's going to need help."

Bell grabbed Brooke's arm and they hurried to the sheriff's office. Henley was in a meeting, but Bell went in ahead. Brooke could hear Henley barking at Bell and then the inner office door came open. Henley stood before her scowling.

"Why am I hearing about this only now?" Henley said waving the arrest bulletin.

"I don't have time for this," Brooke answered. "Neither do you. You need to call CHP right now. You need to get the backup to the farm workers camp in Olimpo before Cole gets killed. Now!"

Henley clenched his teeth and he shouted behind his back to his assistant. "Get me the CHP commander's office in Glenn! Get the chopper ready! Tell operations to scramble an intervention team, pronto!"

Henley gave Brooke a cold stare. "We'll talk about this later."

"Yes sir."

***

A booming roar. A huge tree limb snapping. Wild heat on his face. A gyre of flames, widening and turning.

Cole came to. Duct tape bound his hands to the steering wheel of the pickup. His ankles were tied, too. The fire lapped against the hood. The windshield cracking. Karmen sat next to him, unconscious. Hard to breathe. Too much smoke. The hammering inferno surrounded him.

As the heat inside the cab intensified, the tape's adhesive lost some tension. Cole worked his hands off the wheel. The tape still held his wrists together, but he got the truck door open and fell out. On the ground, he freed his legs. He dashed to the passenger side and pulled Karmen free.

He saw the back of the cottage; they were in the yard behind the house. He could see the culvert on the other side of the yard. Shrubs and tall grasses were burning in front of him, and the furnace-hot air rushed closer. He got the tape off his wrists and threw Karmen over his shoulder and tried to run for the water.

He dragged her in. As soon as he did, she snapped to, coughing and flailing at the water. Cole put his hands behind her head and stood her up. The roar of the fire surrounded them, the flames biting and the smoke choking.

The source of the water came from the other side of the highway. Cole could see a tunnel where the water was being carried beneath the road. The fire raged above the tunnel and all around it. Cole took Karman's hand and led her toward the opening of the tunnel and pushed her inside, there was barely enough room for them both.

"Keep going," he shouted. "Push through to the other side."

There was only a couple of inches between the top of the water and the tunnel's rough ceiling. Dark inside too. They had to wade about twenty yards. The water was lukewarm.

Light at the other end, smokey and dull. There was a wall of flames in front of them. They waited. Five minutes. Ten. The fire filled the tunnel with smoke.

***

The first of the CHP units left the Willows station at eleven fifteen, code three. Officers arrived at the gate of the farm workers camp twenty minutes later. Their orders were to detain anyone trying to leave the camp.

The chopper took off from Sacramento with six aboard along with the two pilots. Except for Brooke, the other passengers were all sheriff detectives. The ride would take about an hour. Everyone wore headsets so that they could hear one another but no one except the pilots spoke.

***

After parking their victims in the path of the blaze, Dixon and Preston made their escape. Preston brought his little dog. Dixon drove. They were going sixty before they saw the patrol cars blocking the exit of the camp. Dixon tried to swerve, and lost control and the car careened into one of the patrol cars. Preston's head hit the dashboard. Dixon pulled himself out of the driver's side door, with his pistol in one hand. He traded shots with the CHP officers. Two.

Three. Four. Dixon tried to run. The cops got off four shots. Dixon fell, mortally wounded in the chest.

***

The wind shifted and pushed the fire south of town. The chopper landed in a parking lot about a half block from the camp. Brooke ran off first and charged through the police tape. She went first to the body lying near the wrecked car; not Cole. She saw the man with the bandaged head, sitting on the ground with his hands cuffed behind him. That wasn't Cole either.

She was frantic, calling his name, running from the car crash site to where some of the police officers were gathered. "Where's Cole?" she called to them. "There's another man! James Cole! Where is he?"

One of the sheriff detectives who had been on the flight with her, put an arm on her shoulder. "They think he's in there someplace," the detective said, pointing toward the camp and roaring flames. "We'll have to wait."

Brooke put a hand to her forehead and stared at the fire and smoke.

A woman officer was in charge of the state patrol units. She called out, urging everyone to work quickly. "The wind could change any moment," she said. "We need to wrap this up. Get the body out of here."

The medics loaded Preston into the ambulance and took off. The lead detective from Sacramento called to Brooke. "We got to follow them to the hospital, I need you to come now."

Brooke listlessly got into one of the CHP units.

They drove across town and to the highway. There were still remnants of the flames along the road. They were on the backside of the inferno. Tears welled up in Brooke's eyes.

"What have we got here?" the officer driving said out loud. "Look at these two."

The unit slowed. A man and a woman were walking along the side of the road.

"They look like they've been through hell," the driver said.

"Stop," the detective from Sacramento sitting in the front passenger seat. "That's our guy!"

Brooke leaned forward. "My god! It's Cole!"

ABOUT THE AUTHOR

Tom Chorneau is a writer, editor and poor poet, originally from Manhattan Beach, California. He is best known for his years as a news reporter for the Associated Press and San Francisco Chronicle, among other stops. He lives today near the Sierra Foothills with a chocolate Lab named Lily.

What does an author stand to gain by asking for reader feedback? A lot. In fact, what we can gain is so important in the publishing world that they've coined a catchy name for it. It's called "social proof." And in this age of social media sharing, without social proof, an author may as well be invisible.

So if you've enjoyed *Victim Eleven*, please consider giving it some visibility by reviewing it on Amazon or Goodreads. A review doesn't have to be a long critical essay, just a few words expressing your thoughts, which could help potential readers decide whether they would enjoy it, too.